# BOY ALMIGHTY

*An Autobiographical Novel*

## FREDERICK MANFRED

*Introduction by Freya Manfred*

University of Nebraska Press | Lincoln

Library of Congress Control Number: 2021937801

For Maryanna Shorba
friend and wife

*A man, yet by these tears a little boy again,*
*Throwing myself on the sand, confronting the waves,*
*I, chanter of pains and joys . . .*
*A reminiscence sing.*

—Walt Whitman,
"OUT OF THE CRADLE ENDLESSLY ROCKING"

# CONTENTS

# INTRODUCTION
*Freya Manfred*

Dear Dad,

The last time I called on you to help me write an introduction to one of your novels was for *Lord Grizzly*, which many say is the crown jewel of your *Buckskin Man Tales*. Now, I again call on the vital spirit of your letters and conversations to help me introduce *Boy Almighty*, the second of your twenty-five published novels. I know you won't mind, because even in the last few weeks of your life you said firmly, "If I happen to go to some other place when I die, I don't want to lie around doing nothing like some of those descriptions we hear about angels and heaven. I want an assignment!"

*Boy Almighty*, first published in 1945, is one of your two most autobiographical novels. As you wrote, "I had tuberculosis once, almost died of it. In fact, I saw my file one time when I was recovering. I was on a gurney, and the doctor brought me to his office downstairs, at the Glen Lake Sanitorium. And then he went out of the office for a minute and I reached over and picked up my file and looked at it, and it said, 'Terminal.'

"I wrote *Boy Almighty* within a year or two of being dismissed from the sanatorium . . . How do you make it interesting for a guy laying in bed for three hundred pages? Well, that's because my memory was keen and I finally unraveled the whole thing and got it all in there.

"I first worked at *Boy* not for the purpose of art (though it became that perhaps later) but for the secondary purpose of getting rid of an obsession. It was a catharsis. A bloodletting. A public confession. An open psychoanalytic purging."

*Boy Almighty* is a remarkable blend of stream-of-consciousness and objective reporting—a novel ahead of its time that foreshadows our present day fascination with memoir. It describes the trial of the human spirit during the body's breakdown and reconstruction, and the spirit's ultimate victory. Or, as you wrote, "It is a profound study of simple people trying to survive under duress" and "describes modern man's relation to his universe with a tuberculosis sanitorium as a background. The main character . . . one

Eric Frey . . . entered the San a broken person—broken in health, broken in love, broken in ambition. I trace the slow evolution of his recovery."

Dad, I was only a year old when this deeply personal saga was published. But I watched you and my mother, Maryanna Shorba Manfred, struggle for decades with the physical and mental aftereffects of tb, so I'll try here to describe what life was like for our family while you pursued your writing career in the decades after you left the San. I'll forgo academic commentary and refrain from trying to place you somewhere in the constellation of other American writers you so admired, because as a writer born in 1912 in Iowa, you chose to stay and work in your beloved Upper Midlands rather than move to New York City or another metropolitan area. Because you wrote during the second half of the twentieth century, when the lands west of the Mississippi were just beginning to produce first-rate writers, you often said, "I had to create my own audience, and then write for it." I also won't quote any political or religious points of view, because you were a maverick, and although you had a liberal bent, you often said, "I don't like to adhere strictly to any one political or religious group—they all think they know the whole truth and that's not possible."

You often spoke about how you lost thirteen roommates during your two years in the San, but you also described how those arduous years gave you time to think about who you were and what you wanted to do with your life. You wrote, "The experience in the San made me. I might have just dissolved had it not come along." When you were strong and lucky enough to be able to leave the San after two years you were upset because Dr. Sumner Cohen told you that writing fiction was too emotionally stressful a task for someone with half of one lung and a quarter of the other missing. He suggested that you could look for part-time work in other venues and added, "Don't become a writer, or raise any children, if you want to live."

Yet you became a writer, even before you and Mom started a family. And when you finished writing *Boy Almighty*, you asked Dr. Cohen to read it carefully to check everything out. You wrote, "When he got all done, he said two things. He was quite curt about it. He said, One, he had never really known how a patient felt, he had never really seen this whole problem from the point of view of a patient . . . Two, everything was plausible. Nothing was overdrawn or too realistic or raw or anything." And so, you came to believe you were going to be doing "something important, as a writer," and you gratefully kept on writing for fifty-two more years. "I don't know why it is," you wrote, "but I can't do things the way other people do 'em. It's got to be new and my way, or nothing. I guess I'm a natural born lawmaker lucky enough to be working over in a safe area, letters."

My sister, Marya, and our brother, Frederick Junior, watched you write in a ten-by-fourteen-foot remodeled chicken coop in our back yard at the home we called Wralda in Bloomington, Minnesota. In 1959 we moved to the home we called Blue Mound in Luverne, Minnesota, and that little cabin moved with us. Years later, we moved it again to another piece of prairie, east of Luverne, next to the home you called Roundwind. You wrote three to four hours a day, five days a week, your face charged with ferocity and exhilaration, a stormy and sunny pattern in which we all grew up. Or, as you said, "When you burn, you burn at 100 percent; you give it all you have, and more. That's why I hate to get sick. I can't write at 60 or 80 percent. I end up with pap. Just pap."

Here in the Upper Midlands you created an epic body of enduring literature. Out of a deadly illness came a new way of life, out of a mighty near-death struggle came forth sweetness. So we thank you for your vital and iconoclastic spirit, Dad.

Love, Freya

One day in 1948 my big-brained, six-foot-nine-inch father with freckles all over his muscular, hard-working arms and back looked at me with pleading blue eyes, and said, "Honey, would you do me a big favor? Would you walk up and down on my back?"

I felt on equal terms with him at that moment, because the expression on his face was suddenly that of a four-year-old boy, and I had just turned a happy-go-lucky four myself. "You want me to walk on your back?"

"You bet. Walk up and down. It will help me so much. I'll lie on my stomach and you can wear your bare feet—you can even hop up and down if you want."

"Okay, Dad! But . . . won't it hurt?"

"It will help my lungs. Help me breathe. My tb made it harder for me to breathe whenever I'm recovering from a flu."

And so, like the helpful little hero I felt myself to be at that moment, I walked up and down on his back, digging in with my toes when I felt I might topple off his shoulder blades, adding a tiny jump now and then for fun, which made my mother laugh, "Fred! What in the world will you think of next?"

"This is the best thing in the world, Maryanna. It's bound to help." "We'll see about that," she said. "You don't want to do anything to make your lungs worse!"

"This will do the trick," he said. "You'll see!"

And after my gallivanting journey on his expansive white-whale back, my father, who groaned and coughed so much every time he got sick, insisted in his typically enthusiastic way that my pummeling had helped him breathe "ten times better."

It was wonderful and scary to imagine how much help I could be in the face of a devastating and mysterious disease that could even kill grown-ups—a disease that still kills a million and a half people in the world every year. But Dad often proclaimed how proud he was that he was getting better and stronger. He was also proud of how I could help him around the yard, weeding the garden, transplanting flowers, or watering trees. His path—and my mother's path—our path—was upward, into a better future.

My mother's reaction to surviving tb was more subdued, but I thrived on seeing her beautiful, wistful smile when I helped her set the table, sweep the porch, or stir the soup for dinner. At other times, when I begged her to run with me across our beckoning summer yard, her eyes would light up for a few lovely, flying steps, and then she'd begin to turn white and breathe heavily. "I'll rest a bit," she'd say, and then she'd hold her chest and tell me about her "adhesions" from tb that wouldn't let her "breathe normally." The first few times this happened, I was shocked that someone so grown up and accomplished and perfect could not run the way I could, but after a while I got used to the idea that she needed to recover more from her sickness. So I went on helping in the house and the yard, being a "good girl" and a "good helper."

In the evenings Mom would sometimes read Emily Dickinson or *Alice's Adventures in Wonderland* to me, or a book for young people called *Huber The Tuber*, by Harry A. Wilmer, md, which explained what tb was and how it affected the lungs in words that a little girl could understand. I learned that because of "tb germs," we all could infect, sicken, or even kill others. To protect my parents, especially my father, I learned when I was ill to wash the doorknobs I touched, and to wash my hands with soap and hot water dozens of times a day, especially before and after every meal. My mother had survived a lighter case of tb, and I didn't have to avoid her when I was sick, but I couldn't be in the same room with my father until I'd recovered from a cold or flu. My parents explained that if Dad caught my cold it could mean bed rest for two or three weeks with high temperatures and constant coughing.

Sometimes Dad would tell us about how he felt when he was first released from the San and found enough energy to walk up a long, steep hill in Eden Prairie, Minnesota—a scene he describes near the end of *Boy Almighty*. He also told us how he "broke his adhesions" by chopping wood, and how it "didn't hurt that much." Almost everything he did since he had left the San was a mental or physical challenge he relished, and he often said that he woke up every morning grateful to be alive. He went on to say that when you were sick you should always listen carefully to every word your doctor said, but at the same time you should not feel obligated to follow every one of their rules, because sometimes "you know your body and yourself best." He believed that doctors should be part of your health team, and that although you need rules to live by, you also need to feel free enough to know when to break them. Meanwhile, you should "sleep at least eight hours every night, take a daily afternoon nap, walk at least one rigorous hour per day," and "drink a lot of milk, and eat a lot of greens and raws and proteins."

When I was sixty years old, I wrote a poem, "Many Things Frighten Me," in which I describe the intense atmosphere in our home during those early years when our parents were trying to heal physically and mentally from tuberculosis.

Many Things Frighten Me

> Many things frighten me as I age,
> especially people with serious illnesses,
> but I can't tell them I worry,
> for fear they'll feel insulted.
> They're more than their pain or crutches,
> but I'm not reassured.
> I'm still a girl waiting for my wheezing father
> to rise from his sickbed,
> where he fights another cold or flu
> that could kill him.
> I always feared the end of Dad
> would be the end of me.
> Mom had tuberculosis, too,
> and gasped for breath
> when she tried to run and play with me.
> They tried to keep their fears a secret
> because Dad said I was too sensitive
> and Mom said it was my siblings
> who couldn't bear the misery of this world;
> but the germs they told us about
> invaded the house each winter,
> dropping with the freezing snow,
> festering in the rutted country roads,
> sucking the color from their cheeks.
> They needed comfort, more than I could give.
> Flailing, whispering, shouting,
> they tried to stay calm, and failed,
> then tried again, linked by the fear
> of watching others die, of dying themselves,
> of losing us, and earth, this precious place,
> this priceless battleground.

In March of 2020, my husband Tom and I found ourselves facing covid-19, and like much of the world we gathered masks, gloves, hand wipes, and plenty of soap and water and began cleaning phones, door handles, and every other available surface. We talked about how we could protect ourselves and our beautiful grown sons, Nicholas "Bly" and Ethan "Rowan," not to mention our dear friends. One morning I woke too early, burdened as usual by my fears of covid-19, and I remembered how my parents had struggled to breathe as they recuperated from tb, and how my father had written about those years.

I went to my bookshelf and found *Boy Almighty* and began to re-read it, and I was soon, once again, riding sidekick to Eric Frey. I cheered for his recovery and rebirth, and watched as the faintly glowing ember of his life was slowly fanned, nursed, and strengthened. I applauded his passion for writing and life just as I applauded my father's passion for writing and for the gift of life. My family and I had lived for decades with the real life version of Eric, who rose from the hell of the San, and finally, near the end of the novel, made a vow to begin a career as a writer. "Eric swore to himself that, to make up for the loss of life at death, he would fill all the moments before it with all the exultation he could remember. He would see, leap, sing." A short time after he left the San in March of 1942, my father wrote to Dr. Cohen, "My life is in the chance that I can become a really fine writer . . . I'm not living just to live." Besides having survived tb, Dad was the eldest of six brothers, a farm boy who had also survived prairie blizzards, the Dust Bowl, and the Depression, and wrote about them in his novels. He understood why it was so very necessary to "see, leap, sing."

Dad always seemed to know when it was time to take action, which reminds me of when I was in first grade and Dad rescued me from Westwood Elementary School during a 1951 Minnesota blizzard.

We weren't exactly leaping or singing in Miss Bly's second grade classroom when the blizzard came up, but by noon I could clearly see every bush and tree outside the windows blowing in a horizontal direction and I wondered why there had been no formal announcement of school closing on the intercom. I'd been assigned to help Bobby Bean with his multiplication, while other students took turns at the blackboard under the measured gaze of Miss Bly. It had become so dark outside that all the lights in our room were blazing.

Suddenly, the door of the schoolroom flew open and there

stood my father wearing a towering black Russian Cossack hat, a hefty grey winter coat, and size sixteen rubber boots. His eyebrows and shoulders were frosted with ice and snow. Before Miss Bly could say a word, my father bellowed,

"Hello, Miss Bly!" And he beckoned to me. "Freya, get your things! We're going home!" As Miss Bly approached him, Dad waved an arm over the class and cried, "I can take any of you country kids home. Who wants a ride?" No one answered. They just stared at Dad and the suddenly diminutive Miss Bly. "Okay, then!" Dad said. Turning to Miss Bly, who was gaping up at him, Dad roared, "Excuse me, Miss Bly, but the roads will be closed in less than an hour. Better get the principal to order those buses out now!" "Your Dad's a giant," my friend Shirley whispered.

"Yeah, the Jolly Green Giant," Bobby Bean sneered, always the sarcastic goof-off.

But I wasn't embarrassed. I could feel Dad's excitement. Something big and important was happening, and Dad and I were going to be part of it.

A moment later we jumped into our old black Ford and started down the winding, snow-covered Bloomington streets, chugging all the way out of town to Normandale Boulevard, and then left onto Auto Club Road where in those days mostly farm houses stood amid the cornfields. But as we approached the big sweeping curve near the Masonic Home we found that huge drifts already covered the road in long swaths, some of them nearly twenty feet long and two or three feet high.

Dad stomped on the brakes and jumped out of the car. "Stay here where it's warm!" he cried, and dashed off through the near whiteout. I watched his tall wind-whipped form flailing through the drifts until he leaped into the ditch, and struggled along, his long arms flapping. Then he leaped out of the ditch and began marching, zigzagging up and down through the field. After a few moments, he returned, panting, his face red, his voice huge in the roaring wind. "We're going straight through the cornfield. The wind blew it clearer than the road! Jump in the back seat and hang on!"

And so I grabbed the back of Dad's coat collar and we flew off the blacktop, down into the ditch, and up into the rutted cornfield, ramming and crashing through the cut-off cornstalks and mounting snow—no seatbelts in those days. Dad didn't seem to mind that I clutched at his neck while he sucked his breath in and blew it out. Three times we almost got stuck, and the fourth time, when we were close to losing our battle with the snow, my father began to sing a song I'd never heard before and never heard again: "Well, gimme a bucket a blood, boys! Gimme a bucket a blood! You can take your whole damn nation, and your whole congregation, and stick it up your ass!"

"Dad! What are you singing?!"

"A song I learned once. To give me strength!" he shouted, tears from the wind while he twisted the steering wheel left, right, and left again. He stepped on the gas and back on the brake and back on the gas, until—bumping, bouncing, and swiveling—we made it across the frozen field to the road, and sailed along one more snowing mile—home.

And at the door stood my beautiful, brilliant, musing mother with a look of relief on her face. "I can't believe you made it!"

"Dad sang a song with swear words in it," I told her, "that's why we made it this far."

"What song is that?" she asked Dad. "Nothing!" Dad said. "It was just the wind!"

The next day we heard that most of the other children had to spend the night at school.

So, that was the living Boy Almighty. I met that guy more than once. Even in the last months of his life, which I describe in my memoir, *Frederick Manfred: A Daughter Remembers*, I believe my father's experience at the San with sickness and death greatly influenced how he faced his own death fifty-two years later. As he lay for six weeks dying of brain cancer, mostly stuck in the hospital, he was disarmingly straightforward about his dreams, his thoughts, and his feelings. He kept his sense of humor and understood what the doctors were telling him, although sometimes he'd present the truth rewritten, the way he wanted to believe it, to gain the courage to get through a bad moment.

When he at first avoided referring to his brain tumor as cancerous, I decided it didn't matter. He was, as usual, adjusting to what was happening to his body in his own authentic fashion. I believed he instinctively knew what attitude would yield the best result.

He enjoyed telling stories as he died, about when he'd knocked out Joe Louis's sparring partner in a boxing match, or how he'd written a shelf full of worthwhile, enjoyable novels. And during the few days he had at home before he had to go back to the hospital, he was so grateful to be in his own bed, gazing out at the waving prairie grass, that he didn't stop talking for hours. Though he hadn't spoken about death before, back at Roundwind he turned his considerable mental fortitude to thinking and talking about something we were all thinking about.

He told us how his father, Frank Feikema, had died. "I've been having long conversations with your Uncle Ed, too, since he died. And with Professor Jellema from Calvin College and others."

I looked into his eyes. "And the people you're talking with are all dead?"

"Yes. That's right. But I wish they'd be more precise about what they are doing on the other side. Listening to them is like watching a bad tv show, badly written. I want more clarity."

"Maybe they'll get more clear with time."

"They'd better," he said, smiling, "because if they don't, pretty soon I may lose interest."

He was beaming with pleasure, delighted to play host. Tom and I drew chairs up to the bed and ate dinner with him. He told us in great detail how Edward McDowell, his former publisher, had died, and more recently, Wallace Stegner. He spoke as if he were steadying himself and learning something by describing each man's death. "I saw many men die in the sanatorium. I remember when Huck Anderson died, sweet Huck Anderson. I saw this red spume erupt from his mouth, and blood poured down his chest. That was something for me to see from the corner of my eye."

He asked our sons, Rowan and Bly, to hang their drawing of a winged fire-breathing dragon on the bedroom wall, and spoke with great joy about how talented and handsome they were. "Wait till they grow up. They'll have every woman in the world chasing them. They'll be president and vice president."

"I'm not sure that's something to wish for, Dad."

"Oh, it will be, when they're ready. Or else, I hope at least one of them will be an artist."

He stopped talking about death when Bly and Rowan joined us, and only continued after they left the room.

I remembered that one day when he'd been writing for fifty years and had twenty-five novels behind him, he was asked during an interview, "If you had one minute to live and were given the privilege of making a final statement, what would it be?" And Dad replied, "I'd say, 'It was all marvelous. I don't regret a minute of it. Even the pain and hunger, the almost broken head and the broken heart, were sweet to have. It was life, not death. And all moments of life are very precious.'" This attitude was probably why, even when he had to go back to the hospital, I savored my precious time with him. His speech was garbled at times, but he often said wonderful things. He was curious to the end, with a sweet disposition, unblaming and uncomplaining, and even reassuring. Whenever he had a setback, he'd look up at me and say, "It will be all right, honey. Don't worry, it will be all right."

When Uncle Henry and Uncle Floyd and their families came to visit, Henry later told me that Dad suddenly said, "You know, Henry. I've got to get this right."

Unsure what Dad was referring to, Henry asked, "Get it right? Get what right."

"Dying," Dad answered. "You get one chance to do it right. This is my only chance."

When I told Dad we had to leave for three days to bring Rowan and Bly home to start their first few days of eighth grade, I promised him that when we returned we were going to do everything we could to get him back home to Roundwind. I stroked his cheek and said goodbye, and he looked at me and mumbled a few semi-garbled words, quoting from something he'd read. I had to bend close to hear him: "Yes. Goodbye, honey. Your path leads upward into life, and my path leads downward to death." He shook his head in wonder. "Isn't that a wonderful saying? A genius wrote that. It's so beautiful. What a wonderful writer. Just wonderful."

Later I learned that the quote came from Socrates in Plato's *The Apology*: "The hour of departure has arrived, and we go our ways—I to die, and you to live. Which is better only God knows."

Looking back, I believe part of Dad knew he was about to die, and another part of him did not accept it. The father, the man, and the farmer in him knew and acknowledged it. The other being inside him, the creative being, the lizard prince and dedicated novelist, did not accept, would not accept, should not have accepted his death.

He was a dying man and he was also—Boy Almighty.

*A Note on Language*

No changes have been made to this reprint of *Boy Almighty*. Since the novel was written seventy-five years ago in 1945, in a different time, you will find a few instances where "negro" is the term used to describe an African American or Black person, and where "quarter-blood" or "Indian" describes a Native American. As my father once wrote in a book of reminiscences, *Prime Fathers*, "The health of a society can be measured by the size and vigor of its minority group(s)." Also, I feel strongly that there are a few paragraphs that no longer reflect my father's later, more mature understanding of homosexuality. He changed, but these sentences do not reflect his growth. I was, however, raised by a man who believed all races and peoples were beautiful, and that we would all be even more beautiful if we could respect each other and love freely, no matter our religion, race, or sexuality.

*Sources*

Huseboe, Arthur R., and Nancy Owen Nelson, eds. *The Selected Letters of Frederick Manfred—1932–1954*. Lincoln: University of Nebraska Press, 1988.

Manfred, Freya. *Frederick Manfred—A Daughter Remembers*. St. Paul: Minnesota Historical Society Press, 1999.

Rezmerski, John Calvin, ed. *The Frederick Manfred Reader*. Duluth MN: Holy Cow! Press, 1996.

# BOY ALMIGHTY

# T I—RETURN TO THE MATRIX

HE BULKY ambulance-driver pushed a thin pillow beneath Eric's head and covered his long body with a clean white sheet.

The bulky man gestured. His stubby assistant hurried. And together the two men lifted the stretcher and carried him from the narrow room.

As Eric passed through the door, he turned his blue eyes sideways to look at his books and manuscript for the last time, turning his eyes so far they hurt in their sockets.

Gravely the two gray-clad men carried him down the winding stairs. For heavy men they were surprisingly gentle. Only when they reached the last turn in the stairwell did they bump his long-toed feet dangling from the edge of the stretcher. The bump stirred the fierce little animal in his left side and it gnawed at him and he held it stiffly against his naked body. The bulky man swore considerately, and drew in his breath.

As they emerged from the tenant-aged frame house on Hickory street, the late afternoon sun filtering through the just-leafing trees splashed sprinkles of light on Eric. He blinked and hesitated and then jerked his joint-knobby limbs a little, like a gray-bellied bug discovered beneath old bark.

Faintly he heard a car drive up and heard the fall of the engine murmur. The car door opened and he heard a woman draw in her breath and exclaim, "Why, it's Eric!"

He recognized the woman. She was the sturdy wife of Bud, a friend, who had given him his only good meals during the hungry months. He remembered she liked to cook.

Vaguely he heard her rush across the sidewalk and the lawn, and ask the men, "What's wrong? Where's he going?"

The bulky man did not answer. He had taken a deep breath to lift his end of the stretcher into the ambulance.

3

"Tell me, what's wrong?"

The big man set his end on the edge of the ambulance floor and said, "Nothin's really wrong with him, Ma'am. Just sick, is all. Got a bad cold, maybe."

"Where's he going?"

The big man hesitated, and then blurted, "Well, Ma'am, he's goin' to a sanatorium."

"What? Eric going . . . not our Eric! Why, he always looked so strong and healthy."

Eric stirred again and blinked. "I was hungry," he mumbled.

"What was wrong, Eric?"

"Hungry."

"Hungry? Didn't you have any money? Why didn't you tell me? Or Bud?"

"Hungry."

They shoved him into the ambulance. The doors began to close.

The warm-hearted woman, crying, turned to the men. "Tell me, tell me what happened? I want to know. Please tell me."

"Lady, he's full of bugs. TB bugs. An' we're haulin' him off to the Phoenix Sanatorium."

"Hungry," Eric mumbled.

The doors clanged to and the motor started.

The driver of the ambulance was a gentle man. He had some concern for the patient. Eric could feel the tenderness of him in the way he drove around corners, the way he eased the machine over rough streets and slipped it effortlessly between grumbling cars.

They went along slowly. Every now and then the driver's assistant opened the panel behind the seat to ask Eric if he felt all right.

Eric nodded. His left side pained him too much to make an effort at speech. He held the side of his body as a separate entity in his arms. All the muscles of his neck and his back on the left side, the muscles over his abdomen

4

and in his thighs, were taut and frightened. A few quivered involuntarily at the strain. He lay stiffly, holding his pain closely in his arms. If the evil beast got away, he thought, it might attack again. He held it closely.

The light in his braincase was dim. It wasn't a flame any-more; it was barely a glow; it was hardly light enough to help him find his way from moment to moment. Only when the ambulance jarred him did the coals in his body's grate flare up.

The brake-drums groaned and the ambulance hesitated. Eric poked at the glow in his brain. He caused it to light up and he worked at lifting his head so he could look through the two small panes in the rear door. He looked, and grayly, dimly, saw they were rounding Lake Calhoun. There was a sharp wind out and the waters of the small, oval lake were full of bared teeth. Some of the waves were caught with fierce white splashes. There were a few boats on the surface, and, far beyond, out where a row of bolle-ana poplars curved slenderly and accurately like a row of trees in ancient Attica, he saw a car moving slowly. He wondered who was driving it. It might be himself. He found it difficult to sense just where he was. His head fell back on the finger-thin pillow and the glow faded and the walls of his braincase receded so far into the distance that his skull seemed miles wide and the ceiling of it a lofty, vaulted dome.

The glow came up again and reached at the edges of his skull and seeped out through its apertures. He was sur-prised to find himself covered with a thin sheet and still lying stiffly on the stretcher within the ambulance. He could not understand his situation. He had a notion that an eternity of living had slipped between himself and the car he had driven on the other side of the lake.

The ambulance twisted beneath him and he heard the heavy tires rumbling over rough brick-paving. He tried to force himself backward, far enough to get at some store-house where he had put away volumes of memory. He got there eventually and took them down and spread them out.

5

He opened the pages. He found recorded that southwest of the city a way lay paved with bricks. This road led out towards Lake Minnetonka, out over the mauve, biscuit hills. And near the lake was the sanatorium.

The glow faded again and he lay deep within himself like a raced-out hound, panting, resting, deep in the recesses of his temple. He could see his brain lying on its side, its head resting on its forepaws and panting, tongue out and gaunt. Could even see the saliva running from its mouth, dripping upon its forepaws. It was very tired and sweaty.

The ambulance shook. It was trying to shake him off its back. The jarring awakened the glow. It brightened suddenly. Once more his braincase was filled to over-flowing with light. He raised his head and looked out of the panes of the door.

They were out on rolling land. He studied it with care. The green he saw, a yellow-green, was spring's first grass, and the ruffles on the tree branches were the first bursts of leaves, curled and opening like just-born babies' fists.

A lift in the road tumbled the ambulance a little and his regard went swiftly to his side. The muscles stood stiffly at pain's attention, tightly holding the clawing little beast against his ribs. He faintly remembered the fox gnawing away at the Spartan boy's vitals, and was pleased that he could still remember stories, pleased that he could still lift himself, feet and all, above the monotonous drift of one moment becoming another.

The ambulance turned and slowed and then sped up and then slowed again and turned, circling, turning, until he was sure he had fallen onto a phonograph turntable. He held his side stiffly, fearing the pain that would spring up when the speed of the turntable slackened.

There were voices about. The glow brightened and he lifted his eyelids and looked at the world. The ambulance doors were opening. He saw two men, a burly man and a stubby man. They seemed vaguely familiar. He saw two other faces, women's faces, as white as the nurses' caps they

6

wore. The stretcher moved and he felt himself moving with it, and he felt the brush of the world's breath upon him, the wonderful touch of spring's breath and spring's crisp coolness upon his face.

The nurses were rough. The stretcher disturbed the beast in his side and the beast ate at him and he stiffened his muscles against it and tried to smother it by hugging it close.

He forced his eyes open again. The sky was too blue to be sky at all. It was an immense blue eye, staring so sharply he blinked.

People seemed stilt-tall as they moved past him. There were too many of them.

Two huge doors opened and a stench of carbolic acid hit him. It was fearful, the stench was, and he almost retched. But he fought it and kept the animal quiet. It would eat no more of him if he could help it.

The two doors closed behind him, like two huge lips of a whale lying on its side, and he was inside the stinking body.

He felt eyes brushing his face. Some of the eyes were square with pity. Some were slitted as if the owners of them were afraid to look out of them. Some were bold and cruel, staring at his nakedness.

He was rolled down a hallway and into an intensely dark room where the glow of his brain, instead of sharpening like a lantern does when night's darkness presses upon it, almost went out. There was a smell of burnt air. He had no feeling of anything about him. There was no sky nor depth, no grass nor stars, no sun, no walls nor floor nor ceiling, no white, but black and black and nothing. He was lonesome here.

A voice, a calm voice spoke, softly, "Can you roll on your side?"

He rolled against the little animal. He tried to smother it. He held himself stiffly.

"Take a deep breath. Hold it."

He heard a click, a buzzing. A strange glow, an X-ray's

glow, lighted outside his braincase. It was so like his own glow that he was sure it was the open skull of another man, accidentally revealed.

"Good. That's it."

Hands lifted him upright, held him against a machine. He heard a murmur of voices. A kind voice was exclaiming, "Bad? Hah! Look. There's a major lesion. There's some more trouble. And that's pleurisy, maybe pneumonia. Or, it could be still another lesion."

"What's a lesion?" Eric suddenly asked, opening a lucid moment.

"It's a . . . trouble."

"A trouble?" Eric looked and saw four white faces peering at him and nodding. The faces were masked. "A trouble?"

"Yes. It's a hole. TB bugs ate a hole in your lung about the size of an egg."

"A hole!" Eric exclaimed. Without moving a muscle, he laughed a little. The glow rose and he laughed still more, still restraining his muscles from mirth. "The little rascals. So they ate a hole in me. A hole. Holy Moses."

The faces quivered. Hands laid him on his side. The door opened. The stretcher began to roll again and he with it. The stretcher rolled down the hall, a high gray hall with an uneventful ceiling.

He saw many faces and smelled much foul air. He heard many people coughing; sometimes so hard he had to restrain an impulse to imitate them.

He was in an elevator. He could feel it ascending. He wondered if God were taking him up to place him on His right hand to sit for a pitiless eternity.

He forced his wick to glow. He forced his eyes to open. He saw a kind face near him. Beneath it stood the body of a man with hands on the controls of the elevator. His face smiled down at him. Eric looked at the face carefully. It was a mirror. On this mirror he saw countless other faces, an endless procession of faded white faces that had come into the San just as he had come this day. It was a kind face, a gentle face, a gentle mirror. Its reflection improved one's looks.

They were pushed into the hall, he and the stretcher and the little beast in his side.

A pusher rolled him quietly down the hall, and through a door.

He heard women whispering. They were nurses.

One was saying, "Out in the hall."

"All right, all right!" The voice was harsh.

He was out in the hallway. He heard some scraping and, when he opened his eyes again, he found himself on a stretcher with white screens around him. There were windows on his left.

The house must be full of visitors, he thought idly; so full I have to sleep in the hall tonight. There is no room at the inn.

He drifted off. The ember fell, fell, fell, and flickered and went out. He fell asleep.

Food was moving in his mouth when the tiny flame came up again.

He waited a moment. Yes, it was food, and it was rolling around in his mouth and his mouth was moving too. He pushed at the glow and awakened it and then lifted up his eyelids again, pushing them up as if they were heavy sliding doors, and saw a white woman feeding him.

The food had no taste, and he took his tongue and scooped it toward the front of his mouth-cavern. The cavern was very wide and high and it took him some time to sweep the food forward to the door. But soon he had it all swept up in a pile and thrust it out.

"Oh, but you must eat," said the white woman's voice. "You've got to eat. You must eat or you won't get well."

That was a thought. Get well.

He held his tongue quiet. Maybe he had better let them store some food in his mouth after all. He took up his tongue and set it over to one side to make room for the food.

9

The white woman loaded in a few shovelsful.

"Chew it," she said. "You better chew it."

He considered this. How could a granary chew its own contents? Of course. The white woman was squirrelly. A corncrib . . . who ever heard of a crib chewing its own corn?

"Chew it," she said. "Chew it. Chew it hard."

Slowly, though he thought it foolish, he opened the sides of the corncrib and began to chew on the corn.

He smiled. This was funny. No one had ever seen what this white woman was seeing. She was actually watching a corncrib chewing its own corn.

The smile widened. He could feel it cracking open the sides of the crib. He would really give her a run for her money. He would give her a treat. He hurried the movements of the crib sides, chewing the corn inside it.

"Swallow it," she said. "Swallow it. Please swallow it. I've got a lot more for you."

He considered her talk. She had more? Holy Moses, Pa must have quite a corn crop this year! Quite a corn crop that he could refill the cribs again and again.

"Swallow it," the white woman said insistently. "Swallow it, swallow it."

What did "swallow" mean? He considered it. He tried to turn up the wick. "Swallow it." Now what did that mean? Did the corncrib have a belly? A sort of cellar-belly?

A cellar-belly.

He would try it. He took his tongue again and swept the huge piles of corn together into one lump and pushed it back toward his cellar and down it went. He waited to hear it fall. He waited.

"Now eat some more," the white woman said.

"Wait," he said. "Wait. It didn't go down yet."

"What?"

"Shhh . . . " he cautioned. "Wait." He waited, listening. But there was no sound.

"Stuff must've landed on some hay down there," he confided. "Cellar must be full of hay. That's why we didn't hear it."

"Sure, sure," the white woman said. "Sure it did. And now, here, eat some more."

He opened his cribs again.

But then the little animal started to eat at him again. And swiftly the glow went up and, pfft, out.

Two file-rough voices were talking.

"Ain't you the new head orderly on Third West now?"

"That's what the super says."

"Nice going. You must be a pet of his."

"What?"

"Yeh."

"Honest-to-God, Joe, I've never played up to him. Just went along. Then all of a sudden he called me in and gave it to me. Really."

"Skip it."

"But . . ."

There was a silence. Eric hoped they would talk some more. It had been beautiful.

"Oh nuts! Skip it."

The protesting orderly asked, "This stiff just come?"

"About five minutes ago."

"Did he look bad?"

"Gray as a dead man."

"Are they gonna leave him here in the hall?"

"Guess so."

"Wonder why they don't give him a room?"

"I dunno. The floor doc says he won't last the night. He'll croak. No use making up a room for him then, is there?"

"No, I suppose not. Christ, them docs are hard-boiled. No feelings at all."

"You can say that again."

They stood breathing together.

Eric stirred. Tomorrow morning, there would be no sun tomorrow morning?

No sun?

11

# A

N HOUR later, at six o'clock, he had another moment of clarity.

He saw that he was in a corridor about forty feet long, twenty feet wide. It was high, and painted a dull gray, and it connected the main building with a wing. The corridor explained the passing of many feet beyond the screen.

He was near a window in the corner. A wash-stand stood near his bed with a tumbler-covered bottle of water, a small box of white paper napkins, and a gray sputum-receptacle on its top. From its side hung a clean towel and a washrag, both boldly marked in red, *Phoenix Sanatorium.*

He took the little gnawing beast close against him and turned slowly, laboriously, over on his left shoulder so that he could see the countryside.

He puffed. He coughed. It was the first cough he had dared to let ride through. He had submerged all other impulses. He panted a little.

Through the window he could see the long high ridge of the opposite wing of the building. Beyond it, still farther west, was the falling sun. The red brick walls on the east side of the west wing were bloody red in the shadow, and the windows glimmered purply.

He shifted his eyes a trifle. Far out beyond the wing of the building, the land swelled into small hills, some crested by trees, some by careful rows of cornstalks, and some by the sweep of grass.

There was one hill with a farmhouse perched halfway down the side of it. Lower, a barn, half-rammed into the chest of the hill, protruded disturbingly over a rock wall. Two cows were entering a door, with a lad following. The lower door closed. The lad leaned over the door for a long time, dreaming.

Strokes of green lay over the hills, as if an artist had just begun to put on the colors after he had sketched in the outlines. Even in the old cornfield where the decaying stalks were yellow-gray, a green was coming through.

12

Eric shifted and saw a gray-brown swamp directly south. Beyond it lay a fan-shaped lake browed by oaks. The waters were darkling beneath evening's black-blue sky. The stubby waves were sometimes white-capped, sometimes deeply purple.

He looked out over the land and the swamp and the lake; and rejoiced, momentarily, in the streaming sunlight, the striding shadows.

He noticed that the oaks were still clinging to last year's faded brown leaves. A few of the leaves were falling as the just-now-bursting sprouts thrust the old ones away. To one side of the lake, new young leaves were silvering a clump of white birches.

Soon his interest in the earth subsided. He wasn't sure he loved the earth anymore. One stroke less of flame in his skull and he could be indifferent to spring itself. He turned his eyes to look to the west again, trying to find the sun, his friend. Eric studied his position. Unless someone rolled him to another part of the building he would never be able to see his sun again.

There was a stir beside him. A gentle voice was upon him, a woman's voice.

"Yes?"

"Are you comfortable?"

"Yes."

She was a thick-armed, laughing nurse, with breasts as big as bowls, as ample as Ma Memme's had been. She rolled him over, gently; so gently, she did not disturb the little animal in his side. She lifted a small thermometer from a glass tube filled with red, antiseptic fluid and thrust it into his mouth. It was cold and the fluid on it tasted unpleasant, like flat water with chloride. Her hand circled his wrist. She took his pulse.

A fancy seized him. He felt himself being swung. The smiling gentle nurse was holding him by the mouth and the wrist, and was swinging him about in the universe just as Pa had once playfully swung him in their farm kitchen twenty-seven years ago. Mounting excitement welled in

13

him, welled up so fast, vague laughter finally splashed from him.

He studied her face. She was sweet.

She dropped his wrist on the white cover and withdrew the thermometer. She read it. Her smile did not change perceptibly as she stepped back to lift a pad hanging on a string from the back of the bedstand. She recorded his pulse-beat and temperature.

"Bad?" he asked.

"Oh, not very."

"Bad?"

"No. Really. It's quite a remarkable temperature for a skinny man like you."

He shivered. He could feel the little beast stirring in his side. "Tell me."

"No. Of course, you've got a fever, you know. But . . . it's not bad. And I've brought a few pills for you. Can you swallow them?"

His nod was faint.

She lifted his head and placed two capsules on his tongue and helped him to a glass of water. He swallowed with difficulty.

"Do you need anything else?"

He felt the need to blush, but was so weak he could not. He needed something. He moved his hands a little. For the first time since the pain had crawled into his side, he was conscious of his hands. What had happened to them all this time? He had held the little beast against his side with them, but nothing more. He wondered if his hands were white, if the veins rain in blue streams across the white on them.

He said, "I can't urinate alone." He was startled by his own calm speech. This was a woman and he was asking her to help him.

"Oh. Of course," she said. She reached down and lifted up a small urinal that looked like a headless white duck. Under the covers, rustling the stiff white sheets, she helped him.

14

"Thank you," he said, "I was a little worried."

She glanced at him. "You're a friendly man with so much sickness in you."

He tried to smile.

"Anything else?" She reached across him to straighten out his bed-covers. Her breast touched his face lightly, swelling out softly as it came down more firmly. "Anything else?"

"Thanks."

She was leaving.

"Nurse!"

"Yes?"

"Nurse . . ." He restrained his panting. His flame was low. Too strong a gust of air would blow it out. "Nurse . . . roll me . . . " he fought his panting . . . "roll me to where I can see the sun."

"The sun?"

"Yes. I'd like to see it."

"Why?"

"Please."

She came over and took his hand. "I'm sorry I can't. I'm so sorry I can't. So very. But there's no way."

"Please!"

"Sorry."

He said nothing and drew his hand from hers and rolled over on his side again. He heard her leave.

This time the little animal stirred and bit at him for turning on it. The little beast was upset for a long while, slashing and gnawing at him. He lay quietly and suffered it vengeance. He had momentary impulses of anger toward it and wished fleetingly that he were strong enough to grab it by the neck and wring it and kill it.

At last the little beast finished exacting its satisfaction and quieted.

He remembered the nurse writing on the pad. He was curious to see what she had marked on it.

He felt too weak to move. He was not inclined to disturb the little gnawing weasel in his side. Even the mere thought

15

of the animal brought breathlessness upon him again. He decided to stifle his curiosity. He told his mind it would have to wait a while. He wrote out a sermon and preached to it. He tried to assuage its fears and its abnormal curiosity. He fed it platitudes: "Be of good cheer." "Fear not, for I am with you." "Be of good hope." "Place your trust in me." "I am with you always." He fed it little stories.

But his mind was restless. The flame in it was stronger than ever. It demanded knowledge. It was hungry. Its forepaws were raised menacingly and its eyes were sharp upon him and it demanded to know. "The truth," it said. "I must know the truth. I must know. There is something there on the pad and I, the Poet, must know it."

He smiled paternally at his mind. His mind was like a child. It was young and did not understand that it must not know all things. He laughed indulgently, thinking that he was a very sane citizen of the jungle. He told his mind, "There's always tomorrow . . . when you're grown up."

"Death is coming tonight."

'Well, in that event, what's the difference?"

"It's coming tonight."

"Now. Don't try to scare me. You're only a child. How can you frighten me?"

"It's coming tonight."

"You don't need to know."

"But I must know. Maybe this is the one fact I need in my search for the Answer. And I want it now. Now. Now. I am the Poet and I want the Answer at last."

Such a mind. Well, maybe he should humor it. Besides, what matter if death did come while he was reaching for the pad?

"All right, all right. Quiet now. There's that little animal in my side I've got to humor. Quiet and tiptoe now."

He smiled cunningly to himself. He would outfox the little animal. He would be cunning.

He moved slowly. The effort was great. He tired quickly. He puffed. Breaths whistled through his moisture-heavy bronchi. Slowly he managed to turn over on his other side

16

and face the stand beside his bed without disturbing the sleeping beast.

With great effort he pulled his right hand up from under the sheet. The arm seemed to be unendingly long. When the hand came past his face, he was surprised to see blue veins running in streams across the flat, white, lightly-freckled prairie of it. He sent the hand toward the stand, curved it behind.

He was disconcerted to find the pad fastened securely to the back of the stand. He held a council with his mind.

He laughed softly. It was a pleasure to feel that he was divided into two people, each with a job to do.

He pulled at the stand. It moved easily. He lifted the pad; lifted his head. He felt the neck muscles, which tied his head to his torso, straightening out like guy wires.

His eyes went down the temperature column. 104.6°.

Down the pulse column. 136.

He dropped the chart. He fell back into bed. He looked at the gleaming red figures neoned in his mind. His temperature was up six degrees. His pulse doubled. That was sickness.

The orderlies had been right. He thought about their use of the word "croak." He had always associated choking with croaking. He remembered how Pa's pigs, dying of hog cholera, a hundred of them in one day, had all choked when they croaked.

He directed his attention to his throat. He listened. He heard a wet whistling. The choking was already begun.

A man appeared at his bedside. The man was dressed in a white smock. He had a professional air. Except for a band of gray-black hair about his ears, he was as bald as a rain-wet gourd. Behind the glasses, the eyes of the man were kind and owl-wise. Eric felt he would like to visit with this new mind. His own mind was dumb sometimes, even utterly stupid. But he did like to share the little light it had, the little glow, the little flame, with the higher fires kept in the skulls around him.

17

The man spoke. "How do you feel?"

Eric smiled. "All right." His flame went up. His skull was like a Hallowe'en pumpkin illuminated by a candle.

The man said, "I'm Dr. Abraham. Your doctor. How do you feel?"

Eric considered the notion of having a doctor. For some prejudice or other, he felt he shouldn't like any doctor. This one, however, was at least pleasant.

"How do you feel?" Dr. Abraham asked again.

Eric thought about the word "feel." The manner in which the man spoke it indicated he had a special use for it. "Feel?" he panted. "I hardly feel."

Dr. Abraham nodded.

Eric could feel the man's eyes trying to give him strength, to reach inside his skull. "I'm pretty sick, Doc."

The eyes warmed.

Eric could read them. Dr. Abraham was making a last call on this patient before recording its passing.

Dr. Abraham asked, "Where is your family?"

"Family?" Eric hadn't thought about them. The flame had been too low. "Why, home, I s'pose. Pa and my stepmother both. Got a brother here, in Minneapolis."

"What's his name?"

"Ronald."

"And your father's?"

"Edward Frey. Bonnie Doon, Minnesota. That's in the southwest corner of the state."

The eyes blinked, shutting off light from him momentarily. "We couldn't locate Ronald."

"Oh?"

"Why didn't you tell him?"

"I didn't know I was sick."

"Hah!" The guttural expression was the doctor's only ruthless gesture.

"My light's far down, doctor." He fought for breath.

"Yes."

The man was honest. He knew Eric. From somewhere Eric found some breath, and said, "I read the temperature

18

and the pulse, doc."

"Oh? Well, you'll be all right."

They looked at each other, and smiled.

Eric said, "Don't tell anybody. Not until . . . "

Dr. Abraham nodded. "All right," he said softly. He took Eric's arm full in his hand and gripped it and left.

Eric relaxed.

So this was it.

He felt pleasant about it. He smiled softly. He thought to himself, "If the sun doesn't come up for me tomorrow . . . well, my carcass will still be around for a few more days." He rested, breathing a little. He mused. "I wish I could be around to watch the undertaker fill my veins with embalming fluid just like I helped fill Ma Memme's, and watch him lay me out, and watch people I know file past me so I could study their faces. I'd know then what they really thought of me. And watch them deck me out with flowers and watch the domeny pray." He breathed slowly. "Thunder, I sure wish I could see it."

After a little time he became sad. He had a small regret. He was dying without something done.

Funny how a man wanted to end life with a little glory, make himself imperishable, become identified with everlast-. ingness.

Man was a trapped flame. This collection of vibrant chemicals called man had been given a flame, a little flame strong enough to reach out beyond the confines of its skull to see that life was impermanent.

Man had been trapped. He had been given a piece of candy and, once having tasted it, wanted it, like a querulous child, to last all day.

Man, like the child, wanted the last horizon, eternity. Man had been given just enough life to sense that life would be good to have forever.

Eric ballooned himself with so much breath he awoke the animal.

Sharp pain.

Bitter is life. Bitter. Bitter.

19

The flame fell down, far. It glowed, was dull red.
Blew the wind then. Blew.

III—FLICKERINGS

THE NEXT morning he awoke suddenly. His eyes
opened wide.

He turned his head slowly and was astonished to find
the brightest sunlight he had ever seen lacquering the red
bricks of the west wing. The row of lombardy poplars
reaching up along the wing from the ground below was
full of crisp yellow sparkles. The birds sang so spiritedly
that an impulse to stir tormented his febrile limbs.
He was about to put his arm beneath himself to sit up
when he remembered the little animal.

But he wanted to leap about. He was sure that he could
dance again. It was ennobling, this sunshine. It was a gift
he had never expected to get again. He wanted to call in a
friend to share this gift. He wanted to call Martha Lonn.

Martha! The name stung him and he dropped deep into his pillows. He had not forgotten her. Like a couchant,
blood-sucking weasel, she had waited for a favorable moment to seize his mind. He cursed her inwardly. Now that
she had thrown him aside for another, couldn't she leave
him alone?

Panting, he closed his eyes again. The moment of wild
glorious exhilaration had vanished, replaced by this memory, and its futility.

A cough heaved up his chest. A heavy wet obstruction
gagged him. Fearful, he struggled to keep from choking to
death. He sucked for breath to expel the obstruction. He
coughed until his skin purpled. He was thoroughly surprised to notice the reserve of power still in his body.

The haystack in his throat rose up and filled his mouth.
He quickly reached around at the stand and found the
gray sputum box with its removable wax-paper container.

He spat a mop-like object into it. He fell back exhausted.

After a couple of respirations his lungs felt remarkably free and open again. He idly wondered whether this lung-freeness meant he was improving, whether it indicated he would live despite the evil predictions of orderlies and doctors, despite the pleurisy and pneumonia and tuberculosis.

The screens parted. He did not recognize the ample-breasted nurse who stepped into the enclosure, carrying a basin of steaming water. She was wearing a smile she had picked up with her gown in the dressing room. She said, "Time to wash up now. You must be clean for breakfast, you know."

He closed his eyes.

Apparently she remembered, then, that he was very ill. She became very gentle in her movements. She carefully pushed the stand aside and, taking a bar of soap and a washrag, worked up a lather in her hands.

When he smelled the sharp odor of tar soap, he opened his eyes.

She was smiling. She was full of concern. Her movements, he decided as she turned to wash him, were of the correct humility and he submitted to her ablutions. She was washing his feet with tears and anointing them with oil.

He had an uneasy feeling about this woman; as if he had known her somewhere before. But his world was only as wide as his eyes could see at any one moment, and he could not place her in the past.

He lay quietly as she lifted his right hand. He could not determine just where the long, loose bones of his arm were tied to his body. He tried to grasp the idea that the arm she was now washing belonged to him.

When she tugged at his left arm he almost sprang from bed. "Be careful!" he said tensely. "There's a little beast . . . a great pain there."

"Oh. I'm sorry."

"It's all right. You didn't know."

She finished washing him. She placed the thermometer beneath his tongue and took his pulse.

When she had recorded both, he asked, "Better?"

"Oh yes," she said very quickly.

He said nothing.

It was good to subside into the pillow again. He thought about the sun outdoors. His mind was still vague, still weak. It was difficult to think very long about any one thing. He forgot easily. He frowned as he tried to remember what had just happened a moment ago. He blinked his eyes, trying to place himself astride each moment. He kept slipping off. He felt diffused, scattered.

But he was glad that he could see things with some little clarity, that he could exercise some little judgement on the passing moments.

He thought about the idea that the world was only minute-wide and minute-high. He was sure that at one time the world had been much larger, much wider, for this world he now had was too much like a playhouse. A heavy fog had crept upon him, obliterating everything except himself and the ground he lay on.

He lay quietly sleeping until an orderly came through the screens carrying a tray. The orderly barely glanced at him, set the tray on the stand, and hurried away.

Eric did not glance at the tray. By the smell that suddenly came, he knew it was good. He sniffed gently, picking out the aromas: hot milk, orange-juice.

The screens parted again and the same nurse came in. He stared at her. He pushed at the boundaries of his world to see if he could remember having known her before. She was freckled. She had an ample bosom. She was gentle. He shook his head. No, he had never seen her before. But she was pleasant and he liked her.

"How'd you like a bite to eat?"

"No."

"No? Aren't you hungry?"

He did not answer. He was struck by her gay manner.

"Here," she said briskly then, "here, you must try. I'll help you." She set the tray beside him on the bed and, taking up a spoon, filled it with orange-juice.

He gagged when the filled spoon touched his lips. A vomiting impulse clutched him, violently, uncontrollably. Again he was surprised by the hidden reserve of strength in his body.

The animal in his side awoke. "Take it away," he gasped.

Her eyes opened widely. She took the tray and set it on a chair outside the screens. "Maybe," she ventured uncertainly, "maybe you'd like to try a little later." She left.

He settled back into the pillow, wishing that the soft sides of it would cover his face and hide him away forever.

He rose out of the deep.

A nurse with freckles and a cap that looked like a bonnet worn backwards was beside him. She was holding a curiously shaped implement. He stared at it. He could not determine what she wanted.

She placed it beside him on his bed. When she saw his questioning look, she reached down to a lower shelf in his stand and drew out a roll of toilet paper.

He understood. "Oh no," he whispered. "Not this morning."

She hesitated. "But you must . . . if you can."

He shook his head. "No, not today. Can't."

She looked at him, studying his words. "You mean, you're too weak?"

He whispered, "Yes. Though I could the other."

"This?"

He nodded.

"Of course," she said, and, matter-of-factly, reached down for his white urinal. She helped him expertly. He was surprised at the flatness of the experience.

"Nothing more?"

"No. Just let me sleep," he said.

She drew away quietly.

His mental glow thrust away enveloping layers of white

sleep. He was surprised to find a nurse with freckles and a smile beside him. She was swishing a washrag in a small tub of water. The tub had been set on the bedstand. "Remember me?" she asked brightly.

He liked her friendly ways, but did not know her. "No."

"You don't? That's funny. I was here just a few minutes ago. Why, I was here a couple of times this morning. And last night."

"You're new to me."

"Why, that's funny." She looked at him closely. "You really don't?"

"No."

"That's very funny. You act clear-headed."

He said nothing.

"I don't understand it. Well, anyway, it's time for your bath now."

He did not stir. The word had no meaning for him.

"Take your shirt off," she said.

He did not move.

She laid aside the washrag and drew down the white sheet. Her fingers were wet and cold, and he shivered.

She took her hands away then and said, "Excuse me all to pieces. I should've dried my hands."

He did not make an effort to talk.

She asked, "Don't you have pajamas?"

"I've been too hard up to have any." He was startled to hear the words. He did not remember poverty.

She seemed skeptical. "No pajamas? No nightshirt? Nothing?"

He was so weak he could hardly move his tongue.

She said, "I did notice last night you weren't wearing any, but I thought . . ."

He smiled weakly at her. "All I was wearing when I came in was a wrist watch Pa once gave me."

She drew down the sheet to his waist and began to wash him with warm soapy water. For a moment it was invigorating, and good, and he felt mothered. He was apprehensive that she might disturb the little animal in his side but

24

she was careful. When she had finished his chest, he lay relaxed, puffing gently.

The flame went lower, lower, beneath the water she poured over him.

Awakening, he was startled to find a freckled nurse washing his leg. She was moving his leg.

Awakening, he was surprised to find a freckled nurse rolling him over to wash his back. He lay almost smothered in the pillow. His neck was doubled and she reached forward to lift it straight. He felt like a broken bird.

She rubbed his spine and his buttocks gently. She rolled him over on his back again. His head flopped awkwardly. She reached forward to lay it neatly on the pillow. As she did so, her breast came gently welling against his bare chest.

She said, placing the washrag near him, "Now, Mr. Frey, do you think you can finish your bath while I make up a bed down the hall?" When he didn't move or betray by his eyes that he had heard, she repeated, "Do you think you can finish your admittance bath now?"

"Finish?"

"Yes. You know, finish."

"Can't," he whispered.

"You must. You've got to be clean . . . there."

He looked at her. "I thought nurses were objective."

She looked back at him. "Well, mister, you asked for it."

When she had finished, he said, gathering all his strength to say it, "Now, that wasn't so bad, was it?"

"No."

They heard someone walk past the door and she said, abruptly crisp, "I'll try to find some pajamas for you and then make your bed."

He was startled to find a man with a bald head and owl-wise eyes beside him, standing over a weird contraption made up of two cylinders and a tangle of rubber tubes.

25

The man was Dr. Abraham. But Eric did not remember the man in his finger-narrow world, nor the full-breasted nurse standing off to one side.

Dr. Abraham said, "You look as if you'd been on a week's drunk, Eric."

Eric liked the words, the tone of them, the idea behind them. He managed to smile.

Dr. Abraham said, "I think you should have a pneumothorax, Eric." He looked at Eric and added, "You see, it's this way. I'll explain." He gripped Eric's arm full in his hand. It was a firm and warm and friendly hand. "No, you don't need to talk. Just listen to me and take it easy. First, we want to put air between the wall of your lung and the pleural lining around it. You've got pleurisy on your left side. That means your pleural lining is being irritated by something as it rubs against your lung and this irritation causes the fluid ducts to secrete fluid. Now, if we separate the two, the irritation may disappear."

Eric nodded. They were going to take the little animal away.

Dr. Abraham continued, "Second, you've got a cavity in your lung. That means your tuberculosis has eaten out some of the lung tissue. But by giving you air and collapsing your lung into a smaller space, we may be able to bring the walls of your cavity together again so they'll have a chance to heal. Third, by collapsing your lung, we'll give it a rest."

Eric's mind picked up each word carefully, going down the long line of words. He nodded.

"Good." There was grim satisfaction in Dr. Abraham's voice. "Now, will you sign this paper? It merely means that you've agreed to take pneumothorax."

Eric shook his head.

Dr. Abraham's face clouded. "You don't want it?"

Eric nodded. His eyes looked down to his thin hands. He tried to move them, to say something with them.

Dr. Abraham understood. He said to the freckled nurse, "He's too weak, Miss Berg. Have him sign it later. He

**26**

agrees to it and that's something."

They rolled him over on his side.

He felt someone plying a wet dab of cloth over his chest. A moment later Dr. Abraham said, "Now this may hurt a trifle. It's a needle with novacaine to anesthetize your side. After that, I'll use a blunter needle to push through between your ribs into the pleural cavity. But you won't feel that one, we hope."

Eric liked Dr. Abraham very much. The man complimented a person by explaining his moves. He quieted unrest by his frankness.

There was a needle prick. There was a blunt broom-handle forcing its way between his ribs. There was a curious ticking. A tightness gripped him. He stirred.

Dr. Abraham's calm fingers were on his shoulder. "Feel out of breath?"

Eric nodded.

He heard the doctor mutter to Miss Berg, "That's 500 cc's already. I think another hundred will do it."

Though his chest seemed to be pressed between a closing vise, the little animal became weaker and weaker. He relaxed. He was thankful.

A steady jostling disturbed him from a drugged sleep. He was lying flat on his back when the glow in his skull burst into a sputtering flame. He opened his eyes and was startled to see a small gray river running overhead. He blinked.

He moved his head a trifle. It was easier to move his skull than his tired eyes. Miss Berg, still not a remember-able entity, was smiling at him from the foot of his bed and she was walking, and then it dawned on him that they were moving him somewhere and that the gray river was the ceiling. He twitched, and then the bed came to a quick stop.

A strange nurse, also capped with a split bonnet, bent over him. "We didn't hurt you?"

He smiled weakly at her.

This new nurse was pleasant; and shrewd, he saw; and

**27**

he was glad she was about. She was tall and prim.

He was overwhelmed by this sudden interest of people in him. It was new, and wonderful. He stirred, and twitched his toe with satisfaction. His chest felt good now, except that it seemed so tight he thought he would never be able to draw in the next breath. And though he always did, he was never quite reassured.

The nurses began to push his bed again and he entered a room just wide enough to accommodate it. They rolled him against the windows, which faced westward, and through which he could see the west wing. The window sill prevented him from seeing the ground, but he knew he was high up, perhaps on the third or fourth story.

Around him the nurses bustled comfortably, rolling his stand into the room, straightening his sheets, and drawing his blinds. His head lay to the north, his feet to the south. The walls of the room were as gray as the corridor's. But the floor was of white tile, a white as bleached of color as the sheets and the bedstead and his blue-veined hands. The whiteness made him feel clean. It even made the gray walls seem white.

"Now," said the new nurse, "now you're safe in your new home."

He looked at her and studied her face. "Who are you?"

"Oh, I'm Miss Florence. I'm the charge nurse supervising this floor. When you want anything, just reach back and push this button. A light'll go on outside your door, and at my desk. That'll be a signal for some nurse to answer you." She looked at him. "I guess we better put this button" ... and she lifted a bulb-like object that was attached to a cord from the wall and placed it near his cheek ... "put this button right close so you won't have to reach."

He nodded. He looked from Miss Berg to Miss Florence. Miss Berg was the best.

"Well, now. Has Miss Berg outlined our routine to you?"

He considered this. Should he memorize the rules now, or wait until he felt better? Maybe he would die anyway.

He thought about it. Well, they had moved him into a room. Maybe they had hope. Maybe his temperature and pulse had gone down.

Apparently Miss Florence took his silence to mean he would listen, for she said, "Well, in a moment, they'll bring in a tray for your dinner—"

"Please," he whispered. He could feel his flame fluttering dangerously. Moving into the room had been a shock.

Miss Florence quieted and she opened the door for Miss Berg and he was alone.

His eyes closed. He was afraid his flame would go out. But once it had sunk to an ember, his worry vanished and he was only curious to know what would happen next. He sat in his skull and watched the low red coals for a long time. He reflected on them. And fell asleep.

He was awakened at noon by Miss Berg, still strange to him, for the flowing moments were still vanishing. She said, "Mr. Frey, I've got something special for you."

His eyes followed her movements near his bed. She had set a small tray on the stand and from it he could see steam rising against the light-gray wall.

"You're hungry, aren't you?"

He did not answer.

She looked at him. She glanced at his feet hard against the end of the long bed. She said, "Well, anyway, you'd better make up your mind you're hungry because I'm going to force you to eat."

When he made a move as if to protest, she added quietly, "Now, now, don't get any fancy ideas. You may be big, but not too big for me to handle." She balled her fist playfully at him. She picked up a pillow from a chair and propped up his head. She took a bowl and spoon from the tray and, filling the spoon, blew on it gently to cool the fluid and brought the sweet-smelling soup beneath his nose. Barely breathing, he smelled of it and felt a faint hunger. He made a slight movement with his lips and she pushed the spoon into his slowly opening mouth.

It was good. It was fuel for his flame. It warmed him. He sipped about ten full spoons.

"That's wonderful," she exclaimed, radiant. "That's wonderful. You'll surprise yourself, so quickly you'll get well."

He said nothing.

When he refused more soup, she seemed displeased.

But he had no more hunger and wanted only to slip down to a level again, deep into the bed to rest. He was tired after that effort of eating.

She helped him with the pillow. Looking up at the wall above his head, she asked, "Have you listened to your radio yet?"

His eyes opened into squares, questioningly.

"You see," she said, and she took a pair of earphones down from the wall, "you see, this sanatorium has a two-way radio switch for all patients. The radio goes on in the morning at seven and goes off at one, when rest hour begins. At three, at the end of rest hour, it goes on until nine at night when the lights go out."

Once more he begged, "Please."

"But . . . I only said it so you'd have . . . I only said it because I thought maybe you'd like—"

"Please."

Her merry face quieted. She picked up the tray and left the room.

A strange, heavy-boned nurse came in. She asked, mechanically pleasant, "Well, are you all set for rest hour now?" She walked around his bed and drew down the buff-colored blinds. Shadows repossessed the room. Again she asked, colorlessly, as if she were talking to a portrait, "Well, are you all set for rest hour?" She looked directly at him.

He gasped. She had the cold hostile eyes of a Martha! of Pa!

When he did not answer, nor stir, nor even move his eyes, she looked at him sharply as she stood by the door. She stared at him for a while and then closed the door. He continued to stare at the door for a long time.

The door banged open and he sat upright in his bed and the flame in his skull scattered like an explosion. He asked, "What's that?"

"Oh," said Miss Berg, coming toward him, "Oh, I'm sorry. I didn't mean to scare you. These doors . . . och! They're without stops and they're always banging." She pulled up the buff blinds. She came to his stand and reached down for his white urinal.

She lifted it, shook it, looked at him questioningly. "Empty?"

He had been watching her. She seemed vaguely familiar. But in his eclipsed world, he could not find a place for her. And he did not understand her question.

"Must I help you again?"

He nodded.

She helped him efficiently and quietly, and carried out the urinal beneath a towel.

A moment later, the clumsy, heavy-limbed nurse came in with a basin of steaming water. "Wash up now," she ordered, and left.

When Miss Berg came back with the emptied white duck, he asked, "Who's that prize gobbler?"

Miss Berg laughed. "She? Why, that's Miss Pulvermacher."

He smiled to himself. The name certainly fit her.

Miss Berg saw the hot water and she laid aside her towel and washed his face and arms.

Eric liked the excitement. He had slept well and his flame was up.

The charge nurse, Miss Florence, came in. She stood close to his bed and asked, "You didn't happen to take your temperature and pulse, did you?"

"No."

"Well, here now," she said, and she placed the tube in his mouth and picked up his flaccid wrist.

In a few moments she had taken both readings and

made a note of them on the pad behind his stand. Still holding the pad, she asked, "Did you raise today?"

He did not understand.

"I mean," she explained, "I mean, did you raise any sputum today?"

He nodded.

"How much?"

"Oh," he whispered, "a saucerful."

"And did you have a movement?"

"No."

Miss Florence said, "Well, now from three-thirty to five you're allowed to have visitors."

Visitors? He had never given visitors a thought. He squirmed uncomfortably. He wanted none of them. They would only come to stare at him, to watch him die. He hated watchers. And wailers. Holy Moses, no. No visitors.

His face was so expressive that Miss Florence exclaimed, "But, of course, if you don't want to see anybody, we'll see to it that nobody comes in."

He nodded vigorously.

She looked at him, and left.

He never did know if there had been company for him that afternoon, for he remained asleep until five when Miss Berg brought in his supper on a tray. Again it was hot soup. He managed to sip a bit more than he had at noon.

The soup soothed him and he felt sleepy again. It amazed him that he could sleep so effortlessly, so calmly, so dreamlessly. He was certain his body had died a number of times that first day.

It was six-thirty when a nurse bungled into the room, carrying a small emesis basin and a glass of fruit-juice. It was the clumsy one. He was surprised to remember the clumsy Miss Pulvermacher with the Martha eyes.

Her actions betrayed either a disregard or an ignorance of his weakness. She banged the utensils on his tin stand.

32

She stood by his bed, bumping it roughly. She took up the pad and asked, "Temperature? Pulse?"

He felt curiously superior to her. He observed her calmly. Her bobbed hair was too short, hanging down the back porch of her head like a clipped rooster's tail. She had a heavy body.

"No," he whispered. It pleased him to say it.

"Why not?"

When he did not answer, she grumbled; and, for the want of something to do to keep her composure, glanced at the chart. Her manner changed. With excessive consideration, she took up the tube and placed it in his mouth and took up his wrist to count his pulse.

His hate swelled. Licking flames covered his face. Fires like swift blushes enveloped his body. Sweat moistened the palms of his hands.

Then, her sudden compassion awoke a question in his mind. Hadn't his temperature improved after all?

He turned his head away from her and was surprised to find himself staring directly into the sun. It was rolling now like a hoop, well-balanced and spinning, on the edge of the west wing's roof.

She left. The hot fire subsided. He took a couple of deep breaths into his tight chest and with great effort reached out to turn the stand around. He picked up the pad and looked down the row of figures. The morning and early afternoon temperatures had not been bad but the marks she had just written in were: 104.8°, 132.

He had just pushed back the stand when Miss Pulvermacher came in again. She handed him two yellow capsules and, taking up his head, helped him drink water to rinse down the pills. He swallowed with difficulty. He rolled his head out of her hands and dropped onto the pillow.

"Is there anything else I can do for you?" she asked.

He stared at her, wondering how he could humble her. Then an idea lighted. "Say, what's your first name?"

"Why?"

"What is it?"

She stared at him. "Nurses are not permitted to give patients their first names."

"What is it?"

"Tina."

"Huh."

She left him angrily.

He exulted for a little time.

Then he began to have misgivings. He felt sorry for her. He had played her a dirty trick. Poor woman. He felt ashamed.

He turned to look for something. He became interested in the sun. It had fallen a little. The roof of the west wing had sliced off the lower half of it. It could not roll. He watched the fiery swirl of flames. The half-ball became a quarter slip; a thin sliver of flame. It sank quickly, swiftly, was gone.

He would not see it again. His friend had left. He stared at the spot where the sun had disappeared. The sun had been his noble friend, shining upon him even when he could not respond to it.

He tried to imagine what it would be like to have the sun come up on the eastern horizon, fresh and beaming and ennobling, coming upon the world, and he not there to welcome it with his flame. It could not be! Were he to go tonight, there would be clouds in the morning. There would be clouds. The universe would sorrow for him. The spheres of heaven would wail. The moon would weep inconsolably for him. The sun would warm the world in vain.

He stared at the west wing's roof. A day had gone.

With a cry he burst upward in bed, sitting erect; and by his action raised the level of his vision to a point where he could once more catch a glimpse of his golden friend. He could see only a sliver of it, but it was good, and golden.

Again, slowly, inexorably, it sank out of sight.

With the desperate anxiety of an animal trapped in closing jaws, he pushed his body upward from his white bed, and again, miraculously, saw his sun!

But, still it fell.

He stood up, tottering, gripping the window frame, gripping it with a mighty effort, gripping it to keep from falling. He coughed. He gasped for breath. Once more he caught a flame.

Then he collapsed.

It was the clumsy Miss Pulvermacher who found him, tumbled in his white bed. She untangled him.


## IV—OLD VOICES AWAKEN

A MONTH went by.

One afternoon he awoke with a clear mind. He heard a clinking sound. He sat up, throwing his shoulders upward and catching his elbows beneath himself. He stared wildly around the room. He saw Miss Berg. Blinking, sucking in his narrowed breath, he stared at her. She had brought in a basin of hot water and set it on his stand.

"Come," she said. "It's time for you to wash up again, Mr. Frey.

"Oh." He understood, and relaxed. A rest hour had gone by. "You had me scared there for a minute." He gave her a slitted look. "Say, I think I remember you. I don't know your name, but I think I remember you." That bosom. It was like Ma Memme's. "Sure, I remember you."

She smiled at him. Her freckle-rimmed, blue eyes crinkled. She folded her soft hands again and again on her stomach. "Well," she said at last. "You'd better wash up. Your company'll be here in a minute."

"Company?"

"Of course. Don't you remember? This is Sunday afternoon and this is the time they come."

He looked at his white frog-leg fingers. "Company." "This is the time they come." He studied the phrases. He asked, "Did I have company before?"

"Why, don't you remember?"

"No."

"Really?"

"No."

"Why, Mr. Frey, you've had company every Sunday for a month."

"Month." Again he jerked up. "A month?"

She had been about to leave, but now she turned and with curious eyes asked, "You mean, you don't remember them coming here at all?"

"No," he said emphatically, upset that he had been cheated, "No, Ma'am, I . . . my mind's a flat blank."

She smiled at him.

He could feel compassion in her gesture. "Guess I must a been sick," he muttered. "Say, do I feel better?"

She laughed aloud. "Well, you ought to know."

"That's right." Smiling sheepishly, he resettled in his deep pillow. "Well." He wriggled his toes and fingers experimentally. "Well, I guess I do. Say, at that I do feel all right." He looked at his arms. Their thinness appalled him. With a start, he threw back the sheet and the blanket to look at his legs. "Holy smokes!" he exclaimed. "Look at those bean-poles. Why, there's nothing to 'em. Nothing. And those little chicken muscles, they flap like wash in the breeze." Out of breath, he puffed and fell back. He murmured, "And I once had a body. Baseball, basketball, swimming . . ."

"You'll get it back some day," she said. "And you shouldn't get so excited. A person would almost think you'd lost a whole year."

"A year? Why, good lord, woman, we just agreed I lost one month already. What do you mean, a person'd think I'd lost a year?"

"You'll have to learn that here, in this world, this San, months are regarded as days, years months, and lifetimes years. Time means nothing in this place. Pretty soon, when they ask you what time it is, you'll look at your calendar, not your watch."

He quieted.

"Yes, it's true," she said very softly.

36

He looked at her for a wide moment. "I've got a long stay ahead, haven't I?"

She said nothing.

"You know," he said, "you know, it's funny. All I can remember sort of vaguely, is coming in here, a little bit. And then I remember that the world, that my life, was about so long, a finger-length, a small minute. I'd always forget what I'd done the minute before."

Her full mouth opened into a teasing laugh. "Well, you were a little squirrelly."

"And Pa . . . and who else was here?"

"Many people. Some from your home town. Your brother Ronald called a while ago to ask if they could come again."

"You mean, he called today?"

"Yes."

"You said?"

"They could come."

For the first time he remembered the flame in his skull. It was bright. Sharp. He felt electric just now, even though he was a little tired, lung-tired, throat-tired. "And my temperature?"

"It's much better. It came down three days ago."

"How much?"

She smiled, but said nothing.

He guessed her thought. As a nurse, she could not tell him. He would have to look after she left.

"What did Pa say?"

"Well, how do you mean?"

"I mean, what did he say when I just lay there, wordless?"

"Why, Mr. Frey, you talked. You talked to everybody. Oh, of course, sometimes you didn't sound very commonsensical, but you talked."

They smiled at each other, enjoying each other's thoughts about the scene.

"Holy Moses, that must have been a sight," he muttered. Pushing his fingers through his slough-hay hair, he exploded, "Say, I'd better get a haircut if I'm going to have company."

She shook her head. "No, we don't give haircuts to patients as long as they've got a fever."

"Oh? Then I do have a temp?"

"Trying to catch me?"

He laughed. "Say, who shaved me?" He rubbed his faint red-brown beard.

"Why, Bill the Barber."

"You mean, somebody shaved me every day I've been here?"

"Sure. Every other morning."

"Well I'll be damned."

"You know," she said, cocking her head to one side, "you sound like somebody who's had so much bad luck he doesn't know what good luck is like."

"Bad luck, huh?"

"Yes."

"Woman, bad luck isn't the half of it. Sometimes I think there's a devil out to do me dirt." He paused. "Of course, that's foolish. Such talk only helps to dig the grave deeper."

She looked at him and shook her head. "You sure are a queer one."

She left. He sat up and tried to wash his face. His efforts were feeble. But once the sticky feeling around the eyes had been rinsed away, he felt cleaner. He was about to look at his small mirror and to glance around the stand to study his chart, when a faintness spread through him. Every muscle cried for rest.

The long moan of the boiler-house whistle, announcing the start of the visiting hours, had barely fallen to a hoarse whisper when his door opened and in came his brother, Ronald, who lived in nearby Minneapolis, and Pa, and his step-mother, and three other relatives, the last from Bonnie Doon.

They came in with a slow, measured tread, as if they were slowly swinging, step by slow step, down the aisle of a church, slowly approaching the bier for one last look at a relative's face. Eric half-expected the line to make a turn at the foot of his bed, half-expected them to lean over his face and, with a trembling tear or two, move on to sniff a little and gather outdoors to fashion a tale of his sorry life. They stood quietly in his room, not offering a word, staring at him, like crows eyeing an empty grainfield.

Eric looked at his father. Pa's familiar features stirred him: the gray iron-hard eyes, the bony leather-cheeked face still as firm and severe as always, the long-limbed bony outline of his body, the gray suit. Eric remembered that Pa and he had once been bitter enemies. That had been when they had lived together on the farm near Bonnie Doon, Minnesota. Eric could faintly remember how it had come about. He was four when the first crop failure had dimmed the passion for land in Pa's eyes. The next year grasshoppers had come to clean Pa out; the year after, the drought and rust. Pa had not been able to see that such things were normal on the prairie. He felt he had been betrayed by something he had loved. And one day, catching Eric in a mischievous moment, he had boiled over and his son had become the innocent victim of months of stored-up anxiety. To young Eric, Pa had suddenly changed from a rollicking playfellow to a bitter-eyed, whip-wielding father. Young Eric had felt that he too had been betrayed by a loved one, that his little play-Eden had been darkened by a Satan. For a number of years young Eric had hoped that Pa would come to his senses, that he was only sick, just as Ma Memme sometimes was. But the sickness had lingered, and lingered. Eleven years later, grown tall and powerful, Eric, to prevent destruction, had had to declare his freedom. Freedom had come with an explosion like a volcano. He had raised his balled fist against his father, had swung it, and had hit him. For the first time he had tasted the sweet fruit of seeing his father cower; though after the curses and the recriminations had fallen to earth, after the hot showers of psychic mud had cooled, Eric came to realize that Pa had only been possessed by the horrible torment that he might be a failure. The declaration, moreover, served to deepen forever Pa's scorn of Eric's hungering after the mysterious unknown. Pa had wanted him to be his smart boy on the farm. Pa was unschooled. Pa's life had been full of starving and hard work. Pa's father, Grampa Eric Frey, had been too much consumed by his bursting ego, too much an individualist, to settle down to one community so that his children might duplicate his own learning.

Eric, studying his father now, said finally, "Hello, Pa."

Pa cleared his throat and his clear, light eyes misted as he said, "Hello, son."

The other relatives stood behind Pa, arms folded. They stood apprehensively. They feared the pestilence of the white plague. They called it consumption.

Eric said, "Well, how are you, Pa?"

"Fine. Good." Pa scratched his gray stiff hair. "Never expected to see you take up this kind of a life, son."

Eric tried to smile. "Well, Pa, as we always said, you never can tell what a Frey will wind up doing."

Pa said, coming closer to the bed, "Eric, we got a letter from your doctor and so we come again."

Eric nodded.

"How do you feel?"

"Good."

"Miss Berg told me you ain't supposed to talk much."

"Oh, it isn't that bad, Pa. I can talk a little. Won't some of you women sit down?"

Two white chairs scraped over the white-tiled floor.

Pa asked, "Who brought you in here?"

Eric looked closely at Pa. Pa had understood something. "I came in on my own steam, Pa. Why?"

Pa rubbed his gray-black beard and fumbled his hands together and forced a smile to his lips. "So. You came alone here."

"Yes. I figured it would be a lot easier for one man to sneak in here and grab a bed than if a whole bunch of us tried it."

The others stirred. Their faces were so grim with determined sorrow, with the fear of consumption, that they couldn't laugh. He was tempted to snort, to skip impishly about the room, to tweak their noses and bottoms, to show them he was far from dead.

The door opened again and in trooped some city friends, including Bud and his warm-hearted wife who had given him occasional meals during his hungry days. They brought in noise. They brought in a pre-arranged show. They would make him feel happy. They were not going to let on that he was gravely ill. They brought jokes and repartee and smiles.

Soon the friends fell to talking about their worldly lives again; the labor leader struggling with the vagaries of economic justice, the teacher with her problem children, the women with their shopping.

The relatives, meanwhile, having been backed against the wall by the invasion, fell to whispering among themselves like pharisees at a crucifixion.

A half hour later, a fat relative arrived in tow of Eric's old minister, Domeny Donner. Eric had long ago given up going to church. He wondered what God's delegate would have to say.

Domeny Donner shook hands with him in the elaborately familiar manner of an immaculate undertaker. Eric half-expected to see the relatives line up, three on each side of his bed, and take it up like a coffin with handles, while the domeny pulled out the collapsible undertaker's carriage.

After the greetings were over, and he had met the others in the sympathy-flooded room, Domeny Donner said, "Well, Brother Frey, how fares it with your soul today?"

Eric said, "Thin. Like restaurant soup."

Domeny Donner did not understand, for with a pleased smile, he went on, saying, "And of course, you've prayed to God today to have mercy upon your soul?"

Eric felt himself weakening rapidly. All the strength he had managed to scrape together this day, was vanishing. Still he rallied to say, "Domeny Donner, what about my body?"

41

The domeny's bright smile sickened; and then, with a determined air, he turned his bald dome sideways, as if to preach a sermon to the others at the same time. "What profiteth it a man if he gain the whole world and lose his own soul?"

Eric rose up from his bed a little, his face smarting with a rising fever. "How can a soul live without a body?"

There were grumbling coughs in the room. The city friends felt ill-at-ease.

Domeny Donner became severe. His white-gray eyes became as cold as Pa's could sometimes become. "Eric, if you, poor humble sinner that you are, don't recognize that you are a sinner, if you don't go to the Lord on your hands and knees to beg Him for forgiveness . . . why! I warn you, it'll not go well with your soul. Brother Frey, death is at your side. Don't you hear Jesus, gentle Jesus, at your door?" Domeny Donner cocked his head to one side as if he actually expected to hear a celestial knuckle knocking.

Eric was too dumfounded to talk. He remembered the old lingo; but he was slow to understand it again.

The relative, a church elder, heavy with white beard and pendulous belly, said, "Eric, you better lissen to your Domeny andt make peace wid your soul. If you don't, as sure as I'm standing here, you'll suffer hell-fire andt damnation."

Weak, cornered, unable to avoid them, Eric stared at the two. They had driven all the way up from southwest Minnesota to save his soul. Smiles they had not; nor understanding to realize that life was a star in the skull, and that death was the slow fall of the star and its diffusion as it dropt from the firmament of light.

The elder, he recalled, might have contributed to his illness. In the Bonnie Doon parish twenty years ago, there had been a controversy between the elder and the young church women. They had objected to his use of the congregational communion cup; for always, after he had drunk of the Lord's blood, his moustache had dripped red wine. Sometimes the women had actually shuddered when they heard him slup up the stray drops hanging to his straggly gray hairs. They had claimed that the practice was dirty, unhygienic; particularly since he always seemed to have a cold. Imperially the elder had waved them away. Hadn't Domeny Donner's blessing made the wine germ-free? Were they questioning the purity of Jesus' blood? So, shuddering, the young women had been forced to partake of the Lord's defiled Supper. And so, too, had Eric.

Though Eric pitied the old man, he became angry at his presumptuousness. He turned to the domeny and whispered, "Look, good Sir, you're wasting your breath. I'm too much of a heller for you to save me now."

The domeny jerked upright.

Eric fixed his eyes on Domeny Donner. "Haven't my beloved relatives told you that I've been a heller from way back?"

"Well, there were rumors."

"No doubt."

"But the main thing is, they said you had consumption, and that you were dying and in danger of hell-fire. So I came to help you."

"Thanks."

Domeny Donner held his head to one side. "Eric, maybe you're right. God always has a reason for the things he does. God doesn't punish people with consumption unless he has something in mind. And consumption is a fit chastisement for helling around, consumption is."

"Aw, I only got a bad cold. Give me a little rest, a little food, a little overhauling, and I'll be all right again."

"Well, maybe so. But it won't do you much good until you've first had a spiritual overhauling. Eric, do you realize that your soul is in bad shape?" Domeny Donner paused dramatically. "Eric, can't you read the handwriting on the wall? That this consumption that God gave you has a meaning? He's trying to tell you something."

"He uses an odd language, Domeny."

"Eric."

"All right, all right. God got disgusted with me and so

He poured some rotgut consumption in me."

The domeny's eyes narrowed. "Do you mean to suggest that it isn't a Holy God who chasteneth His people with consumption?"

"No. Besides, consumption's called tuberculosis now and you get it from a bacillus, a sort of bug."

"Oh, so you're one of these people who explains sickness and death by naturalistic causes, are you?"

"Yes. I have great respect for science."

"Science. Bah!"

"Well, Domeny, I think it's a bit more sensible to take notice of the fossils one finds in nature than those one finds in the church."

"Eric."

Suddenly Eric became angry again. Was this scowler a member of Ma Memme's church? His humane Ma Memme? What were they trying to say, that he was here because a God, a father, a whipper, was punishing him? "Look, mister. Just let me cough a few TB bugs in your face and maybe you'll change your tune."

Trim, newly-suited Ronald stepped forward. "Look, Domeny, can't you see the poor guy's all done in? Let him be."

Domeny Donner glared at Ronald. "But what of his soul? Don't you understand that when his father baptized him in my church he became a covenant child? Even as you yourself became a covenant child? God has given me express orders to come up to Macedonia to save him!"

"Get out! The whole lot of you. Get out!" In his anger, Ronald's well-groomed hair fell down. It was the first time, Eric realized, that Ronald had openly interfered with his life. Years ago they had agreed never to make remarks to each other on how to live. And they had given each other freedom thereby.

Eric said, "Now, Ronald, the friends and relatives, they are all right. They—"

"I said they're to get out!" Ronald roared.

Pa said, as the others got up and filed out with hurt

44

eyes and wry mouths, "I'm stayin' here, Ronald. And so is Ma."

"Of course, Pa. Of course. I didn't mean you."

Eric's step-mother said, "No, I think I'll go too. I'll go get a drink a water."

"I didn't mean you either," Ronald insisted.

She smiled gently. "Maybe you three would like to have a visit. You know." And she left.

When the door closed, Pa and Ronald drew up chairs and sat quietly beside Eric.

Pa said, "You mustn't pay the Reverend no mind, son. He meant well. Don't hold him against religion."

Eric nodded. "I know, Pa."

Ronald asked, "Where's your clothes?"

For a moment Eric was too tired to talk.

Ronald went on. "Still in your boarding house? Books too?"

Eric nodded.

Ronald drew out a notebook and carefully wrote in it. He said, "I'll take care of everything. Don't worry."

The notebook reminded Eric of his career. "My manuscript?"

"Oh, yeh. That. Okay. I'll get that too."

The white room plunged into silence. Pa sat quietly fumbling his hands.

Pa drew out his pipe absent-mindedly and filled it from a leather tobacco-pouch. With a long stick match, which Eric used to call a bull pine, he lighted it. Soon the room was sweet with fresh good smoke.

After a few moments, however, the smoke became too sharp for Eric's tight lungs and he began to cough.

Instantly Pa put out his pipe. His eyes and his manners became apologetic.

Eric lay on his pillow, reflecting. How quiet his father and brother were now. How quiet. How solemn. How soothing it was to have them near. All the others could go forever.

Eric remembered the day Pa had come to the city four

45

years ago. He had become the friendly, open-palmed man again, possessed with impulses to greet everyone, poor or rich, crippled or well, woman or man, and his first visit to the tumbling, grumbling metropolis had disturbed him. He liked to pass a word or two with the men, liked to nod his head to the women. The first day of that visit, as Pa and Ronald and Eric had walked down the street, Pa had nodded his head to strangers, had bade them the time of the day. He could not understand that they did not respond. And he was aghast when Ronald had exclaimed, finally, "Hey, Pa, cut it out. People don't greet each other here in the city. They think you're crazy if you do. It just isn't done here."

"Why not?"

"Well, it just isn't done, that's all."

"Why not? People do in the country. Is they something wrong with a feller if he wants to say hello to a feller? Ain't we all brothers here on this earth?"

Ronald shrugged.

Eric had said, "Ronald, what's the harm in Pa greeting people? There should be more friendly people in the world like him. Let him wave a hand to everybody. It'll do 'em good."

And Pa had concluded, "About the only friendly critters I've seen in town here have been the dogs."

Yes, Eric remembered that day. He remembered how Pa had given him a strange warm smile, and had broken the old feeling of uneasiness that had existed between them. From that day on Pa was not carrying a whip. For such memories life was worth living.

And for the memory too of the day just two months ago when he was hungry in the attic room on Hickory street, the little room he called his coffin, and Pa came.

. . . Eric had been awake but an hour that day, in the afternoon, and was still dimly conscious of the universe about. He had just had a cup of coffee, brewed on a tiny electric plate, and he had had a cigarette. He had pushed

**46**

out of his mind memories of Martha, of the rejected book, of futile job-hunting.

There was a firm knock on the door of his semi-dark coffin.

"Come in."

The door opened. There was a silhouette in the hall-way light.

"Pa! Come in."

The past walked in with a great roaring burst.

"Pa, and where's . . . oh, come in, Ma." Though she was his step-mother, he was fond of her.

"This where you're livin'!" stern-visaged Pa asked.

"Well, yes . . . you see, it's hard to get a room now. These times, you know."

Pa looked about with his gray-cold eyes, his narrow face more severe than ever in the dusky room.

Eric turned on the overhead light. "Here, sit down. And take this chair, Pa. And Ma, take the easy chair . . . I mean the bed." He tried to laugh jokingly about his few pieces of furniture.

She looked at the disheveled bed and promptly began to make it, pruttling like a brood hen scolding her chick.

Pa sat down and stared at him.

Eric tried to be at ease. "Well, how is the farm, Pa?"

"Good. We're going to have a good year, this year. A good one."

Eric nodded. Pa was always optimistic. Optimism was a beautiful thing.

They talked of the old days, avoiding talk of his job-lessness, his room, his clothes.

Pa said, "Son, we drove a long way, and we're hungry. Could you hunt us up a feedbag somewhere?"

"Oh . . . oh . . . well, not in this room. I can't cook here."

"No, no. I mean, find us a good eatin' place. I'll show you how to eat a real meal. Why! my boy, you're thinner than a sicklin' cow that's throwed her calf. You must be eatin' wood-shavin's."

**47**

"Pa!" Ma exclaimed, reprovingly.

Eric laughed. "No, not exactly that."

"But you're thin! I could tell by the sound of them last couple a letters a your'n that somethin' was cookin' you no good. So, I says to Ma, I says—"

"Let's go eat, Pa."

Eric found a cheap cafe. And Pa ordered a meal for all three.

The feast sickened Eric. He fought impulses to vomit.

They called on Ronald and talked until late that night, remembering the old days.

Then, Ronald found lodging for them.

Eric went to his room, and sagged into his chair. The effort to be on their level had been exhausting. He sank into sleep, oblivion.

The next morning Pa came in with a warm, close smile, found him still in the chair. He had been up to something. "Say, you must a fell asleep right after breakfast."

"Yes."

"Well, we gotta go home now. We had a chance to get away from the farm for a couple a hours to see my boys and now we gotta go back. Chickens, pigs, everything's callin' us. Well, so long, my boy. And eat some. Eat."

"Yes."

"Eric, I wanna ask you something. Is Ronald makin' enough to help you?"

"No."

"Don't be too proud, son."

"You can never be too proud around brothers."

Pa smiled.

They went down to the old family Chevie, where Ma was waiting.

They stood talking together. Just before they left, Pa shoved a small package into Eric's hand. Then, waving, Pa drove off with a lurch.

Eric went upstairs and slowly entered his room. He snapped on the light.

He opened the package. Underwear. They had seen, then, that he had none. Pa had seen.

He stared at it. Life, she is a bitch, he thought. There wasn't enough sap in him to cry . . .

Pa got up from his white chair. He drew a package from his suit-coat pocket and put it on Eric's bedstead and wordlessly, firmly shook Eric's hand and left with Ronald. Eric's heart beat against his ribs. It rammed its head against his chest walls trying to get out.

Through the transom over the door, he overheard Pa talking. "We're goin' home now, Miss Berg. Now, I want you to take good care a that youngster a mine. He ain't much count right now. Kind a gant and thin in there. Pretty sick. But I'll bet you a dollar to a doughnut that if you'd feed him some grub every day, good grub, with plenty of roughage, the kind that'd stick to his ribs, why, he might show you a thing er two. He's only been off his feed. He's got some tough blood in him, he has. An' his bones are big enough to carry some weight."

Eric's disease-tamed heart became a wild animal again. He pushed the button. Miss Berg came in. "Nurse, my father's left me a package. Open it."

Miss Berg nodded, smiling. She untied the strings and laid open the leaves of the paper-cover around the box. She removed the lid. With a quick understanding eye she said, "That's real nice, that is."

"Well, what is it?" he demanded, making a move as if to lift himself out of the bed. "Well?"

"A pair of leather house-slippers." She lifted them up.

"Oh." He looked at them. Pa had made them himself.

"They are very nice," she said.

"Yes." Pa had made them big enough to fit his long feet. They were for his comfort when he should get up to walk around again. He smiled and murmured, "Pantofles."

"What?"

"Pantofles."

49

EACH DAY was a gift. Each day came wrapped in sparkling morning sunlight.

For most people, days are all alike. They forget that they are presents from the unknown.

But Eric knew they were gifts, all of them. One by one they came, and he knew they would not come again; that this day he was having, this one short spurt of time, this one was the last of its kind; that once it vanished into evening's melancholy sunfall, it was gone forever.

He caressed them and called them each a name.

This one, this day, he named "a golden drop."

The next one, this day, he named "a water drop."

Again, the next one, this day, he named, "a golden drop."

They were all new and different names, they were, because when a day died at sunfall he forgot it sleeping; and waking, found a new one and named it the best name he knew, "A golden drop, a water drop."

A glowing, golden drop, falling on his hollow skull, from which resounded sepulchrally a sonorous drumming sound.

So infrequently fell the drops for him that he hungered for the next while the drumming of the one just fallen was still echoing in widening circles away from him.

Drum! and a single note from a harp went hurtling into a dead dark silence.

Drum! and it split the dark silence, made the vacated space ring with bright sun, the world crackle with re-stirred chemicals.

Drum! and sunlight plunged into the black night and spread it wide, wave and wave away from him.

He marveled at an old dilemma: the more meaningful the day became, the more meaningful death became.

He lay idly inside his tumbled tower, his fallen temple. His hands were sleeping.

He was a stricken brave. He was a Job fallen on ashes,

not caring how or where he lived.

He was a ruin floating down a river escaped from its banks, a chip adrift on gray, near-stagnant waters.

Gradually his mind cleared; the fog retreated; his world became wider. Sometimes memories crept into his skull and warmed themselves at his fire.

So he lay inside his body, hardly aware of it; occasionally sending a spark to its outermost parts when it came time to rest in a different position, or when it was time to turn over for the night's long sleep, or if a nurse wanted to stir him for a bath.

The flame in his skull was sluggish. He slept, drugged, and sped swiftly through the night. He slept, sluggish, and dragged through the day.

There was so much room to wait in. He luxuriated in the universe, in the space he could wait in, wait in, waiting. He lay luxuriating in the universe.

It was in the morning that he wrung most of his golden water from the world, drop by drop.

And in the evening, when the sun fell beyond the high west wing, he soared from his body like a slim, white note of music.

There was the time when, awakening from a morning's drowsy rest hour or an afternoon's nap, bewildered, angled in his bed—for he was too long for the longest—covered by a white starch-stiff sheet, his giant toes lifting the coverlet into nomad's tents, whiteness surrounding him like the white sands of the desert, he fell to wondering who he was and where he was, and if he was a something or a somebody.

The little flame in his mind became a living thing then and asked the questions that come only out of such a being. "If I am an *It*, what is an *It*?" "Or if I am an *I*, what is an *I*?" And in answering itself, for no one else would answer, the little flame encountered the boundaries that man finds around him, and not those of a son of Jupiter. And it thought, "There's a woman in white who feeds me every day and helps me with my bodily duties."

**51**

Or, "The windows are on my right hand, not on my left." Or, "I eat, and I excrete, and between the two I live."

The thoughts pleased him. He marveled that such illusions came into him at all. His flame was achieving stature again.

Lying there, he fell to thinking about his body, about the pocket of air they were forcing into his huge arching chest; fell to wondering about his limbs, his belly, his genitals. With some effort, he forced his mind to each part of his body; felt each part idly drifting beneath the white sheets.

He wondered whether any part of his body had volition of its own. Could it move itself? He said to himself, his little flame lighting up with eagerness, "Yes, even if it takes until tomorrow, I'll wait to see if some part of me can move of its own accord."

He waited.

And waited.

And then, his eyes twitched.

And, like a frolicsome calf turning to another blade of grass, he pointed his nose toward the window. His eyes, focusing short before him, discovered faults in the pane; swirls of glass like whirlpools in water, wavy wrinkles like sweeping rises in a meadow; and among these, dust-rimmed marks where rain-drops had fallen.

Beyond the window, way out, the vast distance of ten feet or more, swept the sorrowing nod of the lombardy poplar, the Old Lady. A wild wind, hot from the belly of southern America, came up. The Old Lady bristled momentarily; then straightened her clothes and swayed easily. She grieved and her leaves rustled and threw the flat of their faces toward him.

He looked eternal distances beyond the old lady tree. The great world was filled with green-blue leaves and dark barks and heavy grains and just-sprouting corn rows. And people working. People working.

What were people working? What was sweat? He

moved his hand over his hip to feel if sweat were bubbling through the fountains of his skin, just as it once had when he worked his father's grain-laden fields.

What was sweat?

Sweat was . . . sweat was sin escaping from his temple.

And then, upon that childhood whimsy, he curled up on his side, was once again asleep and swimming in Ma Memme's womb.

## VI—BRIEFED FOR BATTLE

TWO MONTHS after he had entered the house of white rest, on an evening just as supper was being served, the door of his room opened quietly and Dr. Abraham stepped in. The doctor was dressed in a long white smock. A nickel-shiny stethoscope dangled from his white belt.

Eric started, and knew he had been caught with his hands up over his head.

"Hey, where are those arms."

Eric, stubborn, kept his arms up. "Aw . . . "

"Down with those hands, mister!"

"What's wrong with relaxing this way, Doc?"

"Wrong? Nothing . . . if you want to stay in bed five more years." Dr. Abraham pointed. "Aren't you the one who bragged that you could keep any rule you wanted to?"

Reluctantly Eric nodded. A week before, Dr. Abraham had said, "Eric, you're facing the toughest fight you've ever gotten into. And if you win it, it will be the greatest battle that you, or any man, can win." He paused. "Look, I'm going to be brutal about this and tell you something. For a while your system will be toxic with TB poisons, and you'll feel bad. And for that while it'll be easy to take the cure. But later, when the fever leaves, and the pulse comes down, and the metabolism becomes favorable, then . . . then the battle will really begin. All day you'll lie here, lazy. The food you eat will be more than enough to hold your own with your TB. You'll feel that you could run the mile, play papa to a dozen fast fannies. Really. And yet, actually, if you tried to walk even ten steps, you'd have a relapse. You'd crack up. You'd have wasted a year's work at healing. It's when you feel that well, with two years of strict bed-rest ahead, that you'll get restless and think you can't do it. Oh, sure, for a while you'll remind yourself of the rules. Sure. 'Don't stretch your arms.' 'Don't sit up on your elbows.' 'Don't laugh too hard.' 'Don't jerk.' 'Don't, don't, don't.' But if you're human, and I'm sure you are, the 'don'ts' will drive you mad. And the next thing, pfft, there you go. Like a child, for no good reason at all, you'll get stubborn, obstinate, and fly the coop."

"Oh, but Doc, I've got too much brains to pull off a stunt like that."

"Hah. Many a man has skipped out of here because he couldn't stand thinking about a five-year stretch doing nothing."

"But Doc, I . . . me, I won't have to stay here that long, will I?"

"I can't say. All I can say is, don't think about it. Think about today. Obey the rules. Take the cure. Be a man. The real man tempers his blind-eyed stubborn battling. Controls it."

"Oh well, Doc, that'll be easy."

"Hah. Let me tell you that there are forces in you that can ruin you."

Eric was not in the mood to be silenced. "Well, yeh. But, I get tired of obeying the rules. Day after day. I tell you, Doc, a day is a long time to be good in."

"Hah."

"Aw, Doc. Really. What if I do put my arms in the air?"

Dr. Abraham came close to his bed and with his fore-finger traced muscle lines over Eric's chest. "You're stretching your whole chest this way. And stretching the new young tissues healing inside."

54

"Aw, Doc. Can't a man do something he likes? Just once?" Eric folded his arms over his bony chest.

"Look. Let's take one of these paper napkins here. This thin filmy tissue-paper." Illustrating, Dr. Abraham saturated the tissue with water from Eric's water-bottle, and easily, effortlessly, tore it apart.

"Oh."

" 'Oh' is right. Every time you cough, laugh, stretch, jerk, you're ripping those new tissues; tissues it took your body months to build. And, your TB bugs, which have all along been boxed up in those tissues, will run free and go to work on you again."

Eric smiled sheepishly. To divert attention, he asked, "Ah, say, tell me, Doc, once the bugs're boxed up, what happens to 'em? Choke? Die?"

"Most of 'em will live as long as you will. That's why we call you an 'arrested', not a 'cured', patient when we discharge you."

"I'll never get rid of them?"

"Most likely not."

"I'll always have to be careful? Always? Can't ever relax, or run, or jump, or stretch . . . make love?"

Dr. Abraham laughed. "Well, you can do those things moderately. Except the love. That's equivalent to a seven-mile walk. And right now, that would kill you."

Eric grinned, asked, "Doc, tell me, how long before I can begin to live this moderate business? And take these seven-mile walks again?"

"Oh, two, three years from now. Depends. If your pneumothorax holds, maybe two years. If it doesn't, and you can't heal by strict bed-rest, well, then maybe we'll have to clip your ribs."

"Clip my ribs? Oh no you don't."

"I'm sorry. But we'll have to. We've got to make that lung inactive some way. If we can't collapse it by pneumo, then it's the ribs." Dr. Abraham's eyes narrowed on a thought. "Look. Here's the point. Suppose you had a sore on a knuckle, an open sore. Suppose you moved it back

**55**

and forth twenty times a minute, sometimes sixty times a minute. Well, how long do you suppose it'd take to heal it? A long time. And a breathing lung is just like that wriggling sore."

"Holy Moses. Cut my ribs. Me and a stove-in boxcar."

Dr. Abraham nodded. "Well, let's not think ahead." He paused. "And another thing. You and your TB are a couple of wrestlers. When it gets the upper hand, you lose. When you get the upper hand by taking the cure, you win. And still another thing. And it's a funny one. Your TB can win, completely. But you never can. You'll be wrestling with it until you die."

Eric settled into his pillow. He saw it coming. "Doc, give me the real lowdown on my case. Am I in bad shape?"

"No. I wouldn't say so. You're all right. If."

"Tell me. Tell me really."

Dr. Abraham studied him intently. He put his hand on Eric's shoulder. He gripped him. "Well, Eric, you had pretty well everything that a body could have and still live. When you came in, you were as sick as a dog. You had TB, pleurisy, a touch of pneumonia, skin lesions . . . a general breakdown in health."

"But I'm a little better now?"

"Yes."

"Tell me."

"Yes."

"And I'll make it?"

"Well, frankly, there's some question about it."

Eric whitened.

"Question, because, as I said before, there are forces in you that can ruin you. You're a dreamer, a roamer. You live in the future. And I wonder whether you have what it takes to live today. Oh, we'll try to save you. We'll keep your fancy busy . . . except that men like you will dream anyway."

Eric was silent. He looked at his frog-leg fingers.

"Hah. One of these days, when the full horror of looking ahead to five years of lying here hits you, I'll get a buzz from your charge nurse, Miss Florence, and she'll tell me you skipped out. Because you couldn't take it."

"Well, I . . . "

"Oh, you have some virtues. You have curiosity. And that's something. You want to see everything but do nothing." He paused. "You know, I got a feeling that you're one of these people that never finishes a job."

"Aw, now, Doc, take it easy."

"Well, do you think you could do a first thing first if you tried?"

"Sure."

"Hah. I've got to see it first."

"Well, what is it I got to do? Tell me, and I'll see if I can."

"What you've got to do is this. First, fix a point ahead. Second, live to get there. No more. Don't look beyond it. Fix the point on something close by. A radio program. The next meal. Anything. Something."

Eric fumbled with his sheet below his chin. The pillows propped his head forward and his beard tickled his throat as he talked. "Well, so both my lungs're shot to hell, huh?"

"No. No. One of them will still make a pretty good lung, after a couple of years of bed-rest."

"But the other, it's pretty well . . . ?"

Dr. Abraham nodded.

A wave of self-pity welled up in Eric. "Doc, when I start to die, you'll stay by me?"

"Why . . . you're still a long way from that."

"Promise me."

"Sure. But what makes you ask that?"

"Because when Ma Memme died, our Doc wouldn't come out that night. It was moonlight, and he wouldn't."

"Maybe he had another case."

"He had a case all right. A case on a nurse."

"Hah."

"And Ma Memme was dying. I called our Doc four

times. And he kept telling me that both Pa and I were too excited, to leave her alone."

Dr. Abraham's face became troubled. "Yes, Eric. Unfortunately, even in our profession there are fools."

Eric said nothing.

"Yes, and ignorant quacks. I've seen patients come into this San here who had about a week left to live. Their lungs were so shot only an act of God kept them going. Yet, their family doctors didn't know what was wrong with 'em. Never knew what was up. Oh no. When I'd call them on consultation and tell them what I'd found, they'd act surprised. 'TB? That's funny. The lungs seemed okay to me. The wind blew in, the wind blew out. That's funny.' I'd ask if they hadn't noticed the general run-down condition, the pallor. They'd say, 'Sure, but that looked like a slight case of anemia.' 'Didn't you notice the cough?' 'Sure, but a lot of people have smokers' cough.'" Dr. Abraham shook his head and gestured.

Eric stirred uneasily.

"I'm sorry, Eric."

"Well, Doc, I look at it this way. You doctors are still like us. You know a few more facts about the body, and you know the averages better, and you think twice before you do anything, but that's about the only difference between us."

"Hah! If only there was that much difference."

Dr. Abraham left.

## VII—THE WHIPPER RECOGNIZED

ALL THROUGH supper Eric mused on the doctor's words. He began to see that his body was mending. He checked off the facts: he was eating heartily again, he was sleeping soundly at night, his mind was clear during the day, and his limbs felt comfortable. "Strange I didn't notice it before," he muttered to himself. "Strange."

He finished eating. As he was about to settle into his pillows for the evening rest hour, it occurred to him that he could quite simply check his discovery against the pulse-and-temperature chart. He licked the edges of his lips. Remembering Dr. Abraham's warning not to do anything violent, or sudden, or to reach, remembering the image of the easily-torn, wet tissue-paper, he contained himself, stirring up his muscles slowly, extending his left arm toward the bedstand while he propped himself up with the other. Just as he was about to roll the stand around, Miss Pulvermacher came in without knocking.

He jumped guiltily and fell back into his pillows. A quick image of Ma Memme and the farmhouse pantry and stolen raisins came up. He recalled Martha's ice-blue eyes.

Miss Pulvermacher looked suspiciously at his ruffled sheets. "Take your temperature?"

"No."

She studied him, snapped, "Now that you're up to exercising in bed, don't you think you can take it yourself?"

His flame became white. Damned female. Insolent.

She took up the thermometer and jammed it roughly into his mouth. She picked up his wrist to take his pulse.

He turned his head away from her, staring out of the window.

She dropped his wrist and withdrew the thermometer. She wrote down the figures on the chart. She went out into the hallway. In a few moments she returned with a small rubber-wheeled wagon on which stood a pitcher of water and a glass of fruit-juice. She poured out the water and set the fruit-juice near him, staring at him meaningfully, as much as to say, "If you can move around in your bed, mister, you can also reach for this drink."

She left, closing the door behind her.

Exasperated, reckless, he jerked at the stand and lifted the pad. The last entry read: 103.2°, 130. He sucked in a nervous breath. The figures were still high. His eye caught last night's entry: 100.2°, 112. He perused the figures for the past two weeks. The readings on the preceding nights had been much lower too. The rates of both temperature and pulse had been dropping steadily from the dangerous 104.6°, 136 of a month ago. What had happened this night? Had his momentary anger generated a temperature?

He dropped back into his pillow. He puffed wildly. There wasn't enough air to breathe. He bellowed his lungs. He clutched his throat, laboring for air.

At nine o'clock when the radio earphones above his bed had ceased their indistinct murmurings for the day, and after he had watched night close in and smother the west wing's lights, he fell to brooding.

On other nights, the moment the nurses had turned off his light he had slipped effortlessly away into oblivion. Only once that he could remember had he looked through the stately lombardy poplar leaves and across the mall to watch the lights in the west wing flutter and go out in the nightfall's dark. But this night he tossed in his bed. He tried to find sleep the customary way by lying flat on his back, his legs spread, his arms folded over his chest, his head turned off to one side toward the window.

He lay watching the late May evening, watching the old poplar just outside his window gather its leaves close around itself, watching the gray-silver along the horizon become a fierce hard black. The faint light along the earth's rim reminded him of Shakespeare's *Romeo and Juliet*—

> . . . . . . *Come, civil night,*
> *Thou sober-suited matron, all in black,*
> *. . . Come, night; —Come, Romeo, —come, thou day in*
>     *night;*
> *For thou wilt lie upon the wings of night*
> *Whiter than new snow on a raven's back.—*
> *Come, gentle night, come, loving black-brow'd night . . .*

The poem brought up sickening memories. It was a mistake to trace out the lines of that poem from the dusky tome in his memory, a sad mistake. Instead of finding sleep, he was disturbing himself with poems, poems that cracked open the sepulchre wherein he had buried Martha. Let her sleep!

He tried another position from which to coax sleep. He turned away from the window to lie on his left side, his right leg falling with a clank upon the bones of the other, his left arm thrust back, his right arm lying awk-wardly around his face with the tendon-stringy hollow of his elbow just cupping his nose. The new position was the correct one, Dr. Abraham had said. By lying on the side where the lung had been folded up by pneumothor-ax, he would be keeping the pus from dripping over into his good side, or better side, which was also flecked with cheesy, tuberculous spots.

He shifted uncomfortably in bed, alarmed by the idea that he would always have to live with those squirming nests of bugs in his chest. In all likelihood he would have to spend the rest of his life running about like a queru-lous old man trying to find just the right spot for his stinging rheumatism. He cringed. That body of his, with its power to lift the wheel of a car, with its whipping pow-er to splinter boards in a backstop with a baseball—had he lost that body forever?

He rolled over to try the other side. Once more his legs with their meat-barren, heavy bones clanked each up-on the other. Once more he could feel the inching weight of his folded lung settling in a new direction inside his chest.

And what of the dripping pus? To hell with the pus! He would rest just as he pleased. A real man couldn't live by rules. Good Christ, a man should be able to ignore rules once in a while, shouldn't he? Sure. T'hell with the rules. Let the damned, yellow, bug-thick, stinking pus run over into his good right lung.

He looked through the window. It had become darker outdoors. The sky was sharp with white tears. The old lady poplar shivered in her clothes, swaying a little, rust-ling.

**61**

He was fond of Old Lady Poplar. She had been with him since he had come in, eternities ago. She had nodded every night to him, encouraging him. She was a wonderful Old Lady.

He laughed at himself. How could he believe in wooden images? How could he play with the childish fancy that a tree was a mother? Yet what else was one to think of this old poplar nodding there, even more blackly dark than the night, like a tamed blackbird in a lampless temple?

He twisted in his bed. By now thousands of poisonous tubercle bacilli should have drained into his right lung.

He lay on his back again.

Tubercle bacilli. Bacilli. A treacherous sounding name. Tuber. Like a pickle or a cucumber. Watermelon. Tuber.

How much of a flame had a live Tuber in its brain? Or in its seat of life? Its center? Its nucleous? Was it an illumination? Actually a perceptible nimbus? Did it think? Did it feel? Did it cognate? How long was the night? He wished he had a radio. Or a friend. The friends outside the San had faded slowly away. They came occasionally, but the visiting hours were too narrow to keep the touch alive. Talk was always too hurried. Their worlds and his veered away from each other.

Where was sleep? Had he come to the time Dr. Abraham had described, the time when he would feel better than he had ever felt in his life, the restless year of bed-curing before he could move around again? Or was he still slipping? Was this the one last burst before collapse?

Lovely Old Lady Poplar. Dear Old Mother.

Sleep, O soul. Obey. Sleep. Sleep. Time to sleep. Obey my command.

But his being rebelled. It wanted action. It wanted to run. It wanted to see; just as years ago when the animal glow within young Eric had been too daring, too curious, too hungry, and he had wanted to grab at the apples hanging out of his reach. It had not learned from the whipping.

**62**

. . . Young Eric had seen his Ma Memme go into the fuel shed near the house with a tub and a pail of water.

"Whatcha gonna do, Ma Memme?" He longed to lay his head between her pillow-breasts.

"Nothin'. None of your beeswax, sonny. Run along now an' play with Ronnie." Her voice was tired. She was suffering from shock too: the pigs had died of hog cholera, the grasshoppers had come three days later. For a week she had been in fear of what Pa might do.

"Whatcha gonna do, Ma Memme?" He loved to say her name. It was also his name for milk. And he had tied Ma and Memme together the day he had seen creamy memme dripping from her breasts as she was about to give suck to little Ronnie.

"Nothin', I said. Go. Go play with Ronald." With a tired shove she had sent him on into a grove of ash where Ronnie was climbing trees in hunt of birds' nests.

But after he had played a while, he wondered what Ma Memme looked like in the dark toolshed. He ran into the cornfield behind the grove and stealthily worked his way up close to the shed. He studied the small shanty. He listened. Water splashed within. He studied the red wall before him. He spotted a knothole just a foot above the ground. Cautiously he crawled out of the cornfield, crept over the grass, through the weeds near the shed. Cautiously he lifted his head. He peered. It was dark inside. Black. But soon the darkness became purple, then gray, then . . . he saw her: white skin, bowl-large breasts, blonde pubic hair, blue eyes sad, washing hands.

And suddenly the Universe convulsed. There was a roar. A shattering thunder of words. A mighty *swissshh* of the whip. A whipper had come.

Agonized, little Eric whirled catlike over on his back to face his foe, his feet and hands clawing the air. Through fumes of fear, he saw Pa with a horsewhip, flailing him, and wailing over him with a strange chant: "You dirty little sneakin' brat, tryin' to see your mother naked. You dirty little devil." *Whang! Whiiip!* "I'll teach you." *Whing! Whiiip!* "You ain't no born son a mine, nor no child a God no more." *Wheng! Whiiip!*

With Pa no longer a friend Eric had searched for a new pal, a kindly uncle or aunt. He never found one. And by the time that Pa had become loving and kindly again, it was too late. The magic and the laughter of their early love had vanished forever . . .

Thinking about the incident now as he lay on his bed, he was almost tempted to believe there was a vengeful God or a Pa-like Satan, a Whipper.

What was there about him that invited hurt? Disaster? Had he not good impulses? And did he not have a natural longing for joy? It wasn't as if he expected grief and therefore got it. No. By inclination he was a happy lad; and a good Lord could have made anything of him. A long nose should have been a blessing. Eric nodded. Malevolent beings always resented curiosity.

He considered his father. Lately Pa had become a gentle old man. But there had been a time when Pa had looked like a Jehovah, a terrible Whipper.

Holy Moses, come to think of it, there had been a Whipper in the religious academy too. The English teacher there had been tall like Pa, had been frustrated like Pa, had taken a savage delight in destroying Eric's dreams. Every theme day, with glittering eyes, the teacher had read Eric's effort to a guffawing class of fools, emphasizing his grammatical mistakes and ridiculing his imagination.

And in the south Minnesota college too, by God, a Whipper had hounded him. There it had been no single person, but a foreboding air; and a few black-coated crows, professors, ready to croak their saws at him should he wander off the straight-and-narrow into the fragrant pastures of fancy.

Yes, it was easy to figure it out now. He had been too curious for a Whipper. Eric re-examined the three greatest shocks of his life, devastating shocks, all coming within the last couple of years; three quakes coming so close one upon the other that they had knocked him into this invalid's bed. When it had come time for him to explore the world of love, a Whipper had presented him with Martha. When it had come time for him to seek a way of earning his own livelihood, a Whipper had clapped him into poverty. When he had felt it was time to try his hand at creation as a way of compensating for his failures, a Whipper had sent him that January letter. Every time his nose had quivered the least bit to the scent of a new adventure or search, a Whipper had been right there with his whip. *Wheng! Whiiip!*

Even after he had been out of work for a year and a month, had worn his last pair of shoes down to the fake-leather insole, even after his hungry body had almost given him up, a Whipper had bothered to toy with him once more. And the Whipper had been clever with the way he had laid his bait.


. . . It was noon, and March, when Eric returned to his boarding-house after a heart-sickening interview downtown.

The lawn before the house was barren, and speckled with rings of dirt where the last snowbanks had melted. Trees were throwing their limbs into the water-gray sky like black-armed octopi.

The house was near the University. Upon coming to Minneapolis some years ago, he had chosen this neighborhood to live in to be among people who pursued ideas, to be near a library full of good books and magazines. The brown house was old. Its foundation was sagging. Its steps were worn. But sometimes, in the evenings, its rooms were filled with laughing, carefree students.

He trudged up the walk, thinking about the interview. The personnel manager had said that he could not hire an active member of the Newspaper Guild, could not hire a man who asked too damned many questions about too damned many things.

Eric stepped into the house. As he puffed up the winding stairway, the word "blacklist" popped into his mind.

65

He entered his narrow attic room. The air in it was as close as a coffin's. He sat down in a wooden rocker.

He covered his face with his hand. He cried. Wasn't he going to make it after all? Already a whole year of starvation, of living on coffee and fried potatoes, and cigarettes that a sentimental druggist couldn't refuse him, had thinned his dangle-armed body to a slat with stilts for legs, had almost weakened him too much to go on fighting.

He bit his lip. He managed to control himself. He rolled a cigarette from an old butt and a few remaining flakes of Bull Durham tobacco.

He considered asking Ronald for help. But Ronald had trouble enough of his own. Ronald had just gotten work and needed every penny to catch up on his own debts, to buy new clothes. No, not Ronald.

Eric coughed. He looked at his beloved books and wished he had enough energy to read them: Tolstoi, Doughty, Whitman, Melville, the Bible.

He recalled the face of the boss when he had refused scab work. To take such work would mean pushing another man out of a job. Our present economic system, he had told the boss, was like a pop-bottle cooler: when you rammed one in, another popped out. There was room for only so many, and no more. The boss had fired up, and in an unguarded moment revealed that he hadn't intended to give him a job in the first place. He couldn't afford to keep a trouble-making union man alive.

Eric coughed. The tobacco in the hand-rolled cigarette was as strong as aged horsetail.

He toyed with the idea of writing a letter to Pa and finally wound up penning a few words on a postcard. He went down to the corner to mail it. There was a smell of spring in the air. He wondered, idly, if his blood would ever again race with passion, with the abundant sap of creation, with the dream of love. He wondered if he would ever again be lucky enough to meet an uncle or an aunt that would match him smile for smile and laugh for laugh.

Coming up the steps again, stumbling a little, he came upon the Whipper's bait, for just then he recalled that his brother Ronald had twice gotten unemployment compensation without having had a job in between. Entering his dark room, he decided to look at the receipt for the last compensation check he had gotten. He studied the dates. The earning totals. Why, yes. He was eligible for more aid. The required year had passed. Well. Well now. He scratched an ear. A little free change was worth looking into. He went to the bathroom, and recombed his hair. He noticed that his hair had changed from a golden straw to a faded slough-hay hue. His comb was full of falling hairs.

The State Unemployment Office was downtown, a mile away. It took him two hours to walk the distance. He had to sit down every block, using drugstores, confectioneries, front-stoops of homes, and the Court House as resting places.

The girl clerk remembered him from last year and she drew back her lips in a sneer. When she could not prove him wrong, she called the manager. The bland-faced man studied the chart of figures, and then reluctantly nodded his head. Eric signed a slip. "Come back next week, same day, same hour."

"How long must I wait for the first check?"

"Just like last year, there's a two-week waiting period. You're supposed to keep on looking fer work."

"Oh."

When the first check came, Eric had hardly enough energy left to go to Charlie's Cafe to order a meal. He walked along. He rumbled like an empty boxcar. While he waited for the soup, he walked over to a scale to weigh himself. The figure, 170, on the indicator shocked him. He usually averaged 210 pounds.

He ate very slowly, rolling the potatoes and hunks of pork chop and shreds of lettuce and swallows of milk around with his tongue, giving every taste-bud a chance at the wonderful flavors.

**67**

When he finally finished the banquet, he felt sleepy. He went back to his room and lay down on the cot to give his body a chance to absorb the energy in the food.

Two days later he found a student co-op eating-house and became a member. And with each check, he began to catch up on the six months back rent he owed.

He lived for the meals. He got up in the morning, dressed, walked a block to the co-op, ate, retired to a wicker chair on the porch, read the morning paper, went back to his room to sleep until noon. Then he got up again, ate, came back, slept. The routine was the same in the evening.

In a few weeks he felt a little better, though his cough was as persistent as ever. Out of curiosity he weighed himself. 180. He had gained ten pounds. "Well," he thought. "Well. Maybe I'll pull out of this after all."

But one noon Jack Upham, one of the boys staying at the house, a University bacteriologist, noticed his cough. "Eric, spit in this little glass, will you?"

"I'm all right."

"I know, I know. But, I'm just fooling around a little at the lab, picking up a little sputum here and there, just to see what's in 'em."

"All right."

At five, the telephone rang downstairs. He went down to answer it.

"Eric? This is Jack. Say, can you come over to my lab a minute?"

Eric paused. "Why?"

"Oh . . . it's nothing. Thought maybe you'd like to take a glim at something I got here."

"I'm all right."

"I know, I know. But come over anyway."

"All right. Just as you say."

It was cold out. He was glad that he had bought good clothes when he had had the money for them. He strode down the street, loping a little, faint.

He entered the laboratory.

68

Jack growled an affectionate greeting.

"Well, what is it?"

"Eric, it's TB."

"Oh?"

"Yes."

"Sick, huh."

"Yes."

"But hell, man, I can't be. I just gained ten pounds."

"Look."

Eric peered through the eye-piece of a microscope. He saw slim, narrow tubercle bacilli scattered on the mounted glass. They had been stained red. He stared at one of them. He wondered if it had teeth, a belly, an anus. "Dammed funny critter," he muttered.

Jack relaxed then. He smiled a little. "They sure are. And they're dangerous. Deadly."

"They are, huh."

"Eric, you'd better get an X-ray of your chest. And get a general all-around checkup."

"No money."

Jack thought a moment. "Well, I got a doctor friend. I don't see why you can't go through the county clinic. When a guy gets TB they usually do something for him. The city health department won't let'm run around infecting everybody else."

Eric sniffed and laughed ruefully. "Seems a man's got to become a pestilence to his fellow citizens before he rates attention."

Jack's dark eyes were sympathetic. "Yes, so it seems. I'm sorry, Eric."

Eric went to the clinic. He joked with the woman X-ray technician. She smiled at him as he stripped to the waist. They laughed when his bone-ridged chest proved to be too wide for the plate. "We'll have to take you in sections," she said, smiling, and fluffling her blond hair.

He waited for the report in a narrow gray room.

A young medic came in. His eyes, like Jack's, were weighted. "Well, Mr. Frey, I think I've got some bad news for you. You've got a pretty serious case of tuberculosis. Now, I'd like to make a suggestion. What you need most and first is a rest, a long rest. A rest, say . . . at the county sanatorium. The Phoenix. You ought to go there for . . . oh, say, three months, maybe not that long even. Something like three months, maybe."

Eric didn't answer right away. He knew what was going through the young medic's mind. Following such news as he had just had, most men leaped into the air, shouting, screaming that they couldn't leave life, couldn't let their families starve. And looking at Eric, the medic must have felt he had another jumping-jack on his hands.

"Well," thought Eric, "since TB's fatal, I can just as well die in the sanatorium as anywhere else." He laughed, remembering how once at a social worker's convention he had, out of a perverse notion, selected the five healthiest people in a panel of ten photos . . . and had picked them right. They had active tuberculosis. The panel was intended to shock the onlooker into the realization that no man knew when he had the unraveling disease.

Another thought came to Eric. It would be too bad if he died before he had re-worked his prose-poem novel. He had something to say. He had a life to record, a little bit of a sermon to preach.

He nodded his head. He had to write an eternal theme before he died, something concrete, everlasting. He had to make his scratch on the rock, to leave a permanent footprint. Every man, when he sees death coming, rushes and storms about to get his will made, to get in his say. He makes decisions that affect the lives of his friends and his loved ones; and sometimes the very universe itself. Diabolical life-force! It gave man just enough light in his brain to sense everlasting life . . . and his own impermanence.

"Can I write in the sanatorium?"

"Yes."

"Sure?"

"Yes." The doctor sighed with relief. "And now, Mr.

Frey, if you'll sign this sheet here . . . it's just a statement to the county welfare board about your being a resident of this county and that you voted in the last election. It doesn't mean much. Just a formality."

Eric studied the sheet. The top line read: *Pauper's Oath.* He laughed. "There's no fake about this."

The young medic's eyes were uneasy.

Later still, the county nurse came around to check up on him, and to instruct the landlady on how to disinfect his room. The nurse was a small, good-hearted little spinster. Seeing his books, she told him by way of conversation that she had once managed to read *Anthony Adverse.*

He studied her silently in the dim light of his narrow coffin.

She told him to keep his mouth covered with a napkin when he coughed. She said too that he would not be able to write in the Phoenix.

He exploded then, not so much because he was being denied the right to create as because he hated letdowns. Just when a shaft of resurrection's light had come through a chink in his coffin, a rude hand had plunged him into darkness again. It was a lowdown trick. "But, lady, the doctor promised I could write before I signed the papers."

"I'm sorry."

"Why, that liar."

"I'm sorry."

"Sorry, hell." He narrowed his eyes. "Look, lady. I've got to write."

"But, really, Mr. Frey, they won't let you. I'm sure of it."

"Lady, there's one thing I've got to do before I die. That's write." He paused, coughed. "Maybe I should tell you what I mean by that. Look. This writing that I've got to do, it's bigger than me. Or you. It's . . . You see, there's a nervous impulse in mankind, a blind Poet trying to say something through our minds. What it is, I can't say. I don't know. But I do know it's there. I have felt it at work in me. Look. Whitman, Rolland, Doughty, Gand-

71

hi, Marx, Jesus, Tolstoi" . . . he paused to point them out on his bookshelves. His head buzzed. He had a vague feeling that he was saying something very foolish . . . "they had it. And they are my older brothers. If it hadn't been for them, I would never have known what it was that was threshing around in my bones. These brothers of mine are waiting for me, their younger brother, to report on what I think that wrestling is. They are waiting for me to do my share of the family chores. So, the Phoenix's got to let me write, got to grub-stake me for a while, got to stretch out this life a bit so I can get the story down on paper. My brothers are waiting for me."

"I'm sorry."

"But, lady . . ."

"Really, I have nothing to do with it. The physicians at the Phoenix make the rules and that's all there's to it."

"But . . ."

"Talk to the doctors when you get there."

He coughed. "Well, hell, then I'll just pull out and hide in the Arrowhead pines. It'll be wild there, and free, and I can be utterly alone and write."

As he talked, and for all his dream of writing, he knew he was pretending. He had not written for weeks. His talk was the last snarl of a coughing, dying body.

But he raved on. He told her of the books he had read. He took out his mind. He flashed what he thought were its powerful workings before her. And when he saw her trembling in fear of his waving arms and flaming eyes, he shouted exultantly. Through her, a symbol of some little authority, he was striking back at the cruel fates.

And then, his passion spent, he felt sorry for her. She really meant well. He was a devil, dying. And coughing. He felt miserably ashamed.

She got up hastily and left.

The next day, the first Saturday in April, a note came in the mail informing him that he could go to the Phoenix the next Thursday.

He went down the street, looking at the buds, noting

72

the green grass-shoots along the sidewalk, listening to the robin's mating calls.

He happened to meet Ronald, his brother. Without warning, without a word of greeting, Eric said, "Say, Ronnie, congratulate me. I've got consumption. Just got the good news."

Ronald jumped back as if a hand had smitten him. And stared. And paled.

But Eric did not enter the San as he had planned. Once more his life-course was to convulse and his way to take a buckling twist. On Tuesday afternoon, while he was reading Whitman, while he was smoking, a pain so severe that it paralyzed his limbs smote him in his left chest. He could not move. It was only with sheer maniacal determination that he managed to call Jack and his roommate. When they tried to undress him, he screamed. They undressed him as he was, bent in pain. They carried him to the bathroom. Despite their care, he flowed over his legs and the floor.

The next afternoon, at four o'clock, the ambulance came from the San . . .

He lay in his white bed, tossing. Yes, looking back on those days, it was easy to see. A Whipper had been pursuing him. Yes, it was easy to recall.

Where was sleep? He must sleep. He must sleep. He must not torment himself. Sleep. He needed sleep now. Sleep would encircle Tuber, whip the Whipper. Sleep would win. He tossed. He agonized over those days.

He wished he had a friend so that he could talk to him about the Whipper.

Sleep would not come.

Old Lady Poplar swayed softly outside the window.

He shifted his bones in his white bed.

He looked at the radiant dial of his wrist watch. It was already far past midnight.

His chest tickled. He smiled wryly. Old Tuber was at work, eating away at the tender pink tissues of his lungs.

**73**

The little animal, though quieted, was still at work. It was the secret agent of the Whipper.

The night was black. Black. Memories as large as cat-sized maggots ate into his brain.

Faintly the white sheets of his bed gleamed in the night; like a white bird he lay whipped and prostrate in a shutter-ed cage.

## VIII—FOOLISHNESS

THE ROOM was warm. He tossed back his bedclothes. He eyed his blue-striped penitentiary pajamas gloomily. Sour Miss Pulvermacher had told him curtly that Miss Valery's Patients' Aid had tailored them for him, just as it had made hundreds of others for similarly impoverished inmates. He shook his head. Couldn't she have let him exult in them, let him think they were a special gift, let his uncombed fancy play with their new smell and crisp edges? If ever a fellow needed the fun of thinking that he had a brand new toy, this was the time.

As he lay glowering, he became aware of a change in his surroundings. There was first a silence, then a loud *thung* against the wall behind him. He heard angry words, another *thung*, a door opening, a scream, a series of startled yells.

He sat up. The hallway resounded with wild blows and cries. The autocall buzz-buzzed the emergency signal. Beneath the saloon-like swinging doors, which had been installed for summer ventilation, he saw white-stockinged legs of nurses scurrying past, heard their muttered speech, heard one say, "It's the Mexican and that Boscoe kid, fighting." And another exclaim, "Why, they've got knives."

Knives? Eric rolled out of his bed and stumbled across the room. He pushed the swing-doors apart. He burst upon two crouching men; one with a swarthy and impassive face and glittering dark eyes, the other with a blond's ice-blue eyes. Both swayed on weak legs, both swung bloodied knives. Their silence was lethal.

Eric tumbled forward. He caught the blond man by the neck and hurled him against the wall so ferociously that his knife clattered to the floor. A henish nurse pounced on it and held it primly at a distance, staring at the blood.

The moment the blond was eliminated from battle, the dark Mexican lad stood up from his crouch and began to smile. Politely he said, "Thank you. Thank you. But me should finish. Not you." He straightened out his pajamas. As he did so, his face became pale, and he fell. His left arm, which he had kept hidden, flopped awkwardly over his chest, spurting blood from the elbow.

Eric, puffing, started to sway.

"Why, Mr. Frey," exclaimed Miss Florence, "what are you doing in the hallway? You, a strict bed patient? Get back in your room."

There was a clicking sound at the end of the hallway. Dr. Abraham came bounding out of the elevator.

Miss Florence saw him and, realizing that it was her floor that was in shambles, moved to clean it up. She leaped upon Eric, dragging at his arm so violently that his legs, unaccustomed to walking, buckled and he went down. The other nurses pounced on him, too. Hands tugged at him. A heavier hand, Dr. Abraham's, pushed him. He was propelled, awkward and uncoordinated, into the bed again. He closed his eyes. The hands left him and he heard the scuffling feet crowd out of the door.

Out in the hallway Miss Florence scolded, Dr. Abraham barked, someone cursed. There was a muffled cry.

A few moments later Dr. Abraham came in again and stood by his bed.

Eric did not move, did not open his eyes. He was too tired to respond.

"That was a very foolish thing to do, Eric."

A silence.

"Very foolish."

"I know."

"Well, it's all right. I know why you did it. But don't ever let me catch you trying such a stunt again. If my patients want to kill each other off, that's their business, and mine."

Eric did not answer.

"Eric, I want a promise from you."

"All right."

"Promise?"

"Sure, Doc." He was worried about his heart. It beat as if a tub of blood were guggling in it.

"That's better. Don't think for a minute I'm angry with you. I just want you to use a little horse sense."

Eric sighed deeply, involuntarily, and he swallowed to ease the action of his heart. To divert Dr. Abraham's attention, he asked, "What made'm do it, Doc?"

"Oh . . ." Dr. Abraham took off his glasses and peered through his narrowed and dusky eyelids, staring out of the window past the poplar. "Oh, they just got restless. Been here about two years. Both good boys. I thought they'd get along as roommates but . . . If only we could put the brain to sleep while the body convalesced, why then . . ." There was a dreamy look in his eye. "But, we can't. So, we have these explosions now and then. And you can't blame the boys. All their lives they've been used to making their own decisions: the Mexican in his beet fields, the other in his shop. And then, suddenly, they've had to lie down, and let others work and think for them. And if a man's got any spunk in him at all, any ego, he's going to show his teeth every now and then just to make sure he still owns a little corner of the world. Yessir, it takes a big man to come out of here in one whole piece."

"Or else a dumb one. A cow could take the cure easy."

Dr. Abraham laughed. "Yes, no doubt."

"Just the same, Doc, I know darn well I'd never lose my temper."

Dr. Abraham smiled a little.

"Really, Doc. I just wouldn't get on edge like they did."

"No, I don't think you would. Got your breath back?"

76

"Sure."

"Good. Let's have no more rescuing of the perishing." He smiled. There was a subtle gleam in his eyes. "You know, a man could expect big things from you."

"Could?"

Dr. Abraham's eyes narrowed until they were thin luminant slits of perception. "Eric, you've heard the old saw. 'The bigger the spirit, the bigger the beast?' "

Eric nodded. His whisker-rough chin tickled his throat.

"Well, my boy, if you can get out of this place with both your TB and your spirit under control, it'll really be a conquering. As I said before, you're right in the middle of your biggest battle."

They looked at each other steadily, peering at each other.

Eric's eyes weakened and he looked off to one side.

Dr. Abraham turned and left the room.

Later that hot June morning, some time after his heart had quieted and his throat and chest had lost some of their fiery rawnesses, two burly men with mischievous eyes, wearing overalls and sweat-soaked shirts and suspenders, swung into the room. Eric was considerably startled. He watched them measure his bed, then the length of his body.

Forgetting the rules, Eric drew himself up into a sitting position. "Hey, what goes on here?"

They looked at him blankly, continuing their computations. They stepped back and conferred in broken talk.

"About seven feet, huh?"

"I'd say about seven six."

"Should we resection the frame?"

"Yeh. Maybe put on some handles too." They looked at him. One said, "Say, young feller, bed's too short for you, ain't it? Feet comin' through here, head stuck between the rods there. Sure." And without waiting for an answer, he turned to the other, "Sure. The box'll be big enough, I think."

Eric rubbed his eyes. "Say, what's going on here?"

The man who seemed to be boss said, "Oh, measurin' you up fer a coffin, maybe."

"What?"

"Why not? What the hell. A lot a fellers croak in here. You don't expect to live forever, do you?"

"Oh . . . aw, nuts."

"Sure. We're measurin' you because you'll need a special. You're so goddamned big. An' you know what? We're gonna make it outer an old pianner box."

Eric forced a laugh. "Well, while you're at it, make damned sure it's a good one then."

Unruffled, they continued their mutterings, their mysterious gestures, their talk about length and depth and width.

"When must you guys have this coffin ready?"

"By noon."

"Aw, c'mon fellows, cut the comedy."

Sitting up made him feel light-headed. He was out of breath. He blinked his eyes.

Then, as noncommitally as they had entered, they left.

Towards noon hour, Miss Pulvermacher walked in. She pushed open both doors, hooked them to the wall. Approaching the bed she said, "Well, young man, you're moving today."

Again he popped upright in bed. "What? Say, what the thunder is going on here? I don't like all these mysterious businesses. I want to know."

"You'll see."

"Does Dr. Abraham know about this?"

Miss Pulvermacher snorted. "What's he got to do with it? We nurses have got the say where a patient'll sleep."

He watched her pull his bedstand and two white chairs out in the hallway, watched her approach the footend of his bed. He burst out, "Say, now, you leave this bed alone. You're not going to take me out until I know where I'm going."

She laughed at him. She pulled his bed toward the door.

**78**

She said, looking at his charity pajamas, "You should talk."

He puffed. He drew himself together. "Don't get me mad. Tell me where you're taking me, or, so help me God, I'll hop out of this bed and knock you down, woman or no woman."

She continued to pull his bed. She laughed at him. She shook her crudely bobbed hair. Her slinging breasts threshed within her starched uniform.

He caught the edge of the door and held on so tightly she almost pulled the bed from beneath him.

She came around to loosen his fingers.

Her touch infuriated him. He shot his face forward into hers. "Listen, you big clumsy bitch, let me alone."

She jerked back. "I'm afraid I shall have to report this to Miss Florence."

"Go ahead. And by the way, I wouldn't mind seeing her myself. Get her. Now. Right now."

She slowed.

"Get her. Now. Right now."

"Well, well, well. What's going on here?"

Eric rolled over. There, coming from the wing's far end, was Miss Florence. She was smiling at him, though the grimace was pinched.

"Miss Florence, where am I going?"

"Miss Pulvermacher, didn't you tell him?"

"No, I didn't. You see, I . . ."

"Never mind." To him she said, "We're moving you down to the first floor. They've got two nice roommates waiting for you there."

He flopped into his pillows. "Roommates? A new floor? Why, say, I don't like this."

Miss Florence laughed. "I'll tell you, Mr. Frey. You were peppy enough to help us keep order up here so we thought it was time to move you to a floor where you could help yourself."

"Oh. So, then this floor is . . ."

"Yes, it's for the critically ill. Up here on Third East, you're on Critical."

"Then I'm really getting better?"

"I guess that's what it means, Mr. Frey."

"Well, what about those fellows who were measuring me up?"

"You'll see." She smiled owlishly.

They began to push him out into the hallway again.

"Wait. Wait. Don't rush me. Moving into another room . . . you see, moving's a big thing. Can't rush into it. Got to kind of get used to the idea, just like I got used to this room. I dunno, I don't . . . What if I don't like the other fellows?"

"You'll like them. One of 'em is Mr. Olson. He's very nice. And so is your other roommate, Dr. Fawkes."

"A doctor?"

"He has an M.D., but he is really a scientist."

"Oh well, that's different. But, I still don't like this moving. Say, why didn't Dr. Abraham come and talk this over with me?"

"Well, Mr. Frey, you don't seem to understand. The nursing staff handles the disposition of patients."

Miss Pulvermacher smiled triumphantly at him.

His brain gleamed with a quick thought. "But if a doc wants it, he can keep a patient in a certain room, can't he?"

"Mr. Frey, there are a lot of sick people outside the Phoenix who are waiting for a chance at your bed here, at your room. So, it happens no one has the privilege of staying where he wants."

"I'll bet the rich have."

"Mr. Frey, in this San here, the rich man and the poor man, the paying as well as the charity patient, has equal rights. We make no distinctions."

"Oh come now, Miss Florence, don't give me that."

"Mr. Frey, I guess you just don't want to understand."

"But, Miss Florence, it's you who don't want to understand. You see, I don't like being shunted around like a steer in a stockyards. I'm not exactly a nobody. I want to be treated like a human being."

**80**

They stood facing him: Miss Florence severely, Miss Pulvermacher smirkingly.

"No, I won't go. Not until Dr. Abraham comes up here and okays this." Adamant, he clung to the door.

Five minutes later, Dr. Abraham came up, looking worried.

Miss Florence outlined the problem.

Dr. Abraham nodded, turned to Eric, and observed caustically, "You don't lose your temper, do you?"

"Well, I . . ."

"Look. I'm the one who ordered you downstairs."

"Oh."

"I thought it high time you had an audience for that histrionic impulse of yours." Dr. Abraham glared at him, then left the floor.

Eric made one last move. It was difficult to surrender, to be big. "Where's Miss Berg?"

"She's not on this floor any more," said Miss Florence crisply.

"Oh, so that's why I haven't seen her lately."

"Yes."

The two nurses began pushing him once more toward the elevator door.

"Too bad. I wanted to bid her good-bye."

As they pushed him along, he caught glimpses of other patients in the wards along the hallway. They were gray-faced. They held napkins over their mouths in fear of the rasping cough that would spray bacilli in all directions. As Miss Pulvermacher had told him, most were dressed in the same kind of blue-striped material from which his pajamas had been cut.

He came to the end of the hall where hurrying nurses cackled with sharp talk.

"So long."

"So long."

Miss Florence pushed his bed through the elevator door which had just opened and she said to the elevator man, the same man who had taken him upstairs that day he

**81**

came in, "George, this young man is going down to Miss Mitchell's floor on First East."

George nodded wordlessly.

Eric watched the nurses' faces through the closing glass door. He was going to miss Charge Nurse Florence; yes, even Miss Pulvermacher. He felt ashamed. He had behaved like an ass.

The elevator started down. Eric looked about wildly, excitedly.

The elevator stopped. George pushed him into the hallway.

A quick-stepping nurse came up. She had red hair. He studied her. He did not know if he should like her.

She drew him down the far end of the hallway. "I'm Miss Mitchell. I've been expecting you."

"Oh?"

She looked at him sharply and then, turning, opened two swing-doors. "Well, here's room 176. Your new home. Boys," she said, talking to the two patients inside the room, "here's your new roommate, Mr. Eric Frey. Mr. Frey, this is Dr. Theodore Fawkes. And . . . Mr. Huck Olson."

Eric nodded. He smiled at them politely. They were alert-eyed men. He had an uneasy premonition about them. Knowledge of the gravely thin and yellow-hued Huck and the very gentle and wise-smiling Fawkes might someday hurt. There was a startling difference between them, too. Huck had milk-blue eyes; Fawkes, shiny brown. And Fawkes wore a dark square mustache.

"I'm sure you'll all get along just swell," purred red-haired Miss Mitchell.

Another nurse came in. Together the two nurses pushed Eric into the same corner he had occupied in his Third East room.

Settled, and the nurses gone, he looked out of the window. There was Old Lady Poplar . . . except that instead of being able to see her nodding head, he was staring directly at her trunk-stiff hips.

He glanced at his roommates. They had gone back to

their reading. He noted that Olson was reading Van Loon's *The Story Of Mankind;* Fawkes, Thomas Mann's *Magic Mountain.*

Eric propped his head up on his pillows to get a better look at them. Huck, like himself, lay alongside a window. The foot ends of their beds were separated by a few inches of space. Fawkes' bed, placed beside Huck's, filled the third corner of the room. The fourth corner was empty. The room like the other upstairs was white and immaculate.

Eric stirred in his bed. He fidgeted. He asked, directing his voice towards Fawkes, "How long you been here?"

Fawkes laid his book down. His brown eyes, almost as black as a setter's, were brooding. They were subtle, speculative eyes. "Two years."

Eric's stomach muscles tightened. "And you, Huck?"

Huck's pale blue eyes twinkled. "Six years."

"Oh." Eric thought a moment. "What've you got, Fawkes?"

"A little trouble in each lung."

"Bad?"

"Oh, some cavitation."

"Holes, then?"

Fawkes nodded.

"When do you expect to get out?"

"Oh, two, three years."

"Oh."

Fawkes grinned.

"And you, Huck? What you got?"

"The same."

"Holes?"

"As big as lemons."

"Holy Moses."

"You running a fever, Fawkes?"

"Some."

"You Huck?"

"A little."

There was a rattling and a clanking outside in the hallway. It stopped before his door. Red-haired Miss Mitchell came in, smiling oddly. "Well, Mr. Frey," she said, "as long as we're settling you down in your new corner, we might as well be thorough about it. Here's your new bed."

Eric popped up. "Bed?" He stared at the long span of it just outside the opened swing-doors. "So that was what those bums were measuring me for. A special bed."

Fawkes and Huck sat up in their beds too. Everybody laughed.

"Well, bring'er in," Eric exclaimed.

Miss Mitchell helped him roll from one bed to the other. He stretched himself in it. He rolled a little from one side to the other.

"Like it?" she asked.

"It's like a sea."

It was near suppertime. Fawkes and Huck were hidden behind their evening papers.

Eric watched their fingers clutching at the edges of the newsprint for a while, thinking about the world that was reflected on the sheaves they held so tightly; and then, turning his head, looked out through the opened window, watching the varnished leaves of the poplar glint and twist in the sunlight. Beyond, the grass on the lawn was a little burnt.

He was glad his roommates were absorbed in their own worlds. Though he had begun to like them and felt they had the right sort of fur for him to rub against, he was still provoked at the abrupt way he had been moved around, and was not in the mood for talk.

For a few short hours, the roommates had been very silent, he thought, and watchful of his manners and prejudices. But gradually Fawkes and Huck had relaxed, and reassumed their familiar attitudes toward each other. Presently they included him too. They were at ease sooner than he had expected.

He liked Fawkes. The man had the wise gentle manner of a grandfather. Eric could imagine that he and Ma Memme would have been the best of friends. But Olson he was

84

not sure of. For one thing, the pale man resembled Martha Lonn.

The door opened quietly. Without turning his head, Eric knew it was Dr. Abraham. The doctor was near his bed before he could turn.

"How's the new house?"

"Oh, good."

"And your new bed?"

"All right, I guess. Big enough. First time I've been able to rest all stretched out." A side-thought flashed within him. He was still piqued about the way he had been handled, and wanted to extract a little satisfaction, even from the good doctor. "Say, Doc, I've seen a few paradoxes in my time. But this bed business is one of the best. When I needed it most, when I was sicker'n a cat with pups, with my knees all doubled up, my head pushing through one end of the bed and I couldn't lay straight unless I'd stick my toes through the other end, I didn't get a special bed. But now, now that I'm on the mend, I get it. Funny, uh?"

Dr. Abraham blinked his eyes. "You're probably worth the investment now."

Eric blinked.

Dr. Abraham looked at his shiny shoes, and scuffed a little at the floor.

"You doctors. You know, you're sure a bunch of calculating devils."

Dr. Abraham looked up, patted Eric's arm and, turning to Fawkes, asked, "He's been behaving, I hope?"

The roommates, who had been pretending they were reading their evening papers, looked up. Fawkes glanced from one to the other with a knowing smile. "Pretty good. He's not quite so high strung as our old roomie."

Eric looked up. "There was? Of course. Where'd he go, the guy that had this spot?"

"Up and around."

"Oh."

"Well, you're all right, aren't you, Eric?" Dr. Abraham asked.

"Sure."

"Good." Dr. Abraham walked toward Fawkes' bed and asked, "Say, Ted, in your chemistry, did you ever run across the idea of 'sympathetic elements'?"

Fawkes' eyes became smoky with subtle thought. He looked piercingly at Dr. Abraham.

Eric could see they were good friends. He wondered if this talk was part of a running argument they had.

"Did you?"

"No."

Dr. Abraham paused. He drew in his breath sharply and slapped the footend of Fawkes' bed. "Well, I haven't either. But I wonder about it sometimes. I had a patient today. She was so bad, a man could almost say she wasn't alive, the condition she was in. And, well, I encouraged her and, somehow, she hung on. Just before noon Stein and Price were operating on her when it happened that I was called out of the operating room to handle a little mishap on one of the floors. And while I was gone, she came out of the ether. Stein said she started to smile until she saw that I wasn't holding her hand. And then, pfft, gone. Just like that."

There was a cold silence in the room.

"Yes, too bad. Well, good-night, men." Dr. Abraham left.

It was after nine, and dark, when Eric thought of something. "Fawkes, awake yet?"

"Yes."

"Say, the fellow that had my corner here, how long was he here before he moved on?"

There was a moment's silence. Fawkes said calmly. "Sixteen years."

"Oh. In this same corner, sixteen?"

"Right."

"And where's the fellow who lived where you are now?"

"Dead."

"And in your's, Huck?"

86

"Dead." Huck's voice seemed to be edged with pleasure.

"But the guy that had this corner, sixteen?"

"Right."

Sixteen years. Suppose, he thought, suppose he had to live sixteen years in the same corner with Martha in his heart? The bitter alum of defeat would pucker him up into a skin of dust. He groaned.

"Anything wrong?" It was Fawkes.

"Nothing. Just that my chest hurts me a bit. That moving today, you know."

"Oh. Want me to call you a nurse?"

"Oh no. I guess I got the habit of groaning just like some people grunt every time they move."

Black quiet settled over them.

Eric closed his eyes against the dark room. Sixteen years. When he was eleven years old, in the seventh grade, and when Ma Memme was still living and they were on that farm east of Bonnie Doon, Minnesota, then, at that time, this man had come into this corner. And had been here ever since, doing nothing but eat and excrete, and breathe and have visitors. During those sixteen years . . . why, he had gone to high school, later to college, had seen his Ma Memme die, had hiked through America, had lost jobs, had gone hungry, had begun his long prose-poem, had met Martha, had . . . why, had lived!

Sixteen years. Eric could visualize the man, praying each night for deliverance; and in the vague dawn, finding his supplications unanswered.

Eric groaned . . . and held his breath, fearing that Fawkes had heard him again.

Yes, he had been living. And if he were going to live, as it seemed he might, now that they had moved him down from Critical, well, what about his writing and Martha? One of these days he had to make up his mind about it and her.

Then it hit. Why, that mishap Dr. Abraham had spoken of, why! that was when he had refused to move from his other room. Eric felt his face whiten in the dark.

And so then . . . ah, that talk with Fawkes. Subtle Dr. Abraham.

Eric rose on his elbows, staring wildly about in the dark room. A life had gone because he had been childish. A life. Guilt swept into his skull like gray-black smog, choking his fire. His chest felt tight. Such sly ways the Whipper sometimes used to humble him.

A loneliness possessed him. He wished he knew his new roommates well enough to talk to them about the Whipper. Perhaps they could talk him out of his obsession. But then, maybe they would only laugh at his notions. He settled deep into his pillows. The black, ponderous, starless universe pressed down upon his brow.

# IX—THE WHIPPER SEEN AGAIN

**T**HE NEXT DAY, before Eric had a chance to feel settled in his new room, the doors parted and Miss Berg walked in. She smiled at him as if she had expected to find him in the corner. He was tempted to exclaim; but still feeling disgruntled, he grumbled instead, "I suppose Miss Pulvermacher's transferred to this floor too?"

"Why, yes. What's wrong with her?"

"Oh, she's . . . Oh, I don't know. She's a bitch."

"Why, Mr. Frey. Miss Pulvermacher's considered one of our best nurses. At least that's what Miss Globe, head of the nursing staff, thinks."

"Well, it isn't what I think."

His roommates chuckled.

Miss Berg fussed with the sheets of his bed. "Well, grouchy, I think you'd better take a trip. Maybe X-ray can brighten you up with a little good news."

He grunted. Yes, it would be interesting to know if the cavity in his left lung was closing. He had wondered about its size. The amount of sputum had dropped to half.

While he was truculently considering this, Miss Berg

brought in a vehicle.

Promptly he sat up. "I'm really going for a trip some-where?"

"Like I said, to X-ray."

"Holy Moses."

"Got your hair combed?"

"Hell no. What for?"

"You may meet some people."

"People? Oh. You mean women. T'hell with the wom-en."

"Say, is it necessary to swear like that?"

He grunted in reply.

She drew a gray blanket from under his bed, where it had been folded over a crosspiece, and unrolled it on one side of the litter.

With considerable groaning and lifting, they together managed to swing his body onto the litter. His long legs hung over the edge. He saw his roommates grinning as Miss Berg struggled to get the blanket around them. She finally had to ask him to double his legs to get them covered.

"Got your sputum cup? Your napkins?"

"No."

"Better take them with you. Got to be sanitary, you know."

"Rules, rules, rules."

"Now, now."

"Look, I don't cough. Nor spit."

"But suppose you did, though? And'd spit TB bugs all over the floor, giving it to others?" She set the box under his blanket close to his chin and slid a few paper napkins into his pajama pocket.

She pushed him through the door, feet first, and started down the hallway, his blanket-covered knees blocking the · view ahead. Her full bosom touched his hair as she leaned forward to push him along. Her vigorous body pulsed its strength into the moving litter. Her breathing stirred the hair over his forehead.

He rode on the elevator with George, who lowered him

to Main floor and shoved him out into the hallway. A pusher came up, a gray man puffing heavily, a patient up on exercise. He moved Eric toward X-ray.

The hallway was filled with ambulant, pasty-faced men patients. Their bellies ballooned out heavily below thin narrow chests. All except one seemed preternaturally sad. The exception was very cheerful. Their eyes spoke little histories.

The pusher rolled him to the door of the X-ray room.

Eric waited.

Beyond the edge of his impromptu, leg-poled tent, he saw another big-wheeled litter coming toward him from the opposite end of the Main Floor hallway, from the women's side of the San. A girl was on the litter, also partially covered by a gray blanket. He turned on his side to flatten his knees to watch her coming. She was wearing pink pajamas and her dark brown hair was upswept from her face. She had green-blue, skinned-grape eyes, with sharply-defined black eyebrows. She had very full lips, carmined with lipstick. She wore red fingernail polish. A pusher rolled her up to the door of the X-ray room too and then turned her litter about and faced her the other way.

Eric considered her. Martha wasn't the only lovely woman in the world. And this one was ill.

He smiled about this new woman. He could see that she was friendly, and good. She was like a farm girl. He acted on an impulse to speak to her. "Well, what have you got?"

The girl on the litter turned on her stomach and faced him.

"What've you got?" he repeated. The expressions on her face pleased him. Here, he thought, is a woman interested in every new turn and twist of life. She smiled warmly, almost excitedly. Her eyes were as wide as open hands. She was a child anticipating gifts.

"Nothing. I'm just having an X-ray. To see if there is any fluid."

"What's that?"

**90**

"Fluid in my pneumothorax. I had a pneumonolysis."
She laughed at his widening eyes. "That's an operation
where they go into your chest with a little knife at the
end of a long thin rod and cut adhesions."

"Sounds like a worm-hunt."

She smiled widely. Her teeth were even and full-sized.
"Yes, doesn't it? I don't know much about it, but the adhesions are the places where the lung gums to the pleura.
And when they pump in the air, those places stick together
and stretch like taffy."

"Oh. How do you feel?"

"Good. Oh, I haven't had much trouble. I really came
here for a rest. They found a spot and gave me pneumo,
but it hasn't been bad at all. I've never been positive."

"Why, that's wonderful."

"Not as wonderful as my getting my four trips back
next week."

"Four trips? What's that mean?"

"That I can go to the bathroom four times a day.
Walk there."

"You mean, you're all healed, and starting the getting-
up program?"

She smiled. "Yes."

"Why, that's great."

"Oh, it'll be wonderful all right to have full bath, and
come and go as I please, and sit at a table again. They say
I can in three weeks."

"I'm glad for you."

"And in two or three months, in the fall, I can go for
a half hour walk each day." She paused. "Just think. Walking outdoors, under the trees, sitting in the grass, watching
the cars go by, and . . . Oh . . ."

Eric tried to hide his face with his hand. But he was too
late. She had seen the envy in his eyes, had seen he felt left
behind.

"I'm sorry," she said.

"It's all right."

"How far along are you?"

"Depends on which way you mean it. You see, I don't know much about things here yet. But I have been moved off Third East."

"Well, that's good. To First East?"

"Yes."

She remained silent. Her eyes were full of sympathy.

"Who are you?" he asked.

"I . . . well . . . why?"

"I'd like to know," he said. "What's your name?"

"That doesn't matter very much."

"Maybe not, but you do. What is it?"

"Mary Lehar."

"Mary Lehar," he repeated. His eyes lingered on her face, on her dark hair framed by the white pillow. He noticed the red lips and red fingernails. "A beautiful name." He was pleased with her country-girl ways.

She laughed. "I'm glad you like it."

The door of the X-ray room opened then and a white-gowned man emerged and he began to draw Eric's litter inside. Eric reached out his hand.

She hesitated, took it in her own.

He held hers a moment, released it.

As the door closed behind him, he heard her call, "Good luck."

That night, after the lights had gone out, when he and his roommates were trying to coax sleep into their skulls, he lay in thought. Mary Lehar was vivid in his mind. He recalled the touch of her pad-firm hand. It reminded him of Ma Memme's. He recalled the song, *The Touch Of Your Hand*. He was disturbed and also a little pleased that the face of a strange woman, seen only fleetingly, should prove so exciting to him.

He considered writing her a note. A new woman would help him forget Martha Lonn. He mused about Mary for a while, dreaming of chance meetings, of accidental tete-a-tetes.

Then misgivings arose. Writing her would not be fair

92

to her. Nor to himself. "When I get up, if I ever do, I'll be nothing but a wrecked old man, an old lunger, coughing a little, half-waving my hand, and trying to get safely across to death."

No, from now on it would be best to ignore women. He could give them nothing. Most members of society still expected a man to support a woman, to surround her with comforts and beds and children and money. No, he had better toss marriage out of his scheme of things to come. He sighed, and turned, his leg bones clanking. His pillow had settled into a hard lump and he leaned on an arm to fluff it and double it. He resettled into the soft folds. He stared out through the night-darkened window and traced the outlines of Old Lady Poplar's stiff belly. He sighed.

Why hadn't death come? Why hadn't the Whipper finished His job? Life would have been as simple as sleep then.

But if he should live, he would have to adapt himself to a world which would not, and perhaps could not, give him a job; would not accept his book; would not bring back Martha.

How bitter her leaving had been. How bitter.

. . . He had been driving down the street that September Sunday afternoon. He whistled, trying to focus his mind on the only pleasant thing he could think of: that, after a month of sullen silence between them, he was seeing her again. They were going to see an afternoon performance of *Of Human Bondage;* and, he hoped, going for an evening ride into the fall country.

He whistled. He pushed down certain aching thoughts as if he were putting his hand over the mouths of bawling children and shoving them down into a black cellar. He found it hard to forget that he hadn't a job, that the finance company was about to take possession of his V-8.

Like a wary animal, he sniffed the September air. He drove carefully, with quick eyes, with quick reactions to the complexities of the street traffic. He sensed a crisis ahead.

He probed his memory to understand what was happening to his relationship with her. He tried to understand her. For one thing, she was really not his type. She came from a wealthy and a society-minded family while he was a farm boy who had acquired a taste for truth and beauty. For another, her father and mother despised his convention-breaking attitude, looked down on his ambition to write. They were afraid that he might ruin her.

He smiled wryly. He ruin her? Why, she had been the pursuer. She had singled him out at parties. She had been the one to ply the compliments, with her "Oh what a mass of man you are." In fact, he had been just a little afraid of her. Her passion had been almost harsh. And when she drew him close, she always seemed to be on the point of screaming.

He smiled to himself and drove along. Such was life. He remembered the day when her parents discovered who he was, and what he wanted from life. Like a black-browed Jehovah and His Wife, they had peremptorily ordered her to stop seeing him. They tried to lock her in the house. They took her on a trip to New York. They took her out to the country place. But she had persisted and finally the family retreated and watched sullenly from the sidelines.

Eric drove along carefully. He tried to analyze what it had been that had attracted him. At first it had been her lovely, apple-sized breasts, their ample swellings so like Ma Memme's. Later, he had been fascinated by her ice-blue eyes. They were so like Pa's cold eyes. But what had really opened his heart was her determined fight with her parents to keep him.

Eric nodded as he remembered their days together. Then, blinking, he noticed the street numbers and realized that he was almost there. He resettled in his seat. He set his mind in order.

He pulled up before her house on Park. She was waiting for him on the steps. When she jumped up and came swiftly toward him, he knew she was trying to prevent an accidental meeting with her family. She hurried toward him. She was wearing a tight dark-blue skirt and a close-fitting

94

light-blue blouse. She was carrying a blue purse that matched her shoes. The various blue hues caught the blue in her eyes.

She got in beside him. She was smiling. Her ice-blue eyes were Pa-cold today. He saw instantly that she would not kiss him. He held back.

He shifted his long legs underneath the dashboard and lighted up his yellow-stemmed pipe. He brushed his hair out of his eyes.

He started the car. "Did you have trouble getting away?"

"No. But mother was furious. She had invited the Bulkleys over for dinner."

"Oh. Russell too, I suppose?"

"Oh sure." She rubbed her hands together.

"Haven't you eaten, then?"

"I took a bite in the kitchen."

"I'm sorry."

"Oh, that's all right," she said looking down and pulling at a loose thread in her skirt. She rubbed her hands, and stroked first one arm from wrist to elbow and back again, then the other. Eric noted the feverish gesture.

He said, "Maybe we better have a bite before we go."

"No." She put her hand on his arm. He trembled at the touch. "No, we better go now."

He hesitated. He had only two dollars in his billfold. "No, let's eat. We got time."

"I'm . . . but I'm afraid we haven't got the time.

"Why not?"

"Well, I promised father I'd go to church with him tonight."

"Well, I'll be a son of a bitch."

She stiffened. "I don't like your swearing."

"Well . . . but, thunder, woman, this is the first Sunday we've spent together in months." He drew furiously on his pipe. The billowing smoke almost obscured the road ahead.

"I know. Come. Let's go to the *Bondage*."

He parked near the theatre, and locked the car doors. They walked down the street toward the Minnesota. He

95

bought two tickets at the outside window and entered the dark foyer with her. They found two seats in the last row. The newsreel had just come on.

When the main feature started, he leaned over and gently took her chin in his hand and kissed her. When he felt what he thought was a lack of warmth, he kissed her again.

Once more, near the end of the picture, just after Mildred had accepted Philip's care without a word of thanks, he turned to kiss her. Martha drew away.

"Say," he whispered, "what's up? I got a bad breath or something?"

She said nothing. She began to stroke her arms again.

He shrugged. Perhaps tawdry Mildred had momentarily banished emotion from her mind. Well, if that was it, he had to give her credit for having consistent moods.

When they left the theatre and were once more in the car, he said, as he lighted his pipe, "Martha, you don't know how wonderful it is for a bird like me, with no job, no money, to have a woman like you."

She moved uneasily beside him.

"Really, Martha, I . . . "

"Oh shut up." She twisted in the seat; then was instantly contrite. "I . . . I didn't mean . . . " She hid her face in her hands and cried to herself, "Oh, you don't know. You'll never know."

"Know what?"

"Oh, take me to Adele's."

"Why, I thought you were going to church with your father tonight."

"Well . . . yes I am. I'm going to meet him there after I see Adele."

He darted a glance at her, saw her stroke her arms nervously, then studied the silver leaping hound on the radiator cap.

He started up the car, turned toward Adele's house. He drove along. There's something screwy here, he thought. First she says she's going to church with her father, then she asks me to take her to Adele. He shook his head. He lighted his pipe as he drove. He puffed on it. He remembered that on another occasion she had not kept her stories straight. Last June, when he had tried to get a Sunday evening date with her, she had said she was going to church with her father. And an hour later, driving along by himself, he caught her with a short, laughing, dark-haired youth on the Mississippi bluffs near the University. When Eric questioned her later, half-laughingly, half-embarrassedly, wondering if the youth were Russell Bulkley, she haughtily refused to explain. Eric puffed on his pipe. He bit into its yellow stem. He rolled his yoke-wide shoulders nervously.

Suddenly he pulled up to the curb, turned to face her. "Martha, I think you're lying."

She blinked.

"Martha, you are lying."

"Why . . . ! " She shivered, and slowly her pale blue eyes became ice.

"Martha, what are you trying to tell me?"

"To tell you . . . oh, you make it so hard to be diplomatic, to get in the mood, to . . ."

"You mean, you've been building me up to let me down easy?"

She stared at him.

"Look, woman. If what you've got to say can't be told without a buildup, it's rotten." He hauled up a comfortable cough.

She looked down and drew a handkerchief from her handbag and wiped a tear from her eye. "Oh, Eric, I'm a hussy, I guess."

"Oh, come now."

"Look, Eric. What do you want from life?"

"Must we go through that again?"

"Tell me."

"Why, I want the right to create, to love, to breathe. To wonder what an ant thinks about when he runs up and down and all over a leaf or stone. I want just enough

**97**

food to keep alive and just enough bricks to build a fireplace. No more, no less."

"Well, you'll never have those if you marry me."

"Why not?"

"Look, Eric. Look. I want a family, and I want to meet people. Parties. And . . . oh, I want things you don't want. We'll never get along. We're too different."

"This is a hell of a time to find that out."

"I know. That's what makes it so hard."

"And I suppose Russell can give you these things?"

"Oh, Eric, that's not big of you. Please."

"Aw, nuts."

"And besides, where you want to go, I can't follow. Nor can a family."

"Where'd you get that stuff?"

"Why, just look at all the creators, all the dreamers. They didn't have families. In fact, they lost their loves. They thrived on unhappiness."

He snorted. Coughed. "Such as?"

"Beethoven, Tchaikovsky, Whitman."

"Nuts."

"Really, Eric." She rubbed her hands furiously.

"Martha, what are you trying to say?"

"Oh . . . nothing, I guess."

"Martha, you're lying."

Her eyes became icy, Pa-cold. "I didn't go out with you to be insulted."

"But to insult me, huh?"

"Nononono. You see, you don't know. You'll never know."

"What's that, a new song hit?" He gestured and filled his pipe. "Martha, if you've got anything to say, say it now, or forever hold your tongue."

She picked at the loose thread again.

"Say it now."

"There's nothing, I guess."

"Sure?"

"Yes."

"Good. Now. Kiss me. I love you. I love you more . . . Martha, if you possibly can, try to see me tonight. Call me up after church if you can make it, and I'll come right down. I want to have a real talk with you tonight."

She looked up and her light-blue eyes held his steadily and she said, "I'll try." She kissed him. And he tumbled into a happy mood again.

He took her to Adele's and drove home. He went to his dim room and turned on the radio. He brewed some coffee on the electric plate and ate two old nut-rolls and then lay down on his cot to listen a while to the music.

But he was restless. The waters within him were rolling.

When she did not call at eight-thirty, he got up and began to pace in his narrow coffin. Perhaps she had had an argument with her father and had given up the idea of seeing him that night.

When the symphony hour came on at nine, he lay down on the floor, his favorite resting spot. The orchestra began the program with Franck's *Symphony in D Minor*. The deep notes made the floor-boards of the old house tremble. He cried and laughed as the music tumbled into him.

He leaped up. He loved her so much. So tremblingly. He had to tell her. Now. This instant. There was an agony of love in him, an exultant, painful crying in him for her, a love so abounding that silver-framed images of all the lovely things he had ever seen on earth rose like visions from the white flames within his skull: the red-wine oak leaves and the purple-shadowed Big Horns and the impersonal majesty of Yellowstone and the whale-large redwoods of California and the white pillars of the United States Supreme Court and the white marble pillars of Attic temples and the green sheen on the grain and the silver sheen on the silver spruce in the afternoon sun.

He had to see her now. Now. She was the golden drink contained within his life-vessel. It would be unfair to her, and to him, if she did not know, now, of this vivid aureole within himself. This knowledge a woman should have. It

**99**

would be her greatest prize. Oh, he loved her now, just now, creative, burgeoning, up! up! soaring!

He called her house. She should be home by now with her father. He heard the telephone ringing, heard it click, heard her father's flat voice. "Hello."

"Is Martha there?"

"Martha? No." Eric could hear impatience in the man's voice. He could hear a newspaper rattling and guessed that the old man was reading the *Sunday Journal*. Eric could see him bent over, listening, his vest unbuttoned, the paper brushing his leg.

Eric said, "Oh. Why, I thought she was with you tonight."

"And I thought she was with you."

"She not there?"

"No."

Eric dropped the receiver into its black cradle.

What now? What was up? An evil notion, a blood-hued, hate-fed flame, rose in him and raced into and filled up every cranny of his skull; and then struck down, and seared his veins, and burned him until his manroots ached.

He rushed from the house to his car. He switched on the dashboard light. Not enough gas. He fumbled in his pockets for loose change. Thirty cents. He hurried to a corner filling station on the East River Road, near Franklin, for a gallon. Thoughts raced within him. He was sure that she was out with Russell, kissing him, loving him. He shuddered. The flames in his skull swirled in a whirlpool.

He drove madly across town.

He called from a drugstore near her home to make sure she had not come home in the meantime.

"No," said her father, angry now. "No. She's not home. I thought I told you that before."

Eric hung up before the old man could say another word. He ran out to his car, got in, whirled it around the block, parked before her house.

He crouched in the front seat. Ten minutes went by. Twenty minutes. Thirty.

And then he began to have misgivings. Perhaps he had been foolish to come chasing all the way out here; probably turn out to be a wild-goose chase. Martha was all right. It was only his crazy imagination. He had been nervous lately. Upset. Defeated. No, she had not lied. Something had happened, something she simply could not avoid, and that was why she wasn't home. Maybe her girl friend, Adele, shy Adele, had invited her over for the night. He lighted his pipe, smoked a while, began to feel happy again.

He looked out of the car to study Martha's house. He saw, why, there was a faint light in the living-room. Who was that? Her father? Mother? Were they waiting up for her too? He looked at his watch. It was eleven o'clock. No. It must be Martha. Maybe she had come in the back way.

Well, if it was Martha, he had to see her. He would call her softly through the window. The window would be open, for the day had been warm. He would go up to the wistaria bushes beneath the living-room windows and call her and tell her how great his love had been earlier in the evening, how foolish he had been since. She would laugh at him, and tell him where she had really been.

He stepped quietly out of the car.

He approached the house. He stopped to look around. He had to be careful. Should someone see him in this neighborhood stealthily crossing the lawn, he would be reported as a peeping-tom. But there was no one on the street; not even a car.

Then he heard footsteps. There was someone coming after all; to his right.

Eric strolled down the street, turned the corner, and as soon as he felt he was out of sight of the other, rushed around the block and once more approached the house.

He looked again, glancing up and down the sidewalk. No one. Now. Now. He crept across the grass. Carefully he stepped on the walk where it curved around the house. He parted the bushes quietly. He neared the window. He stood up, shooting his body up through the bushes. He

**101**

rammed forward through the prickly branches and looked down through the screen, through the open window.

He saw something he did not understand right way. When he did see what they were doing, he turned around and ran to his car. He started up the motor and roared off before the impulse to kill them possessed him completely.

He sped blindly down the street. He remembered the baboon lovers he had seen mating in a Como Park cage one day. He recalled the red of their tumescent fleshes.

"I should have killed them," he gritted to himself. "Killed 'em."

He drove through a red light.

"I should've killed her. I should've grabbed her and ripped the head off her neck."

He drove along. The steering-wheel cracked inside the powerful grip of his huge clutching hands.

Later, when he undressed for bed, he found a dollar-bill in his side-pocket. He stared at it, knew what she meant by it, and tore it to shreds . . .

. Eric, lying in his white Phoenix bed, twisted and groaned.

Someone stirred in the room and a voice, Fawkes', sounded, "Anything wrong, Frey?"

Eric sucked in his breath, embarrassed. What else had Fawkes heard? "No. No. I just couldn't get to sleep and I just sort of groaned, I guess. That habit, you know."

"Oh." A pause. "Guess we all got sleeping trouble."

"You mean, the Whipper sometimes whacks you too?"

"My God, what's that?"

"The Whipper."

"Who's that?"

"Oh, nobody. Just . . . well, something in the universe, a hard-hearted God."

"Oh."

"Forget it. I was just muttering in my beard."

Eric lay thinking about Fawkes a moment. About Huck. What tortured lives were in their heads? What was the panoramic sequence of them? Where had the events occurred? Were they trying to survive a Martha too?

Eric lay on his left side for a while, according to Dr. Abraham's instructions; then, turned and rolled over on his right side. He tried to outline Old Lady Poplar outside his window. A breeze wisped in through the screens, and brushed his hair, and brushed the fuzz on his arms.

Yes, with that fearful Whipper on the loose, waiting to torment him, it would be best to die. Going back to tree-shaded, lake-girded Minneapolis would mean that he could not go down some of its streets without torturing himself. For somewhere in that city lived Martha, now another man's wife.

He lay staring upward, brooding. Except for the finger-length of flame in his skull, the universe was very dark.

He tossed. Coughed. Rolled over on his back. Wasn't it curious that both Martha and this new Mary should use almost the identical words to express such a difference in personality? Martha with her arrogant "Oh you don't know. You'll never know." and Mary's humble "Oh I don't know. I really don't know"? Curious. Jesus must have noticed somewhat the same difference in the Martha and Mary of his day.

Just before he went to sleep, he was not surprised to see, in the dim window where ordinarily a white curtain moved, the vague phosphorescent figure of Martha. He was not afraid of her and he murmured sleepily, "Martha, now that I have lamented you, depart, begone, and go."

# I X—ENTER SATAN DEEBLE

T WAS SATURDAY morning, and early. It was pneumo day; the day of the stabbing needle; the day of pain.

Into the dark room the sputum-cup collector came with his barely suppressed flashlight. The first nurse brought in hot water and emesis basins.

The roommates awakened: Fawkes very tardily, as if he had sunk as deeply into sleep at night as he was brilliantly awake during the day; Huck with great explosive coughs lasting a half hour and dissipating whatever energy he might have stored up during the night's sleep; and Eric, slowly too, gradually sensing the crisp smells of July that came in through the open window: the hay, the slough grass, the meadows, the corn, the sunburnt tree leaves.

Breakfast was served. Orange-juice, cereal, milk, sugar, toast, butter, eggs, and coffee.

Then came the leveler of society, the bedpan. Sensibilities were suspended and the room's shades drawn.

Then, the shades once more up and the room cleared, the day began.

Eric lay with his nose toward the window, watching the tree leaves on the mall slip over and under the morning wind-drifts.

One of the doors parted and a lanky stranger walked in. Like Dr. Abraham he wore a long white smock and a dangling stethoscope.

"Good morning, gentlemen."

"Hi, Doc," Huck greeted, smiling oddly.

"Hello," Fawkes echoed.

The newcomer turned to Eric. "I'm Dr. Deeble. I presume you are Mr. Frey? Mr. Eric Frey?"

"Yes."

"Well, well," said the stranger. He was tall. His hands and face were gaunt, his skin blue-white. His dark eyes were quick. Mockery lurked in them.

"And I presume you are on Dr. Abraham's service?"

"Yes."

"Good. Good." Deeble stood by Eric's bed and drew his stethoscope from his belt and fitted its earpieces into his ears. "All right, all right," he growled. "Uncover your chest. Come, come. I haven't got all day. A lot of other patients are waiting to die, too, you know."

Eric stared at him. Though he sensed something was wrong, he opened his pajama tops to expose his chest for

104

examination. He glanced at his roommates; they seemed to accept the stranger as a doctor.

With little mutterings, and mysterious noddings of the head, the newcomer went over Eric's chest.

He seemed to reach a conclusion. He withdrew the stethoscope earpieces, hooked the instrument on his belt. With a red-leaded pencil, he drew a large irregular oval on Eric's chest, cutting the skin in places.

Eric, almost witless with fright, his head pushed awkwardly forward by his pillow, his chin whiskers tickling his throat, asked, "What's that?"

Deeble shook his head forebodingly.

"Tell me."

"That, young man, is the outline of your cavity."

"You mean, that hole in my lung?" Wild-eyed, Eric bent his head forward to look at the outline. It was nearly six inches in diameter. "Moses, Doc, that's practically my whole left lung."

"Yes," Deeble sighed.

"Holy Moses." Eric flopped back on his pillows. He panted. How could a hole that large ever heal together? Why, the edges would never touch. All was lost.

But something occurred to him. "Say, that X-ray Dr. Abraham had me take, did that show the hole too?"

Deeble nodded.

"My God!"

Deeble said, "Well, I don't suppose there's much use of my continuing this examination, but . . . well . . . since it's routine, strip to your knees."

Slowly Eric unbuttoned his pajama bottoms.

"Hurry, hurry."

Eric pushed down his bottoms.

Deeble leaned forward, his dark eyes narrowed in scrutiny. "Yessir. Just as I expected."

"What?" Eric's mind flicked.

Deeble turned to Fawkes, as though he, too, like Dr. Abraham, shared scientific interests with him. "Notice how the patient pretends innocence? I've often observed that the most diseased protest the greatest purity of heart."

Eric grabbed Deeble's arm. "Listen, Doc, tell me, what've I got?"

"Syphilis."

Eric sucked in his breath. "Syphilis?"

"Yes. We must isolate it." Turning to Fawkes again, Deeble observed, "Interesting statistics I'm working up, Fawkes, on this relationship of tuberculosis and syphilis. Very interesting."

Eric exploded at that. "Say, I want you to get this straight. I'm not . . . I've never monkeyed around with whores. Bad women."

Deeble's lips curved slightly.

Eric narrowed his eyes. He began to hate the new doctor. It was a vile trick to smirk over a patient's sores. A vile trick.

Just then Miss Berg stepped through the doors. As Deeble's body was between himself and the nurse, Eric did not catch the momentary look of consternation that opened her face, nor the quick winks in the room.

Deeble turned and said professionally, "Good morning, Miss Berg."

"Good morning."

"I have finished my examination."

"Oh."

"And . . . and, I'd like to have you dress him three times a day."

She blinked.

"I want you to attend to Mr. Frey personally. It's a serious case of lues."

She blinked again.

Deeble left then, bowing, smirking, his stethoscope earpieces clinking on the belt of his white smock as he stepped through the swing-doors.

Miss Berg looked after Deeble and sighed. "That man. He's going to drive me crazy yet." She turned to Eric. "Well, young man, get out your sputum cup and napkins again. You're going for a ride."

"Where to?"

"It's pneumo day."

"Oh, that's right." He had forgotten. The week previous Dr. Abraham had told him that henceforth he would get his pneumothorax treatments up on Second East along with the other patients on his floor. He stirred in his sheets. He braced himself. He remembered the last time the stabbing needle had scraped his tender ribs, had plunged into his chest cavity. Nervous sweat dampened his pajamas. Then he recalled the six-inch cavity in his lungs and thought, "What the hell. I'm going to die anyway with a hole that big."

Miss Berg helped him onto the litter and bundled him underneath a gray blanket. Again his knees hid the view ahead.

She pushed him down the hall and into the elevator.

George took him up to Second East, and pushed him into a hallway leading off to the left.

He counted fifty patients lying on litters around him. A swirl of nervous, hysterical talk filled the shade-darkened hallway. Men and women patients, pouring out their repressed hurts and lonesomeness, were so intent on their own stories they hardly heard each other. It was a great occasion.

Eric studied the women. Except for the elderly, they looked well; too well, for patients. They had rosy cheeks, and their lips, like Mary Lehar's, were bright. For a full minute he was puzzled that they should seem so much healthier than the men. Then it came to him. Makeup. Real women, though now prostrate, they were still practicing their arts. He admired them.

Reluctantly he remembered his condition: a six-inch cavity and lues.

And Mary Lehar. Where was she? On Dr. Abraham's service too?

Then, like a dog on the alert, he became suspicious of his own judgment. And laughed. Of course. Of course the women were beautiful. He had been isolated from them so long that even a Miss Pulvermacher could be beautiful.

A white-haired male patient-pusher came along and shoved him into a dark room. He looked around nervously for the pneumo needle. Would they stab him in the dark?

He recalled his first day in the San. This room too had faces half-covered with masks, had that strange, eery light of the fluoroscope, that smell of ozone, of burnt air. He remembered his concept of seeing a light in the open skull of another man, accidentally revealed.

A voice sounded in the dark. "Well, Eric, how do you feel?"

"Oh, is that you, Dr. Abraham? I feel good."

"How's your temp been?"

"Almost normal."

Strange hands were tugging at him. They helped him sit erect. Someone, it seemed Dr. Abraham, pulled a heavy object from the ceiling and pushed it against his chest beneath his chin. Looking over it into the dark, Eric could see illuminated faces moving around in the semi-obscurity.

The faces leaned forward, peering. His eyes adjusted themselves. He recognized Dr. Abraham surrounded by nurses.

"Well, Eric, your chest looks good."

"It does?"

"Yes. Of course, there are adhesions. And they can cause a lot of trouble. A lot of trouble. Fluid. Empyema."

"That dangerous?"

"Hah. There can be very serious complications."

Eric had another thought. "Say, Doc, suppose a cavity clears up, does the sputum turn negative too?"

"No, not necessarily."

"Is yellow sputum positive?"

There was some laughter. "Are you becoming a spit specialist, Eric?"

"No." After a grudging laugh with them, he rushed on to ask, "Say, how did my X-ray turn out, Doc?"

"Good. Good."

"The cavity?"

"Well . . . there's no evidence of it anymore . . . but don't get any notions about quitting the cure."

"It's gone? Say. Holy smokes. Somebody's off the beam. There was a Dr. Deeble in and he outlined a cavity on my chest with a red-leaded pencil. See?" In the dim room he opened his pajama jacket and tried to trace it out.

Dr. Abraham and the others in the room blatted laughter. "So, Satan Deeble's been at it again, has he?"

"What? What?" Then Eric guessed. "Isn't Deeble a doc?"

"Hah. That crackpot?"

"Why that dirty son of a bitch . . . oh, I'm sorry. I didn't mean to swear before you nurses, but . . . "

The door of the fluoroscope room opened and Dr. Abraham, still laughing, began to push him out and said, "Speaking of quacks, Eric, there is a real one."

Eric blushed. Say, that reminds me. That syphilis . . . oh . . . "

"What?"

"Nothing. S'nothing."

"Hah. Did he get you on that too?"

Eric growled. "I'm going to get that guy for that."

"Now, now, Eric, Deeble meant well. He just likes to play. Don't be hard on him. He's been here for ten years. Can't seem to cure himself. And, with an active mind and a still busier imagination, he's bound to get into trouble, pull some stunts."

Eric growled some more.

"Now, Eric, it's a compliment to have him pull one on you. He usually picks on the strong." Dr. Abraham smiled. "Well, I'll see you in a few minutes in the men's pneumo room."

After all the patients, both litter and ambulant, had been fluoroscoped, Eric was rolled into a bright green room. The walls and the floor were built of lucent green tile. Three flat operating tables dominated the center of the room. Around each of them stood a series of small instruments, so shiny the nickel on them flamed. There was

109

a sharp smell of collodion and the wrenching aroma of Novak's solution. Nurses gestured fussily, ordered efficiently. It was a wonderful room for torture.

A negro patient lay on the middle table; a white man on the one to the right. They lay quietly, like dumb dogs awaiting a master's pleasure.

The third table was folded back on its end and Eric's litter was pushed in its place.

A nurse unbuttoned his shirt, rolled him over, propped two hard pillows beneath his right side, drew his arm out and over his head in an inverted V, and told him to hold that position. She dabbed his left chest with cold, pink Novak's solution.

In a moment Dr. Abraham came, grinning, his fingers as gentle as a mother's upon Eric's chest. "Novacaine today?"

The question was an old one. Each time Eric was about to get pneumo in his ward, Dr. Abraham had asked him if he were tough enough to take the blunt pneumo needle between his ribs without an anesthetic. And each time Eric had sucked in his breath, thought it over, and had taken the novacaine.

Eric said. "All right, I'll start today. Go to it. Since it's going to hurt, you might as well make it hurt big."

"Really?"

"I said it."

Eric tensed on his litter. His arm, tiring in its awkward position, began to sting. His toes curled up tensely, his fists became tight with fear. He drew in short, fluttery breaths.

Plungh, and the blunt needle was through. He winced.

"Now, was that so bad, Eric?"

"No. No, it wasn't bad at all. I like it this way. And you only get stuck once, too."

"Sure."

Eric lay dumbly.

After a few moments, Dr. Abraham said, "Guess I'll give you about 600 cc's of air today, instead of the usual 500. Start pushing the adhesions a little."

There was a sudden tightness. His short breaths became faint puffs. His chest seemed to be the size of a thimble. He coughed.

"Something?"

"I . . . pret . . . ty . . . short a . . . breath."

Dr. Abraham jerked out the needle and slapped a dab of collodion-soaked cotton on the puncture. "And that's enough for today." He turned around. "All right, next."

There was a sudden splat of movement, a rustling, a scream; a voice, a negro voice in a deadly purr, "Now don't you come behind me like that again, Mistah Doctah. I just cain't stand havin' a fella comin' behind me like that, is all."

"All right, all right."

Eric turned around to see what was up. A thin, a very emaciated negro was sitting upright on his litter, panting, a razor in his lifted fingers, his arm shaking like a black stroke of lightning. "Now, Mistah Doctah, I meahnt thet. They knifed my pappy in the back an' no sonofabatchin' doctah is goin' to knife me theh."

Eric watched the negro a moment, saw Dr. Abraham smile as if nothing had happened, heard him say, "All right, all right. I'll give it to you in front, where you can watch every move I make."

The negro subsided. But he did not close the razor. He held it grimly while Dr. Abraham injected the novacaine. The negro did not seem to notice the prick.

A nurse rolled Eric out into the dark hallway, past the women's pnuemo room, and on, until the white-haired patient-pusher came to wheel him to George and his elevator.

As Miss Pulvermacher pushed him into 176 again, he smiled diffidently at his roommates, and said, "I guess I'm a prize sucker."

Fawkes and Huck grinned. They were relieved by his attitude.

A confidential mood possessed him. "You know, boys, what really had me worried was that syphilis. I'd just met a nice girl the other day, and by golly, I thought, here, here

I've got a dose of syph and can't do anything about it."

Fawkes and Huck laughed.

Miss Pulvermacher, who had been helping him into his freshly-made bed, observed, "I didn't know there were any nice girls around here."

No one answered her.

"Really, I didn't know there were any real, high-class girls around."

Fawkes laughed. "Don't lose your corset, Tina."

She turned. "I've been here ten years, nursing. I ought to know."

"Ever see Mary Lehar?" Eric asked.

"Her? That bohunk?" She sniffed disdainfully.

Eric glared at her. "So you think you're better?"

"Of course."

"Oh, one of those" . . . Eric relished the moment . . . "so that's the reason I haven't liked you. For your information let me tell you that I'd marry a woman as black as the ace of spades, if I loved her. There are good people in all races . . . except for the intolerant biddies like you."

She shrugged angrily and left the room.

# T XI—RELAPSE

HE DIRECTION of existence veered. He had been lucky too long.

The next morning, he felt a sharp pain in the left side of his chest. He felt awkward in his bed. He felt off-center. He was either too serious or too merry.

The quiet of the Sunday morning, with its subtly pervading reverence, evident even though he could not see a city's silenced streets nor observe the leisurely air of people strolling to church, did not calm him. The gentle hymnal quality of the music in the earphones did not soothe him. The middle line of living along which he felt he should travel was too evasive to follow.

All morning long he tried to control himself, to forget his pain. He drank innumerable glasses of water to rinse away the odd taste in his mouth. He swallowed forcibly to expel the buzzing in his ears.

One moment the flame in him was so bright that he found himself cackling noisily to his roommates; the next moment so dull he found himself withdrawing to the somber quiet of his skull. Nothing was right. He shook his head.

When the fat Sunday morning paper came, he turned to it eagerly, hoping that the news it held of the world outside the San would level him into steady flight.

Momentarily it did . . . until he read the funnies. Stirred by what he thought was an olympic mirth in Li'l Abner, he roared so loudly that presently the little animal in the left side awoke and began to attack him viciously. He held himself against the little beast. He knew he should report that it had come again, but he was afraid.

He turned the page to Dagwood Bumstead. The strip pictured Dagwood driving a baseball through a neighbor lady's window, a stunt Eric had also pulled one day after he had bragged too loudly about his slugging powers. He cried and shook with helpless laughter as he watched Dagwood run before the lady's wrath. He could not control himself. He noticed his roommates looking at him wonderingly, uncomfortably.

It was Huck who first laid aside his section of the Sunday paper to say, "Hey, brother, you'd better cut out the nutzy laughing. You'll bust a lung."

Laughter left him as suddenly as it had come. To have heard the otherwise silent Huck break into speech was something of a minor shock. "Huck, I just can't seem to stop. Just screwy this morning, I guess."

Huck's pale blue eyes filled with concern. "Take it easy, boy."

"I'll try Huck. Thanks." A wave of self-pity rose in Eric. "Thanks. It's good to know I've got a friend in here."

"Well . . . that's all right." Huck's voice crispened.

"Friend or not, I'd pass that advice on to anybody."

"Anybody?"

Huck ruffled his paper irritably. "Sure, why not? I'm friendly with everybody, but make real friends with nobody."

"No? Why?"

"A guy can't afford to make friends here."

Puzzled, and holding his clawing animal close, Eric turned to Fawkes. "Do you feel that way too?"

Fawkes looked from Huck to Eric. "He probably means that San friends have a way of dying a little sooner than others."

Huck nodded.

Eric settled into his pillows. Perhaps the man was right. The way the animal was digging into his side, he might be next on the Whipper's list.

He felt feverish, hot. His toothroots began to ache. A few minutes later he felt cold. He drew up his sheets and, though it was summer, thought about covering himself with a gray blanket.

He felt his pulse. It was fast, and irregular.

Quickly, though he hid it from his roommates, he took his temperature. Up two full degrees.

A half hour later, sweating, his ears buzzing, he took his temperature again. Up three full degrees.

"Fawkes."

"Yes."

"Something's wrong."

Both Fawkes and Huck sat up. "Yes?"

"In the last hour, my temp . . . it's jumped three degrees."

Fawkes blinked.

Huck's face became angelic with concern.

Again Eric began to swell with self-pity.

Fawkes said, "I'll ring the nurse for you."

By the time Miss Berg answered the bell, Eric's ravenous animal had worked its way into his brain. He groaned unknowingly.

The flame in his skull flickered, became dully orange.

Dr. Abraham came in. He listened to a recital of symptoms, nodded. "Fluid," he said crisply. "That complicates his pneumothorax."

Eric put up a hand. "You'll stay by me?"

"Of course."

Eric relaxed.

# W XII—THE FLAME CLEARS

HEN HE awoke, a tall orderly with concerned brown eyes stood by his bed, balancing a fat roll of gum on his thick lower lip. He held a tray in his hands.

Eric moved a little.

"Breakfasst?" The man's fat lips blurred his speech. "Breakfasst?"

Eric blinked. Gradually pulling himself up on his pillows, and staring bewildered at his roommates, he asked, "Breakfast? Already?"

Fawkes smiled at him encouragingly. "Sure. Time to get up. We've been wondering when you'd come to."

Eric rubbed his eyes. Something was amiss. Though his senses seemed to have their normal appetites, he felt out of step with time.

"Breakfasst?"

Eric glanced up at the orderly again. The man was as awkward as a grasshopper. He slouched a little. His clothes were spotted and torn, his fingernails ringed with dirt; his teeth yellow from lack of brushing. His whiskers, even after a fresh shave, formed a black muffler around his face. A high brow rose cleanly through sparse hair.

"Breakfasst?"

"Yes. Set it down." Eric was pleased to notice he felt hungry.

The orderly looked at him briefly, glanced at the row of books on Eric's window-ledge, and then went out.

Eric sighed. Weak, he fumbled with his bedtable and lifted the food-tray on it. The effort was almost too much for him.

He glanced out of the window. The last time he had seen the mall, the grass had been lightly singed. But now July's sun had burned it severely. For a little time he watched the sprinklers waving lazy arms of water over the greens. He exclaimed, "Say, where the hell have I been? It seems weeks since I last was here."

Huck said, "You was nutzy, my boy."

"Oh." Eric remembered. "I got sick, didn't I? You know, I do feel kind of white around the eyes. What happened?"

Fawkes said kindly, "Nothing serious, I guess. You had a fever for a couple of days. And you were unconscious."

Huck chuckled, and, tracing an imaginary spiral with a finger, said, "Brother, you was as cuckoo as a nest of squirrels in heat."

"But what happened? What really happened?"

Fawkes said, "Well, I don't know for sure. But your laughing jag the other day broke an adhesion in your chest and you developed fluid. Dr. Abraham's been aspirating, that is, draining your chest, about a thousand cc's every other day."

"Holy Moses, that's more than a quart."

"Yes."

Eric fumbled with his pajama top, lifting it. He spotted a series of raw, still-red needle-pricks on the skin of his left chest. Rubbing his ribs near the pricks, he felt small areas of soreness. "Is he still aspirating me?"

"No. I heard him tell Miss Mitchell they're going to let you fill up."

Huck added, "Until you choke."

A spurt, a thought came. "Thunder, I've lost my pneumo then, haven't I?"

Fawkes' eyes became kind. "Well, they really won't know until your fluid dries up."

"Huh. So, instead of two years of bed-rest, I've got four

or five coming. And then a rib-cutting."

"Now, take it easy."

"Five years of bed-rest. Of rotting. Holy Moses."

"Don't get excited. Some fluids dry up quickly. And when they do, the doctors resume the pneumothorax treatments."

"Sure?"

"Yes."

"Say, I wonder what my temp is?"

A few minutes later he drew the thermometer slowly from his mouth.

"How much?" asked Fawkes.

"99.6."

"Hmm. Good! You were up pretty high, you know."

"Think he'll live?" asked Huck, his eyes merry.

Fawkes grunted. "If he sticks to the rules."

## A XIII—THE FLAME QUICKENS

FTER breakfast, Eric asked, "Say, who was that new orderly that came in here this morning?"

Huck looked up from a magazine. "Calisto Sly. A dirty old Jew that nobody likes. He . . ."

Fawkes interrupted. "Now, now. No race prejudice here. Let Eric find out for himself, Huck."

"Okay."

Later, Calisto came in to sweep the room. And again, first off, he glanced at the books on the window-ledge. As he absent-mindedly dusted the chairs and sills, he cast quick, appraising glances at Eric. He coughed and chewed rapidly on his fat gum.

He came to the books. He brushed each volume meticulously, lovingly. He picked up the last book in the row, Darwin's *Origin of Species*. He paged through it a way, asked, his thick lips curiously mangling the words, "You like thiss."

"Yes."

Setting aside the broom which he had been dragging after him, Calisto looked with narrowed and reflective eyes through the window. "Yess, it's pretty good at that. Good. Life iss like what he says it iss. Yess." Fixing his eyes intently upon Eric, he asked, "Ever read Veblen? No? Great. Great. He was a great man. Hit the nail right on the head."

Eric caught his roommates exchanging glances. So. This was what they meant. This rare creature. A janitor who read Veblen. Eric narrowed his eyes, reflecting. He remembered that Einstein had worked out his leaping theory of relativity while earning his living as a humble little hireling in Switzerland. No one had suspected greatness in that creature with his unpressed pants, his naive manners, his self-effacement. Eric's flame brightened to white heat. Was this another unheralded genius? "How do you mean, hit it right on the head?"

Calisto gestured at the windowsill a few times as if he were dusting it. "Well, you know" . . . and he bent his eyes sharply upon Eric again . . . "Veblen claims men are bloodthirsty egotists, that they have very little time for brotherly love, that they will never get together and live happy."

Eric drew his sheet up close to his chin to protect himself from the sprinkles of spittle that Calisto spewed in all directions as he talked. "Yes, I know, Calisto. But there's where I think I disagree with him. I think we can get together, by teaching man to live like a brother with his brother."

Calisto's eyes became as large as white-petalled daisies. His mouth fell open so far he resembled an idiot. "No, no," he began vehemently, still dusting the same spot on the window sill, "no, no, that's . . ."

"But really, Calisto, man can. Look. Suppose you and I, and Fawkes here, and Huck, suppose we're living in the same valley. Suppose I get an idea about . . . oh, say, imitation rubber breasts for flat-chested women. Suppose instead of me trying to get you three to help me in the name

118

of democracy while actually owning the works myself, suppose we build this together, own it together, make ironclad rules that to eat you must work, and, if we get an oversupply of riches, save'em to back another idea that Fawkes or Huck might get, don't you think we'd all feel we belonged together and were brothers?"

Calisto's eyes opened even wider on this notion. His thick mouth trembled. Eric spun on, "You know, really, I think that if we could teach mankind that it was criminal to collect money and wealth for one's self, we could get them to live like brothers. Education is awfully powerful."

Calisto broke through, words emerging muddily from his heavy lips, "No, no. You're all wrong. Yess, education, yess it iss powerful. But not that much. It's really only just a whitewash. Just a little covering." He gestured violently, tearing at his own shirt, unbuttoning it. "Man, we, me, we're animals. We're blood and bone and shweat and testicalls. We breed, eat, shleep, and try to beat the other guy out of a fair living. The earth? It iss covered by wrigglink, strugglink appetites."

Eric, tiring, and trying to conserve his energy, protested quietly. "But Calisto, look. If . . ."

"No no. The only way socialissma works, iss thiss way. We must show each man how he can get more out of it than out of capitalissma. We must appeal to his selfissh ego. See. Look. Me and you, we argue, huh? Right here. Are we hunting the truth? Or, trying to win a fight? Uk. It iss the last. A course. Look, as long as each man thinks he iss better than the next man . . . like, you think Fawkes iss all right, but deep down, you think you are the better dreamer. And Fawkes, he sits sure and proud behind his eyes and he tells himself he iss better than you are in one thing. He thinks he iss a better scientist. Even a shanitor, me, thinks there's always somebody worse off than me. Maybe it iss a garbage collector, or something, a sewer cleaner, anybody."

Huck and Fawkes were listening intently too. Huck had sat up in his bed, and began to cough a little.

"But Calisto," continued Eric, "don't you believe in the dream that someday we'll have a brotherhood, a Christian heaven here on earth, socialism?"

"Yes. Yes. Someday. Perhaps. But not by thiss crazy brotherhood education alone. We must be realisstic. We must be realisstic. We must see man as he iss, an animal, with good instincts." Eric had to strain his ears to catch all of the syllables. "When you go to plant a crop in a field of stones, you don't get a crop unless your plan includes the stones. Won't do no good to throw the stones over in the neighbor's field either. He iss trying to do the same thing you are. No, you gotta go underneat' the stones, dig up a little earth, a little earthy instincts, and out of that . . . see?"

Eric lay back in his pillows. Maybe this man was right. Eric had accused his old boss of being heartless; and Martha and Russell too. Perhaps they had just been realistic —real animals from which he could expect no kindness.

Calisto watched him, smiling. His eyes were gentle. "Do not understand me wrong. I do not mean to hurt you feelings. I . . . I can see that you are a good man. Me and you, maybe, with a little realistic education, maybe we could get along all right. Maybe."

"Calisto, did you ever go to school?"

"School? Uk, that don't mean much."

"Did you?"

"I went to a rabbi school once. But I got so many questions in my head, I qvit."

"Married?"

Calisto laughed, spraying over Eric's sheet. "No woman wanted me."

"What do you do for excitement?"

"You mean, shex?"

"Well, yeh."

Calisto grinned at him. "That's none of you businiss."

"Calisto, how come you're a janitor? Why don't you get a job that fits your brains?"

Calisto, still polishing the windowsill, shot out a flame, asking, "What job did you have before you came here?"

Eric blinked.

Calisto instantly became gentle again, and said, "Maybe . . . maybe I'm just a misfit. Maybe I belong with the common animals. I just don't know any better. I am just like them."

Fawkes asked, "Calisto, what would you really like to do in life before you die?"

Calisto smiled, and rubbed the sill, and dreamed, and said, "I would . . . but oh, it iss foolissh."

Huck leaned forward and coughed. He lifted a thin white finger. "Calisto, really tell us. What would you like to do?"

"I'd like to write a book. Be a book writer."

Fawkes pursued. "But why? What for?"

The door opened. Miss Mitchell, obviously angry, asked sharply, "How many rooms have you cleaned already, Calisto?"

Calisto jumped guiltily through the door after her.

Then, before the roommates could look at each other to exchange comments about the man, Calisto popped his head into the room again and said excitedly, "For what? I'd write the book to help start the brotherhood of man so that we could liquidate this charch nurse here." He looked down at his feet. Quickly, almost magically, his momentarily merry face became deeply earnest. "Yes, I would write a testament to tell the truth I found in my life, so that, maybe, I could help my fellow animal a little. Only, I will never write it. You see, I am a coward and I lack the brains. For to write the truth, a man must have a brave brain. A man must be strong to write about himself honestly. It takes great bravery to write about the things people respect. A writer must be able to ask, did a spiritual spermatazoa quicken Mother Mary?" He paused. "You see, all three of you guys shumped when I said that. And why? Because I touched you on your taboos."

# XIV—THE WHIPPER: ANOTHER VIEW

THE DOOR opened and Deeble stepped in.

"You!" exclaimed Eric.

Deeble laughed. "So you caught on?"

"Skunk."

"Satan is the name, sir. Satan Deeble." Satan grinned and asked, his brown eyes now warm with interest, "You're not sore?"

"No. Except that . . . "

"I didn't think you'd be. Had you figured for the kind of fellow that didn't get his water hot. Who could take a little kidding about short-arm inspection."

Eric rubbed his nose and grumbled.

Satan went on. "Get's kind of dead around here. Nothing to do. Got to have some fun. All the old patients know the tricks. So . . . that leaves the new birds."

"Oh skip it," Eric said. Just as before, Satan's extreme pallor caught his eye; a faint blue fire seemed to be burning beneath his white skin.

"Well, you can't blame me. Ten years is a long time to stay in here, waiting for The Brain to finish me off."

"You never get away?"

"Balls of fire, no. I'm one of these cases where a man heals well enough to stay alive, but not enough to turn negative. So, I can't get my leaves." Satan shrugged; then found a handy smile. "Yep. This is my home, my native jug."

"Ten years."

"Yep."

"Holy Moses, how can you stand it?"

Satan grinned. "Oh, you know the old saw: I cussed when I lost my shoes . . . until I saw a man who'd lost his feet. Still, it does get tiresome and so I work a little. A couple of hours down in the morgue each morning."

"Morgue?"

"Yeh. That's where the lungs of the dead and gone are kept on ice. It's down in the ground, three floors down. Get there by a tunnel."

"You work with dead people's lungs?"

"Sure. You get used to it."

"Huh. Not me."

"Sure you do. Someday I'll take you down there, if you want to see it."

"Thanks."

Satan shrugged. "It's nothing."

"Lot of lungs down there belong to guys you once knew?"

"Sure."

"That ghoul's work appeal to you?"

"Well, there's other things I do. I edit the San mag. And then too, I dilly around with psychology. And astronomy." Satan's eyes lighted. "You know, it's fun telescoping the vaulted heavens."

Eric smiled at Satan's flying phrases. "And what does the telescope tell you?"

Satan's face became very serious, almost fanatic. "That religious concepts of the universe are utterly ridiculous."

"How so?"

"To think that man, miserable bag of germs that he is, a collection of glands on crutches, has the guts to say that he knows The Brain that runs this show as well as the other galaxies in the vast beyond" . . . and Satan stretched his arms so wide Eric thought for a short moment the man's fingertips would reach infinity itself . . . "that, sir, is the most colossal conceit of all!"

Huck said, growling, "Satan, you must be nuts to wanna monkey around with the stars. Hell, man, I'd think you'd feel small enough battlin' TB, without tryin' to look at the stars to see how small a speck you are."

Satan's eyes, cleared of mission work, became considerate again. "I like it, that's all."

Eric asked, "Tell me, is that what keeps you going?"

"No. Music does that."

Eric leaned forward. An idea spat a flame inside his skull and burned sharply on an emotional oil that had been repressed for days in the subterranean folds of himself. "What kind of music? Puke-box jazz?"

"Oh no."

"By God, I sure wish I could listen to the opera on Saturday afternoon. And to the symphony on Sunday. But the bastards turn off the radio during rest hour."

Satan's eyes glinted with mischief. "You fellas haven't a radio, a small radio hid in your bedstands?"

"No. You?"

"Sure. Listen any time I want to."

"What if you get caught?"

"Buy a new one. Shucks, what's ten bucks in my life? I can't get music after I'm dead." Satan became reflective. "Say, I got an electric phonograph they let me play. Play anything I want. Tschaikovsky, Dvorak, Beethoven, Cesar Franck. You know, the whole works. They don't care."

Though his chest pained him and his back hurt, Eric leaned forward in his bed. This was music. Music. "Fawkes, Huck, you guys like music?"

"Sure."

"Damn right."

"Then why the blazes don't we . . . "

Satan looked from one to the other, asked, "Say, would you like to borrow mine? I'll bring it up if you guys can get permission to use it on this floor. Okay?"

"Mister, go down and get it. I'm ringing Miss Mitchell now."

But Miss Mitchell, the charge nurse, wasn't so easily persuaded.

"But why not?"

"Well, I'll have to bring a report of your request to Miss Globe, the head of the nursing staff. And then, she'll have to take it up with Miss Valery, director of Patients' Aid. And then, if they think the request reasonable, they'll bring it up to your doctor. And then, he takes it up with the general staff at staff-meeting next Monday. Oh no, I don't think you'll be able to have a phonograph in here. At least not today."

Eric could feel a fever mounting in his veins. A fire

burned in his cheeks. He roared, "Miss Mitchell, we're having music in this room today!" As he faced her, he could also see, off to one side, Fawkes and Huck turning their glances downward, as if they were ashamed of him. Satan, however, was grinning.

"No, I'm afraid you can't," she said, shaking her red hair.

"Satan, get your music."

"No." She crossed her arms.

"Then I'll get it."

She laughed at him. "You couldn't walk five steps."

"Not?" Eric glared at her; then, tossing aside his sheets, swung his legs over the edge of the bed and started toward her.

"Don't, don't," she fluttered. "Don't. I'll take it up with the authorities right now."

Eric lifted a gaunt arm. "Get. And no beating around the mulberry bush." He glanced at his wrist watch. "In just five minutes sharp, at nine, I'll expect you back with an answer."

"But that's ridiculous. There's other patients to be considered." She stepped into the doorway. "I'll think about it when I've finished with them."

"Nurse, call Dr. Abraham."

"No."

"Why not?"

"Because . . . because" . . . she coughed apologetically . . . "well, you see, we nurses're supposed to keep all trivial matters from getting to the doctors."

"But this is serious."

She stared at him, her eyes slowly narrowing, and slowly firing again. She turned and walked out of the room.

Eric leaped after her and stumbled on buckling legs into the hallway. He fell.

She heard him crash; and turning quickly, gulked a little cry.

And, just as once before, struggling nurses dragged him back to bed.

125

Miss Mitchell brommed at him. "You foolish man. You might've broken another adhesion."

"Can Satan bring his music here?"

"Yes yes."

And so the boys had music. They put aside their books and lay dreaming upon their pillows.

First there was Beethoven's *Emperor Concerto*. The deep notes trembled like great whales in a blue ocean. The golden flame in Eric lifted its white plumes and spread them widely. He looked through the window, listening, dreaming. Old Lady Poplar curtsied. The many blue-shadowed spruce and pine upon the mall quivered in the hot sun. A sparrow plummeted down, down, till earth came up to meet its breast; and then the sparrow lifted, and turned sharply upon a flock of breathren who had congregated to feast upon some bread crumbs. Trains rumbled upon the hollow belly of the earth.

There was Franck's *Symphonic Variations for Piano and Orchestra*. Eric was beside a river. Down it came memories, floating islands, once a part of his life-land. There was the Bible—

*Ho, every one that thirsteth,*
*come ye to the waters;*
*and he that hath no money:*
*come ye, buy, and eat:*
*yea, come, buy wine and milk without money, without price.*
*Wherefore do ye spend money for that which is not bread?*
*and your labor for that which satisfieth not? . . .*
*Hearken diligently . . .*
*Let your soul delight itself in fatness.*
*Incline your ear . . .*
*Hear and your soul shall live . . .*

And there was Whitman too—

*Come lovely and soothing death,*
*Undulate round the world, serenely arriving, arriving,*
*In the day, in the night, to all, to each,*
*Sooner or later delicate death.*

*Praised be the fathomless universe,*

126

*For life and joy, and for objects and knowledge curious,*
*And for love, sweet love—but praise! praise! praise!*
*For the sure enwinding arms of cool-enfolding death.*

*Dark mother always near with soft feet,*
*Have none chanted for thee a chant of fullest welcome?*
*Then I chant it for thee, I glorify thee above all,*
*I bring thee a song that when thou must indeed come,*
*come unfalteringly.*

And Housman—

*From far, from eve and morning*
*And yon twelve-winded sky,*
*The stuff of life to knit me*
*Blew hither: here am I.*

*Now—for a breath I tarry*
*Nor yet disperse apart—*
*Take my hand quick and tell me,*
*What have you in your heart.*

*Speak now, and I will answer;*
*How shall I help you, say;*
*Ere to the wind's twelve quarters*
*I take my endless way.*

The river scene faded.

His strong flame leaped higher, feeding greedily on the fats of his hates and his hungers as they melted in the warmth of the music.

He ached that his prose-poem had not yet been published. He ached that he had not yet proven himself to Martha, even by her values. He sorrowed that Ma Memme was not here to glow at the song of his creation. He thought of grave-eyed Mary Lehar and her friendly hand.

There was a man singing then. Robeson. A negro, with the width of sadness, with the sweet-sweet ache of a little freedom greatly struggled for, with sorrowful humility.

He thought about the poor in the dust-brown valleys of America. They were like him. In pity for them, he cried. In pity for himself, he cried.

Hesitantly a new flame fluttered in him, at the foot of the great white pillar of flames, within his arched and lofted skull; hesitantly, for the words in his mind regarded each other with suspicion. Hesitantly, a little, he caught a few of them with the fingers of his mind, and stroked them into friendly moods, and braided them together to fashion little strands, verse, songs of his own—

> Have you not heard in some idle moment,
>     or pause between some immediate talk,
>     old voices awakening within you?

The new flame, cello-rich, purple-tipped, rose—

> What will you do
> with this gift of life?
> This Kingdom stolen
> from water and sunlight
> and favorable metabolism?
> This empire, which,
> skull-bound,
> spreads beyond
> the borders reported
> by patrolling senses?

And then the flame filled out a little, darkening—

> My day is filled with a terrible aching.
> I try to write a poem, this poem, a lament . . .
> But each word must fight its way to utterance
> Through rolling floods of virus.

Too—

> Sometimes I am impelled by I know not what urge
> Or mighty power using me as its voice
> To tell you all the wonderful things I've seen.

Abruptly he remembered. He had once dreamed of becoming a writer. But he had been broken.

. . . For a month after he had stumbled upon Martha's love-nesting, a darkling wind blew fiercely upon his flame. He cared for nothing. Women, friends, jobs, children, sunlight, all of them, were as nothing to him. His skull was filled with wisps of smoke, cinders, blackness.

The finance company took his car away. He hardly noticed it. He was too far gone to be ashamed of poverty.

Yet, miraculously, after a time, there was a stirring in his mind, a vague impulse. Despite the hunger of his belly and the vast vista of ashes in the world around, a little plant of hope thrust its slender curving stem up towards the sun. There was an impulse to write.

An unfinished manuscript lay in a suitcase under the bed. He took it out. He read it. Sometimes he caught a good phrase, a good echo of song. He puffed slowly on his yellow-stemmed pipe. Soon he began to nod. Yes yes. It was good enough to publish. He made up his mind. He added a few pages and called the whole a novel. Excited, his hair wild, he sent it East to a publisher.

In three weeks it came back with a letter:

Dear Mr. Frey:
   I regret to say that the final decision went against your *Roots in the Soil.* I do hope this does not discourage you from writing another book. You can write. Someday you may even write a great moving novel. You have an eye for realistic detail. Your work has an honest ring. But over-all, it does not quite make it. When you finish your next book, be sure to send it to us if you are free to do so.
                                        Sincerely,
                                        R. H. McMurray

"Does not quite make it." Huh. Why, there were no more vital fibers in him. He knew he had reached his limit. If what he had written about the farmer with gummy black dirt on his hands, with yellow-brown manure on his pants-cuffs, with fist-hard lust in his thighs for his wife, wasn't good enough, then nothing he would ever do would be.

He muttered to himself as he sat in his rocker, smoking his yellow-stemmed pipe. Those bastards in New York were queers anyway. New York was an alien country. It was provincial. It did not reflect the America west of the Hudson River. People living west of the Hudson knew both their own province and, through the radio and the press, the ideas current in New York. But the New Yorker knew only his little province.

129

Eric nodded. Sure. He had once been there on a hiking tour. It had struck him then that many of the artists he had seen had had a curious resemblance to those hens Pa had always wanted to kill, those eggless hens that sat in the dust ruffling their feathers magisterially and blinking their eyes and eating food thrown to them because working hens beside them had to be fed. In Greenwich Village he had almost vomited. The dives were crowded with parrots. Broken wings, split throats, faded feathers, gray dung, lay everywhere. Birds of paradise fornicated under each other's wings. Sour belches exploded in his face. And at Columbia University, professors and bugs wore saucer-large spectacles. Students wore scaffolds on their shoulders to support the rising structures of their brains. Cerebrums and cerebellums buzzed everywhere. Even the lovers sitting in the chapel-quiet, trellis-darkened love-nooks had humming brains. No, New York was a hell of a town.

Eric nodded again and got up and put on a top-coat. He went outdoors. It was the first week in November and he was surprised to find that the air was still warm and that the trees were still heavily clothed with orange and yellow and red-brown leaves. He walked slowly down the Mississippi towards Fort Snelling. It was almost dark when he had left the house and, by the time he had walked a mile, night had come on. He watched the wrinkles on the river's waves; observed that the reflections of the willow leaves lay like splashes of black ink on the pale gray waters.

He came home. Picking up a hundred pages of the manuscript at a time, he tore them to shreds. Then he went to bed.

But the next morning he was surprised to find that his ideas about New Yorkers had changed. Maybe they were right. After all, he had rushed through the book, hadn't bothered to edit the clumsy phrasings, nor to cut away the scaffolding that a writer uses to construct an edifice. And those two remarks of the editor "You have an eye for realistic detail. Your work has an honest ring." were excellent compliments. Yes, those New York editors should know writing when they saw it. They sold books. They made money or went broke depending on how well they knew their stuff. Besides, if a piece of writing did not stir someone, then something was lacking, no matter how many theories or quirks he may have rammed into its making. He stoked his pipe and nodded. Yes. He jerked open the old portable typewriter and started a new draft. "By God," he growled as his fingers jigged on the keys, "by God, if they want realism and honesty, I'll really spill my guts. I'll give'em the very blood from my bones."

In three weeks he turned out three hundred pages, half of the new draft. He sent the half to R. H. McMurray the editor.

In a week he received a note. "Please send me the rest of the new draft."

Eric shouted. He sang with the spheres in the firmament. He knew he would survive. Let the cruel world send its frosts deep into him. Let the frosts try to pinch the toe-roots of his life. Let them. He would not care. His soul, like Pa's glorious and perennial alfalfa, would only deepen its root and outreach the frosts each winter; and in the spring, send up a new shoot. O soul. O life-force. O sun. He would yet triumph. He would yet write the song of the midwest prairies. He would yet write the one poem of the blue-joint grasses rolling and twisting west of Bonnie Doon.

The book would become a key. It would find him work. For no boss, no matter how prejudiced he might feel about the phrase "Frey's a trouble-making union man," could help but be impressed by an author. The book would place him on a level with employed friends. It would give Pa, who had never had a chance at education, and who could not read nor write, a chance to be proud. Pa had always hated educated gents. But a book? And by his son? Ah, a book would become Pa's temple. Pa would worship the book; and his son.

Yes, the book would open many doors. It would give him food. It would give him a chance to gloat over Martha.

It would tell her that she had made a mistake when she had taken that rich bastard's son.

Yes, if this editor, McMurray, who sounded like the good uncle he had been looking for ever since Pa had whipped him, would take the book, then, then all the eye-darkening hurts would fade to memories; memories that he could chuckle at when he should have aged into a gray old American Shaw. Yes.

In two weeks Eric finished the second half of the book, sent it off. He waited. He puffed on his pipe. He strode beneath the Mississippi cliffs. He waited. This time for sure. Yes sir.

He waited a whole month and a half. And then his hope began slowly to shrivel. And his body to thin.

It was a January morning. He sat in his armchair by the window, holding a fading hope close to his heart, the hope that somehow, despite the evil forces that beset him, he might succeed as a writer. He noticed idly that the neighbor's hearty child had come out of the house to play in the sun on the snow. It was dressed in a blue snowsuit.

He moved his chair a trifle and the shadow of his wide shoulder obscured his heavy, long hand. Outside, the bright sunlight burned on the new morning snow like a white sweeping flame. He remembered the olden days, long before he had met Martha, when sunlight had made him happy, enthusiastic. No matter how morosely he might have felt about his drab dull job or his lonesomeness at night, in those days sunlight had always lifted him. He was a son of sunlight. He felt, sometimes, that he understood completely why the Egyptians, and all the pagan peoples, had worshipped the sun. Of course, there were days when he enjoyed the sad heavens too; the heavy clouds, the lineless skies, the dripping rain, the swirling snowstorms; because when he was low in spirits he enjoyed the lowering spirit of the earth, enjoyed melancholy music. Even self-castigation could be pleasant if there was the prospect of sunlight ahead.

He heard the child playing with the dog outside the

132

window. The child shouted. The dog barked. He thought about the contrast between the child and himself. The little boy (or was it a girl?), playing on the snow in the biting cold, had red cheeks and was full of life. It romped. But in the room here, there was a bitterness, a soured life with a few books bought, a few pictures hung, and second sheets of the uncertain manuscript, *Roots In The Soil*. Who ever heard of soured wine being useful to anyone?

He looked up and noticed that the mailman was coming down the street. He was surprised at the question that flashed through his mind. Was this the day he would hear about his manuscript?

He was sure of it. He jumped up and went downstairs. He stopped at the front door. Anxiously he watched the mailman go up the neighbor's steps, drop something in the slot, turn, and come down again. Eric shifted his feet. A fever heated his face and he wiped sweat from his brow.

The mailman was coming up the steps of his boarding house, nearing the mailbox hanging on the doorpost.

Eric's mind boiled. Should he meet the man? Or should he be nonchalant and wait until he had gone? Yet, be nonchalant for whom? Wait for whom? Ridiculous. Go now. Get it. Take the mail from the mailman's hand.

Eric opened the door. "Here. I'll take it."

The impersonal face of the mailman creased with a smile. "Okay. Nice mornin', ain't it?"

"Yes, isn't it." Eric felt he could afford to be neighborly now. His right hand was filled with mail.

Dropping all but four letters on the hall table, he climbed the stairs to his coffin. He settled into his rocker. He turned it so that the light from the outdoors would fall over the letters in his hands. The great sun. Sunlight now. The world was full of sunlight.

This . . . this was a card from a mail order house. This . . . this was a letter from a John of college days. This . . . this was a letter from a publishing house, asking: would he be interested in the world's greatest classics at just 59c a volume? And this . . . why this was it.

He opened it. Read. Crumpled it.

He looked out of the window. He could feel his face turn gray.

Yes. Sunlight.

Holy Moses, how he hated life. Life, she is a bitch . . .

The music had stopped. The trees stilled.

The room became raucous with talk. "Hey you. Eric! Didn't you listen?" Satan Deeble was pulling at him. "Hey you. Didn't you like the music?"

"I . . . I liked it. Yes. I liked it very much."

To himself, he thought: the Whipper sure poleaxed me that time, that barren day in January.

## XV—HUNGER FOR THE RED BONE

EVERY MORNING fat but quick Benny, a fox squirrel, came scrambling to the end of a bow-like limb on the poplar, hopped onto a window-ledge running the length of the East Wing, lifted the unhooked screens with his powerful forepaws, and began his panhandling.

Benny had many friends. Every morning he scurried along his route like a mad mailman late, hurriedly slipping into rooms and gobbling crumbs that patients offered him and swiftly going on to the next, until he came to 176, the last stop on his route.

Each time Benny finished his meal and left Eric and his roommates at bedpan hour, an hour obviously disgusting him and making him contemptuous of human civilization, Eric watched him go with nostalgia. How wonderful to hop from limb down to limb, escape to the earth, and be free to scatter nuts and breadcrusts and confusion over the mall.

Benny sat on Eric's bed, his gold-bronze tail plumed up

134

behind him, his gray belly bulging, his head bobbing above a crust of bread, his needle teeth crunching and cracking noisily.

Benny cocked his head sideways. He considered Eric. He cocked his head back, and considered him; cocked it forward, and considered him. Even when Benny reached for another bite, his eyes never left off considering Eric.

And Eric, in turn, considered Benny. Fat rascal. Daring. His gray-furred belly, his gray-brown hair, his varnished brown eyes, his gold-bronze undertail, underbelly, underneck so temptingly near for a fondler's hand. For an animal Benny's skull flame was quick. And high. Could he have been literate, what a tale he could have told of his dim past emerging from the sloughs of the Cenozoic Age.

Benny finished his breakfast at Eric's board. He hopped over the bed ends into the sheets beside Huck to sit down to a piece of doughnut.

Through again, he leaped across to Fawkes' bed, to finish off, chucklingly, four whole peanuts.

Then, preening himself, he investigated the air with a subtle black nose. Sure he had exhausted the alms-givers of their crumbs, he hopped back to Huck's bed, then to the window ledge, then to Eric's window.

At that moment, an ignoble impulse seized Eric: imprison the squirrel! Was Benny more deserving of freedom than himself? Had an animal more right to frolic in the August sunlight than he? The sun was his friend. His own very personal friend. Yes. Eric held the screen shut.

Benny became frightened. He whacked his tail on the ledge. He whacked it at the books, tumbling them to the floor. He squealed a little, whiningly. He nosed the closed screen. He pushed it. He could not understand. He hurled himself against the screen, his vigorous body swirling frenziedly. He twisted and turned and finally, desperately, jumped for the hand that held the screen. Eric sucked a breath of fear, jerked his hand away. And in a whirl of brown and gold and gray, the fox squirrel vanished.

Eric sighed; then closed the screen against the flies and

mosquitoes of August. He leaned on his elbow to watch the descending fox squirrel.

How happy it was now, frolicing in the hot grass of August, cooling itself in the swift breasting winds of summer.

How happy he would be someday when he could be free again, free and out among the hot warm breezes of late summer, upon the brittle grass, beneath the hard-leaved trees, amongst the rich, smelly, red-berried bushes, the lushly weeded roadsides, the full and hanging apple-trees.

The whole animate world waited for this time of the year: harvest-time. Impelled by eternal urges, butterflies as thick as wishes fluttered on flowering swamps. Cows as fat as squirrels fed on seeding blue-grass. Horses cropped the tops of oatsheaves. Farmers ate from tables garden-laden. Children gobbled enormous strings of apples. Rich, rotting plums lay purply red and ripe in the wind-combed grass. Ah, yes, this was the time for a man to live.

And yet, here he lay now in his bed, wan, thin, restless, neither dying nor living, a vague collection of cells, drifting nowhere, unorganized, sometimes choking bacilli, sometimes being choked by them.

And the sun. The great sun. These were the sun-days when a man's face tanned a godly golden-red, a lion's pelt, the ripened slough-grass hue of reddened gold.

Yes, now, this moment, he should free himself. He would demand that a nurse fetch the suit of clothes that Ronald had brought a couple of months ago. Eric would demand his clothes and go. And go.

On whose legs? Yes, the legs. A man needed legs to go. Twice he had essayed to walk on his own; twice had crumpled to the floor. He made up his mind to strengthen them. He would walk around the bed every night, one minute tonight, two tomorrow, three the next, and so on, until he could walk ten minutes, long enough to stagger outdoors where he could fall upon the grass, and lie beneath the sun, and feel once more the nervous walk of ants pulsing on his arms and legs, and have the pleasure of cursing them.

Oh for the pleasure of sitting in the grainfields again, in the shade of a golden shock of grain, or binder, or some forlorn single tree; to talk with sweating men, wet to their suspenders, to commingle his thoughts with theirs, to roll cigarettes with them. Just once to smoke a pipe with the good men of the soil beneath the sun. Once more to reach the grassed world and lie upon the belly and drink from a water stream and eat the grass upon the curving bank. And watch the water-lives, the fish and frogs and waterbugs, and drink with them, and live with them, and ponder on their worlds. And eat the grass upon the banks.

Benny. Benny. Your freedom. Blessed freedom to fight and to live and to quarrel, to tire and to grouch, to hate, to laze. Benny the freedom man. Eric slave of sheets. Eric, a living tank, wherein good and evil battled.

The flame in his skull leaped, became a violent red burst, an angry loud flame, searing his nerves down to his toes, until he lay trembling, until he thought he would roar out of the room like a rocket zooming to the sun.

He made a move in his bed. He pushed aside his books. He reached forward to the window and raised it. He unhooked the screen, calculating the distance to the tree. In his mind, he weighed himself upon each succeeding branch. He judged them strong enough to carry him safely to the sun-loved earth.

The door opened behind him. Caught, startled, his heart swelling and thumping once, soundly, loudly in his chest, he turned. It was Miss Mitchell. Red-haired Miss Mitchell.

"Mr. Frey, what are you doing? What are you doing?"

He did not know what to say. He was surprised to see himself perched ludicrously on the window-ledge, poised for flight like a wing-short ostrich. He murmured, "Oh, I dunno. I . . ."

"Get down. Get down. This instant." She was upon

him. Her clawing hands dragged at his arm.

He did not resist her. He fell back into bed.

"Now you lie right here. No monkeyshines no more." Catching her breath, she added, "No monkeyshines no more, you hear? Goodness. You had me scared half to death, sitting up there like that. As if you were going . . . what's wrong?"

"Nothing."

"Oh come now."

"All right. There is. But I'm not telling you. This is something for the doctor's ears alone."

"But . . ."

"Can I see him?"

"Right now?"

"Yes. Right now."

"But . . ."

He sat up again. "Do I get to see him?"

"Oh yes, Mr. Frey. Yes. I'll get a nurse to bring you there right away. Yes."

In the doctor's office, Dr. Abraham sat back in his chair smoking a cigar. Eric lay leaning over the edge of his litter.

"What's wrong, Eric?"

"Oh I dunno, Doc. I dunno. I feel like tangled yarn." Should he tell the doctor about the Whipper? He was afraid the doctor would not understand.

"Eric."

"Yes."

"Tell me."

"I . . . like I said, I'm all tangled yarn. The big cat of the universe has snarled me up."

"Eric, take your time. Relax, my boy."

"Doc, can I start writing again?"

"No. That's something you can't do yet."

"Why not?"

"Because writing will stir you up too much. It's hard work, probably the hardest work there is. And you're stirred up too much already. No, what you really need is quiet. Look at yourself there, trembling like a harpstring, seething like a brewing chemical. Look at yourself."

"What must I do?"

"Try to be quiet. Keep your hopes close to your belly. Fix on a point close by. Then, live only to get to it. First things first."

Always these platitudes, Eric thought, always. No, the doctor would never understand about the Whipper. "Doc, can I smoke?"

"I should say not! I've been glad you quit when you did."

"I didn't quit. I was just too sick to keep it up. Then I can't start again?"

"No."

"Why not?"

"It'll irritate your lungs."

"Doctor, just what is my condition now?"

Dr. Abraham studied him solemnly over his cigar, took off his spectacles, wiped them, returned them to the ridge of his nose, put his cigar in the ashtray, quietly drew forth from his files a folder of sheets and graphs. He began to read to himself.

Dr. Abraham leaned forward. "When did you weigh last?"

"I haven't. The nurses weigh my roommates, but not me. I guess I'm too damned sick."

"Well now. That's something we can do right here. Now."

Together they piled his body on the scale. He weighed 150.

"Hm. You weighed 180 when you came in. What's your average weight, Eric?"

"Oh, 210."

Dr. Abraham shook his head. "You've been slipping steadily. Steadily."

"But, Doc, that can't be. I've been eating good. And my temp is normal."

"Yes, I know. And your sputum? Do you raise much?"

"A little. Just a little bit of a yellow speck in the morning."

Dr. Abraham perused a sheet. "Well, it's still positive."

"And my X-rays?"

"I have them here. We'll look at them."

They examined his plates. Dr. Abraham outlined the shadows indicating trouble areas, outlined the fluid level in his left lung, pointed to dark spots.

"Where's the cavity outline, Doc?"

"We can't see it. We don't know if it's there or not. It's hidden behind all this fluid. But, since you're still positive, there must be a little bit of it left open there."

"The left lung's shot to hell then, huh, Doc?"

"Oh no. There's still a lung there. But since your pneumothorax failed, it hasn't improved any. We'll have to try something else. Maybe."

"Rib-cutting, huh?"

"Hm. Maybe."

"And the right lung?"

"Oh, that'll be a good lung, good."

"When?"

"Oh, five years, six years from now."

"Must I stay in bed that long? Forever?"

"Quite possibly."

"But what of me? Of me? I almost flew this morning. What of me?"

"Wait. Sleep. Rest. Wait. Wait, Eric. Quiet now. Not so loud. Plan for the close-by things."

"But six years of year-long days. No, Doctor. I'll go. Go."

Dr. Abraham laughed. "No."

"Why not?"

"You're too strong. You're too strong a character to go."

"That's candy. You're handing me candy, Doc. Candy."

"You are, though."

"Yes. But six years of year-long days. Year-long days."

"I know. I know."

140

"What can I do?"

"Read. Sleep. Rest. Eat. Wait."

"No cigarettes? No writing? No singing? No woman?"

"No. No woman. A woman'd be that seven-mile walk, you know. It'd kill you."

"But my roots, Doctor. They're swollen."

"Yes." Dr. Abraham narrowed his eyes. He drew out a pencil and jotted a note on a prescription blank.

"That a prescription for saltpeter?"

"Hah. No, just some pills for your nerves."

"Nerves."

"Yes. And I can't help you. I can give you sedatives, and smiles, and palpate you, but I can't help you, unless you help yourself. It's only you who can."

Eric lay breathing, pulsing; his flame leaped about in his skull. He thought of something. "My last sputum test?"

"Oh. Oh, that's right. The report should be here to-day." Dr. Abraham sprang up, relieved. He rushed from the office.

Without thinking of the wrongness or the rightness of his act, Eric sat up on an elbow, reached for the folder containing his case history. When he had finished reading, he put it back and lay down. He coughed a little. He ticked off the facts: metabolism low, sedimentation high, blood count up. One notation had caught his eye. A consulting physician had written in a bold hand: "Suffers from nervous disorders. Too much fire."

Dr. Abraham re-entered the office. His face was sad. "I'm sorry, but it's positive. Though the Gaffky count is lower. That's been dropping steadily since you came in, you know. Almost down to zero now."

"That mean anything?"

"Not much. A little."

"Going down, huh? Say, maybe that means four years instead of your six?"

"Maybe."

The door of 176 opened. In came two women: one,

tall and immaculate in an overly starched uniform with darting hard brown eyes; the other, pumpkiny and friendly with lips ready for chatter. They introduced themselves to the roommates: the tall woman, Miss Globe, head of the nursing staff; the other, Miss Valery, Patients' Aid.

Looking at Miss Globe, Eric realized why she was feared by the nurses, why Miss Pulvermacher should be her favorite. Her dark eyes glowered like an angry Pa's, like the Whipper's.

It was Miss Valery who took charge of affairs. She approached Eric directly, laughing at him a little. "Hear you got a case of the nerves?"

"A little."

"Ever try to do anything with your hands? Good way to get rid of the jitters, you know."

He laughed uneasily. "It depends what you mean."

"Handicrafts. Like knitting, leather-work. So forth." She looked at his gnarly fingers. "Maybe you'd like to cut statues from wood? Or make linoleum cuts?"

"No. No. Books're my outlet."

"Try knitting."

"Fingers're too clumsy."

"Bah. I've seen men with fingers as big as crossbeams do hardanger."

Eric looked at her, half-persuaded by her direct manner, her easy way of looking warmly into him. "Well, all right. Bring out the yarn and needles."

She looked at him, smiled deeply. "Try it. Won't hurt to try. Once. Knit your mother, or your sweetheart . . . your grandmother, that's it, your grandmother, a sweater. Many a man's done it. Good for him. Try it."

He was too stunned to speak.

After they had left, he asked, "Is she married, that Miss Valery?"

Fawkes shook his head. "No."

"Well. I'll bet you she's gets its benefits, though. Holy Moses, what a female."

Fawkes laughed.

142

Huck said, "Boy, and that other toots, she's a cool pickle, Miss Globe is."

"Yeh," Eric agreed. "But, fellows, that Miss Valery. Wow. I'll bet she gets what she wants. I'll bet you she eats raw beefsteak for breakfast."

They laughed.

"Bet she's a good woman, though," Eric added reflectively. "Good."

In a day, with Miss Valery teaching him, he was busy with needles and yarn; and eventually finished a plain scarf. But he was satisfied for only a time.

One morning his skin began to itch. Flushes of rash broke out. Little white, clear-watered bubbles popped up beneath the epidermis, wherever his skin was thin, weak; between his fingers, in his arm and elbow pits, along the scalp line, below the gently tufted hair of his pubis. He lay writhing in bed. He could not keep his fingernails off the itching, fiendish rashes.

He rang Miss Mitchell.

"Look, nurse."

"How long have you had that?"

"Just noticed it this morning."

She looked at him oddly. "You've been taking sedatives?"

"Yes."

"Don't they make you feel dopey, the nembutals?"

"No. Not at all. And I itch like a man buried in ants."

"Maybe you need a bath. It's time for your bath today."

Miss Berg came in with a small bathtub. While she soaped up a wash-cloth, he undressed beneath the sheets. He lay tensely, itching; all the while enjoying the beauty of her brassiere-cupped breasts. He watched them loll as she washed his chest and stomach. He flushed as he thought of fondling her billowing softnesses. He shivered.

A fire lifted swiftly from his braincase and ran like lava down his veins and fired his roots and swelled them. He lay aching and longing to touch her bosom.

Gritting his teeth, he forced another thought through the fire. "Nurse, what's your first name?"

She hesitated.

"Go ahead. Tell me," he pleaded.

"Thusnelda." He saw that she too was fixed in a rhythm stronger than her will.

"Thusnelda." He whispered it. It had the sound of a lover's stroke. It was the name a man gave a naked woman.

She touched his legs, bathed them, his toes and knees, his thigh.

He trembled. He ached. He was ready to leap from bed.

He wondered why Fawkes, or Huck, did not interrupt them. Were they blind?

She touched him, and he thought his roots would erupt.

They were interrupted. There were voices in the hallway. The door opened.

Dr. Abraham led the way. Behind him came three other men attired in white smocks, stethescopes dangling. Dr. Abraham began the exchange of smiles, of introductions. The newcomers were San doctors examining odd cases.

They knew Fawkes. Nodded to Huck.

"This is Mr. Frey. Dr. Dallesandro. Dr. Stein. Dr. Price."

"Hello."

"Hello. Hello. Hello." Dr. Dallesandro, stumpy, black-eyed, was the superintendent of the Phoenix. Dr. Stein, heavy, with a pale face, and fat with scowls, had the butcher's manner. He was a surgeon. Dr. Price was gentle, kindly, almost angelic. He too was a surgeon.

Eric surmised they had come to see him as a prospect for rib-cutting.

Miss Berg, who had quickly covered him with a sheet when the medics came in, stood silently to one side, her head down, a draft horse waiting for its driver.

Eric listened to them vaguely. He was glad they were too absorbed in their talk to notice his heightened color and Miss Berg's heifer-like flustered eyes.

**144**

He itched. He thought a moment. "Doctor. Dr. Abraham. Look. I want you to look at this. I don't know what's happened to me, but I'm breaking out in all directions. White pimples, red rashes."

"Oh." Like fox on the scent of fowl, the medics quickly leaned forward to study his skin.

Dr. Dallesandro nodded a quick head. "Acne. All of them get it before they leave."

Dr. Price smiled gently. Dr. Stein growled unintelligibly.

Dr. Abraham began, "It's . . ." and then, severe in mein, he turned to the nurse. "Has he been taking his prescription regularly?"

"Yes."

"Better make it P.R.N."

Eric's mouth fluttered. "What's that?"

"Those are the initials of a Latin phrase, meaning 'Whenever necessary.' "

"Oh."

"And, I guess you . . . yes, no more baths for him. Bathing may spread it."

Miss Berg nodded dumbly.

"No baths, doc?"

"No. No baths for a while. And if you need some handholding to take it's place, we'll put that on P.R.N. too."

The room jangled with laughter.

Eric angered. They were clods to laugh at his hunger. He swallowed and said, "Okay, you're the doctor. But I'm warning you, I'll stink myself out of here."

"Well, you may wash your armpits, and so on. But no more baths until I prescribe it."

Eric nodded. "Okay. Maybe it's just as well. I always did itch after I had them."

"Oh?"

"Yes. For about a half hour."

The medics looked at each other and nodded together. "Deficient in skin oils."

They left.

Later that day time poured swiftly again. Adele came;

Martha's friend. And promptly, according to their mutual agreement, his roommates disappeared behind their papers so that Eric could feel he was alone with her.

"Why, Adele." Her honey-blond hair was like Martha's; but her blue eyes were softer. They were like two oval flowers.

"Hello, Eric. How are you? You look well."

A battle started in him: he should send her away, for he would hurt her; he should keep her, for she would soothe him. He scratched himself, rubbed. "Adele, I'm glad you came. Take a chair."

"How are you, Eric? You look very well. Very." She examined him eagerly, almost the way Martha used to explore him with her digging eyes. Her soft eyes sought him amidst his ruins, his fallen temple. Then, looking at the others in the room, she shrank back on her chair.

"Never mind them. Come close to my bed. Talk to me." Inside him the battle reopened old wounds. She should go; she should stay.

Hesitantly, a little, she leaned forward then. "Aren't you feeling better, Eric?"

"Some."

"You look well."

"Adele, you're a good girl to have come. I was lonesome."

"Oh. Could I have come before?"

"Yes. No. I . . ."

"Well, I really wanted to, but, you see, Martha told me not to." The words entered him like slowly driven piano chords.

"Yes."

They sat silently, looking down at their hands, rubbing each on their own laps.

She said, "I saw Martha last week. She talked about you."

"Oh?"

"And she has a baby."

"Tell me, what's your father doing now?"

146

"A baby, she had."

"Your father?"

"He started a new business. And we moved. To the edge of town. Why, we can practically hear the cows moo."

"So close you are to the country?"

"Yes. And mother, she's . . ."

"Adele."

"Yes."

"Go."

"Leave you?"

"Yes."

"Shouldn't I've told you about Martha?"

"Go now. Please."

"Oh I'm sorry. I've offended you."

He said nothing.

"Eric, I thought you would like to know about her. She's been thinking of leaving her . . ."

"Go."

The door closed behind her. He could hear her swift steps clicking down the hallway.

A fire was on his skin, needling, scratching, itching.

Huck tore down his paper wall. "Holy Hell, why'd you send her away? She was beautiful. Beautiful. I was having a wonderful time enjoying her."

Fawkes said, "Holy Wassail, do you realize what you did? You sent a woman away. A woman. A blond!"

"Yes."

A fire was on his skin, needling, scratching, itching.

He heard voices in the hallway. "Who's that?"

Fawkes said, calming, "Library girls. With books."

Books? Books? Yes, maybe new books would help. He rang for them. They came in, pulling a little four-wheeled cart loaded with books. He sought through the titles while the girls, ex-patients, half-stood, half-leaned on the beds of his roommates, gossiping.

He found Byrd's *Alone*, paged through it, was sure that his lonely vigil was like his own.

He found an account of the first flight over Mt. Everest.

147

That too could lead a way. These two books would satisfy.

The girls left, a little disgruntled that he would not talk to them about the latest tag: that he and Mary Lehar were sweet on each other.

Hurriedly his eyes led him to the white wastes of the Antarctic. Swiftly his eyes lifted him up over Mt. Everest. But the fire still burned. He still scratched and rubbed.

He lay looking out of the window. He wondered where Mary Lehar might be. By this time she should be far along in her getting-up program. Perhaps she was already out there wandering on the mall. Mary Lehar. Had she talked about him that girls should gossip about them?

He quelled an impulse to write her. It would be unfair. He had a rib-sectioning to face; and that flower of a woman was too delicate to be embraced by a broken boxcar, too fine to feel the rough knotted edges of cut ribs pressing into the peaches of her bosom.

That night he and Fawkes and Huck were caught up in a hot funnelling argument on politics. They hit a crescendo two hours after the lights had gone out. Twice the kindly night nurse tapped on their door.

Then, the door opened, sudden, and Miss Haxxo, the black-haired, hard-nosed supervisor, who had eyes like Miss Pulvermacher, lashed out harshly, "Shut up!"

Eric jumped.

The door slammed shut.

For a few seconds he was speechless. Then he flared up. The idea. That female bitch. Did she think he was a child? That bitch. He broke into a loud tirade. He was so angry he hoped she was still near enough to hear him. "Why, the guts of her. By God, the next time she comes blasting through that door without knocking first, I'm heaving a water-bottle at her. That raggy bitch."

"Oh come now, Eric," Fawkes soothed.

Huck laughed. "Hell, Eric, they've got a right to come busting in here. Remember that *Pauper's Oath* you signed? Hell, brother, you better not yell too loud."

148

"Listen, Huck. I want it understood right now that not even the Whipper can come in here without knocking. I'd hit Him over the head too, the bastard."

"Aw, come now. Don't act like a kid."

The next morning he called Dr. Abraham. Miss Mitchell came with him. "Look, Doc. You're busy, I'm busy. So, I'll come to the point. Last night some bitchy snoopervisor popped her head in here and tried to scare me. Now look. I know we were disobeying the rules, talking so late. But I'll be a bastard if I'm going to let any old bitch stick her head in here without knocking. People can knock if they got some business in here. And if they haven't, they can expect a bottle over the head. Now, go tell that Haxxo super that she'd better knock next time, or so help me God, I'll conk her over the head with my water-bottle."

Dr. Abraham reddened.

The angered face infuriated Eric still more. He popped up in bed. "Look. That goes for you too, Doc."

Dr. Abraham chewed his teeth, and wheeling, left the room.

Miss Berg came again the next day.

"Thusnelda."

She blushed. "Your backrub. It's time to rub away your aches."

"Oh yes." Eagerly, just as always, as every day, he turned on his belly to have her administer the soothing strokes of a cool, alcohol· backrub.

She rubbed him gently. The flames in his skin glowed softly, gently, almost creamily thick.

She stroked his shoulders and rolled his shoulder blades around and pushed down on his spinal column until shivers of pleasure, of mad delight, rippled and pulsed through his flaccid muscles.

She rubbed the small of his back. She rubbed it warmly, closely, intimately. She rubbed him like a lover. Her hands were like Ma Memme's, like Mary's.

A glow rose in his thigh, swelling his roots again. He

could feel the veins gorge with blood.

He forgot. He slipped away. Lying on his belly, he seemed to have dived into an ocean of goosedown. The itching was gone.

How beautiful were her breasts. A potter's delight. How scented they would be were he to kiss them, fondle them. They were like Ma Memme's, like Martha's.

How golden her hips. How golden the peach-hair upon her thighs. How gentle her hands. Mary.

The fire in him thickened, rose, swelled; orange, purply.

There was a sudden gathering in his thighs, an urgent message gathering into a longed-for storm, into longed-for rain. It rose, potent as sap in spring, swift as a fountain, gushing from his roots, lifting, searing him . . . and then beneath him, his roots ached and flooded and throbbed.

He sighed. How soothed. Soothed.

He felt faint, a little sick. There was a faint smell of freshly cut flesh.

Miss Berg slapped his back lovingly. "There, there's your backrub for today."


# XVI—WHITTLINGS

THE SUN rose. It became hot.

With a weary sigh, Eric removed his pajama jacket. He resigned himself to the monotony of living through another heavy summer day. No one, except possibly the Whipper, would care to make a mercy call on him in this heat.

All forenoon he lay fretting on a sweat-dampened sheet, panting. He tried to read; but his moist fingers spotted his beloved books, his eyes stung from inrunning sweat.

Turning in upon himself, he sorrowed that he had to forego so much of the good life that lay outside the walls of his ward. He brooded. He lay flat on his back, his face turned sideways, staring at the mall where the sprinklers waved futile arms of water over the burnt, orange grass. Sometimes a little wind rose from the scorched growths and sighed through the screen and brushed the fuzz on his bared chest.

He grieved about his existence. He worried. His nerves became taut.

By afternoon, before the visiting hours came, a wild ferment was bubbling in his veins. A craving for freedom was a lively yeast in his brain. He cursed the hidden power that was inexorably preparing his ribs and soft lungs for a terrifying, macabre operation. He groaned. He had to lie abed another five years, waiting for it. It was a horrible prospect. He could grasp enough of the sense of it to see many a rebellious day ahead.

He brooded. Looking at those five dreary years of misery stretching on and on, he recalled the time when, as a lumbering though swift-handed lad of seventeen, he had faced the gigantic task of husking a hundred acres of corn alone.

He had stopped to figure it then. A hundred ears of corn made one bushel, seventy bushels made an acre, and a hundred acres made a year's crop: a total, roughly, of nearly a million ears to husk. An eternal task. With such a desolate prospect of drudgery ahead, he had thought, then, of refusing to get up in the morning. But somehow, groaning, agonizing, he had found courage to go on. That last ear of corn had seemed forever a time away.

And now this cure-taking. The last minute of it, too, seemed far away. He studied the idea of it, the length of it. There were sixty minutes in the hour, twenty-four hours in the day, seven days in the week, four weeks in the month, twelve months in the year. In five years there would be, roughly, a total of five and a half million minutes. What a flat algid swamp of inactivity it would be. It was outrageous to ask a man with fertile glands and a hunting brain to wait that long. Too much.

He shook his head. Where would he find the fortitude to wait?

The visiting-hour whistle blew.

The summer doors swung open. A stranger stepped in. Eric made a guilty motion toward his pajama jacket. But when he saw that the newcomer was a man, he forgot the modest impulse.

The man was tall; and huge. Folds of mattress-thick fat blurred the outline of his skeleton. His legs were of such girth that Eric knew instantly he suffered from a heart ailment. He presented, as he entered, the effect of a silo walking on staggering sacks of cement. Toppling above this unsymmetrical mass was the huge globe his head, heavily thatched with white patriarchal hair. Red pimples pocked the man's potato nose. His mouth was uncertain and wistful, as if it were associated with a brain that speculated more on things than it commanded them. His cheeks were as gray as soiled flour.

But the eyes were the man. They were twin dreamers.

Eric was startled to hear Fawkes exclaim, "Father! Why, you've come."

"Bbllbbll. Woll. So, there you are. Bbllbbll. Hello." Eric noticed the father had a white mustache as curt as his son's black one.

"Father, you shouldn't have come."

Before Old Fawkes could mouth a reply, a sudden piping voice, strident and bossy, emerged from the region of his hip. Unnoticed, a little mite of a female had entered the room with the giant. From the ensuing talk, Eric gathered she was a henish, frustrated secretary, laden with the task of trying to get this empire of a man to put his thoughts down into the form of a scientific treatise. She squealed, "I told him he shouldn't come. His heart, you know. Weak. Can go anytime. But, huh. You know him, of course. And I told him you would be angry. But, huh. And then his work. It's so important. So important to humanity. We must catch it before he . . . you know."

Old Fawkes gaped at the little wren as if he did not understand her.

Young Fawkes smiled wrily. "It's all right, Miss Baxter.

152

It's all right. He's here now, and I'm glad he's come. Take a chair, both of you."

"Occh. You don't know what a trial he is to me. You don't know."

The old man shrugged.

"Really, he's such a problem." She waved her hands, and broke into a seething babble of words. Old Fawkes would not do this, nor that; broke this rule, that rule; locked her out of the laboratory, locked her in the bathroom; locked her in the cellar, locked her in the broom-closet; and always, when she would finally manage to escape, there he would be, back at work in the laboratory, "when he should be resting and thinking about his book."

Old Fawkes grinned. He winked at Eric and Huck, who were listening avidly.

"Why, one time last winter he even had the cops in on us," she exclaimed.

"Cops?" Young Fawkes narrowed his eyes.

"Yes. The cops. Didn't you hear about it?"

"No."

"Why." The little wren leaned forward. "It was a disgrace. You see, your father's lately been interested in the nature of fish diseases. And some woman friend of his, some society woman who has nothing more to do than worry about her goldfish Dolphy, called up and asked him if he would take a look at her sick goldfish. Poor Dolphy had some kind of rash, she said. Well, of course, you know your father. He doesn't know any better. He lets the most ridiculous people take up his time. His valuable time. And so, like a fool, he goes over there, never telling me about it so I could make an appointment at the proper time, and looks at her goldfish. Studies it. Then he decides to take it home and examine it at his leisure. So, he soaks his handkerchief in a pan of water, wraps the fish up in it and starts for home. Well, on the way home he, of course, has to stop and blow his nose. In this handkerchief. You know. All the time forgetting he's got a goldfish in it. And, of course, the fish has to roll out and fall into the snow."

153

Young Fawkes chuckled. He looked covertly at his father. The old man said nothing. He sat quietly, his eyelids hooding a merry expression.

"Well, when he gets home, he remembers that he's gone out to get a goldfish. When he looks for it, it's gone. Well, cussing and roaring, he finally figures out that he must have blown his nose somewhere along the way, and so lost it. And so he goes back, kicking through the snow." She paused, wetting her thin lip with a quick aspish tongue. "Well, about this time a patrol car comes along. Two cops in it. They start following him around, watching him. There he goes, kicking through the snowbanks. Pretty soon, to humor him, one of them gets out and asks, 'You lookin' fer somethin', mac?' 'Yes.' 'What you lookin' fer, mac?' 'A goldfish. A sick goldfish.' 'Oh. Well, that's . . . did you say a sick goldfish? In that snowbank?' 'Yes.' 'Oh.' The cop looks hard and then gets a wise look in his eye and then, to humor your father along some more before he gets dangerous, gets out of the car and starts looking too. They kick around together for a while. And, of course, the cop has to find it. You can imagine what that cop thought. Well, anyway, the upshot of it was that they took your father home and turned him over to me. But can you imagine?"

Young Fawkes winked at his father. "That true?"

"Woll. Bbllbbll. Well, yes, I guess so. Substantially."

"Of course it's true," she shrilled.

The old man cleared his throat. He rolled his eyes. Then, with the greatest of kindness, and with an air of having a secret understanding with her, he leaned over and whispered to her, "That reminds me, Miss Baxter, isn't it about time for you to go see Dr. Abraham? Like we said?"

She jumped up. "Oh sure. I forgot. Sure." Her eyes gleamed. She had the look of a woman who has been promised a trip to get away from drudgery.

After she had gone, the old man drew up his chair and placed his hand on Young Fawkes' arm. "Woll, bbllbbll, son, how's your health?"

154

"Huh. Miss Baxter will tell you that later."

"No, really, how is it?"

"Good."

"How long before you can get to work, son?"

"Oh, it'll be about two years, two more years before I can get to work there."

"Two years? Bbllbbll. No."

"Yes."

"But, you'll be allowed to do a little work, won't you?"

"No. None at all."

"But son, that's terribblll. Terribblll. We can't let you lie here and rust."

"Well, if I don't, you won't have me at all."

"Occh. It can't be that bad. Why, look at Darwin, son. He was mortally sick too. Yet he worked a little each morning. Two hours a day. For many years. And we got the *Origin* out of him."

"Yes. But I'm more ill than he was."

"Occh. Bbllbbll. Son, we need you as bad as we needed Darwin."

Fawkes shook his head, blushing a little. "No, father, it isn't that bad."

"Son, you don't seem to understand. Here you are. A great brain. And we're not using it. We're wasting it." The old man's eyes became milky with dreamy thought. "Son, let me tell you something. Do you know that our civilization may be plunging into another Dark Age? All the signs are there. Yes. I'm positif, son. So hurry, son, hurry. Get well before we're buried away in our little monasteries again."

"Oh, come now, father, isn't that loading it on?" Young Fawkes' eyes became smoky with thought.

"Son, I'm positif. Come, let me bring you a little laboratory apparati, and some books, so you can work a little. And keep the darkness back a little while longer."

"Aw, you . . . Well! Now I know how Miss Baxter feels about you and your heart. Father, father."

The old man rolled his white head about. "You know,

son, I'm beginning to believe you've turned soft on me; that you've turned . . . well, let me say it bluntly, that you've turned lazy. Yes. Lazy." His eyes became sly, watchful.

"But father . . . say, what the hell do you mean, lazy?" He glanced at his father a moment; then quieted. "Father, don't get me worked up. Father, please don't. Please. With these two ambitious birds in my room here and my own ambition being what it is, I have a hell of a time staying quiet without you stirring me up. So don't." Young Fawkes coughed.

In the other corner of the room an imitative impulse stirred Huck, and he cleared his throat and wrestled with a wild cacophonous fit of coughing.

Eric felt the impulse too. He swallowed and sneezed.

All the while the old man studied his son. Nodding to himself, his eyes becoming mellow and warm again, he said, "Of course, son, of course." He patted his son's shoulder. "Of course. I only wanted to see if there was still a little fire left burning in you."

"Don't worry."

"Good."

After a pause, Young Fawkes asked, "Father. Do you know what I don't get, though?"

"What?"

"How the hell can you get along with that exclamation point of a woman, Miss Baxter? She'd drive me nuts."

The old man laughed and rumbled. He rolled his eyes. "Oh, she's all right, son. I find she's an excellent thought-sucker. Thorough. Very accurate. And she writes clearly. And, if they do want a book out of me, that's the only way they'll get it."

"Huh. Seems to me you might pick a thought-sucker with a little more architecture. One with a little more front-porch to her."

"Bbllbbll. Son, I am not yet a David that I need a fresh maiden to rekindle my fires."

Young Fawkes laughed.

156

"No, son, no. Bbllbbll. No. There may be snow on the roof" . . . he rubbed his white head . . . "but there's still fire in the furnace."

"Aw, father, you know you're getting old."

The old man stilled. Laughter vanished from his eyes. "Well, so you can't start work for a while yet, huh?"

"No, father."

The old white giant stood up. "Well, I must get back. Well, I had to see you, son. Had to. So . . . well . . . " The old man shook his son's hand and, slowly turning away, tottered out of the room.

For a long time Fawkes lay quietly, his eyes closed, his fist hidden beneath the sheets.

Twenty minutes later, a frail woman came into his room. Her clothes, a faint gossamer, were all of a piece with her cobwebby hair and her vague gray eyes. The smile of the martyr curved her lips with rue. White tendons and blue veins ridged the backs of her hands. She seemed cool and unflustered in the heat.

She came toward Eric's bed. "Are you . . . Mr. Frey?"

"Yes." With his right hand Eric hunted vaguely about on his bed for his pajama jacket.

"Oh, that's all right," she said knowingly. "You needn't cover up. It's too warm anyway." She paused. "I wonder, could I visit with you a little while?"

"Why, sure. Yes. Here, take a chair. Mrs . . . ?"

"I'm Mrs. Deeble. Wybren Deeble's mother."

"Oh." He brushed his hair. "I never knew that was Sa . . . that was his name. Wybren."

"Yes. It is a strange name. It was once the name of a famous devil-banisher in the Old Country. In Europe."

"Oh."

"Wybren has often spoken of you. So often that I had to see who it was that had caught his eye."

"That's nice of him."

"Yes." She drew her chair closer. "Yes. Poor boy. Poor boy. He has had such a time of it. He's been so restless here.

He was beginning to turn bitter. And then you came. And it's a good thing you did. I was so worried."

"Well, that's nice. I didn't know I had such an effect on Deeble."

"Oh but you have. It's wonderful. And now, looking at you" . . . she surveyed the entire length of his body . . . "I know why. One can see right away you're a kind one. A deep one. One who can keep himself quiet till the day he's well. And that's one thing my poor boy couldn't learn. He hasn't learned to wait. And I can see now that he may learn it from you."

"Me?"

"You must be a deep one to be so willing to lie here day after day waiting for health to return, patiently waiting and waiting." She nodded.

Eric twisted away. He did not know how to act. Mothers always embarrassed young men with their gush.

And then, just as softly and as mysteriously as she had entered, the gray-eyed mist of a mother stood up and said, "Well, I must be going now. I only visit my poor boy once a month and I want to spend most of it with him. So . . . but, I did want a look at the man who had caught his eye so."

"Oh."

"Good-bye."

"Good-bye."

The doors parted again.

"Pa. Why Pa! Come in."

Pa stood chucklingly in the doorway, leanly gray and bronzed. A smile arched up into his cheeks. Seeing Pa stand before him Eric was amazed to think that he had ever considered Pa the Whipper.

"Come in. I'm so glad to see you. Where's Ma?"

"She's home. She stayed t'home this time." Pa came closer, nodded gravely to the others in the room; and, taking a chair, took Eric's hand in both of his and shook it. "Yeh. So, son. Well. You're still good, huh?"

"Sure. You came alone, Pa?"

"Sure. Alone. I had to make a business trip t'Minneapolis and so I thought I'd look up my son a minute an' see how he was gettin' along."

"I'm glad you did, Pa. Glad." He paused, then asked. "Isn't it too hot traveling?"

"No, it's not bad. It's tolerable." Pa smiled. "Why, son, you know we've shocked grain together when it's been hotter'n this."

"That's right. I forgot."

"Well, how be y'u?"

"Good. Good. So good, in fact, I'm thinking of running away."

"No! Well, that's fine. That's wonderful. Now I know you're fittin' again. I always did say that as long as you got your vittles regular, you'd be the runningest kid alive."

"Just you try lying here. It's a hard job."

Pa nodded. "I suppose it 'tis at that. A hard job." Pa's face became solemn. He stared through the window. A tear of sweat ran out of the forest of his gray hair and down the bronzed slope of his forehead. It poured over into his eye. He blinked. "Yes. I guess it is hard work at that."

Eric drew himself up in his bed a little and rubbed his knee. "Oh, well, if a man has to, he can."

Pa looked at Eric's arm, his legs, his bared chest. "By God, son, you're gettin' to be as fat as a barrow. You ain't never been that hefty, has y'u?"

"No, I guess I haven't. But it don't mean much. A man can be fatter than all get out and still not be healthy, you know."

Pa leaned forward to feel his arm. He pinched his biceps. "You're pretty hard too. You ain't exercisin'?"

"No. Except to lift up the top of my body when I sit up to eat."

"You're pretty hefty, all right. That's right good. Well, then it really looks like maybe you'll make it now?"

"Sure."

"How's your appetite? Can you eat?"

159

"Oh sure. Lately I've been eating like a horse again."

"Oh well then. Now you're gonna make it. No matter how sick y'u get, if you can eat, you can lick leprosy itself."

"Sure." Smiling, Eric asked, "What did Dr. Abraham tell you, Pa?"

"Oh, he agrees with you."

"Huh."

They were silent and uneasy for a moment.

"Well, Pa, how are the crops this year?"

"Fairish. The oats went good. Corn's gonna be nubbly."

"This business trip you talked about. What was that?"

Pa smiled mischievously. "Oh, I had a little business up here. A li'l business."

Eric grinned. "Pa, I'm always glad to see you."

Pa shifted, made a motion as if he were about to fill his pipe, remembered the rules, and coughed. "Well, it's sure a good sight to see you lookin' so good. Just as fat as a barrow."

"Huh. I don't feel like a barrow. I feel more like a boar loaded with Spanish Fly."

Huck chuckled. The sound broke the family wall that Eric and Pa had thrown up around themselves.

Pa laughed too. "Yep. As I always said, when the grazin' gets good in the pasture, Ol' Tom the Bull starts sniffin' the heifers."

There followed a mellow moment of smiling.

"Yeh, son. I'm glad you're takin' it so good. Like a real Frey. Takin' it like a man. Waitin' your time. It's good to see."

Eric looked off.

"And Ronald, does he come yit, son?"

"Sure. Sure. He's all right."

Suddenly Pa said, "Goddang it anyway. I wish I didn't live so far away from here. I'd sure like to see you more. A mortal man only gets a few years to appreciate his own son."

"Yes, Pa."

"G'dang it anyway."

160

Later, after Pa had gone, Eric opened a package, the third one, Pa had brought him. In it Eric found a stout, bone-handled jackknife.

"Fer whittlin'," Eric murmured to himself. "Fer whittlin'. To pass the time away."

# F XVII—GREENS, REDS, BLOODY REDS

OR A TIME it was a pleasure to talk with Calisto Sly about Life. It was a way of making the otherwise torpid days a little meaningful. The two men, with Fawkes and Huck sometimes joining, explored each other's knowledges and pet ideas and loves. Sometimes they examined each other's private fears, and acknowledged that on certain occasions they had been cowards. The talks, beginning aimlessly, would always end up by opening the tight door to their inner lives.

But presently the dialogues began to irritate Eric. Invariably they became long searches into the meaning of death. And just now death was too uncomfortably close to think about it.

Each day the janitor hurried through his work on First East so he could spend the time gained in 176. Each day Eric became less and less inclined to explore the universe with him. Calisto irked him. Calisto's flame had been a failure too. It had not found a place to shed its light. Gradually Eric became cool, then rude, to Calisto. He hoped his frosty manner would discourage the man.

Calisto was not slow to understand. He went about his work with a dark, mournful face, his eyes eloquent with flashes of resentment, his thick lips and white teeth vengefully belaboring his fat roll of gum.

One morning Calisto came nervously into 176. He set down the mop-pail and stick, fussed with the ventilation of the room, picked up bits of paper from the floor, grumbled a vague phrase now and then, scratched himself, sniff-

161

ed, and started mopping. He moved about the room like a peregrinating volcano, rumbling and grumbling to himself, occasionally flashing grieving eyes at Eric, sometimes studying him with glowering brows.

He was mopping the same corner for the second time, when he erupted. "Eric, you're a fool!"

Eric jumped. Fawkes and Huck drew themselves up in their respective beds, readying themselves to enjoy the scene.

"You're a fool. A dumb fool."

"Why, what do you mean?"

"Uk. If you'd use your head, you wouldn't have to rot here like this."

"I don't get you."

"Uk. Everything iss wrong with you."

Eric grunted. "Just what, for instance?"

"Your health."

"For godsakes, what . . . Good Lord, man, what the hell do you think I'm in here for, to get sick?"

Fawkes and Huck snickered.

Calisto assumed a meek expression. He cast hurt eyes at them. "Well, I don't mean that. I mean, you got a fine appetite, a wonderful appetite, a lion's, and yet you waste it eating d'wrong foods."

"I eat what you serve me. Isn't that good enough?"

"Uk. No. Them San dietitians, they don't know from nuthin'. Uk. If only you would eat d' right foods, then you would work a mirawcle."

"Well, what've you got in mind? C'mon, spill it. You won't be happy until you do."

Calisto lifted his mop carefully from the floor, dangled it dripping over the mop-pail, settled it slowly into the open wringer as if it were cold syrup he were pouring, and then, gripping the wringer handle, said, "Thiss. Them dietitians, when they go to school, collech, do you think they learn much about the real world? Uk. Not at all. The collech profs just rivet the old notions tighter to their bones."

162

"What old notions?"

"Well, look. The young kits start school thinkin' that the human being iss a good guy, don't they? That he's full a nice thoughts about everything. That he ain't no animal. They don't know they are little animals; that their pa's and ma's, and Bible readin', and grade school teachers, has been splashin' whitewash over'em ever since they wass born. You know how it iss when you grow up?" Calisto slammed down the wringer handle, pressed out the oily gray water, released the handle, and, with the wrung mop, began to clean the floor a third time. "Now. It's the same way for them kits that go to school to be dietitians. They start off thinkin' they're human beings and, for all the profs tell them, they keep thinkin' so."

"Well, what of it?"

Calisto shrugged. "Well, they never learn that man wass once an animal, eating grass and fruits. That people wass once a bunch a Nebuchadnezzars, eating the grass in the pastures."

Eric paused. He glanced at Fawkes, saw that he too had begun to speculate inwardly. The janitor had something. "In other words, what you're trying to tell me is that I should go back to the menus of my savage grampas, the very menus that helped bring the human race up to its present level?"

"Exsactly!" Calisto roared.

Fawkes and Huck laughed.

"Raw foods, then?"

Calisto dropped his mop and came quickly to Eric's bed. "Eric, with that lion's appetite of yours, I tell you it will work mirawcles. Get yourself raw foods of all kinds. Raw vegetables, raw lettuce, raw asparagus tips, raw green peppers, raw eggs, raw meat, raw everything. Milk, and so on. Eat. Eat them all. And then. Boisst! Just watch yourself run up and down the hall, full a health, like a lion roaring."

Eric pursed his lips. "You know, Calisto, maybe you got something there."

"I know I have. I know it. Just watch. You will be su'prissed."

"Well, maybe . . . "

"Mr. Frey, don't be like them fools who never eat the green lettuce in the salad. Don't. You must eat that too. Oh, I tell you, my fren, my heart iss heavy when I see them salad plates come back to the kitchen with all them lettuce leafs still on them. The best part of the meal. Oh, I tell you, it hurts."

"I don't like to burst that pretty bubble," Fawkes broke in, laughing, "but aren't you forgetting about bacteria, Calisto?"

Calisto whirled to face Fawkes. "What bacteria?"

"Sanitation. Cooking does kill a few of them, you know."

"Uk. Sure. But it kills vitamins too."

"Well . . . all right. But sanitation is important."

"Uk."

"Besides, just why must one eat all that green stuff?"

Calisto stared at Fawkes. "You ain't heard a photosynthesiss? You, a scientisst?"

Fawkes narrowed his lips. "What about it?"

"Photosynthesiss?"

"What about it? Don't act so damned mysterious."

"Why, that's where the sun . . . why, it's where . . . anyway, greens iss where the energy of the sun iss captured, and we eat that, and then . . ."

"That's no more than a guess, Calisto. And you know it."

"Why, I reat it in *Science*."

"You mean you read what a certain man guessed it was."

"Why, it iss a truth, man."

"Well, all right. Suppose it is. Aren't you forgetting something? That Eric's stomach, there, isn't fit to handle all that roughage? In fact, you might upset his bodily processes and kill him. No, Calisto, I think that menu of yours is too horny, too drastic."

164

Eric felt himself siding in with Calisto. The idea that mankind had been fooling itself with the dream of being a pack of angels on a picnic appealed to him. It fit his current philosophy of life. "Well now, Fawkes, Calisto may not have argued his points well, but he's got hold of an idea there."

"Oh my God, Eric. You know better than that. Where's that critical mind of yours?"

Eric wavered. He liked Calisto's theory; he wanted to keep Fawkes' respect.

Calisto waved a hand at Fawkes. "My fren, just let him try it once. You will be su'prissed. Su'prissed."

"Look," exclaimed Fawkes. "Look. If he concentrates on raws, he may get into the same trouble Huck got into. A mass of allergies."

Eric nodded. He remembered the afternoon Huck had come back from an allergy test, his arm and back striped like a tiger's hide with inflamed scratches where tests had been made. When Huck drank milk, or ate raw eggs or fresh greens, his cough became more violent, his temperature rose, and gas on his stomach increased.

Fawkes continued. "No, best thing is a rounded diet. Otherwise it can be dangerous."

Huck winced.

Fawkes narrowed his eyes then. He turned quickly to Calisto. "No, Calisto, I think Eric had better wait a little while before he tries those raws. He's at low tide there now, and it could be dangerous." He looked from Calisto to Eric. "If you don't believe me, ask your doctor." He paused again. "But why the hell should I open my mouth, anyway? I'm just a patient too."

"Really, you will be su'prissed. All that power in them frash greens, them raws . . . I tell you, you . . ."

"Oh, the hell with it."

Calisto stared, dropped his hand. He turned and picked up the mop-pail and stick and meekly left the room.

But Eric continued to ponder the idea. He reflected on

the ways of his life on Hickory street a year ago. He had been downright poor. Even had he wanted, he could not have bought a dime's worth of greens. And when he had a little money . . .

Suddenly it came to him that he had had wretched eating habits even before he had lost his job. Ever since he had left the farm, he had eaten but a doughnut and a cup of coffee for breakfast; mosttimes only a cup of coffee for lunch; a hurried dinner in the evening . . . sometimes no dinner at all when he had found a book he wanted to own. And always cigarettes.Back there on the farm Ma Memme had always laden the family table with heaps of raw lettuce, cucumbers, radishes, cabbage, beans, and peas. Why, holy Moses, his belly was adapted to a menu of fresh greens after all.

The next morning, when Miss Mitchell made her rounds to collect statistics and complaints, Eric asked to see the dietician, Miss Twill.

And swarthy-faced Miss Twill came, dressed in white: cap, smock, stockings, shoes. Little Miss Twill had such dusky pigments that her freckles were as dark as fly specks. Her eyes glistened like two drops of black lacquer. The faint moustache that flecked her upper lip was like a smudge of charcoal.

She was a flustered little creature. As she talked, she pushed her stringy thighs against the side of Eric's bed and rhythmically pressed her low-hanging bosom against a pad of papers she held in her arms.

She joined him in a nervous argument about Calisto's theory. She resented the implication that her education had been slanted. Her eyes rolled and darted little angry protests at Eric. Her quaintly large lips phrased hot exclamations: "If I ever get hold of that Calisto. Oh!" "Oh, you're way off, Mr. Frey. Way off!" "Darn, that's not true!" "Oh, that's not so at all!" "Oh nonononono!"

Eric admired her loyalty to dietetic canons. And he was sorry that she was lonesome. It was lamentable that such a lively spirit had been templed so unbecomingly.

Eric tired of the banter. "Look, Miss Twill. Look. The point is, do I get some raws on the side?"

"No."

"Why not?"

"Because you don't need them. Besides, I'll have to see your doctor about this."

"Look, woman, if it turns out I'm wrong about this, I'll take the rap. Don't you worry about the doctor."

"No."

"Look. I'm losing weight fast. I'm just wasting away. Maybe the greens'll be just what the doctor ordered. Besides, I'm tired of this white-white around here." He waved at the bed sheets, the walls, the floor. "I want some color. Some greens. Some reds. Some bloody reds."

"You've been losing weight? How much?"

"Why . . . don't you know? Don't you keep an eye on our weights? What kind of a dietitian are you anyway?"

"Well . . ." she blushed, her freckles darkening. "Well, I just can't think of your weights off hand, just like that." She snapped her fingers.

He growled at her, "Some dietitian you are. Well, I lost over sixty pounds."

"Since you came in?"

"Well . . . thirty since I came in, and sixty altogether."

She studied him. "Oh, that's not so bad. You must remember, Mr. Frey, you're a muscular man. And when you men take bedrest, your muscles atrophy. Isn't that right, Dr. Fawkes?"

Fawkes waved his hand. "I'm not saying anything. This argument has gone beyond my comprehension."

Eric shook his head. "Well, I don't know. I . . ." Stiffening, he said, "Anyway, the point is, I want raws. Bring 'em."

"No."

He sat up, said bluntly, "You know what you need? A good night with a good man. And if I were healthy this minute . . ."

"Oh!" She jerked back a few steps. Her face clouded in

167

struggle, reddened, finally broke into a vexed smile. "Well, of all the . . ."

"Sure. Of course you do. Hell, we all need something. And I need raws. Now! Do I get 'em?"

Her arms relaxed against her hips. She leaned on one leg. "Well . . ."

Every week she brought him a sack of raws. Later, she brought him sweet, purple raisins.

Three weeks went by.

Miss Berg came into the room pushing a scale on rollers. "Time to weigh, boys."

"Me too?" Eric asked, wondering if Dr. Abraham considered him strong enough to stand up.

"Yes, you too."

"Dr. Abraham say so?"

"Yes."

She weighed the roommates first.

Then, with a laugh, she pushed the scale near his bed, saying, "All right, you big bag-a-bones, throw yourself down on this."

He tossed back his sheet and cover, pushed himself along the bed, puffing, feeling a little dizzy. He dropped his white, veined feet over the edge of the bed and then reached for the scale's upright. He was so excited that he did not notice Miss Berg supporting him with her fleshy arms.

Carefully, as if he were a stilled top, he tried to balance himself. He stood swaying. "Hurry, weigh me," he whispered. "I haven't got all day time."

"Can't you stand alone?"

Fawkes and Huck sat up to watch. "Jeepers," Huck exclaimed. "I always thought I was tall. But you, Brother."

"Hurry, nurse, hurry." He looked down and saw his feet slowly turning purple as the blood rushed down. The veins bulged and became black. "Hurry."

"Oh, don't get funny. Keep your shirt on."

"Put it on 150. That's what I weighed last time."

She did.

He tipped it easily.

She slid the marker along the arm of the scale. 155. 160. 165. 170. 168.

"Holy Moses. I gained eighteen pounds. Wow!" He gasped for breath, tottering. "Holy Moses, fellas, eighteen pounds." He stared at Fawkes, at Huck. He sagged.

Miss Berg grabbed him. His long body teetered over her. He knocked her cap off.

He shook his head. "Thunder in the Whipper's britches! Eighteen pounds."

Miss Berg untangled herself from him. She pushed him backward onto the bed with an exasperated gesture. "Well, really. And such language."

"I'm sorry. I . . . but you see . . ."

She laughed at him. All three laughed at him.

"I . . . you see . . ." He collected his wits and said, "Maybe Calisto's right after all, hey?"

"Could be," Fawkes grunted. "Could be. Except that you're still positive."

"Oh. Oh yes. That's right."


He ate great quantities of food both raw and cooked. He ate raisins. He gorged himself with the fruit that visiting friends and relatives brought. Calisto covertly brought him second helpings, sometimes thirds, of eggs and milk.

And always, even after his stomach was so full it hurt, he felt hungry. Every day, little by little, his navel began to sink from sight. Slowly a handful of innertube-like folds of fat collected around his waist.


He studied his sputum every day. The little yellow speck fascinated him. It came usually in the morning. The food he ate to break his night-long fast squeezed up against his lungs from below, forcing the speck into his trachea where the cilia caught it up and thrust the cursed bit of matter into his throat. Then a cough shot it out.

169

One morning it did not appear. At noon, when Dr. Abraham happened in, Eric mentioned its absence.

Dr. Abraham grinned. "You are getting to be a spit specialist, aren't you, Eric?"

"No. But I'll bet you a cookie, Doc, that if I spit in my cup I'll be negative."

Dr. Abraham's eyes twinkled. He rubbed his bald head. "All right. I'll take that bet. Spit in your cup and I'll take it down to the laboratory. Right now."

Eric spat. "Doc," he said, clearing his throat, "Doc, I'm sure it's that little speck that makes me positive. If I could get rid of that, I'd have my TB licked."

"Hah. Maybe."

But the next morning the speck was back. It was larger than ever.

When Dr. Abraham came in an hour later, Eric's hopes had already fallen to inert embers.

"Well, Eric, you were right. Without the speck, your sputum is negative. Here's your cookie."

Eric forced a laugh. "Thanks." He was surprised to have Dr. Abraham take him so literally. "But I think I owe you the cookie now. Just look at my cup today."

Dr. Abraham examined it quickly. "Yes. Well. I expected this. Well, I'll have this specimen tested too."

The report the next day was: Positive.

Eric nodded. He closed his eyes to hide them from his roommates. He continued to eat the greens.

A month later, October, he was astounded to see his weight jump from 168 to 192, a gain of twenty-four pounds, or almost a pound a day. A faint hope, a tiny ember blazed up within him.

"But your sputum?" Fawkes reminded.

Eric nodded. "Yes, you're right. It's still positive."

Again Eric ate raw greens, took the cure, waited, watched a testy summer run before a rusty fall, watched the leaves swirl to earth like colored snowflakes drifting.

November. Weighed again. This time he jumped from 192 to 218, a gain of twenty-six pounds. The ember became

170

a scarlet spark. He waited. He watched. One morning he awoke and found his bones aching. He was surprised to notice that the silver stripe in his thermometer had risen to 101.6. He called Miss Mitchell. She called Dr. Abraham. He looked at Eric, inspected his throat and eyes and finger-nails.

"Did I catch a cold, Doc?"

"I dunno. Maybe."

All day Eric lay deep in his pillows. It was a sort of hol-iday from being ill with TB.

The next morning the temperature was back to nor-mal. "Must've been the quick-flu, Doc."

"Maybe. Whatever it was left without leaving its calling card."

December. White leaves of snow swirled over the mall. At noon the shadows north of the blue-needled pines reached the foot of the Phoenix. The film of fatty tissue on his body swelled. His neck thickened. His cheeks pudged. Sheaths around each thin muscle fattened. Splits opened the envelope around his abdomen as if he were pregnant. His skin fissured. Again he weighed: this time a staggering 247. Still the speck came.

His roots ached. He wrestled with himself in the black night. He wondered if there were any harm in masturbat-ing. But, at last, he managed to control himself. Besides the miserable feeling that was sure to follow, there were always the ear-sharp roommates to face the next morning. Some nights he awakened just as a fast throbbing died away in his thighs. Relieved, he lay miserable, and wondered about existence.

## XVIII—LAMPS IN THE NIGHT

ONE NIGHT, after the lights had been extinguished and after the somber night had risen blackly from its crouch in the corners to repossess the room, pushing each man far into his corner, Eric asked, "Fawkes, how long before you can get up and go?"

"I really don't know."

"How's your weight been? I've been so busy with my own sore I never thought to ask about yours. How's it been?"

"Oh, fair. About normal."

Eric wished he could see Fawkes' eyes to know if he were telling the real story. He knew the man was on guard. He had heard the rustle in the dark of a creature preparing itself for defense.

Eric turned. "How about you, Huck?"

"Oh, fair. I'm holding my own. Gain a pound here, lose it there."

Suddenly Eric became very curious about Huck. All he had been able to learn about him was that he was an orphan, that he had gone to college one year, that he had drifted from job to job. "Huck, what really makes you tick inside?"

There was a silence as if he had spoken a vulgar word.

But Eric was hungry for talk. "I don't mean that in a nosey way. I mean it . . . I mean it only as a problem."

"Uhuh."

"Really now. What do you live for?"

"I dunno. Just drift along I guess."

"That all?"

Again a silence with the flames trembling.

Eric swallowed. Another prying question escaped him. "Huck, that letter you get every day, who's it from?"

He heard Huck draw a quick breath.

"I wish I had a friend like that, a tie with someone dear somewhere who'd write me every day."

Huck coughed. "Wull, the letter's from Joan."

"Where's she live?"

Huck stirred in his bed. He coughed in the dark. He growled, "Do you have to know?"

Eric subsided, "Well, just as you please."

Huck cleared his throat once more.

Eric waited. He could feel Fawkes waiting too. His breath whispered in the black night.

"Joan's a . . . wull, I met her four years ago. She's . . . well, one day I met her when I was up. You see, four years ago, when I was ready to leave this dump, I met her walking one day. She lived near here. A school teacher. And swell." Huck drew in a rattling breath, and rushed on. A strong force was pressing up against the floor of his words. "We got acquainted. God, after these dumpy nurses, like that Tina Pulvermacher, why, I thought Joan was the Queen of Sheba herself. Broth-ther. Gold hair, and her body like so. Real good, you know. I just went nuts about her, I guess, and forgot myself. We went canoeing one day. I knew it was bad for me to go paddling around, jerking my chest muscles. But . . . I did. And, something happened. I sprung a leak and then, down, down, and so here I am, once again in bed."

Eric sat up, leaning forward, trying to catch a glimpse of Huck's face in the dark. "You mean you ripped your lung?"

"Guess so. Yes."

"Holy Moses. That was tough." He paused. "Where's Joan now? Why don't she come to see you?"

"That's the whole point. She's got it too. From me, I guess. God damn it."

Fawkes interrupted. "Now, Huck, that's something nobody knows."

"Well, there is a chance I gave it to her."

"Nobody can prove it."

Huck cleared his throat as if he had been cheated out of some credit. "Well, anyway, she got it and now she's upstairs. Up there on Fifth Main."

Eric was aghast. "You mean, up there . . . ?"

"Yeh."

"Oh."

"Yeh 'oh' is right." There was a rustle in Huck's bed. "You know, fellas, I don't know what to do about her. God damn it, fellas," Huck began to rock in his bed in the

**173**

dark. "Poor woman, she's got bone TB, and lung TB, and just about every kind a TB there is, an' yet, she won't give up. There she lays, hangin' on, hangin' on. And always cheerful. Always. Writes me wonderful letters. Hell. And then, and then . . . she's always thinkin' about the day when we'll get married, when we'll have kids . . . God damn it, fellas, and all the while she thinks I don't know she's already lost one leg. And gonna lose another."

"No!" exclaimed both Eric and Fawkes. "No."

"Yeh. Christ. She figgers on me. And I . . . hell, I can never take care of her. Never. What she needs, if she ever gets out, is a man with dough. It'll take a hospital full of nurses to take care of her. I can't do it. Besides, I'm gonna croak. And that's what hurts. When I go, she'll croak too. I know it. That's what hurts."

"Aw, hell," Eric growled, "You're nuts. You're not going to croak, man. You look good to me. Cripes, you're as healthy as a fish."

"No," said Huck firmly. "No, I know I'm gonna croak. I know that. You see, I can't eat. I can't keep my food down."

"Aw . . . "

"And that's all right. I don't mind, for myself."

"Aw, hell, Huck. You look all right to me." Yet Eric wasn't sure. Lately, with growing concern, he had noticed that Huck's morning coughing spells had lengthened, that his tray was often returned to the food-racks untouched, that when he did eat he belched as if he had swallowed beer foam. "Sure. Aw, man, you'll be all right. Just sit tight."

"Huh. You don't see my sputum every day like I do."

After a long silence, Eric asked, "You know, Huck, those letters, what're you going to do with them?"

"Why?"

"Well, I dunno. That was a wonderful story you told about yourself and Joan. People should know about you two."

There was a violent movement in Huck's bed. "Look,

174

you blood-sucking son of a bitch, that's none of nobody's business what Joan and I've got. Nobody's." He coughed. "By God, I'll make goddamn sure that you don't get them, you blood-sucking weasel you. Live off your own blood, you blood-sucker!"

Startled, Eric fell back into his pillow.

A half hour of nervous silence went by.

Again the impulse to talk pushed up like welling lava. Eric knew he was being offensive; but the hunger in him was stronger than good sense. "And you, Fawkes, you living for a woman too?"

"Me? Oh no. Not me."

"Really?"

"No."

"You didn't leave something behind out there?"

Fawkes said nothing.

Eric sensed in the dark that Huck had quieted and was listening closely. "Tell us, Fawkes."

"Well. There's really nothing. As my father hinted, I like science. And I was working on a problem another fellow started. He went off to do something else, and left me with it. I was just about to finish the job over at the U path lab there when this TB came along."

"And this problem of yours, is it important?"

"Maybe. I . . . there was a chance that it might have become a specific cure for TB."

"Holy smokes, man, really?"

"Well, I had hopes."

"A real cure? Are you sure?"

"No. But it looked good as far as I got."

"Holy Moses, man, does Dr. Abraham know about this?"

"Yes. I guess so."

"What's he say about it?"

"Oh, nothing."

Huck broke in. "Don't be modest, guy. Tell him. You might as well. That son of a bitch will suck your breath if you don't."

Fawkes chuckled. "Aw, it's really nothing."

"Tell him, fer chrissakes."

Eric heard Fawkes swallow.

Huck said, "Well, let me tell you then. The docs here say it's got more possibilities than any other cure in sight."

"Oh." Eric blinked his eyes in the dark. No wonder Old Fawkes had made such a fuss over his son. In this room, then, lay a saint. Eric felt humbled. He coughed and said, "Fawkes, I want to apologize."

"What for?"

"I . . . oh, I've been such a conceited jackass. I've been lying here thinking all this time that I was the big shot in this room. But now . . . now I know you're it. You're the one."

"Aw, Christ."

"Fawkes, you're the man in this room that's got to come out alive. You. Not me."

"Don't get so hysterical, Eric," Fawkes exclaimed. "My cure isn't ready yet. I'm not yet ready to give you free treatments."

"Hey, what about me?" exploded Huck. "Don't I get out too?"

Eric said, "Oh, I didn't mean that. I meant . . . anyway, Fawkes, you're too humble about things. Why! you've actually started something for humanity. Made a step. Can't they do something for you? We've got to save you."

Fawkes coughed nervously in the dark. "Thanks, Eric. Thanks. It's good of you to wish me health." Fawkes became silent for the length of a thought. "Yes, it is too bad we can't help each other, isn't it? But, it seems each one of us has to fight TB all alone. Oh, another can concoct a drug for us; but in the end there, it's what healing power we're born with and what we nurture through life that wins or fails for us. You can't slip your energy inside my skin to help me along. Nor I you." He paused. "Yes, and when we die, no man can go along to help us die. Ever hear the song—

176

> *You got to cross that lonesome valley,*
> *You got to cross it by yourself.*
> *They ain't no one goin' to cross it for you,*
> *You got to cross it by yourself.*

Remember? That, Eric, that is the bare bone of death, with the skin off."

Eric's flame lighted up powerfully.

Just before he turned over to go to sleep, Eric muttered, "Well, I guess I'd better get set for the rib-cutting then."

After a moment of silence, Huck growled, "Who the hell gives a damn."

Eric held himself tensely; then slowly relaxed. He nodded to himself. Once again he had driven away a friend with a bull-clumsy thrust of hand, a friend whose candle might nigh be burnt but whose flame was good and steady.

Other thoughts rose in Eric. Perhaps Huck felt that his humbling before Fawkes had been but a passing mood. Or perhaps Huck came to this revenge because no one had bowed down to him. Or perhaps it irritated Huck that someone could eat so heartily. Eric nodded. He promised himself that for the next few days he would be careful not to smack his lips.

Outside, a little wind came up, and blew upon the windows, and the bare eel-arms of the poplars sleazed upon the panes.

# A XIX—FANTASY IN THE STORM

T FOUR O'CLOCK, the strong wind that had been pushing against the building all day long suddenly became vicious. Gray streamer clouds swept down from the northwest and emptied great flour-sacks of sand-hard snow white upon the land. The tumultuous gale bullied the building, and blustered at it, and drove white breakers of snow against it, and iced it with zero cold.

Eric put aside his afternoon paper to watch the noisy

177

elements outside. Old Lady Poplar had gone crazy. She lashed from side to side, against and away from the window. She tipped sideways, almost to the ground. Then, with a snap so loud he could hear it over the thunder of the blizzard, she whipped back to the other side, almost touching the ground again. With the huge broom her body she swept the side of the building.

The tall trees on either side of the mall within the V of the building's wings, like a set of snarling whips, with handles fastened in the earth, lashed wildly about. Sometimes they whipped the earth; sometimes they fouled each other; sometimes, in blind madness, they beat their own kind, the blue-needled pines, who stood shivering beneath them like grandmothers in fear of their grownup grandsons.

Sometimes the sky hurled down snow so thickly the window panes became squares of pallid gray. During those moments Eric could see nothing beyond them.

Speck-sized snow sifted through the cracks, piling little drifts onto the narrow width of the window-sill. When Eric closed his eyes to the point where vision blurred, he felt himself to be some far-off Wodan watching snow drift across a highway.

A fierce cold entered the room. It came pinching into his woolen retreat. And though the clanking steampipes sizzled, he rang for the nurse to bring them each a hot-water pig and a round of blankets. Then snuggling deep, and hugging himself, he continued to watch the storm.

Eric said, "Fawkes, wouldn't you like to be out in this? Battling away? Struggling? Moses, it would be wonderful."

Fawkes tipped his head to one side quizzically. He shrugged.

Huck sneered, "Still out tryin' to be the hero, huh?" He grunted, "Go ahead. Be one. As for me, this is one day I'm glad I got TB. That I'm safe and warm in bed. I'm gonna enjoy this."

"Well, hell, who gives a damn about your safety? Rot in bed for all I care. I'm for the battle."

The windows drummed. Eric, after his momentary flash of anger, began to muse. He recalled the olden days. He fumbled with the worn pebbles of the past. "You know, Fawkes, I'd sure like to be out with Pa now, out there on the farm. The horses and cows and calves and colts and chickens, they'll all be standing around in the snow, waiting. Their hair'll be all matted, and iced. And they won't want to move when you shoo 'em up inside the shelters. Moses, what fun it would be to help Pa right now."

Neither Fawkes nor Huck answered.

"Yes. About ten years ago I carried a fresh, long-legged calf four miles through a storm. A storm just like this. Carried it, following fences, figuring my course by the way the weeds grew. Carried it with a nervous ma-cow right on my heels, bellering and nosing the calf, and generally worrying my backsides all the way home. Once a coyote came along and I've never in all my days heard such a beller from a cow. It was human, like a horse's. And that coyote? Pfft! It was gone like that! Like a puff of smoke in a hurricane."

Huck croaked, "Boy, what a hero."

Taken aback, Eric stilled and snuggled further under his blankets. He lay watching the bending window panes.

Miss Mitchell came in. "You boys comfortable?"

"Yeh."

"Sure."

"Okay here."

"No more blankets? Pigs?"

"No."

"Good."

Eric wondered, "Say, how cold is it out?"

"Calisto says it's twenty below."

"Brr! That much? Say, if it keeps up much longer we'll be marooned out here."

"Might." Worried, in a hurry, she edged toward the door.

"Why, maybe we won't even get our Christmas mail."

"Oh, it won't get that bad. Christmas is still two days

off and by that time they'll have the roads open. No, that's nothing to worry about. I'm more worried about my nurses. A lot of 'em were off duty and up in Minneapolis when the storm broke. You know, Christmas shopping and such. Well, they can't get back. And so here I am, short-handed."

"That's too bad." A pause. "What about the milkman? Groceries? Eggs? So on?"

Huck said, "There you go again, Eric. Worryin' about that gut of yours." Turning to the nurse, Huck added, "You'd better make sure that the eggs and milk and raws get through or that Nebuchadnezzar there will make a meal of us."

Eric growled, "Aw, lay off, Huck."

Miss Mitchell opened the door to leave. "Well, I can't be talking here all day. Well . . ." She left.

"Holy Moses, how I wish I was out there," Eric repeated. He turned, twisted, scrouged nervously beneath the warm blankets. "Just think, here I am, stinking under my blankets, when out there the real life's blowing by."

Again Huck pounced on him. "Well, what's holdin' you back, hero?"

Eric glared at Huck.

Huck's lips thinned to a hint of a snarl. For a brief second he resembled a hissing weasel. "Sure. Put or get off the pot."

"Take it easy there, mister," Eric warned.

"Aw, you make me tired, you big blowhard. You're always gonna do this, gonna do that. Yet all you do is lay there blowin'. Why, you couldn't break a bag of wind, you couldn't. Hell."

Eric sat up. He clenched his fists. "Take it easy."

"Aw . . ." Huck coughed, choked, coughed once more; and then, his face reddening, sat up to point. "Listen, brother, you're the most conceited blowhard I've ever met."

"Take it easy."

"Aw, fer chrissakes."

Fawkes interposed. "Come come, fellows. What the hell.

Sounds like you two need a little fresh air."

Huck said, "I'll say I do. God, how it stinks here."

Eric hit his upraised knee. "Dammit, Huck. What the hell's on your mind? Tell me. C'mon. All I can see is a bunch a froth at the mouth. Froth."

"Aw . . . "

"Tell me what's griping you?"

"Well, jissus, the other night, what'd you say? You said" . . . Huck pitched his voice to a querulous falsetto . . . " 'I thought I was the big shot around here. But now I know. It's you. Forgive me. Oh, forgive me.' " Huck drew back his lips. His teeth gleamed. "As if you meant that, you big faker."

Eric drew back his sheets and said quietly, "I'll ask you to take that back, Huck. I can't let that stand."

"Aw, go peedle up a rope."

"Huck!"

Again Fawkes broke in. "Say, you two birds. You look like you might get into a fight."

"We are if Huck doesn't take that back," Eric gritted, panting. He swung his legs over the edge of the bed.

"Aw, Eric, go pick on your own size."

"Tell Huck that. That's his lookout."

"Aw, go pick on your own size."

"Dammit, Fawkes, I can't let that little curl of garlic stink up my life with those smelly wisecracks of his. I just can't."

Huck tossed back his sheets. He threw his legs over the side of the bed. He panted. He doubled his fists.

Fawkes sat up. "Well, damn you two birds. I'll have to ring for the nurse if you don't get back in bed," he crackled. "Hey, what the hell is wrong with you two crows?"

Both men hesitated.

"Aw, c'mon, Eric. Get back in your hole. And you too, Huck. Both of you. Two swell cocks like you two shouldn't get your feathers up over nothing."

Eric grumbled. "What gets me hot is that I didn't mean to be a blower. All I did was open up my heart and say what I thought. The truth. Suppose it did sound cocky? What of it? I can't help that. All I did was to say exactly what I thought. The truth. And then the roof had to fall in on me. Holy Moses. Why, if we were to know what Huck really thought, we'd see that he was an egotist too, let me tell you." He paused for breath. "Why, inside, if a man didn't think he was really pretty good, the best in sight maybe, why, he'd never get anywhere."

"Exactly," Fawkes agreed, "now get back to your bed, you two short-armed cocks. And pull down your feathers. You look naked."

The storm grumbled outside the window. It tugged at the wing of the building until Eric felt the floor move underneath the bed. The walls crackled. The air in the room became crisp. It burnt the nose. Bones ached inside the warmly clasping blankets.

Eric lay looking at the frosted windows. There were etchings on them of castles, of dinosaurs, of giant redwoods, of children playing down a slope of hill. There was even a calligrapher's scroll. He lay dreaming.

Eric mused on the size and shape of the earth, its spinning through the cool ether, its vast distance from the sun, its gently throbbing rotation through the spaces. He visualized its surface. He placed himself on the moon to study the earth. He spun around it. He saw snowstorms gathering at the North Pole and spreading downward through the great refrigerator that was Canada. Enormous storms hung off Spitzbergen and Hammerfest, pounded the Nordenskjold Sea, thundered on Ellesmere and Land's End. He heard the ice booming in the North Passage above Siberia. On the opposite side of the whirling sphere, he saw the Antarctic heave with its freezing continents of ice. He saw the penguins running about like white-fronted diners lost in a blizzard.

He saw the warm climes. The fertile humus of the jungle seemed unreal.

He dreamed of mountains. He remembered Sven Hedin's trip through Tibetland. He remembered the swift, well-mounted Mongols preying on each other. He heard the lamas chant. He contemplated their vast, airy religion. He remembered how cold the country had been, how Sven had huddled about his fire of plentiful yakdung.

Suddenly, grinning a little, he spoke to Fawkes in what he conceived to be Tibet-talk. He talked of "yakdung" and "lamas," of foreign things. His speech was filled with many an "ung" and "ing", of "chingung-un-chunging-un-ungahdunging." It was good Tibetan. Good.

And then astoundingly, Fawkes answered in equally facile Tibetan. "Ung-yung-yakdung."

"Ung-yung-ung-hunk-hung."

"Whung?"

"Huck-hung."

They spoke rapidly, swiftly, laughing.

Eric cried, "Strange, that in this land of Amerikung I should find a fellow Tibetung. Yung-gung-yung."

"Yung-ging-yung."

"Wungderful!"

Fawkes, to prove he spoke an excellent Tibetan, explained that he had once spent twenty years there. "Tibetung-ung-tung-yakdunk."

"Wungderful." And Eric explained that he had learned his when he had traveled with Sven as his servant.

With a bashful smile, as if he had trouble forgetting his last grievance against Eric, Huck spoke up in good Tibetan too, that, why! he was Sven Hedin himself. "Chung. Sveng Hendung."

All three roared. It was a wungderful reungion of old-time Tibetungs in Amerikung. And what a miracle that they should happen to meet here, of all places, in the same lungroom.

Outside, in America, with a loud and continual cry, the hurricane growled out of Canada, shouted across Minnesota, and slapped its heavy hand upon the San.

Eric snuggled beneath his blankets. He cuddled the hot-water pig. His bones ached a little.

**E**RIC guessed right. By Christmas Day the storm had blocked the highways with tons of drifted snow. Deliveries of groceries, meats, drugs, and mails stopped. The Phoenix was a village snowbound.

In the emergency Dr. Victor Dallesandro, the San superintendent, installed a system of rationing.

Nurses worked overtime. Doctors hurried through the institution to treat cases of hysteria. In the west wing of the San many women patients, whose husbands could not make their regular visits, disobeyed doctors' orders for the first time. In the east wing indolent men patients suddenly lusted sulphurously after their nurses. Younger patients, both boys and girls, thrilled by the excitement of the storm, ran on weak legs around their beds, and fought a little, and played games. Life was significant again.

When the storm left and the last few straggling clouds had been herded eastward by a clearing wester, the sun came out. The salt-clean snow suddenly flamed into a Sahara of golden white. All traces of man's hand upon the earth had disappeared beneath the bleached and billowing sheet. Magically the San had been transported to the center of a desert of white sand, with mile-long, blue-shadowed dunes stretching and rising and falling away in every direction.

For a little while Eric studied it eagerly, absorbing it, memorizing it. To be outside. To work at restoring the ties of the San with the rest of the world.

He sighed. It was a blunting thing to know that this Christmas Day he was miles away from family and friends. This Christmas might well become the worst he had ever had. He grunted. He sneered, when he thought of the song now current on the wireless—

> *I'm dreaming of a white Christmas*
> *Just like the ones I used to know . . .*

Eric looked out of the window. He watched Old Lady

Poplar sigh, shiver, and sigh from all the exertion she had had.

At ten o'clock Miss Berg came in to ask if they would like a Christmas tree in the empty corner of the ward.

Both Fawkes and Huck shrugged their shoulders. "Makes no difference to me," Fawkes said. "Nor to me," Huck echoed.

Miss Berg turned to Eric. "And you?"

He curled his lips. Sentiment on a day like this? "Nah. I don't want none. All that fuss. Ridiculous. Nah."

Miss Berg looked at him crossly. She had been overworked the last few days. "Just as you wish. I was only offering it. The nurses got together and bought a tree for every room. Because you've all been such nice boys."

Eric snorted. "Nice!"

"All right, all right. But you needn't get mad about it," she said, reddening. She opened the door to go out and then, as she began to close it, snapped, "After all that work we went through, you have to act like that."

At eleven, the door suddenly banged open. Miss Berg pushed in a litter. Her eyes were cold. She said impersonally, "X-ray for Mr. Frey."

He growled at her. "Say, can't you leave a guy alone on a holiday?"

"I thought you didn't believe in holidays?"

"I don't. I just don't like being disturbed today."

"X-ray. Come." She pushed the litter alongside the bed, threw on a blanket, set up his sputum cup and some napkins, stood waiting.

He grumbled at her. But one glimpse of her fleshy bosom and her chubby arms softened the point of his fret. He cursed a little as she helped him onto the litter. And when she pushed him down the hallway toward the elevator door, her scented flesh welling against his head almost made him relent. Perhaps there should be an aromatic balsam in the room after all. But his flame would not clear brightly and he said nothing.

Returning and entering the ward again, he discovered that 176 had undergone a magic change. The nurses had set up a five-foot balsam in the empty corner anyway, had decorated it with tinsel and pop-corn balls, had placed three small packages of chocolates beneath it, and, on each bedstand, had placed a fiery poinsettia.

Staring, Eric felt his roommates covertly watching him, alert for his reaction. He set his face. He would not let them see he liked it. He rolled off the litter onto his bed. He covered himself with his blankets. And though he knew Miss Berg was waiting for him to make a pleasant remark, he picked up Housman's *Shropshire Lad* and began to read.

"Say something," she demanded.

He flicked his eyes.

"Say something, you big dope."

"There's nothing to say."

"Och, you. And here we're shorthanded and did this thing for you. Och."

He grinned inwardly. And cringed a little as he reflected on his satanic impulses.

During the afternoon rest hour, Huck's shout brought Eric up from a nap. "Hey, look, guys, the snowplow's come through. And right behind it . . . say what the hell is that behind it?"

Eric blinked his eyes and stared through the window. The snow gleamed sharply. He leaned on an elbow, peering. "Why, that's a mail truck. By God if it isn't. Boys, we're back in the world again."

The marooned Phoenix welcomed the outside world with a whoop. When good old Victory Dallesandro, the superintendent, called for volunteers from among the ambulant patients to deliver the mail, twenty cadavers responded. With a cough and a skip they made hourly deliveries.

Cards rustled and swirled down upon Eric's bed like clusters of fall leaves shaken from trees by whirlwinds. By

186

five o'clock he counted a hundred. They came from every-where. Somehow word of his illness had reached homes he had stopped to smile in during his wanderings: farmers for whom he had worked a day or with whom he had stopped to have solemn serious talk about their pigs and crops, former professors, fellow newspapermen, three girls he had completely forgotten, and an old college sweetheart who had remembered he had always liked apple-turnovers and who now sent him one stony with the blizzard's cold. There was also a card from Martha.

As he read each message or looked at the gifts, the flame in his skull shot up like a nervous geyser, reaching, spilling. It burned deeply, down to the subterranean oils of prejudice, hate, love. That people had remembered him! "Fellows, fellows." Tears streamed down his face. "Fellows."

Dr. Abraham came in. He nodded first to Fawkes and Huck, wishing them a cheery Yule; then turned to Eric.

Eric narrowed his eyes. Had the nurses been talking again? "Yes?"

Dr. Abraham pinched Eric's arm playfully. "Had a good Christmas?"

Cautious now, watching the other's eyes, seeking the flame behind their veils, he said, "Well . . . most ways . . . yes."

"Most ways?" Dr. Abraham drew up a chair to sit beside the bed. "What else do you want?"

"Oh . . . " Eric blinked his eyes to keep back the tears of shame. Across the room lay the man who should be having Dr. Abraham's attention. Now Huck would surely think him a greedy ghoul. "Oh, nothing."

"Tell me."

"Well, I wouldn't want anything my roommates couldn't have."

"Well, what is it?"

"Oh, I'd like to go outdoors."

Dr. Abraham nodded.

Eric leaned forward. He forgot his roommates. "Doc,

being in bed here . . . maybe it's not so bad in your book because you think we got novels and star-life and Christmas cards and people's love to entertain us. But Doc, I'd give up all those things if only I could go out in the snow for one day. To be out there. Moses, man." Eric took a deep breath. "To walk in the snow. To fight it. To tumble in it. To battle it. To wrestle the wind. To clap your hands against the frost."

"Umhuh, umhuh." Dr. Abraham nodded. His eyes became alive with inward pleasure. "Well, well. So."

"Really, Doc."

"Well, why don't you get up and go?"

Eric sucked in a breath. "What?"

"Sure."

"You don't mean . . . ?"

Dr. Abraham snapped shut his eyes a moment; then opening them, fixed Eric with a watchful glance. "Look. I came in here to bring you a gift. You see, I've been looking over your record again." He shook his finger. "Do you know you've got a pretty good chance to be up by next Christmas? Free of this bed? Not free of the San, but up? You see, you've improved so rapidly it begins to look like you'll lick your TB naturally." He paused. "And if you do? Hah!"

"You mean there won't be a rib-cutting?"

"Maybe."

"Really?"

Dr. Abraham nodded. "Nine hundred and ninety-nine cases out of a thousand would have died if they'd had as much TB as you had when you came in. And yet . . . here you are, gaining more weight than our best patient."

Eric ground his teeth to keep from making a fool of himself. "So I can forget the rib-sectioning then, huh?"

"Well, I can't promise it for sure, because that speck is still there. But if that goes, why then, yes."

"Holy Moses."

"But remember, you've got to get rid of it."

"Yes. Yes."

"Play your hope close to your belt now."

"Don't worry."

"Maybe if you'd take the cure just a little better, just a little more calmly, put in another little tittle of an effort, you could get rid of that speck."

"Doc, a dead man couldn't take the cure any better."

Dr. Abraham gestured. "Like this? Sitting up?"

"Oh yes." Quickly Eric flattened himself in bed. "I forgot."

Dr. Abraham studied him a moment. "How'd you like a couple of shot-bags? You know, they're pound bags with lead shot in them. You lay them on your chest to keep reminding yourself to stay horizontal."

"Holy Moses, Doc, get'em. Anything."

Dr. Abraham's eyes reached deep into him.

Then stunningly, in the last delivery of the Christmas mail, came a letter from Mary Lehar. The hurried, slanted handwriting on the distinctive gray envelope suggested she had written it on an impulse.

He forgot his roommates. He drew down shutters around his flame.

> I had an idea you might be as lonely as I am this Christmas. I happened to talk to Miss Berg on your floor today—you see, I'm really up and around now as I'd once dreamt I'd be. It can be done!—and she said you'd refused a tree. That tore aside a thin veil I'd been keeping between myself and you. Now I come.
>
> Besides, I've never forgotten the day I met you at the X-ray door. I had heard of you from others, that you were a dreamer, something I am too. But I never expected to meet you. And then, suddenly, there you were.

He breathed hard. A hiccough kicked in his bowels. Was he really interesting to a woman who might have the flame of a Sappho in her skull? He could hardly believe it.

Yet, if she had the soul of a dreamer, and wanted to know him, why then . . . why, life! To hell with the Whipper.

A glorious adventure lay ahead.

# B XXI—THE FLAME IS DAMPERED

UT FIRST some cure-taking to earn the right to see her.

After a couple of hours the shot-bags became heavy, oppressive. At 10:30 a.m., when the nurse brought in his in-between-meals nourishment, a glass of milk, he still had an hour and a half to go before he could sit up for his noon meal. As he drank he always stirred his hips a little, deliciously, cautious not to disturb the weights; and then, finished and cracking his teeth, went back to his books.

To lie completely inert for prairie-long forenoons and afternoons and evenings and nights, to cease all conversation, to cease all movement, to breathe but fifteen times a minute, to damper the flame in the skull, was a task he loathed.

When he was tempted to disrupt the glacier-like stillness of his limbs, he thought of Mary. He had to get well for her. She would not want a man with half the ribs of his chest missing. She would want a whole man. And yet, how could a burning bush become a cake of ice?

Sometimes his books did help him forget. It was when he investigated the mental illumination of Buddha, Brahma, and Confucius that his spirit escaped the corked bottle his bed.

One day he investigated the idea of yoga. He hypnotized himself into such a state of lethargy that only his slow-bubbling heart showed life at all. He emptied his mind of all memories, images, thoughts—even the thought that he might have a thought. He closed all the ports, all the windows, all the apertures to his braincase. He shut down his flame to an ember. Strangely enough, he discovered that he was not lonely in the murky chamber where the Whipper kept his holy of holies. When his soul neared extinction, fears, loves, hates, all vanished, and only the last live coal of vitality glowed on the pan of the brain.

Another time he followed the arm-swinging, baggy-trousered Thoreau around on his clearing beside the pond Walden. He studied the flash of Henry's thorn-sharp eyes. With Thoreau he heard the solitary train rattling along in the night. With him he dreamed on the rippling pond silver in the quarter-moon.

Even the speck helped him keep quiet. Each morning, after it had come again, he peered at it lying on the wax bottom of his sputum cup. He studied its circumference, its depth. Carefully he drew a picture of it in a notebook. In two weeks the pictures began to tell the story of his battle with Tuber. Some weeks he won, some weeks he lost. Some days the speck became so minute he wondered if the fragment of pus was an illusion. Then, in a few days, it slowly increased in size, slowly enlarged. When the speck was small, his spirits rose; when it became large, his flame sank low and sullen.

"Temp taking" became self-induced agony. Withdrawing the stick from his mouth, he clamped a paper napkin around it. Holding it close to his eyes, he slowly drew the stick through his fingers, counting off the figures 105°, 104°, 103°. He chanted, "Well, it's not 102°. Well, it's not 101°. Well, it's not 100°. Well, it's not 99°. Well, it's . . . well I'll be devil-damned! It's only 97.8° tonight."

With a little effort he could easily become a cold-blooded reptile.


## XXII—THE NEW WOMAN

HE BEGAN to write Mary. Lying flat on his back, doubling up his legs, he used his thighs as a table so that the scribbling would not interrupt the horizontal cure-taking.

To seek out her knowledges, her prejudices, her loves, he set traps in his letters. As was his wont, he asked the last question first. He sought out her opinions on trade unions. She wrote she had thought about them only vaguely. In reply he wrote a long missive about their origin, history, and function in society. He said he believed in them. In her rebuttal, she observed that, viewed idealistically, the union was more of a reaction to an evil in society, to a barbaric lust for excessive profits by a few top wolves who could not be voted out of power, than a response to a good. Poor and unlettered toilers joined it for protection, not for the gospel that the union leaders preached. And while the union gave the humble some economic power, in many instances it also served to choke the development of talent. Eric pondered her theory and let it go. She could be right, she could be wrong: in either case, she seemed willing to probe the fleshes of reality.

He sought her attitude toward the Jews, Negroes, Chinese, and Russians. She replied that she would marry any man of any race, provided she loved him.

He told her that Whitman was his favorite dreamer. She said Keats was hers. She quoted him. She mentioned that he died young, and of tuberculosis. She mentioned it as if, secretly, she were identifying herself with him.

Despite her reluctance to write about her family, he discovered she was an orphan. In pre-San days she lived with her Uncle Peter and Aunt Anna and her cousin, Raymond. They lived in a farmhouse near Lake Minnetonka, just four miles away. From her tones he felt that they were not pleasant foster-parents; that Raymond, now a flier in the U. S. Navy Air Corps, was an unmentionable subject; that the whole family was poor of both money and soaring spirit. Of her own father and mother she did not write. Looking at all of this, Eric was sure that her eyes were sad because some tragedy had terrorized her childhood.

She always seemed shy, uneasy in her letters. A phrase of hers, oft-used, "Oh, I don't know. I really don't know," was poignant with the meaning of her. She had the ability, she had the good flame; but the fuel it fed on was mixed, and the flame burned smokily, like a peat fire, and she seemed uncertain of what she wanted of life. She was like him, tormented by the knowledge that, though she had superior sensibilities, she knew of no way to use them. She was frustrated before she had fairly begun. He worried about her, worried that someday she would seek outlets that might hurt him.

This last thought released a furious burning in him one day. What if she became another Martha? What if she, too, left him? Was it this flying Raymond she loved in vain? For a week a fear gripped him. It cramped his bowels like a violent purge.

He questioned everybody about her. He compared their reports. He was tempted to ask Dr. Abraham to look up her San file.

When he discovered she was on a three-meal exercise schedule and that she could visit any floor once a week, he begged her to come. And, to the gossips' delight, she did.

She came every Monday. On Saturday some visitor from the city usually dropped in to see him. On Sunday reflective music came over the wireless imparting to the subtle Sabbath air the illusion of a holiday. Then on Monday she came, glorious. Saturday. Sunday. Monday! Three festive days capped by ecstasy. Three successive movements of ascending music.

Besides his own fears and ecstasies, the torments of others helped to raise his temperature. With mocking, kindly mien both Fawkes and Huck offered prophecies each Monday morning that Mary could not come because of some catastrophe. Nurses tattled old gossips.

The charge nurse, Miss Mitchell, was his greatest thorn. She was jealous. After Mary had come the second time, she suddenly became interested in Eric herself. One day, after he had been fluoroscoped and was waiting near the elevator for some nurse to get into the notion to take him back to his ward, Miss Mitchell happened along. She smiled warmly. He was startled. And the more so when she began to roll him toward 176. It was an unheard of thing for a charge nurse to push a litter around. Just as she came to the door she brushed his neck gently, caressively. When he did not respond, she pushed her hand deep underneath his pajama jacket and stroked him softly, lovingly. Instantly he drew away from her and stared, stared until a hue of red deeper than her hair swelled her freckled face. Her lips became grim.

When Mary came the third time, Miss Mitchell's lips became cruel. She would not permit Mary to come onto the floor a second before the 3:30 whistle, nor allow her to stay a minute longer than 5 p. m. Twice she strolled casually into the room, interrupting their hallowed tryst. Eric cursed inwardly. But he did not dare protest. She could cancel Mary's visits altogether.

Because he was still infectious, he touched Mary only as she was leaving; when he held her hand for a moment the touch always stirred up memories of Ma Memme.

At 3:15 p.m. each Monday, he listened for her footsteps. At 3:30 he heard their steady falling *clock, clock* upon the tiled floor of the hallway, coming, coming, nearer to his door.

And always she came in with a wide smile, her eyes half-sad. The conflict in her eyes perturbed him. She was the kind of woman, he decided, who by her moods would bring him either heaven or hell.

Once, a Monday, after he had futilely sought sleep during the afternoon rest hour, had carefully shaved and dressed in his best pajamas, he heard her coming. For every *clock, clock* upon the hallway floor, his heart beat a thousand times.

The steps came nearer, louder. He tossed aside his shotbags and sat up to greet her flashing smile, her sad eyes in the doorway.

Then oddly, the sound of her footsteps vanished. He heard the door of 175 open, heard a splash of talk, heard the door close.

He smiled to himself. She had made a mistake today. It was too bad that they had lost those few seconds, but she was only human and he could forgive her. She had probably been over-anxious to see him.

But she did not come.

He heard her voice. He jerked his head around to listen. He heard her laughing, heard the deep and garbled drone of a man's voice in answer. He pushed his ear against the wall behind his bed. He strained to hear.

She did not come. She did not come for an eternity.

When she did come, twenty minutes later, he greeted her with a burst of angry questions. "What the hell happened? Holy Moses, woman, do you realize you lost us a whole twenty minutes? What the hell were you doing in that room?"

Her smile vanished. Her face became a circle of questioning astonishment. She asked, "Why, what do you mean? Can't I deliver a message?"

"No. Not on our time. Woman, you've wrecked our whole afternoon!"

The laughing roommates stilled.

She blushed. Her sad eyes became more drawn with hurt. "I didn't come here to get bawled out," she cried. She snapped her red nails. "I didn't." She flashed away from him, slamming the door behind her.

"Mary. Mary." he called. "Mary!"

He waited a few moments, cried out again, "Mary!"

Then, realizing that everyone on the floor would be laughing, he slammed himself down in bed and covered himself with bedclothes.

Later, after supper, he wrote her, apologizing, begging her to come the next day.

She did not answer for a few days. When she did, she explained that her request for another pass that week had been denied by both Miss Mitchell and Miss Valery in Patients' Aid. "But," she added, "I may try again next Monday." In a postscript she wrote, "I want to warn you, though. Somehow I feel that you and I are destined to be unhappy together. Our spirits are too similar in nature. We are both too fiery, too jealous."

The letter soothed him. He laughed at the postscript. He wrote, "Too much alike? Look, lady, I intend to marry a human being, not a cow. I intend to propose to a Mary, not to an Elsie."

When he went to sleep that night, a sudden thought roiled his calm. His diaphragm fluttered in his belly. For a man who still raised positive sputum he certainly had ambition.

Both were embarrassed when she came the next Monday. For the first time while having company he became aware of his roommates' ears and eyes.

But finally his benumbed brain did manage to suggest an idea. "Do you play cribbage?"

"Yes."

"Good. Huck, can we use your board?"

Huck nodded and the game was set up.

They played wordlessly for a while—he on his back, she on a chair close to his bed with her legs held primly together. He won the first game, she the next three.

It was almost five o'clock. The slanting sunlight fell sharply upon the white sheets and bedspread. The linen became golden. The hairs on his arms gleamed like myriads of tiny scimitars.

He took her hand. He whispered, hoping his roommates would not hear him, "Mary, it's terrible to think I can't see you more often."

She looked at him for a second; then shifted her glance to his forehead. The maneuver permitted her to read his eyes without seeming bold. "Can't you come to the movie Wednesday night?"

"No. I'm still strict bed."

"Lots of strict bed patients go."

"They do? Why, I didn't know that."

"Sure. After you've been here three months, and aren't too sick, you can go. Ask your doctor."

"Thunder, why don't they tell me these things? Did you always go?"

"Sure, though I had to wait my turn. There's only so

196

many litters for each floor and that means you can't go more'n once a month."

"But even once a month! Why, that's wonderful. I'll ask Dr. Abraham right away. Tomorrow morning, in fact."

She smiled, said, "Of course we won't have much time to talk there. Everybody's around."

"But to see you!"

She blushed a little. Then, looking at him directly for a moment, she asked, "Have you had a ride outdoors yet?"

"No."

"No ride? Doesn't your brother Ronald take you for a ride?"

"No."

"Didn't you know you could get a ride after you'd been here six months? What kind of deadbeat roommates have you got?"

He stared at her. He heard his roommates chuckle. "You mean we can ride together? Out there? We?" He leaned forward in bed to grip her arm.

"Well," she laughed, "ask Dr. Abraham."

"Holy Moses, why doesn't Miss Mitchell tell me about my rights? That bitch." Coloring, he added hastily, "Oh, I'm sorry."

She smiled slyly. "Maybe Miss Mitchell isn't sure you're ready for a ride yet."

"Huh." He gripped her arm again, "Mary, if I get permission, will you . . ."He paused. "Oh that's right. Ronald has no car."

She hesitated a moment. "I tell you. You get your permission, Mister, and tell me the date and hour, and I'll take you riding myself." She laughed. "I'll probably get kicked out of here for doing it, though."

"But why?"

"Patients aren't allowed to drive cars. But that's all right. I'll get my Uncle Peter to bring his car here and I'll drive it anyway."

"I don't know," he cautioned, "I don't know. We don't want to get you into trouble. But the ride . . . Mary, if

**197**

you're willing, I'll risk anything." He probed her eyes for a hint of reluctance. He could scarcely believe that shy Mary could be so forward all at once.

"All right."

"And can I meet your family? See the farmhouse?"

She shook her head. "No, not that. But I'll take you for a ride."

"But why not?"

"Well, maybe later. Maybe."

He narrowed his eyes.

She looked at him, glanced at his brows again.

Miss Mitchell came in. "It's five," she said, quickly glancing down to see where their hands were.

That evening he became a fervent disciple of yoga.

The sun went down like a sliced red beet, inflaming the western horizon.

He lay quietly. Beside him lay his roommates listening to the news broadcasts in their earphones. His heart swelled and emptied with soft slushing sounds. Slowly, slowly, he curbed his fires, herded them back into his temple.

There were a few struggles with Miss Mitchell before he got permission to attend the Wednesday evening movie. First, she said she had forgotten to give his request to Dr. Abraham. Eric threatened to crawl on his knees to the doctor's office. She delivered the request.

Second, on Wednesday afternoon, two hours before show time, she told him he would have to wait his turn. She had only three litters for the twelve patients eligible to go.

"Haven't they ever gone before?"

"Well . . . yes."

"Doesn't that put me ahead of them? I haven't gone at all yet, you know."

She colored. "Well, they had their requests in before you did."

He looked at her steadily. "I think I'll have you call

Dr. Abraham again. I'd like to have him take a look at your sense of justice."

Caught, she said, "Well, I'll see what I can do."

"Look, female, if I don't get a litter tonight, I'll go down there on my hands and knees."

"The love-bug has really bitten you, hasn't it?"

He said nothing.

The show was to begin at 7 p.m. At 6.45 Miss Pulvermacher, now on night duty, came in. "Ready?"

"Yes." He smiled. He could be pleasant to her now.

"Your sputum cup?"

"Yep."

"Where is it?"

"Here." He pulled out a flat receptacle he had invented for the occasion. He did not like the idea of trysting with a bulky cup beside him in the blankets.

She looked at it, nodded reluctantly, grumbling. She fluffed his pillows on the litter. She tied down a blanket. She shook her head a little, rustling her bristly hair. "Napkins?"

"Pocket's full."

"Well . . . all right. Get on."

She did not offer to help him. The effort tired him.

As she started him for the door his roommates sat up in their beds. They were happy for him, smiling, lending warmth from their fires. "Say hello to Mary," Fawkes said. Eric felt honored that Fawkes should like her.

Miss Pulvermacher pushed him down the hall. He was so happy he could overlook her foul breath, her pumping, knee-knocking legs.

They neared the elevator.

George opened the door for them, took the litter from her, and drew it into the elevator. The doors clanged. George took him up.

"We aren't going through Pleurisy Alley, are we?" Eric asked, referring to an odd aspect of the buildings. An alley separated the auditorium from the main building and an overpass connected the two structures on the third floor.

"No. We go over the top."

"That's quite a name, Pleurisy Alley."

George nodded and smiled impersonally. "But a guud one. The wind it blow like sixty through it."

Up on third, near the auditorium elevator, on which he was to descend, Eric found himself amongst tens of patients reclining in a sea of gray blankets and white pillows. Litters jostled each other like fat logs in a slow stream.

Eric studied the ailing ones. They were almost pop-eyed at the excitement of seeing people. They were hungry for attention. When he smiled at them, their faces almost ruptured in response.

And just as at the Pneumo line-up, these females seemed to be lazy queens riding royally upon their litters. Close up, however, and under the sharp hallway lights, he recognized the Cleopatra touches, the thick layers of powder and rouge and lipstick, the faintly hysterical grimace about the eyes, the twitching nostrils, the veined hands. He smiled at them.

He descended to the auditorium in another elevator. A pusher drew his litter out of the elevator, wheeled it about. People's faces whirled. He heard someone call out, "Take it easy, Caspar, you old lion-tamer. You ain't in the circus now."

Eric caught a glimpse of his pusher. The man had a reckless face. He gestured in the grand manner. His face had once been torn by claws.

There was a flutter of clothes about. From a wide doorway nearby with a sign above it reading, *Phoenix Emporium,* emerged many faces and robed creatures. Some were drinking pop and near-beer, some eating ice cream cones and candy bars. Their voices were edged with anxiety.

Some of the ambulant patients were dressed in streetwear, some in bedroom clothes; the women in housecoats, the men in ill-fitting bathrobes. Almost everyone had a sallow look, a heavy belly, and an unnaturally narrow chest. There were few normal-sized people. It was a sorry lot.

**200**

Fires there were but the fireplaces themselves had crumbled.

The pusher edged his litter through the pressing crowd, wheeled it across the asthmatic floor of the auditorium, and lined it up feet first against the backs of the last row of chairs.

Eric propped up his pillows and looked around. Some ambulant patients were already seated ahead in couples and groups. Compared to the narrow sides of his own room, the small auditorium with its buff window shades seemed as wide as a universe.

He was afraid of the crowd, of the curious eyes. He was afraid to read on the faces the histories of the tubercular wars.

A touch on the shoulder. He whirled. "Mary."

"Hello. You must've talked fast."

"And furious." He rested on his elbow, admiring her. Dressed in blue, her eyes had deepened. Her brow was grave. He held her hand. It was as comforting as Ma Memme's.

"Well . . . "

"Well . . . "

Eric said impulsively, "Well, Mary, tell me. I want you to tell me for sure now that you're free to see me, that you're not engaged to another man."

"Why?"

"Well, once I swore I'd never hurt a man by busting in on his woman. I did. So, if you're another's, then . . . "

She looked down at her toes. "Do you expect a woman to answer that question truthfully?"

"If she's a real woman, yes."

"Do you think there are any?"

"Sure. I'm looking at one."

She smiled. "And you? Are you free?"

"Yes. Oh yes." He looked at her. "So, you are free?"

"No."

"What?"

She jumped a little. "Oh. I mean, yes. Yes, I am."

The crowd bulged against their talk. They looked at each other, looked down.

"Yes?"

"I guess . . . "

A litter bumped into his, almost jostling his elbow from beneath his head. Ambulant patients swirled around them.

A sudden stream of light shot across the auditorium and hit the screen on the stage. The house lights went out. Blackness engulfed them.

He squeezed her hand in the darkness.

"I guess I'll have to go now," she whispered, releasing her hand.

"Yes. Will you come after the show?"

But she had vanished.

An hour later, when the lights went on again, he sat up to look for her. To his dismay, four heavily made-up women came up to his litter to talk.

He glared at them. Snippets. Male-hungry snippets. The nerve of them, breaking up his tryst with Mary. Deliberately he ignored them and looked for Mary.

He spotted her coming down an aisle to the right.

She saw him at the same time. She saw his female escort. Her eyes lighted with a question. She walked away. Fleetingly he caught a sly grimace curving her full mouth.

Tricks. Tricks. Women and their tricks. Holy Moses. He had no time for tricks. Either a woman came up to him frankly; or frankly she went away. But no Cleopatra tricks. Snippet! All women were snippets. Damn'em.

When he came back to his room his temperature was 104.6°. The blood in his veins had been replaced by flames.

With Miss Mitchell serving as the bearer of messages, Eric's request for a ride was refused.

When he asked to see Dr. Abraham in his office, he was refused again; and, moreover, was ordered to take sedatives.

**202**

A few days later when Dr. Abraham made his weekly round on First East with Miss Mitchell, Eric clutched at him with anxious eyes. "Doc?"

"Wait 'til your next X-ray."

"Why, Doc." Eric was stunned. The good man had nev er been this unfriendly. "What's eating you?"

Dr. Abraham's dark eyes held his steadily.

"Aw, cut the act, Doc. You look like hell trying to act tough."

Dr. Abraham growled.

"Do you really mean to tell me I've got to wait until my X-ray, two months more?"

"Exactly."

"But, holy Moses, Doc. I'll go crazy if I have to wait that long."

"You'll be all right.Take your sedatives."

"T'hell with the pills. Doc, I'm telling you I'll go crazy if I don't get a ride. Besides, if I don't get it, I'll take it anyway."

Dr. Abraham hesitated; then softened, "Well . . . well . . . I'll see. Give me a few days to think it over."

"Okay."

After a week of tremulous waiting for Eric, Dr. Abraham sent word that he still had not been able to make up his mind about the ride.

Eric settled his chin into his throat and ordered Miss Mitchell to bring up his suit from the locker-room.

She refused.

"Miss Mitchell, if you don't bring up my suit, I'll get my brother Ronald to bring me a suit of his. I'm telling you, if you people don't come across with that ride, I'll leave."

"Leave then. We've heard your threats before."

He glared at her; then tossed aside his sheets, and stood tottering beside his bed. He muttered, "I'll call Ronald on your telephone."

"Oh, but you can't do that."

"We'll see," he said grimly.

"Why . . . " she was breathless with fear. "You can't! Why, that's the nurses' line and the nursing staff will give me hail Columbia if a patient uses it."

"Good."

"I think I better report you to Dr. Abraham."

"Do that."

She hurried away.

He stood waiting, tottering by his bed. His soft feet flattened beneath his weight; the arches sagged. They cracked like knuckles snapping.

In a moment she came back. "Please lie down again, Mr. Frey. Please. We'll bring you down to see your doctor." She took a deep breath. "My! Such a trouble-maker. And I always thought you had some intelligence."

Eric, still standing, puffed a little, trembled, and nodded. Without a comment he turned about and fell on his bed.

Dr. Abraham twisted in his chair. "Eric, I can't let you go. I can't. Your case history doesn't warrant a trip outdoors yet. Look, my boy. First, here you've come so far. Why, you've even turned negative this . . ."

"Negative?"

"Yes, and . . ."

"Thunder. Negative?"

Dr. Abraham looked at him ruefully. "I shouldn't have said that, I guess. Well . . . Now, don't get excited. You may still throw a positive. Besides it's possible the lab technicians made a mistake."

"Oh, Doc, come now. Mistakes? Technicians?"

"Well . . . "

"Look, Doc. All I know is that I want to go. And I'm negative. Negative. Just think. I'm clean again. Clean. I feel like that leper Jesus healed. Ah, you can't hold me now. Please let me go."

"You want to lose all you've gained in one little fling?"

"Oh, Doc, I need it. Listen, Doc, I'm not going to a

whorehouse. I'm going out with a good girl."

"Hah."

"Sure. I'm not like those other guys who look forward to that first ride so they can go whoring again after all those months in bed. Not me."

"Hah."

"Please."

"No."

"Then, Doc, I'm going anyway."

"You'll lose the right to your bed."

"I don't give a damn. Look, Doc, I'm going to take that ride. And, I warn you that if I find some other bastard in my bed when I come back, there'll be trouble."

"I can have you arrested for such talk. I can force you to stay in bed. We have the law out here, too, you know."

"Go ahead. I don't care. This place has been a jail to me anyway."

Dr. Abraham leaned back in his chair and folded his hands. His eyes were rectangular with hurt. "Go then, you damned fool. Go."

"By God, I'll do just that. And I'm riding with Mary too. And alone."

"Hah."

"Doc, you see . . . Doc, she's so much to me. And I never yet had a chance to see her alone."

"Well . . . "

"It's not wrong to see her, is it, Doc? I mean, because of our TB? I'm not marrying her today."

Dr. Abraham laughed shortly. "You're sure a fast worker, aren't you, Eric?" He paused. "No, I guess there'll be no harm in it. Medicine doesn't approve of TB love affairs. But it really depends on who's involved. In some cases it's an advantage to both to have been ill. You'll understand each other's problems better."

"Then I can go?"

Dr. Abraham hesitated. "Eric man, you don't know how much I'd hate to see you battling this whole thing all over again for one little foolish hour."

"Doc, if I don't get that hour, there'll really be a foolish-ness around here." Then, softly, Eric said, "I need that hour, Doc. I've been penned up in that corner for almost a year now. Same sheets, same window, same tree, same hills, same sky, same fox squirrel, same nurses, same nightmares. Give me one hour of the world and I'll be happy for a while."

Dr. Abraham laughed. "You know, I'd sure hate to be the unwilling virgin you've decided to seduce."

"I can go, huh?"

"I don't know . . . You know, Eric, I've been sort of hop-ing I'd weaned you away from life a little."

"Me forget the outside? Doc, my memory is like a stone cut with inscriptions. I could never forget." He paused. "Besides, I've got too many arrows in my bow."

"All right, all right, go." Dr. Abraham grumbled. He fussed with his papers.

A pusher took Eric back to the elevator.

He returned to the room and hurriedly wrote Mary:

I've got the word. When can I see you? Where? What time? Can it be Saturday, St. Valentine's Day?

She replied:

Be ready at 3:25 p. m., Valentine. Have your nurse bring you to the door in back, the one that opens on Pleurisy Alley. And be five minutes early so the nurse'll have gone back to her floor before I come along. As I said before, patients are not supposed to be seen driving cars. Mary.

Exultant, he dipped into a five-dollar bill that a friend from the city had given him for spending money. He asked Calisto Sly to buy him a heart of candy.

St. Valentine's Day came cloudy, but he hardly noticed the overcast sky.

When he tried on his old suit, his roommates and Miss Berg laughed at his splitting trousers and vest. Even with his fly unbuttoned, his trousers barely covered his fat hips. His coat was too narrow across the back. His shirt collar

**206**

was a size too small. He was a fat giant crawling into a pigmy's suit.

With a foolish, nervous grin, he staggered into a wheelchair they had brought him. He dropped the valentine of candy into his pocket. He waved his roommates a good-bye and, a little dizzy, rode into the hall. It was a surprise to see the hallway from an upright position.

He tried to start a gossip with Miss Berg as she pushed him along toward Pleurisy Alley. But she had become cool. Curious, he looked at her; then looked down. Women were fighting over him already. He smiled.

He waited near the glass door for Mary. He watched the road nervously. Each approaching car upset him. His heart rumbled in his chest. He could count the pulse in his neck.

The fifth car was hers. But she did not stop. He managed to catch a glimpse of her face as she sped the V-8 Ford through the archway. There had been fear in her eyes as if she had suddenly seen some evil.

Eric looked around. There, across from him, on the other side of Pleurisy Alley, stood a civilian wearing a deputy sheriff's badge. He swore to himself. This was the law Dr. Abraham had referred to.

Eric considered. He bit his teeth. By God, not even the law was going to interrupt their rendezvous. He waved to the deputy.

Suspicious, the man came over. He was slight, had brown hair, and had eyes so closely set together that his nose seemed no wider than a pencil. "Yuh?"

"Say, my people don't seem to be coming for me today. And waiting here, it's making me hungry. Could you go across to the Emporium there and buy me a bar of candy?"

"Can't you walk?"

"No. I'm still strict bed. This is my first ride."

"Huh."

Eric became nervous. He wondered if Mary were implicated in some crime. She had always been so silent about her ways. Perhaps that accounted for her sad eyes. He peered up at the runty man. "Say, what's goin' on around here that we need a deputy?"

The deputy stared at him, stirred his jaw. "You're new here, huh?"

"Well . . . yes."

"Well, mister, this San here is full of toughs. It's a rest home for most of them Washington Avenue bums from Minneapolis."

"Oh."

"Yuh."

Eric stirred in his chair. This deputy, who stood talking as if he had just wetted his trousers, might catch Mary the next time she ventured through. "Say, you going to get me that bar?"

"Where's your nickel?"

"Oh. Oh yes." Eric flipped him a coin.

The man left.

And just then Mary spurted into the alley. She stopped so shortly that the car lifted up from its braked wheels. He hustled and stumbled himself off the wheelchair. He felt the skin on his belly ripping. He leaned through the door. He pulled along his clumsy feet. He drew them, bumping and crumbling a little, into the car. As he closed the door, he threw the box of candy onto the back seat.

She glanced at the box, smiled, said nothing, and sped swiftly away.

He was bewildered by the moving earth: bare trees, white-white snowbanks, white birches with black rings of peeling bark, gray grass-tufts. The earth whirled past him like a movie run off too rapidly. She drove so swiftly he felt like a fugitive.

He glanced back at the Phoenix. It was even larger than he had imagined. The edifice and its wings crested three small hills. Scattered groves of pine, oak, and clean birch surrounded it.

Two miles away, she slowed. She smiled, asking, "Like it?"

He breathed deeply. "Oh, Mary, it's a song. The song."

**208**

"Yes." She nodded. "Yes, that's what it is, all right. Yes. I'd almost forgotten how beautiful that first ride was."

He drew in another breath. "Thunder. That's the first good air I've had since I got in." He sighed so deeply that he shivered. "And that time I bet I stirred up a nest of moths in my lungs."

She laughed.

He remembered something. "Was that deputy waiting to catch you?"

"Yes. And any other patient out driving."

"That devil."

"Hadn't you heard of Deputy Brannon before? He's our police force. You see, a little city like the Phoenix needs policing too."

"So he said."

They drove on.

He looked at her closely. The blue ribbon in her hair, the bright red sweater, the blue skirt, sharpened the contrast between her pink lips and her gray-blue eyes. He looked at her. His eyes misted. Yes, a consuming disease might have crippled them, even shortened their lives; but they would touch eternity.

They drove on, slowly. Sometimes the car slipped on the icy pavement and the motor roared up.

He looked through the car window. Bare trees. Brown bark. Limbs that fumbled the breasts of clouds with numb fingertips.

He smiled. He did not need the sun today. Everywhere he looked the earth was clean and vital. Everywhere white snow curled in gentle eddies at the roots of trees.

Mary drove around a corner. She drove up a twisting, climbing lane. Branches of chokecherry bushes brushed the car. She shifted gears. The rear wheels spun. He chuckled to himself as he watched her expert clutching, her calculative eyes as she picked her way along the winding lane.

Soon they emerged from the chokecherry trees and were upon a hill. The car coasted over its summit a way, then stopped near a crossroad.

"There," she said, "there. This is the highest hill in the county. I thought . . ." She looked at him shyly.

"Mary, this is wonderful. Wonderful."

He sat wordless. He trembled.

She snapped on the dashboard radio. Over the wireless came a tune that entranced him.

"That's Tschaikovsky," she said.

"I know. Nowadays they call it *Tonight We Love.*"

A sad expression came into her eyes. It deepened them.

He could wait no longer. "I brought you something. It's there. I threw it there," he said, half-turning toward the package lying on the back seat, knowing that she would be turning too.

Her turning brought her face close to his. He kissed her.

He kissed her once again and recalled that he might still be positive.


## XXIII—DRIFTING

IN college, irascible Schopenhauer's ideas meant very little to Eric; they were mnemonics memorized to get a passing grade in philosophy.

This crab-slow winter he suddenly became curious about them. He had a vague remembrance that they might be similiar to his own current thoughts. Calling the San librarians, he had them bring him *The World As Will and Idea.* He read. He smelled deeply of the resinous fire. He ranged the dim vaults of the universe with the sage's lamp. When Schopenhauer lashed out wildly, he chuckled, and nodded his head in agreement.

It was on the idea of Will that Eric fastened most of his attention. As Schopenhauer used it, Will was not the mere whim to leave one spot to go to another. Basically it referred to animal powers, to the desire to stay alive, to the impulse to reproduce. It referred to the same process that today's science describes as the action of the sun's energy

210

upon, and afterwards within, the elements on the surface of the earth. The earth happens to be, among millions of other interstellar lumps, the one clod that has settled into a point in space favorable for such an action. And, after millions of years, the once inert but now activated elements are constantly channelling themselves into creatures, both plant and animal. The inner forces that move these creatures, that make them hungry, that cause them to eat their neighbors, Schopenhauer saw as manifestations of his notion of Will. Thus Schopenhauer, it seemed to Eric, had come a step closer to seeing the real nature of things on earth than had Hegel, Kant, Fichte, and many another philosopher before and during his time.

Eric pondered the theory. He related it to himself. He fingered through the ashes of his life. He himself had been at the mercy of this impersonal energy. He had stumbled through life, drunken with dreams, eating here-there, running after every butterfly and rolling apple with a child's curiosity and a grown man's energy. Only once had he sat long enough in one spot to write a book. And when the energies around him had begun to close over him like jungle humus, swallowing and engulfing his shout, when the Whipper had closed in for the kill, he had not fought back fiercely enough. He had sunk from view. His intellect had not been strong enough to tower above his times and his people like a totem pole. He had not been able to generate enough light to impress his neighbors. He had lacked the power to hang onto his piece of the garment of life with which the earth had been clothed. It was only when he had become a diseased hulk and dangerous to his neighbors that he had been snatched up out of the dark night of evolution and had been singled out for brotherly care.

He lay reflecting. Now that he was beginning to understand a little what the true fabric of reality might be, he was also beginning to understand why he, like Schopenhauer, had become interested in yoga, had pondered on how he could leave this cut-and-wound-anguished life called sansara, had wanted to enter nirvana.

211

He mused. Five years from now, his wounds healed against the world, he would probably once more allow himself to be at the beck of this impersonal will, his skull still as ever a vast black night of ignorance where occasional thoughts twinkled like tiny fireflies. Schopenhauer and his ideas would have vanished.

He smiled as he remembered how one of his college professors, an earnest man, had tried desperately to prove Schopenhauer mistaken. The professor had combed the dark heavens for his proofs. But he had found no flaming meteoric rebuttals—perhaps because he had been too fastidious, for a man had only to see what happened to the food he ate to smell the story Schopenhauer described.

From Schopenhauer he went to Nietzsche. He read *Thus Spake Zarathustra*. He read how Nietzsche, also a sun-worshiper, had failed in health, in love, in profession. It was at once soothing and wrenching to relive the misunderstood philosopher's sorrows. With a shiver he realized that if his own life did not straighten out, he too might begin compensating by dreaming up what he was not.

Eric mused. He stared out of the window. He watched the gray days of February become the blustery days of March. He brooded. He dragged along, a fossil in an inert bog.

And slowly the speck disappeared. Sometimes it did not come for a week. Sometimes it came vague and almost colorless.

And every day he warmed himself with the memory of that St. Valentine's Day with Mary. She had accepted his kiss and his heart of candy like a little girl given longed-for treasures. She had opened her trembling hands and had taken the gifts. For a moment the sadness in her eyes had been erased. With a possessive gesture she had clasped the treasures to her breast and had been happy.

# O
## XXIV—THE DOOR OPENS AGAIN

NE DAY, the second week in March, Dr. Abraham came in.

Eric pushed aside his shot-bags and sat up. "Doc, I'm ready for the wheelchair privilege."

"Oh?"

"Yep. Open up that black book of yours and write it down . . . so Miss Mitchell won't get confused when I give her the high sign."

"Pretty cocky, huh?"

"Well, all I know is that my sputum's been negative for two months, that I've gained about a hundred pounds, that I don't have nightmares no more."

"No nightmares?"

"Not one." He grinned. "Well?"

Dr. Abraham placed his hand gently on Eric's shoulder. "Well, my boy, maybe your spirit is ready, but . . . your flesh is not."

Eric shook off the hand. "I don't get it."

"You wouldn't want to infect a dozen housemates again, would you?"

"What a question. Of course not."

"I guess you don't know then that all the boys in your house on Hickory street came up with positive Mantouxs while you were there, do you?"

"No."

"Well, they did. The University tested them right after you left."

Eric paled. He stared at the doctor. And he suddenly recalled that in college days he too had had a coughing roommate. They had often brewed a midnight cup of coffee together.

"Yes, my boy. Even if I didn't give a damn about getting you safely to your feet, I'd still have to think about others." He paused. "I told you it was touch and go. Tougher'n any struggle you could name. In the action of battle, a soldier's mind is often obliterated. But here, in this cold-blooded siege, it is not. A mind is a millstone here. I know. I was in a World War and a TB war, both."

Eric's tongue became numb. He could see the faces of his old housemates, of Jack Upham who had found his bugs. He could see Jack's heart and veins guggling with infected blood. Had Jack already joined the long row of lungers down the hall?

Dr. Abraham relented. "Well, I tell you, Eric. First, if your next sputum test is still negative; and second, if your X-ray next week looks good, I'll give you the wheelchair privilege."

Eric nodded, hardly noting the promise.

"Remember now. Put those shot-bags back on your chest there and take the cure."

"Yes, doctor."

Then, an evening, the door opened. Dr. Abraham came in. His dusky eyes gleamed. Something momentous had come. "Well, how do you feel?"

"Oh, pretty good, I guess."

"Yes, but how do you feel?"

"Well, hell, Doc, what do you want me to say?"

"You're sure you *feel* all right?"

"For God's sake, yes."

"Good, I just came in to tell you: first, that your sputum is still negative; second, that your X-ray was good. We still can't see through the pleura or behind that fluid where your cavity is supposed to be, but it looks good. So . . . well, I tell you. First, tomorrow you can start sitting on the edge of your bed. Second, next week you can sit on a chair while they make your bed. The week after, you can use a wheelchair whenever they cart you around in the building."

Eric stared. He saw Fawkes sit upright in his bed, his face alight with joy. Huck, too, for the moment, was smiling.

"And . . . say, how are your legs? Thin, huh? Well, be careful with 'em. With all that new weight, you're probably

214

going to have a lot of trouble with your arches. A hundred pounds, you said, huh? Well that's good. Let's see your belly." Dr. Abraham pushed back the blankets and the San-made blue-striped pajamas. He pointed at the tube-like folds on Eric's belly. He patted them possessively as if he had grown them there himself. He chuckled. "Well, well. Just remember now to expect the worst. That you're just giving your body a tryout. Just remember that all we've done is set up a delicate balance between your body's resistance and your TB. That now we're going to try to sneak up on this balance without disturbing it, try to divert a little energy into your legs, gradually filling 'em out. And that all the while we're going to hold the wrestling pair, your resistance and TB, to a tie." He patted Eric again; then left.

Eric turned to his roommates. In Huck's eyes he saw envy mixed with joy. He tried to hide his pleasure.


# S XXV—THE FOETUS STIRS

PRING CAME. Easter. Old Lady Poplar covered her stiff limbs with gay, trembling leaves.

May came. Sparrows laid eggs.

Following the next favorable X-ray report, Dr. Abraham prescribed a new work-up routine for Eric. The first two weeks he could walk to the bathroom once a day. The second two weeks, twice. The third two weeks, thrice; until, at the end of eight weeks, at the Full Bath stage, he could leave his bed, but not the First East floor, as often as he wished.

The first steps were an agony. His arches had fallen. His back muscles had weakened. His neck cords had become slack.

To add to the confusion, he discovered one day that his right leg was shorter than the other. With all of his body muscles relaxed, it had now become apparent.

It was Huck who noticed it. "Say, why in hell's name don't you try standin' up straight once, huh?"

"Why, I do."

"The hell you do, brother. You walk like a dog runs. Sideways."

Eric hid his irritation. He said quietly, "Well, I did notice that my right pajama leg drags a little."

Just then Dr. Abraham came in. "What's up, Eric?"

"Why, Huck says I walk crooked."

"Oh? Take off your jacket." Dr. Abraham stood back, sizing him up. "You do lean over, all right, Like Pisa's Leaning Tower. Let's see, let's push this. No, that won't do it. Well, try this. No, that either. Huh."

Huck chuckled. "Sell him to the Arabs, Doc. With all those humps, he'd make a good camel."

Despite the barb in Huck's words, Eric grinned. He knew he looked lumpy. When he thought he was standing straight, his left hip stuck out like a misplaced potbelly.

It was only after Dr. Abraham had placed an inch-thick book under his right heel that the planes of Eric's body finally fell into straight lines.

Dr. Abraham stood back, exclaiming, "Well, I'll be damned. You have got a short leg, by a good inch."

Eric thumped his heel down on the book. Yes, now his body really felt relaxed.

Dr. Abraham narrowed his eyes. "You say you played basketball?"

"Yes."

"Ever feel odd on the floor? Awkward?"

"Awkward? Say, I was as clumsy as a camel. People used to come to the games just to see me thunder to the floor."

"Backaches?"

"Always. On the farm, I could never understand why other farmers could husk corn all day long without getting a backache."

"Sure. Lordosis. Well, only thing to do is to build up the heel."

216

"A higher heel? Seems to me I ought to cut down the left one. I'm always just bumping the door."

They laughed.

Huck offered, "Why build a heel any higher than it is."

Eric bit his tongue.

Dr. Abraham sobered. He glanced at Huck. "Eric, don't you ever get tired of us normal people?"

"Well . . . not really. You see, I feel normal myself."

Dr. Abraham gripped his arm. "Well! I guess that fixes that."


But Huck continued to snap.

Eric was putting on his Pa-given pantofles for the first time when Huck remarked, "Well, Fawkes, if we get flooded out of here, I know where we can get some rowboats."

Another time, after Eric had cracked his head against the overhead doorstop, Huck cracked, "Holy hell, the Lord God sure piled it high when he made you, didn't he?"

Again, when Patient's Aid surprised Eric with a gift, a long blue bathrobe, Huck growled, "Teacher's pet."

Eric glared at him a moment. He had an impulse to call Huck a jealous sickling. But he turned away instead. And sighed. If Huck only knew how considerate he tried to be; how each morning, after the nurse had carried out Huck's and Fawkes' bedpans, he had deliberately coached himself to re-enter 176 as though the room was as sweet as roses.

He comforted himself with the thought of the new privileges. The new rights would permit him to get away from his roommates. It would be a pleasure to see new faces.


# XXVI–ADVENTURE

I T WAS TIME to adventure again. The spacious world of the First East hallway beckoned him. Behind each closed door lay disease-numbed patients, once nomads, lonely now in their ailing hours for the oldtime wandering days. Within the First East bathroom stood bowed and cautious convalescents who each morning joined in cynical talk while awaiting their turns. From where had they come? What wondrous tales would they tell of themselves? Once more he was a boy, asearch through the world for the good uncle or aunt. He was afoot in a meadow where the secrets of the Universe lay waiting like speckled eggs in hidden nests.

Now that he had turned his face away from the solitude of his room, from the pained and envious eyes of his roommates, he wondered when and where he would find the Whipper again. He had yet to see Him in his ward. Would He be lurking in some bush to which he might come aberrying, mouth and hand astain with the purple of juice? He had no doubt that the cunning Whipper was near, perhaps hiding behind some mask of a face in the hallway or bathroom. Eric prepared himself for a new manifestation.

As Dr. Abraham had predicted, many of the patients that Eric met had lost the spiritual battle.

There was Judge Cripps, an irascible, seventy-year-old man who sat every morning on a high stool, welcoming each furtive, bowel-rumbling ambulant to the bathroom forum with derisive remarks. He explored them for their motives and prejudices. He jabbed into them with a pitiless tongue.

He was called the Judge because, perched all crabbed and hunched upon his stool, and puffing like an angry Mt. Olympus, he hurled his judgements upon the near-dead with all the bigotry of a magistrate who forgets that but two moments before he himself had removed from off the mouth of a toilet his sorry, wrinkled bottom.

Except for a circlet of nicotine-stained white hair that caught at the approaches to his dome, he was bald. He had cruel lips, cruel eyes. And he had been crippled by an arthritic condition that had bent his feet and hands into crab claws.

The Judge hated women. Sometimes he defended Hitler because he had relegated women to their proper role of "baking bread and being bred." The Judge had reached the age of impotence. He could look at sex with a cool eye.

Cripps laughed at success. He cursed ambition. He coughed and spat and disobeyed all the health rules.

Though he was hated by the patients on the floor, Eric was interested in him. Maybe the Judge did not have a very clear fire in his skull, but at least he had an ember.

And because Eric had a ready smile for him, the Judge had, in return, a ready offer of liquor and cigarettes. The Judge carried a bottle of whiskey in one pajama pocket and an endless chain of cigarettes in the other.

"How about a slug, young feller?"

"No. Not today. A little later."

"Huh. That's funny. And you looked as if you might have some intelligence."

Eric shrugged and laughed.

"Godalmightychrist," the Judge roared, "you don't mean to tell me you believe everything that old fogy Abraham tells you, do you?"

"Well, Judge, don't you? Else what the hell you doing here if you don't?"

The Judge looked down, muttering.

Eric smiled.

The Judge coughed, spat in a washbowl, and asked, his lips drawn into a crafty smile, "How about a cigarette then?"

"No."

"Don't tell me you had the will power to quit?"

Again Eric grinned. "No. No. I was just too damned sick to want to smoke. Lost the taste for it. And now, I haven't got enough guts to start again."

"Ah, ha! That's better. Fellows, I drink to an honest man." The Judge lifted his bottle, wiped his lips, snorted once, drank, belched.

The other bathroom senators did not understand the Judge. They snickered at his talk. And they looked at Eric strangely, as if they thought he, too, was squirrelly.

Soon Eric discovered the secret of the Judge. A visiting newspaperman friend, a court reporter, recalled that Cripps has been disbarred from law practice. One day, on an impulse, Cripps had been honest enough to admit his underworld connections. He had been reviled. He lost his business. Had starved. Had broken down with tuberculosis.

Eric nodded to himself. He knew what the Judge was doing. With no hope of ever leaving the San alive, he was trying to amuse himself in his remaining hours with ridicule, cigarettes, whiskey, and last testaments.

Another man in the bathroom, a former workman, Maurie Knecht, tall, cautious, had a quality that Eric instinctively liked. Knecht had not lost his battle.

"How come you don't smoke, or drink?" Eric asked as they stood side by side, washing their faces.

"Well, it won't do me any good, will it?" Knecht paused, went on. "You see, I'm gonna get outa here. So I'm obeyin' all the rules, mister."

"You're a courageous man, Knecht."

Knecht shook his head. "Not at all. I'm just scared. I hate dying, hate being sick, hate TB, hate nurses. I'm too scared to do anything except what the doc tells me."

Eric nodded.

"I'm anxious to get back to my family."

"Oh?"

"Yeh. My two boys. An' my wife. Boy, it'll be wonderful to be back agin', earnin' my own way, growin' up the kids. Boy."

"How long you been here?"

"Three years."

"Got it bad?"

"Both lungs."

"How do you manage to take it so calmly?"

Knecht laughed nervously. "I . . . ain't so calm, mister.

Why, from Monday morning to Saturday noon, I lay tight as a fiddle-string in my bed, sweatin' an' puffin'."

"Oh?"

"Yeh. I always feel guilty them days. You see, them're my workin' hours an' I feel guilty takin' it so easy. Saturday noon comes, an' Sunday, an' why! hell, then I'm all right again. Because nobody else's workin' then, see?"

Eric quickly looked down. He blinked his eyes.

One man frightened Eric.

Bud was thin, blond, freckled. He smiled like the Sphinx. He was a veteran of and a malingerer in the first World War, an amateur artist, and a morphine addict. Though he had been broke and jobless since War I, he had always managed to get his Miss Emma by playing the gigolo. Now as an inmate, despite the postman, doctors, nurses, despite restrictions on his visitors, he still managed to get all the slumber shots he wanted.

Every day he turned down Dr. Abraham's earnest appeals to try the turkey cure.

Eric shivered whenever the man came near him. Perhaps a man could not be blamed for trying to hide himself from the Whipper, but to escape into a swamp where writhing water-moccasins became darlings—God, no!

A small man, Jerk Sneed, who had quick rolling eyes, and who posed constantly in the Sullivan fighting-stance, was forever wanting to do a round with Eric. Jerk claimed Eric "must a been a dumb cluck all his life or else he'd a known how to make some kale wit' that frame a his, boxin' er somethin'." Snorting, Jerk said, "I figger I kin take on the Big Boy myself, because the bigger they come the harder they fall."

Eric was tempted to grab the runt by the rump and hurl him out of the window. But he remembered Dr. Abraham's demonstration of the easily torn paper napkin. And Eric, laughing at the Whipper for being so obvious, decided on another tack.

One morning, when the forum senators were assembled and the Judge was on his throne, Eric went to work.

Sneed had said, as he was drying his face, "You know, you never see a Jew woman takin' a common job, like mop-woman, er so. Them Jews, they're sure to get the best there is."

Eric said, "That's because the Jews are home-builders. Most of their women make careers out of being mothers."

Sneed, surprised at seeing a spark in the dumb cluck, slowly let out his breath. He stared. "Well!" Snorting and looking down at his feet, he blustered, "Well, yeh, I guess you're right about that. Yeh." Sneering and plunging on, he added, "They sure do know how to breed kids, don't they? Them bastards. They breed like rabbits. Fust thing you know, they'll be all over, an' shovin' us out a our country. Just watch. Mark my words. I know. You'll see."

"Oh hell, Sneed, they don't breed any faster than those ignorant Irish or Swedes or Germans in your family."

Again Sneed's face was broken up by a startled look. "Well!" He snorted. "But dammit, a Jew is a dirty bastard. Dirty. Them Jews . . ."

"Not any dirtier than the dirty Swedes, Norwegians, Germans, Dutch, English, and Slovaks living around your Seven Corners in Minneapolis."

"Well, dammit to hell, but a Jew, he's crooked. He's a crooked businessman."

"Sneed, are you tryin' to tell me that all other business-men have morals?"

"Well . . . a Jew, he ain't got no conscience."

"And everyone else has? Try again. You'll find the good and the bad wherever you look."

"Well . . . at any rate, a Jew's a dirty sneak."

"Aw, hell, Sneed, what you really mean is that the Jew is smarter than you. Hell, man, admit it. Centuries of perse-cution by little Hitlers like you has hepped up the Jew, made him sharper. He's had to be sharp or he'd 've died out."

"Say, you a Jew-lover?"

"No. Nor his hater. I like everybody."

Sneed stammered. He stumbled about on his legs. He rolled his eyes. He balled his fists. He stared up at Eric towering over him. He reconsidered. He turned and stood staring out of the bathroom window.

Just as Eric was about to leave the bathroom, Sneed flashed around, spat, "Probably you don't know it, but it's the Jews who own all them houses around Seven Corners, and they're the ones who really make them poor whites live like dogs."

"Bull."

"Well, I know for a fact that it's a Jew what built that wobbly bridge down there by Seven Corners. By cheatin' on his contract. An' as sure as I'm standin' here, that bridge is goin' down some day, loaded with people. White people, too. Them Jews, they don't care fer nuthin' but profit."

The Judge broke it up. "Aw, Sneed, why don't you shut up. You haven't got any brains anyway. The only possible excuse the good Lord could have had for givin' you a head was to let your stomach use it as a periscope."

There were two men who both intrigued and repelled Eric. He had heard vague and uncomfortable rumors about Pinky Bones and Hairlip Borst long before he met them. Once roommates, and now separated because they had been caught in the act of Grecian love, they held timid trysts in the bathroom despite the senators.

Pinky was a mild, excessively silent fellow, thirty years old, and fat.

Hairlip was near forty and noisy. He exacted noticeable satisfaction from the phrase, "Shoot the bean-ball to me, Fatty" and from "What you need, kiddo, is to have somebody give you a first class job of lovin'."

A careful eye was kept on the two by the nurses, who feared that some day they would come upon them in the midst of some loathsome mingling. Though the touch of men irritated Eric, even the touch of some women, he felt sorry for these two lost souls with their addled genes.

223

One day he heard Hairlip say to Pinky, "Kiddo, you should have seen me take that bitch for a ride. She was a dumpy floursack, but oh, so lonesome. I had her hangin' on. I fooled with her. Then, just when it came time to sport her, I laughed in her face an' left her. Boy, was she mad. Kiddo."

Eric thought to himself: when minority groups get a chance to be cruel, they become first class whippers.

The cure-taking rules, Eric was sure, had been devised by the Whipper. An irrepressible impulse to break them bubbled, worked like yeast, in him. Forbidden to visit patients in their rooms, he swore he would see them anyway. He waited until evening when only the night nurse was on duty. With all the glee of a boy on a night-prowl, he dressed stealthily in his blue bathrobe and pantofles, peered through the door down the hall to make sure that the nurse was out of sight, then stumbled quickly across the hall into the room opposite, and sat down to enjoy the stolen fruit.

From one room to another he went. He found some patients gray, and in their last hours, and prone, and gasping whenever they stirred a little. He found some asleep. He found some mending perceptibly. All were eager for talk.

Frenchy Le Clerc roomed with the Judge. He was bedridden. The boys called him Canuck. He was from Canada.

Outside the Phoenix, Frenchy had been a decent citizen. He had been a railroad carpenter, kept his bills paid up, and treated his wife well.

Inside the San, however, he had gone to pieces, defying the institution's discipline. When he felt hungry for a woman, he would stagger out of his bed to the nearest phone and call a whore to the amusement of his roommate, Judge Cripps, and the consternation of the nurses. When the nurses caught him and sounded an alarm, he would lift his black bushy brows to ask, "Jealous, Tootie?"

One day Eric said, "Frenchy, you fool, don't you know you're hastening His coming?"

Frenchy laughed. "When it comes time for a man to die, he dies. Me, I want some wimmen before I go. I still got some ginger left."

Judge Cripps, who had been listening, snorted and returned to his newspaper to hunt for the death notices of friends and enemies.

Eric laughed, and reflected that Frenchy had about as much light in his skull as an aged bull.

In the next room down the hall lived Turtleface, a creature who never talked. He was an appetite out of the jungle. Calisto Sly called him Mister Slop Barrel, because no matter how much or how little food was left on Calisto's food-truck, Turtleface was willing to clean it up.

One noon Eric peered in at the door to watch the monster eat. His wide bottom straddled the width of the bed. His slab-flat belly and back and broad head rose like an up-ended turtle out of the snow-white sheets. His mouth opened and clamped together like a mechanical device. Great piles of food disappeared into the devouring and snapping hole at the top. The eyes blinked slowly, impassively. Sometimes vague subterranean rumbles stirred the massive bulk.

With Turtleface lived a gunman, Whitey. He hadn't a chance of surviving. His lungs were as porous as a pound of cheese tunneled by a dozen rats. A bystander could hear the tattered ends of his lungs fluttering in his chest. He slept with his fingers tensed around his gat.

Sometimes Whitey gave the boys on the floor spreads of beer and wine and whiskey, and candy and fruit; and sometimes even a woman when they wanted it.

When Whitey heard that Eric was a writer, he said, "Write me up, bub, an' you'll have a best seller. There's more wars an' whores, an' dead bodies in my life, than in any play Shakespeare ever wrote."

There were few that Eric disliked. Johnson Jones, the black sheep member of the bathroom forum, was one.

Johnson Jones always entered the bathroom wearing an aggrieved expression. He took off an old worn bathrobe, hung it beside the other robes behind the door; and then, sighing, as if all men in the world were fools except himself, began his toilet.

The forum senators knew he was waiting for someone to mention the word TB. One morning Eric accidentally mentioned it.

Instantly Johnson Jones fastened himself onto Eric. "TB, huh? I know what that is all right. Huh." His eyes became feverish, fanatical. "Boy, do I."

"Oh?"

"Sure. Look at me."

"Yes. Well?"

"Do I look sick?"

"Not that I can see."

"Yeh. Yeh. Sure. You wouldn't know then that I was the worst case a TB that ever came in here. Just absolutely the worst. There was never nobody worse. Nobody."

"I didn't know the San was a racetrack."

"Huh? . . ." He smiled feebly. "Oh, I getcha. Well . . . no, I didn't mean it that way." He paused. "Just the same, I was the worst case to ever come in here. Worst. An' look at me now. Strong. Muscles like a smithy, full a pep, clear eyes . . ."

". . . an' an empty head," interrupted the Judge, snorting, belching, and tippling at his whiskey.

"Huh? Oh. Yeh. Yeh. Well, as I was sayin', I was the sicken'est man to ever come in here. Cavity as big as a tennis ball on this side, an' another as big as a golf ball on this side. Sixty pounds underweight. An' . . ."

"About to pup," snickered the Judge.

"Huh?"

"Godalmightychrist," shot the Judge, "What the hell is sixty pounds? Why, Big Boy, here, has gained more'n a hundred pounds."

226

"Huh?"

"Hell, yes," growled the Judge, lighting another cigarette and scratching his seat.

For a moment Johnson Jones was stopped. He shagged about the bathroom, puffing.

But he recovered and, rolling up his shirt sleeves and patting his powerful forearms, continued, "Well, as I was sayin', I was almost dead. An' now look at me. I'm like a tiger, a lion. Strong. An' why?"

"And why?" sneered the Judge.

"Because I take Dr. Garrison's antigen. It saved me. These doctors here . . .bah, they've closed their minds." Johnson Jones' voice rose to a whining, persecuted pitch. "They're out to get me. An' Dr. Garrison, too, an' him a great saver a mankind from TB. It's a good thing Dr. Garrison retired, or they'd a wrecked his practice." He cried. "Why, if they'd let us, he an' I could save every man in this room here. Everyone. Just let us get you a bottle of this antigen, an' a hypo needle. All you do is hold the needle over a match to purify it an' then give yourself a hypo. That's all there's to it. Next thing you know, you're as strong as a lion. Just like me. Strong." He became sad. "Oh, if only the doctors here'd only let us save you fellers. But they won't. They're afraid our cheap cure will work, an' ruin their fine-salaried jobs. They're out to get us."

Afterwards, Eric questioned Fawkes about the man.

Fawkes laughed. "How big a hole did he say he had now?"

"Tennis ball."

"Yeh. Well, it used to be as big as a pingpong ball. I used to spend hours with that guy, pulling his leg. I'd get him to tell me his condition, and so on. And so help me, no matter how many times I'd ask him, he'd tell it to me all over again."

Eric nodded.

"It's too bad about such fellows. He's been in awe of his well-being ever since he had his close-shave with death."

"But are you sure his cure's no good?"

"Why, the lab men here've given the stuff to guinea pigs. It kills them off. Why, he's induced about twenty other fellows into trying it. They all died."

"All of 'em?"

"Every one. Perhaps not in every case from the antigen. But at least it didn't help a solitary one."

Eric jumped. "And the San lets him run around?"

"Well, as long as he's on the cure, they can't send him home."

"He still positive?"

"Sure."

"Holy Moses, and I washed in the bowl he used without rinsing it with disinfectant."

## H XXVII—A LANE AND A PASTURE

**H**IS LIFE-WAY spiraled upward, a sweeping bolero. Every two weeks his way began to take on greater sonority. His life began to have depth, to have sweep. In each new movement he found new notes of delight, new lyric tones, new alto murmurings.

Upon his third privilege, he began to walk to the weekly movie. For months Mary and he had dreamed of strolling together through the hallways and the alleys, of standing in the summer's warmth beneath the cool archway of Pleurisy Alley, of entering the movie and sitting deliciously excited in the dark. Now the day had come. They fitted their steps into a strolling rhythm. He discovered she was tall, and that as a couple they were well-matched. As he walked about with her, he wondered if any other human beings with death entombed in their chests had ever dared to choose each other for mates. What could half-rotted, half-defeated lovers expect from each other?

At the movies they sat pressing close to each other, sometimes neglecting the fiction on the screen to kiss in the shadows. She pressed close, flushing; he pressed near, blood trembling in veins.

The bolero opened, swirling, expanding, the tense strings searing, the clarinets lifting.

Then a new strain entered. Mary was leaving.

She had passed all the tests: X-ray, gastric lavage, physical, guinea pig. They had given her a lecture on the life hereafter; warning her to seek easy work, to break up each twenty-four hours with two sleeps, to get her pneumothorax treatments with clock-like regularity, to avoid excitement, to banish all thoughts of motherhood. She was "free."

Eric was upset. To him the Phoenix was a large family, where jealous brothers and sisters spied on their lovemaking. And now she was going, leaving him to fend for himself against the prying relatives.

And yet he was happy too; as a worldling she could see him every afternoon if she wished. The charge nurse could not pass on her coming, nor punish her if she stayed a minute too long.

*Going home.* What epic words they must be for her, he thought enviously. Epic words. Song words. She could be with Benny the fox squirrel now. Free. Freedom woman.

On the afternoon she was to leave, she came to bid him good-bye. He was alone when she came. Both Fawkes and Huck had been taken to the bathroom for shampoos.

She came in hesitantly; and as always, smiling a little, yet with the grave ways that accentuated the sadness in her eyes. She fingered a wild rose. A light-blue ribbon set off the brown of her hair. As she settled on the foot of his bed, he caught hints of child gestures in the movement.

He wished she had leaped to embrace him when she saw he was alone. "Your Uncle Pete here with the car?" he asked.

"Yes. And we've got my stuff all loaded up. I . . ." she hesitated.

"Yes?"

"I wish you could go too. It's cherry time."

"Yes." He paused. He wanted to tell her to kiss the cherries for him but he was afraid she would laugh at him. He held back. The winds coming over the hill would have the smell of blue pasture in them. The grass would be purple at the roots. And the sun would be shining in the manes of the black stallions and glistening in the tails of the red mares. He swallowed and blinked his eyes. "What'll be the first thing you'll do when you get home, Mary?"

"See Rebecca."

He started. "Rebecca?"

"She's a young filly Uncle Pete owns. Beautiful, with doe's eyes, and a yellow mane and tail, and a red coat. A lovely filly. No stallion has ever touched her."

He was amazed to notice that their minds could talk without speech. "Oh? Life says one shall."

"Oh no."

He laughed.

Her eyes fired.

He envied her. She would be visiting the streets of the village. She would be seeing the faces of normal people again. "Aren't you glad to be going?"

"Yes, I guess I am. These people here, they make me feel gray inside."

Again he started. Was his mind hers that she should know it so well? "I know."

She looked through the window. The trees waited in the hot sun. "But then, living with Uncle Pete in the country isn't going to be anything to shout about either."

"But Mary, at least you'll be in the country."

"Well, maybe that doesn't mean much to me."

He asked gently, "What's wrong at home, Mary?"

"Nothing."

"Tell me."

She rattled her red-polished nails. "It's really none of your business."

"I'm sorry. I didn't mean . . . you don't understand."

He reached for her. "Kiss me. No one's here. Look. Kiss me."

230

She leaned away from him.

She puzzled him. She had the country-girl way of staring directly at him. But when he looked at her, she glanced away as if she couldn't stand the light. Just where did the red nails and the carmine lips of the flapper fit into her character? He narrowed his eyes, considering her. He began to understand that he had a blind spot when it came to women. When they frowned, or sulked, he was upset. He did not want them behaving as troubled human beings; perhaps because he had no sisters and because he had not known his Ma Memme long enough to learn that she was human too.

Again he reached forward. She escaped him. He crawled along the length of his bed and held her. She laughed and looked down. He touched her lips. Then he drew back, startled. "Mary."

She blushed.

"What have you been up to?" he demanded.

"Just . . . celebrating."

"Yes, but . . . I thought it was sort of understood that we'd never break the cure or the rules unless we two together . . . unless . . ."

She said nothing.

"Mary, I didn't know you drank."

"What's the harm in a little wine?"

"Nothing, really. It's that we had an idea together." He became angry. "Tell me. Where? Tell me."

She stood up.

"Mary. Look. Get this once and for all. When I agree to an idea, I mean it. When I say 'yes' I mean 'yes'."

She broke a little. "Yes."

"Now. Tell me. What happened?"

"I don't know. I really don't know. It just . . . happened."

"Oh." He drew in his breath nervously. He recalled Martha. "Mary, who was there? Tell me."

"A girl. A girl and a man."

"And?"

"Oh, I don't see what that's got to do with it anyway."

"Another man?"

Reluctantly she said, "Yes."

"Who?"

"Eric, I was born under a vine. I like wine."

"So do I. So do I. But that's not what we're arguing about. It's the idea we had of ourselves. That we'd always do things together. A pair."

"Yes."

"Tell me. Who was it?"

"Deeble."

"Satan?"

"What's wrong with him? Besides, he thinks you're swell."

He stammered. He swallowed. He could see Deeble and her walking along, holding hands.

She got up to go.

"Good-bye."

"Good-bye."

She was gone.

He lay silent. He watched the July sunlight upon Old Lady Poplar's glistening leaves. He watched the sunshine glinting in the drying grass on the mall. Some day, he thought, some other wonderling would come across her strange moody flame, and desire it too.

Abruptly he pulled out paper and pencil, wrote her a long letter, regretting the soured parting, urging her to visit him soon.

As he was about to seal the envelope, he thought of something. He could see her even more privately than he had this afternoon. She had a car. While the other patients went to the cinema next Wednesday night, he could escape from the Phoenix for a couple of hours and ride with her in the country.

He added a postscript. He told her he would stroll down the hall at 6:30 p.m. as though he were on his way to the auditorium with the others and then, stealthily, would let himself out by the side door off Main East, would wait in the blue shadow of the Norway pine near the winding highway until she came. "You see, Mary," he added, "you are my life to me."

She came. He was standing near the blue pine, fingering its needles, smelling its tangy resin, scuffing the grass and the cone-studded earth with his pantofles.

She came unexpectedly swift, breathlessly. He had no time to see whether Deputy Brannon was about. He only knew she was upon him, that the car came to a quick stop, that the door opened, that there was a sudden smell of burnt rubber and oil and dust, that she was wearing a blue ribbon and a pair of blue slacks, that when he looked up, they were rising and dipping swiftly over the hills near Lake Minnetonka.

"Mary, can I see your farm?"

Smilingly, she shook her head.

"Can I?"

"You don't care to see my family."

"Mary. I do."

"No, I'm sure you don't."

They breasted another hill, rose on it, slipped effortlessly down into a valley green with oaks and maples and brush, and purple with evening shadows.

"Can we?"

"I thought we'd go somewhere else."

"Mary, look at me. Look. I'm going to see your people. I want to see them. I want to know you better."

"Huh. That's what I'm afraid of."

"But why? Mary, you're mine, and your folks had better get used to the idea."

She laughed nervously.

"Say, by the way, Doc says I can have a week's leave next month."

She turned quickly, almost driving off the highway. "He said that?"

"Sure. A whole week. If I behave." He grinned. "Huh. I better not get caught out tonight."

"You won't. I'll see to that."

"Mary, stop the car."

"Why?"

"Well . . . I . . . stop it."

"Wait. There's a place a little further along here, near a lake. A lane and a pasture. I thought we'd stop there."

"Good."

She drove down a chokecherry-shaded lane. She stopped. They stepped out into the evening.

They walked along, fitting their steps together, treading through the long grass. A snake ran off to one side, hissing at them. A frog legged it into the bushes. Behind them a car slugged past on the highway.

He held her Ma Memme hands. They were soothing. They were a child's. They were honest. They did not wring like Martha's did. They were glad hands. They were always ready to clap.

"Mary, when I get that week's leave, I have no place to go."

She said nothing.

"No place . . ." he hesitated, hurt that she did not pick up his hint. "Mary, must I beg it?"

"Oh . . ." she was startled, cried out, "I didn't think you'd want to come."

"Mary, I don't understand you. You sound like somebody's given you a beating. Hurt you."

"Oh no. It's only that . . . well, I can hardly believe you'd care to spend a whole week."

"Mary, look. May I come that week? Say, the last week in August? The moon will be full then, and the apples ripe, and the plums and grapes and currants. There'll be a harvest all around. Can I?"

"Well . . . I s'pose so. I'll see."

They walked along the lane.

To the left, the corn stood in military rows, waiting. The stalks were sharply green, almost blue where the quick fresh winds from the west flipped over the leaves in the falling sunlight. The palm-like leaves spread curving shad-

234

ows on the black dew-wet earth. A thin veil of wavering yellow-gray tassels rippled on the field.

To the right, burgeoning barley rolled away as if some god were gently blowing upon it. Waves of green, silver, green, raced over it, the various hues chasing each other across the tossing land.

Eric breathed deeply, looking, and clasped her hand.

They entered the pasture near the blue, ruffled lake. A prepotent bull surveyed them; then strolled on to sniff a herd of young heifers. Reindeer-eyed calves came up to stare at them and snuffle their hands.

Silently they strolled along, moved by the immense summer-time efflorescence of nature, by the burst of cease-less exfoliation on the sea of rich loam: quack-grass choking itself, thistles spreading silk-threaded seeds, field bind-weed winding delicate tendrils around priapic cornstalks.

Barely perceptible phosphorescent glows awakened and quickened in Eric's mind, grew into tiny flames, grew into half-remembered events. Little winds blew; the sparks became flames. He became wistful, filled with many unnamable urges and wishes. The past was a strong brandy burning. He recalled calf tracks in the rain-soaked earth on Pa's prairie farm, recalled horse tracks leading to the barnyard. He remembered himself as a pale-legged child running underneath a glowering thunderstorm at dusk, running down a lane with the delirium of a child's wildness, breasting a swift wind and sudden raindrops, ignoring Ma Memme's clucking calls to come in beneath the eaves.

They walked along. The lulling hum of libellulid, the drone of the threatening bumblebee, brought him upon the brink of eternity. In a moment he would hear its singing.

There was the stealthily growing grain. There was the immeasurable fury of cellulating corn. There was the im-measurable fury of expanding, crackling chemicals, which now, after eons and eons of passing beneath the sun, had evolved into multitudes of creatures.

The fires of sunset burned at the edges of the sky's blue

dome, ate into the shoreline across the lake. The broad shoulders of the earth rose. An aurora of perception lighted his mind.

Coming upon a flower garden, they stopped to wonder at the flared purple of the iris. They paused beneath apple trees to touch the green nubbin fruit. They hesitated to breathe upon the young currants and gooseberries in the bushes, and to caress the green spheric grapes hanging in clusters.

They scuffed through the grass. The sweet-sweet smell of a fermenting manure-pile and of half-rotted cherry windfalls in the tangy grass rose about them like incense. They brushed through a swarm of flies hovering over an aged, crusted cow-dunging. Gleaming spider threads tickled their faces.

They pushed their feet through the stringy grass. They watched the waving wild roses.

A wild fancy, a radiant fire lifted in him. How long had the grass been growing?

"Mary. Mary. Kiss me. I want many kisses."

She fired too. "Many? Oh, but you'll tire of me then."

"Never."

"Oh yes. I know." She nodded, as if she were thinking of some sad truth she had learned.

"Come."

Her lips were as smooth and as sweet as melted butter.

## XXVIII—THE WHIPPER STRIKES

FOR NEARLY twenty-four years, a constant unwavering momentum kept the spinning top upon its point. To the casual watcher's eye, the momentum seemed eternal. Perpetual motion had been found.

But then, oddly, in the twenty-fifth year, and the sixth, the seventh, the eighth, and the twenty-ninth year, the top wavered, skipped about, wobbled. The powers of the coiled momentum had at last met their match in the forces of resistance.

Yet mysteriously, miraculously, the spinning top straightened, and went on whirling as before.

And then, in the thirtieth year, the top suddenly jumped here-there. It fell on its side. It shuddered convulsively. It lay still. And all the flaws of the top, and all its graces, lay exposed to the eye.

Huck was in his thirtieth year, and everything seemed to go wrong at once. First his kidneys became infected with tubercle baccilli. He began to moan painfully upon each voiding.

Next, pus began to emerge from his ears.

Next, his testicles began to teem with bacilli. One night pain jarred loose some memory of intercourse in his brain and he awoke screaming. It burned him like an acetylene torch.

Then his already bad coughing spells became violent; so violent that after each session his mattress was dislodged. A day came when he streaked; his sputum became pink with little strings of blood.

And finally, his heart began to stumble

Dr. Abraham came to see Huck twice a day; always as if Huck had only a mild stomach ache and needed but a smile to right himself again. A silent language rose between them. Sometimes they played at a game, Dr. Abraham pretending that he was patting Huck's feet to encourage him, Huck pretending that the gesture tickled him—when all along both knew that the Doctor was watching for swelling feet, the first sign of impending heart failure.

Huck's sharp tongue became more caustic. Even though the dice had rolled him snake eyes, he fought to keep his seat in the circle of play. And Eric, though hurt by his sarcasms, could not find it in his heart to push him out.

One night Eric was just entering the fronded way of a dream when he heard a strange rasping sound in the room. For a few seconds he thought some paralyzed man was desperately trying to call him. Then he understood. He snapped on his light, hopped from his sheets, and ran to Huck's bedside. He jerked on the bedlamp and, seeing how pale Huck was, began to shake him. He shook Huck until a faint white yellow color rose in his cheeks and he came to and stirred and faintly smiled.

Blinking and sitting up, Fawkes stared at Huck a moment and then, cursing, searched hurriedly through his bedstand for some sedatives Dr. Abraham had allowed him, an M.D., to have on hand for emergencies. Finding a packet, he handed Eric two pills. "Pour out a little water in his glass," he ordered, "and hold him up so he can swallow."

Eric did so.

A week later, Huck's legs began to swell; at the toes, over the instep, at the ankles.

As though no spectre stood by his side, Huck became more and more curious about the world. He read until his weak arms could no longer hold up a book. With famous wanderers he travelled over the world; with psychologists he inspected the human heart; with historians he observed man's blind stumbling. He was fascinated by the story of man's sluggish climb out of the virus age. He explored the surface of the earth. Remembering their hysterical Tibet-talk that day of the winter blizzard, he sought out the lamas of Tibet with Sven Hedin, watched the natives on the plateau of Tibet cook their meals over burning yak-dung, watched them covet and rape each other's wives. With Jeans he studied the mysterious galaxies, with Eddington he traced new paths of knowledge. He threw his light farther and farther into the universe.

Eric saw all these things, and marvelled, and loved Huck.

It was the afternoon rest hour. Eric, lying on his right side and idly watching the twisting leaves of Old Lady Poplar, heard a gurgling sound in the room, a sudden cough. He jerked upright and looked over toward Huck's bed. Fawkes, too, awakened and glanced over.

Bright scarlet blood was gushing upward from Huck's mouth and spilling over his bed-cover.

Fawkes' hand struck the emergency button with the speed of a hitting snake.

"What is it?" Eric whispered.

"Hemorrhage. Massive hemorrhage."

Miss Berg came bounding down the hallway, jerked at the door, entered. Her eyes were like blue marbles circled by rings of ivory. One look and she whirled and ran bounding down the hall again. Eric had a quick, abortive vision of her large bosom bobbing as she ran.

Both Eric and Fawkes ran to Huck's bed; Eric supporting Fawkes when he saw that the other's bone-stilt legs, unused for a year, were beginning to buckle.

Fawkes grabbed up a hypodermic needle from his bedstand and bent over Huck. He wiped streaming blood from Huck's limp arm. He gritted his teeth and jabbed the arm.

The needle prick caught Huck just as he was trying to cover his erupting mouth with a napkin, and he jerked convulsively, rolling a little, kicking and choking.

He quieted. He looked at them with faintly accusing eyes and sank away. Another geyser of blood shot upward, higher than the other, leaping. Abruptly it fell. Bubbled. His mouth throbbed with the slow blood of an opened heart.

Dr. Abraham burst in; then Miss Berg.

Eric stood back quickly. He vomited.

# E XXIX—ALARM IN THE NIGHT

RIC TURNED and twisted in his bed. The Whipper had cornered him. The Whipper had lifted His paw menacingly over him, was watching him until he should quiet down and offer a still target.

Eric drew himself up. He waited. Where could he go? The week's leave was light-days away, too far off to be an escape. By that time something would happen.

The morning after Huck died, when the earth was awakening, and the sun had begun to pink the walls of the room, and the west windows had become sheets of red-gold, he awoke and heard a death-rattle. For a moment he thought it was Huck, still alive, and shaking out his shredded lungs with a morning cough.

As quick as an opening camera eye, he saw himself: legs crouched up under his bottom, body on its right side, and face to the gleaming windows. Now, where was that sound coming from?

Then he knew. It was in his own chest. Vibrations were tickling his throat.

Like rats, ideas of disaster milled in his braincase. He lay tense. What should he do? He ran to his memory to get some advice. He got none.

He lay as still as silence. Maybe the rattling would go away. He waited, breathing as slowly as he could.

But the ruffling sound became louder. A weight swung back and forth in his left lung. It crawled up the bronchial tube. It—abruptly he choked. He bounded up, coughing, sucking air, pawing. He grabbed for his sputum cup. He drew another breath underneath the obstruction and, coughing again, hurled up a pancake of straw-coarse sputum. He looked at it and knew it was empyema and knew that the week's leave was off and knew that his ribs would be cut and knew he would lose Mary and knew he would never write his book and knew that he would go insane.

Fawkes, awakening, called, "What's up?"

There was a long moment.

"What's up?"

"Nothing." Eric covered the sputum cup with a white napkin and lay down.

"Spring a leak?"

"No. Oh no."

"Good. Awwwkk. God, I'm sleepy." Fawkes turned over.

240

Eric closed his eyes and looked directly, fearlessly, into the eyes of the Whipper. He whispered to himself.

When he coughed up another long string of smashed yellow tomatoes the next morning, he drew on his blue bathrobe and pantofles, and went down to see Dr. Abraham.

Listening, Dr. Abraham whitened and became very grim. He looked at the sputum for a long time and then asked. "You got a temp?"

"That's the funny part of it. I haven't."

"Hah. Well, the only thing to do is: first, make a smear of this; second, guinea-pig it; third, culture it." He shook his head. "What a mess."

"Mess is right," Eric exploded. "Holy Moses, Doc, what the hell now?"

"I dunno. I really don't know." He paused. "Look, you better get an X-ray, too. We'll keep hunting till we find it."

Eric was sitting on the footend of his bed, moodily staring out of the window, and feeling that the silent room was very spacious without Huck, when Fawkes broke into the parliament of his clamorous thoughts.

"Doc going to take away your privileges?"

Eric whirled. "How'd you know what was up?"

Fawkes smiled. "When the sputum-cup collector came around yesterday morning, I thought he'd collapse when he looked at yours."

Eric tried to grin.

"Really, what's happened?"

"Oh, I dunno. I guess I got a Vesuvius in my chest. It's erupting yellow lava all over the place."

"That's funny. You look as healthy as a pup."

"Huh."

Fawkes pushed himself up in bed, breathed heavily a moment from the exertion, and said, "It can't be bad."

"Huh. It's probably empyema."

"Oh hell no."

"Or galloping consumption."

"Miliary tuberculosis? Oh no. It doesn't work that fast."

"Well, whatever it is, I don't like it."

Fawkes looked at him narrowly. "Did you ever have a major infection before?"

"Oh . . . blood poison once."

"Bad?"

"Yes. I stepped barefoot on a piece of rusty barbwire. In two days I had to tie my leg up on a windowsill, it hurt so bad."

"No doctor?"

"Nope."

"No lockjaw?"

Eric smiled wrily. "I guess not. I could talk like a blue streak when Pa came in to argue with me."

"You were a lucky man." Fawkes paused. "No, I don't think you have to worry. You're probably one of these birds that, given enough rest and food, can throw off most infections. No, I wouldn't worry, Eric. Just take it easy. Relax."

"Huh."

A day later, his raising did begin to subside. And, in four days, there wasn't a trace of phlegm.

The sixth day, Dr. Abraham came in beaming and bowing. "Well, Eric," he said, glancing at Fawkes to draw him into the talk too, "for a long time I've never been able to agree with my colleagues that pleural fluids dry up and become thickened pleuras. And, in this case at least, I was right. What the X-ray boys thought was a thickened pleura here" . . . he placed his hand over Eric's left chest . . . "was only a bag of fluid encapsulated by fibrin, all of it too thick for the rays to penetrate. You know how the body encapsulates a bullet lodged in it? So too here." He paused, smiled, slapped Eric's shoulder. "Well, that bag broke and emptied into your chest, and you coughed it up. The best part is that the X-ray penetrates that spot now and we can finally say that your cavity is closed."

242

Eric straightened.

"And" . . . Dr. Abraham laughed and sniffed and rolled his eyes . . . "and, though I haven't seen the guinea pig test yet, nor the culture, the slide shows that the precipitated fibrin you coughed up is negative. Negative. And that same fluid a year ago was as full of bugs as a dead tomcat full of maggots."

Fawkes whistled.

Eric sat wordless.

Dr. Abraham stood back, smiling, laughing. "Well . . . well . . . aren't you going to say something, boy? I just got through giving you a reprieve."

"I . . ."

"Got your clothes packed for your leave?"

"You mean?"

"Sure. You can go. Only" . . . and now the doctor's face quickly darkened with mock severity . . . "remember, no seven-mile walks. Things can still go wrong. You've still got a long pull ahead."

"Then it isn't empyema?"

"Not yet."

"Thanks," Eric whispered.

"Don't thank me. Thank your bull of a body."

# M XXX—A SONG IS SUNG

MARY CAME to get him in the morning. Trembling, he stepped down the flight of stairs, carrying a suitcase, and feeling bulkily masculine inside the red college sweater and a pair of blue pants.

They drove toward her home. Yellow-purple mists rose from the damp land.

They were nervous together. He knew her thoughts. She was anxious to touch him, but she was worried too. They would have many hours alone this holiday; and the last few times they had been together on movie night he had been too importunate for her. Eric sighed. What did she expect? The doxology? He had lively manroots. And when a man loved a woman and opened his heart to her as he had, inhibitions were about as effective in restraining him as floating spider threads a swiftly running miler. Until a man has had his satisfaction from his woman, love-making is a reckless and an amoral advance into the unknown.

They drove onto the yard. A spread of apple and plum trees lay before him. A long hill was ridged with a vineyard. It was a truck-garden farm.

He met her foster parents, Uncle Pete and Aunt Anna. Uncle Pete, Eric saw after a few days, was a man of bitter and vengeful impulses. He was short-armed and short-legged, and his coarse black hair hid a low curved forehead. He had mean, darting eyes. He took special delight in embarrassing Mary. He hated Mary because she was of his brilliant brother George's blood; and from pretty Anna's womb, an Anna far more beautiful than his own ordinary wife, also named Anna. As he hauled manure over the fields, or sat whittling in the barnyard door, his resentment at the dead brother and sister-in-law for having left him the orphan, Mary, was always pimpling to a head. And jumping up, he would find Mary, seek out her pet hopes, and torment her. Lately he had discovered her love for Rebecca, and he threatened to have Rebecca serviced by the neighbor's stallion, Black Joe. When Mary flared up, he would laugh a bitter and an exultant laugh.

The foster mother, Aunt Anna, was a good woman, always trying to understand her husband, her son, her foster daughter, her garden, her cooking, herself, and always failing. She did not even know that she did not understand. She had a melon-smooth face and an enormous sow-mother's puff-belly.

Cousin Raymond was a mystery. From a picture on the piano Eric learned that Raymond was very sure of his powers, sexual and mental; though the drawn corner of the right upper lip revealed frustration and pretense. The mother said that he was "a good boy. Good. Yes." The father thought him a "no-good," too much like his Uncle George, and forever getting girls into trouble.

"And you, Mary?" Eric asked. "What do you say?"

Smiling, expecting a gay answer, he was surprised to see her blush. He narrowed his eyes. Some day he would question her closely about this Raymond.

The earth was lovely. It burst with fruits.

He stood at the head of a long avenue that had no visible conclusion. Compared to the few hours of freedom on Wednesday nights, the week of days ahead seemed endless. He was free; free to see Mary and kiss her as often as he wanted; free to eat apples; free to break TB rules and regulations.

In trying to see and taste and feel all of the clustering growths in the real world the very first day, he collapsed in the orchard. Mary dropped on her knees beside him, her eyes wide with fright. He laughed at her. He tried to pass it off as a joke. He was too fat, he told her. His legs still weren't strong enough to carry his bulk around. Why, he was so fat, he said, that a half hour after a fit of laughing, he could still feel his lard-face dimpling.

Rested, and his breath caught, he went on with her, searching through the vivid world.

Smiling, shy, her eyes illuminated by purple-gray indirect lighting, Mary kept out of his urgent reach. When he touched her, she trembled, and jumped a little.

And he trembled. He was a sweating, nervous stallion.

They ate together. He was delighted to see her sucking a bone for its very last bit of succulent nourishment, for its last phlegm of marrow. He was glad to see that she loved life with a peasant woman's yearning.

He had moments of remorse, too; of agonized memories. Mary's "I don't know, I really don't know" recalled Martha's "Oh you don't know. You'll never know." Damned phrases! And he was haunted, too, by the love phrases he had whispered to Martha and wanted to whisper now. "If you only knew how I love you at this moment." "You are my heart." "I tremble upon your coming." "You. You only. You."

Arm over hips, he in his red sweater and blue trousers, she in her light-blue slacks, they pushed over the land. They tramped through sloughs thick with ancient razor-edged tall reed grass and floating milkweed down and silver-plumed foxtail. They struggled through fields of corn and found themselves sprayed with golden pollen falling from the waving tassels above. They sweated. They kissed each other. They kicked at the soft, cultivated earth. They brushed phallic corn ears. They touched each other. They pulled pigeon-grass stickers from their clothes. They strode through haylands red and yellow and white with clover. They smelled ambrosia. They stepped aside for flowering daisies. They stepped carefully through heavy windfalls of tomato-red apples. They plucked soft, oozing, over-ripe purple-black plums. They laughed. They tagged through ragweed, forests of it; through cup plant, its elephant-ear leaves flopping in their faces. They kicked through the crabgrass whose blue claw-arms were arched and opened.

An incandescent fever glowed in them. They walked close together. He thought her touches on his arms erethic. He recalled Ma Memme.

The seventh day, the last day of the leave, they went out to the pasture to have a last look at Rebecca. Already the pretty red filly with its yellow tail and mane, and white hooves, had become acquainted with their palms spread wide with lumps of sugar. Once Rebecca had even tried to push her soft, velvety nose into Eric's pocket.

She did not come when they called. When Eric stumbled through the tall grass toward her, she snorted, threw up her tail impudently, and ran off.

"Whatever can be the matter with her," Mary exclaimed. The sadness that had been erased from her eyes these past seven days returned momentarily.

"Oh," said Eric, laughing, "she's probably in heat."

246

Mary looked at him, irritated.

"Sure," he said, "sure. It's natural."

"Oh, you men. You and Uncle Pete."

Eric shrugged and brushed the hair out of his eyes. "I'm just saying it. I only worked on my dad's farm where it was my job to catch mares in heat and call for the neighbor's stud to service 'em."

"Eric."

He looked at her, still laughing. But when he saw that she had become angry, he forced an expression of humility to the surface of his face.

"The idea," she said. "Anyway, Rebecca's a civilized horse."

"I wonder," he mused, "I wonder if storks do actually propagate civilizations."

"Oh." She whirled away from him, her long waving hair lashing about her neck and almost dislodging the blue ribbon.

He stood admiring her. She was trim and athletic in blue slacks. Except for a slight pallor along her temples, no one would ever have known that she had been gravely ill. He chuckled to himself. Mary was a lovely filly herself.

A whinny, a searing, haunting whinny startled him. He looked around. There, near the fence, stood slim and red Rebecca, her head lifted and pointed, her tail arched and her body thrust forward. She was staring to the south, intently listening for an answering neigh.

Eric looked southward too. But he could see only a rising hill of golden stubbles. A line-fence and a row of wild box elders crested it.

Again Rebecca whinnied.

This time there was a response, a shrill, almost human call.

Eric looked at Mary, said sharply, "Why, that's a stallion. A neighbor got one?"

"No. Oh . . . yes. Hank Hoff's got one. Black Joe."

"Well. So. Say, we might see a tryst."

"No!"

"Well, if Rebecca gets anxious enough, we will."

"She won't. Don't worry."

Seeing a higher knoll near at hand, Eric walked up it, with Mary slowly following. He climbed a fencepost. Then, looking, he spotted Black Joe. Rebecca's whinny had awakened the old boy and he was running back and forth along the pasture fence, snorting, tail up, impatient. In the sun his black coat rippled with purple waves. From the gaskin down, his left rear leg was vividly white.

Rebecca neighed again and again. Each call made Black Joe more frantic; until finally, with a loud noise and a snort, he ran back a few steps and turned and hurled his huge locomotive body over the fence. He stumbled a little as he came up and then, regaining his feet, thumpumped, thumpumped, thumpumped across the intervening stubble-field.

Mary gasped. She drew in her breath so deeply that Eric looked to see what was wrong. She was so pale he thought she would faint. He heard her moan softly through her hand, "No. No. Not Rebecca."

Nervous, Eric put his arm about her.

Mary jerked away. With wide, frightened eyes she stared at the coming, looming stallion.

Black Joe had come up to Rebecca. They nuzzled each other across the fence. They bit each other's shoulders and withers. Black Joe moaned in ecstasy. He bit her poll. He tried to bite her quarters. But Rebecca was too quick for him, too excited, too frivolous, and she wheeled away with a little squeal and a murmur, and bit at his barrel and croup. She could barely reach his glossy black shoulder, so massive he stood beside her.

Black Joe resented the fence and he stomped at it and kicked at it. When it still did not vanish, he ran back a way and with a jerky, impeded run, managed to clear the second fence.

Mary turned away, wincing. She drew in nervous, terrorized breaths. Impulsively she jerked at Eric's arm. He drew her close. He cupped her breast. She jerked away again.

Black Joe stumbled around Rebecca.

And Rebecca was afraid, and anxious, and eager. Sometimes she allowed him to caress her, to touch her croup, then slipped away.

Again and again Black Joe came charging for her, his thighs crouched.

Almost Rebecca let him have his will. Almost. But at the last moment she slipped from under him.

Enraged, Black Joe bit at her throat-latch angrily.

Rebecca screamed and ran away from him; and then, reconsidering, came back to him in a series of little trots, and whinnys, and whimpers.

Black Joe stared at her and, of a sudden, was upon her.

Rebecca shuddered. Her pasterns trembled beneath the great weight of the powerful male. Her forearms and stifles rippled under Black Joe. Her chestnuts danced.

Black Joe fumbled and trembled. His wild eyes rolled like black plums and his nostrils flared like the ears of two bass horns. When she would not receive, he bit viciously into her withers and her poll.

In pain, in ecstasy, she surrendered. When the great purple-black stallion struck her flame-point, she screamed again, sagging and trembling.

Dimly Eric was aware of a voice sounding near him, and he listened, and remembered Mary. She had hidden her face against his side.

She was saying, "Tell me, tell me, is it true yet?"

"Mary, you mustn't act so funny. He isn't going to hurt her. It's natural. It's only a little of bittersweet. That's all."

"Is it true yet, then?"

"Mary."

"Oh it's terrible to think of it."

"No, no. It's wonderful. It's Life."

"Is it true now?"

"Yes. Now the thing has begun. And it is very wonderful. She has seized him."

"What? She?"

"Yes. And now the great song is singing."

**249**

"How awful. How can you stand it?"

"It's wonderful."

"And now, then?"

"The song is sung. The head is hung. The flower is fading."

After a few moments Black Joe withdrew, fell off her back. He snorted, clearing his nostrils. He looked at Rebecca a moment; turned away as though he had never known her. He began to crop the grass at his hooves.

Rebecca turned too, surprised that he had left so soon. She nuzzled against him. He jumped and kicked at her and ran from her a way. Puzzled, Rebecca whinnied and followed slowly. Black Joe drifted farther away. Soon Rebecca began to crop grass too. She walked about awkwardly.

Eric lifted Mary's face and kissed her and brushed away her tears and held her gently. He felt sorry for her, for her dreams. It was good to see a woman who believed that chastity was a flower pretty enough to keep. It made a man desire her more than ever.

He wanted her. He drew her along a few steps. He stumbled with her and drew her down into the long grass.

He reached for her. She resisted. Slowly the pain in her face left and she became aroused. Her eyes flashed. Her lips swelled and softened. She pressed her breast against his hand and kissed him. Excited, he pressed her backward until she lay stretched upon the ground. A sweet earth, a grassroots smell, a smell of delicious white sweet-clover balls, mingled with the aroma of her hair. He kissed her. He unhooked her slacks. She held his hand but he was stronger. She held his hand with both of hers. His one hand was still too strong. He touched her bare thigh. He jumped a little when he discovered she was wearing only the blouse and slacks. He soothed her and kissed her. Sometimes she pressed against him; sometimes she drew away. She was swollen and wonderfully soft in his hands.

Involuntarily she sighed. Again. Deeply.

The sigh disturbed him, and awakened misgivings. He remembered her anguish, her dream to keep Rebecca inviolate. In a way he was no better than Uncle Pete. Like him, he hoped Black Joe would overpower her.

He hung for a moment balancing.

He felt her shiver beneath him. And sigh again.

He closed his eyes. "Dear girl, dear girl," he whispered to himself, "this day I'll let you keep one dream . . . though I know it's wrong to let you keep it." He stood up.

He saw her eyes widen and her mouth open in surprise. Tears swelled along the rims of her eyes and she blinked. She jumped up and drew him dearly to her, whispering, "You're so good to me. So good. So very good."

He hid his face in her hair, smelling the white clover in it.

He felt suddenly worn out; the long walk and the excitement had tired him. His legs began to tremble. He ached as though someone had cut him across the thigh with a horsewhip.

XXXI—THE WHIPPER DESCRIBED

AT THE DOOR of the Phoenix, Eric looked once more at Mary in the soft light of the sedan, at her sad-sweet mouth, at her gray-blue eyes, and abruptly left without kissing her, and entered the wide door with his suitcase, and trudged to his ward.

He entered 176. He greeted Fawkes shortly. He set his suitcase down and settled on the edge of the bed. He fumbled with the heavy fold of his red sweater. He looked about the room and discovered he had trouble remembering it.

He snapped on the bedlamp. He began to unpack his suitcase. There was a faint odor of decay in the room, almost as if Huck had just finished using the bedpan. Eric glanced at the empty bed and turned quickly away. Maybe the smell was his own bad breath. Dr. Abraham had told him that TB'ers often had halitosis.

He heard Fawkes rustling in his sheets. Out of the corner of his eye he saw his roommate lower his book and place it open and upside-down on his chest.

Fawkes asked, "Well, what's wrong with you?"

"Nothing."

"I expected to see you come in here dancing a jig."

"Huh."

"What happened? Mary give you the gate?"

Eric grunted. "I wish she had."

Fawkes coughed. "Of course it's none of my damn business, but what kind of vacation did you have?"

"Oh, it was wonderful," Eric said, sneering a little.

"Really now."

"Fawkes, I completely forgot I ever lived here."

"Well, then what're you crabbing about?"

"Oh . . . nothing." Eric folded up his sweater and put it away in the trunk under the bed.

Fawkes quieted.

Eric took off his trousers and folded them and put them away too. He took off his shorts and jersey, hung them over a chair, and slipped into his pajamas. He said, "Well, I know it looks funny, coming in grouchy from a week's leave, after I've had a lot of fun, but it all seems so futile to me."

"Why? You should be disgustingly exuberant."

"I know. But I can't help thinking it's all for nothing."

"Oh?"

Eric got into bed. He fluffed his pillow and lay down on it and looked at the ceiling. "I'm up against it no matter which way I turn. If I get my health back, get discharged, I won't be able to find a job. I couldn't find a job before I came in, so there won't be one now. Especially since I'm both a lunger and a liberal."

"Aw, now." Fawkes scratched his square black mustache.

"No, really. You don't know. You little spectacled scientists grubbing away in your cubbyholes, looking for the answer to the riddle, you don't know what it is to pound the streets looking for work. Especially when you have no particular trade or skill to sell and yet you're twice as intelligent as the man you've approached for a job."

Fawkes said nothing. His eyes brooded. His face became kind.

"I tell you," Eric cried, lifting a hand, "I tell you, it's terrible. Here I am now, got a girl again, got a chance to live like a normal human being, home, children maybe, and so on, and yet, what is there ahead? Defeat. A licking. Oh, hell, what's the use."

Fawkes shifted in his bed.

"And if I don't get discharged, it's death. Like Huck."

Fawkes said, smiling a little, "Well, that just about closes all the doors, doesn't it?"

Eric ignored the remark. "You know, I was just thinking on the way back here. Here I am, a healthy man. At least fairly so. I love life, the outdoors, grass, animals, stallions. I crave sunlight. I am a sunshine boy. And yet, here is a car taking me back to . . . to this, gray walls, gray curtains, gray, gray, gray. Death. And the smell of a dying man's voiding. And why? According to Dr. Abraham, it's so that I can have my teeming world again . . . in time. Which is a lot of bunk. Because the nearer I get to being discharged, the closer I get to defeat on the outside once more. And, God! I'd hate to go through that again. Oh, it's all mixed up. It's just a mess."

Fawkes laughed at him. "Man, you don't know when you've got it good."

"Good?"

"Sure. Why don't you sit back and enjoy this king's life. Look, man. Can you think of any king who ever got service like we're getting? Why, nurses as pretty as princesses carry out our dung for us."

Eric growled.

"Man, take it easy. Enjoy this rest while you can."

"Well, you may enjoy it, but I hate it. Me, I like life."

"Okay, then don't growl when you get a week of it."

Eric sat stubbed.

"Eric, do you know that you're probably the only one

on this floor who's anxious to get out? There isn't a man here who, if he told the truth, would tell you that he hates the San. Hell, he loves it. It's the first time he's had a chance to take it easy. All his life he's had to work for somebody else, punch clocks, work, work, with not one chance in a million of getting something meaningful out of life besides sweat. You know that. But now, coming in here, he's in the clover. Just ask him. He'll tell you he's never had better food, never seen nicer women, never had cleaner beds, never had more time to sleep, never had baths in bed. Really. And here you are, kicking."

"Just the same, I hate it."

"Well, what are you going to do about it?"

"I don't know. I'm thinking."

"Skip out?"

Eric grunted.

"If you do, the draft board will be waiting for you."

Eric sat up. "See? That's what I mean. It's a mess everywhere you go. Just think, this society that I'm supposed to get ready to live in, what's it doing? It's got itself into another blood-letting orgy. I spend two years carefully nursing along my little spark, getting myself on top of a couple of trillion TB bugs, and outside, in the world, they're spilling lives away by the millions."

Fawkes subsided. After a moment of thought he said slowly, "Well, maybe you've got something there."

Eric waved an arm, his brooding eyes aroused. "Why! this earth has had so many wars, wars, wars, it's a wonder some of us have ancestors."

Fawkes laughed.

Eric closed his eyes. The thought was a walk to the edge of a precipice. It was like another he often played with. Had either his father or mother died before they had mated he would never have been.

Eric gestured. "What a terrible thing they're asking us to do. Sign a draft to kill. Kill. If only we could sign up for a draft to create. Like I want to do." He waved a hand. "They tell us it's for freedom again, to save us from the

254

Beast. Well, it's probably against the Beast all right, but I'm not so sure it's for freedom. For him who is to die there is no freedom. Once the dust has filled his mouth, or once his heart has ceased its quivering, freedom has vanished for him." Eric shook his head tollingly. "And in this coming war, they'll kill millions. Ten millions. Twenty, even. And destroy the spirits of millions of others. And all for freedom."

Fawkes shot a question. "And yet, if we don't fight, who'll have it?"

"That's just it. That's why signing the draft is a terrible choice. Sometimes . . . sometimes I wish the governments of the world would let us lungers fight this war, let us spit bugs at each other. We'd get rid of both the warriors and the bugs. The young and the beautiful lads, the Mozarts and Shelleys, we could let them live."

"And the Einsteins and Galois."

"Right. God, how I hate war! God! We get so little from the Whipper in the first place, a mere fifty years or so—Huck got only thirty—and then we got to go around blood-letting to hurry it along. Moses!"

Fawkes nodded.

Eric went on. He was inwardly a little amazed at the powerful fountain that was throwing up this whirl of words and ideas in his skull. "And yet, I wonder. I wonder. Suppose all of us were Einsteins, what would it get us? I wonder. Did you ever stop to think that man, as a species, has been in existence for millions of year? Yet that only the last six thousand he's been scribbling down what he does and wants to do? Did it ever hit you what'll happen, say, six thousand years from now if our historians keep busy? Why, kids in English classes'll skip over our time like we skip over the time of Shakespeare. We know he lived. But who else in his day? Hell, this whole age, the whole thousand years to come will vanish from books forever. And six million years from now? What a thought. What a thought. Man, it makes your . . . your . . . "

Fawkes smiled. His mouth twisted mischievously. "It

draws the pucker strings of your anus into a tight little knot of a hole, doesn't it? Like when you feel your car skidding into a ditch?"

"Ha. Exactly." Eric laughed. Then, pursuing a flame, he added, "We talk of immortal bards. To whom are they immortal? And when? Ridiculous. That's why it's idiotic to seek fame. Why, if a planet should hit this earth and bust it t'bits, who'd catch our books, our tomes, our etchings? Who? No one. Unless it'd be monsters on other worlds whirling about other suns beyond the eye-dimming reach of our galaxy. And they'd not understand us. Phht. Foolish."

Fawkes nodded. His eyebrows became as slanted as a Buddha's. His face became mystic. "Yes, this earth is pretty much of an accident at that, isn't it? Elder Huxley's monkey finally hit the right key and wrote the earth."

"You see what I mean? That was what was in my mind when I came from Mary's farm just now."

Fawkes looked at him steadily. "You know, Eric, maybe it's time for you to begin writing."

"Aw, nuts."

"No, I mean it. Take notes. Think about people, like Calisto said."

"Aw . . . "

"Or, are you afraid of your doctor?"

"Oh, hell. If I decided to write, he couldn't stop me."

Fawkes peered at him. "You know, you've just now admitted you're lazy."

"Nuts."

"Didn't you?"

"No."

"Eric, maybe it isn't the world that's off the beam. Maybe it's you."

Eric looked at his frog-leg fingers.

"That book you once started, what was it about?"

"Oh . . . people."

"What kind?"

"Common people."

"What about them?"

"Well, they had dreams."

"Haven't they?"

"Well, I thought so at the time I wrote it."

"Don't you now?"

"I dunno. Maybe it's like I said. I'm all mixed up. Like everybody else. Everybody. Society's all mixed up."

"Come, come."

"Sure. All the old values are going. Just look around. In here, in this Phoenix even, I get echoes of it. Look. People's notions about government are changing. And about economics. Religion. Morals. Everything."

Fawkes grinned. "You sure like to preach, don't you?"

"Well, isn't it the truth? Just take religion. Who believes in a personal God anymore? Oh, we've got churches. Sure. But the pews in them have become mating exchanges. No, Fawkes, God's not in his heaven any more. God is either Hitler, Churchill, Mussolini, so on. God's come to roost with us. On our earth. And it's mixing us all up."

"Oh, I wouldn't say that. Maybe we're going to get somewhere, thinking that. After we get used to the idea."

"Take the matter of liberals. After the war, people will go for either radicalism or conservatism. And in batches. There'll be co-op this, combine that. There'll be very little middle ground left for the independent thinker. And if he doesn't declare himself for some camp, he'll get killed."

Fawkes stirred.

"Fawkes, the liberal lamps are going out."

"Well, my father thinks so too. But I don't know. I can't see it. I see another vista ahead. I see a future. And a good one."

"Well, I hope you're right." Eric shrugged.

"Really, Eric, why don't you write a little?"

"I don't see you working, do I?"

"Not? Look." Fawkes reached out to his bedstand and lifted a sheaf of papers.

Eric grunted. "What's that? A treatise on love among the bugs?"

"No. Notes. Remember my father, hinting that maybe

257

I'd gone to seed? Well, I've started putting down a few thoughts."

"Well." Eric brightened. "Can I see them?" Before Fawkes could reply, he threw back his bedcovers and stepped across the room. He held out his hand for them.

"Hey, hey. Not so fast."

Eric stopped. "Well, I . . . I just like to see what they're like, is all."

Fawkes laughed up at him. "Now, at this point, if I were Huck, I'd give you a tongue-lashing."

Eric blushed.

"Well, it's all right. Sure. Go ahead and look at them. Just so you don't consider them scientific thinking in process. They're summations. The end results of years of brooding."

"In other words, if it came to a pinch, these are what you'd take your stand on?"

"At the moment, yes. Tomorrow, maybe not."

"You guys just won't stick your neck out, will you?"

"Huh. One look at them will tell you differently. As I say, they're really nothing. Just notes. At the end of the week, I usually drop them in an envelope and mail them on to father just to let him know that sometimes I do get pencil on paper."

"Uhuh."

"And, of course, I write 'em to satisfy a guilty conscience."

"Guilty? You?"

"Yes. My system's been trained to work, and it feels uneasy when it's not in the usual groove."

Eric took the sheets and sat down on Fawkes' visitor's chair at the footend of his bed. The writing was neat. The lines looked like rows of numbers.

*Doctors, physicians. They should be forced to read more outside their field. Many have become narrow, almost ignorant: have become mere skilled technicians, skilled artisans, confusing mule-headedness for caution. And they've become little dictators, probably because the habit of being in charge when they come in on a scene*

258

*has seized control of their entire personality. In fact, in politics, they are oftentimes more than conservative, almost fascist, missionaries from the Chamber of Commerce. Exposure to unusual conditions in the coming war should do them some good.*

Eric glanced up. "You thinking of Dr. Abraham?"
"No, he's an exception."
Eric read on:

*Well, TB has at least settled one problem for me. A lunger is automatically 4F.*

Eric grunted.

*War is a malignant ulcer in nature. War is an unraveling. It unravels the web of culture that nature has been patiently knitting for thousands of years. Each time she gains a little on the cruel rocks and wastes and deserts, a war comes along to undo part of it.*

Eric breathed quickly. The idea hit deep in him, opening clarion-ringing ripples, wide and far wide flowing in his mind. How true. How powerfully true. He turned to Fawkes. "You see what I mean about wars? That's just what I mean. Yessir, we common fellows are just opening up each other's bowels for nothing again. And you ask me to be complacent about it. You ask me to get ready for the normal life with a tune on my lips and my toes ready for a jig. Hell."
Fawkes smiled.
Eric read on:

*Hunger. Hunger is the great cause of war. It is the big push in nature. Hungers live in temples and to keep the temples from crumbling, hungers must be slaked. If they aren't, the temples wind up in quick graveyards like all those endless millions of white skeletons that make up the cliffs of Dover.*

Eric cocked his head sideways, thought, nodded.

*Thoughts about the black and the white. Factories turn out sewing-machines or guns. Education gives suck to*

*dreamers or fascists. Et cetera. Complicating the picture,
each of these forces has its contrasting shades. For example,
guns give us power over nature as well as over each other.
Etc. Every time the sun stirs a bit of earth into becoming
a tree or a creature, it casts a shade. Every time you lift a
light, you throw a shadow. Still, it's good to have the
light.*

Eric glanced at Fawkes. "Say, this stuff isn't bad at all.
Not bad."

"Well, they're just random thoughts."

"But they're good." Eric turned his chair a little to
catch more of the light from Fawkes' bedlamp.

*About writing. Plots tend to kill characters. If plots
kill 'em, why use 'em, since it's the characters and the personality of the writer behind them that makes the book?
Structure, the rest of it, is crossword puzzling.*

*A scripture should record how people eat, breed, sleep.
Look at the* Old Testament, Arabia Deserta. *It's just an
orgy of people eating and breeding and sleeping. And a
crying unto God. The* Old Testament *is good psychology.
It helps us understand our failures and lets us feel that we
are not the only ones who've been unable to get what we
wanted. Come to think of it, in that last idea there, you'll
find the germ of most good novels . . .*

Eric asked, "You ever think of being a writer?"

Fawkes waved a hand. "Oh, a little. Sometime or other
in his life, every man wants to be a poet, you know."

Eric looked down at the notes again:

*Man is a beast, pundits say. Yes, he is that. But he is
more, too. In rare moments he is a gentle creature, a shy
child, singing, hoping, giving a little in charity, sometimes
wishing to climb upward with the best of his kind.*

Eric snorted. "I suppose that's why he's getting into this
war?"

Fawkes cleared his throat.

Eric went on. "Fawkes, I know what you mean, though.
I too have been looking for this poet with the capital P.

If I could find Him, see Him, why, I think I might take up writing again."

"Well?"

Eric turned over a few pages:

*Science. In my field it's become applied science. Mechanisms, mechanisms, mechanisms. The only frontier we've got is the one concerned with giving us more comfort, more speed. But as far as the philosophic scientist, the pure-thought scientist, who really dreams up the world for the others to work in, is concerned, he's on his way out. There's no room for him in the universities. Nor in the big factory laboratories. (I wonder if it's true that Russia is the only country where they're spending money to encourage pure-thought scientists? If so, that's almost reason enough to fight in this war.)*

*Pure-thought scientist. Follows his nose into every hole in the universe. Nothing is sacred to him. He is very lonely. He is curious. He can laugh at himself even as he hurls his star into the heavens. He is scrupulously honest, even at the grocery store. Even with his wife. Even with himself. He is a perfectionist. He is suspicious of people with pat answers. A slow answer may mean that a question has many angles. He is willing to work like the very devil. Really sweat. Work. He should not get praise from his age so he won't feel he owes it anything. If he does, the age, like a plot, might bend his thinking.*

Eric glanced up. "This nut you've created here, with all these godly qualities, can he expect to find the truth?"

"No, he'll never find more than an approximation."

"Then, in the last analysis, life is meaningless."

"Yes, the stone we write on erodes in time."

Eric sat up straight, staring at Fawkes. "Why, then the universe is a chaos? Fundamentally a chaos?"

"It may be."

"Really? Chaos?"

"I am prepared to accept the notion."

"But Moses, man, if it's true, think of the consequences."

"Sure."

"Why, you sound like you hope it's chaos!"

"The thought 'hope' is in your mind, Eric. Not mine."

Eric narrowed his eyes. He bit on the corner of his lip, pondering. "Just what or how do you see chaos? I mean, what's it . . . how does it shape up for you?"

Fawkes laughed a little, "Well, if you'll page along there a little, you'll find some notes on that too."

Eric found it:

> *To understand (maybe!) chaos, define order first. Boiled down, when anything has order, it has meaning for us. Our mind, trained by tradition to think in orderly terms, by what it is used to, can conceive of nothing else. And, to remain sane, our mind must continue to believe there is order, that is, that things are arranged so that its passing existence is not immediately jeopardized. Our mind cannot give up order because it cannot give up the mark it thinks it has cut on the eternal stone. But that, of course, does not prove order. The problem the thinker must set up, if he is to negate his own ego's desire to see itself in the universe, is to wonder what will be the nature of things after the earth has blown up with him on it. What will the universe be like then, say, to the super mind?*

Eric took a deep breath. "Wow, you sure got the universe by the tail here, mister."

> *The intelligence of man is but a flicker in eternity. Thus, if order, if a cosmos, is to exist, it must be related to and have meaning in an intelligence that is as everlasting and as comprehensive as the cosmos itself, and that is capable of measuring and judging in eternal sweeps. We have no evidence of such a mind or intelligence, either amongst us, or outside us. All we know is the flickers.*

Eric shook his head, forcing himself to follow the thought.

Fawkes said, putting out a hand, "You better give me those notes. Really, you shouldn't look at them. They're not finished. They're not thought through."

262

"Please. Can't I read a few more? This stuff is all right."

"Oh now, you know that's not true."

Eric ignored him, read on:

*It's when I try to think with the mind of this super-mind that I find chaos indicated as often as cosmos. For I discover that whenever I see order, I find chaos close behind. To us, butchering hogs in a packing plant may seem an orderly way of supplying meat to a complex society, but to a super-mind, it may mean something else. Key your brain to its highest pitch of perception, banish as much of the clouds of faith as possible, let the sun shine at its brightest, and what do you find? You find that you are confused. Uncertain. And what should that tell you? That maybe you're reflecting reality. That is, chaos.*

Eric protested. "But nobody's happy when they're confused."

"Well? What of it? Maybe it takes a man to be happy in the midst of confusion."

"Well, maybe."

"Really. I'm often most happy when I'm uncertain. Because it tells me that I'm not seeing what I expect, but seeing what is most likely there."

Eric pushed his mind ahead to understand. He looked down at the papers again:

*Sometimes I think that the universe is a chaos of parts, pieces, fluids, into which organizations are working their way, making a living off the countryside as they go, and dying after an effort. Measured against the strongest concept of duration that we have, what is a life? A civilization? Both, as with organizations and organs, collapse, and the parts, once hitched to each other, separate, and break up, and commingle again with the gray immensity of waste . . . until another temporal organization arises.*

Eric looked at Fawkes, narrowing his eyes. "Heck, aren't you loading the same old gun with the same old powder and shot?"

"How so?" Fawkes smiled, as if he already knew what Eric was after.

"Well, take your words 'parts,' 'pieces,' 'fluids,' here. Aren't they the same old cookies, units, stamped out of the same old mass of dough?"

"Yes. Of course. And that's the trouble. Science has not yet been able to work out a language, a set of tools that will come to grips with chaos. The evanescent organisms have a voice, but chaos does not. The only way we'll ever be able to describe chaos is to jump our world. Leave it."

"Chaos, huh. Well, that means that the Whipper wins again."

"Who?"

"The Whipper. The whip of the universe."

"Oh, that bird again. You've got Him on your mind, haven't you?"

"Well, sometimes I really believe He exists. I mean . . . He's like a person to me."

"Maybe so. Such persons make good scapegoats."

"Oh, but I'm not rationalizing."

"Oh, but you are."

"But I'm not."

"Sorry. I'm saying what I see."

Eric pondered. "Don't you believe the universe hates you?"

"No."

"You don't fear the universe?"

"No. Why should I? In fact, it's just possible that the universe, or the Whipper, fears me."

"Huh."

"Sure. Because I'm trying to be a scientist. And I look at Him as impersonally as He supposedly looks at me."

"Oh."

Fawkes' eyes became smoky with thought. "You see, the true Whipper is neither concerned nor unconcerned about us. He is a universe that has no knowledge of us. He can't have. Because he neither feels, nor hears, nor sees . . . nor probably knows."

Eric nodded. He looked vaguely into the dark corner of the room where once Huck had lain. An idea occurred to him. "You know, Fawkes, reading this, a man'd almost think you were writing your swan-song."

Fawkes grunted and sat up and reached for the papers and pulled them from Eric's unwilling hands. "Maybe I am."

Eric crossed his legs. "By the way, what has your temp been lately?"

"Oh. All right. Up a little." Fawkes dropped the notes into the bedstand drawer.

Eric grunted. Empty questions begot empty answers. He studied Fawkes, wondering what was going on in his mind. The light on Fawkes' bed shone angularly across his thin face, accentuating the out-thrusting forehead and nose and mustached upper lip. Eric was startled to see how bony-thin his remaining roommate was. Could Fawkes have slipped so much in one week? Or had the seven-day absence allowed him a fresh impression of his roommate?

"Fawkes, don't you feel well?"

Fawkes' eyes clouded. "Oh, I feel all right." He shifted the book from his chest to his raised knees.

"You look good." Eric recalled the smell of decayed excreta he had noticed as he came in from the fresh outdoors.

"I better look good. I'm going to have an operation tomorrow."

Eric gripped the edge of his bed. "Serious?"

"Extra-pleura pneumonolysis. Nothing really. When they get done, I'll be able to take treatments something like those you were getting. Your doctor was trying to collapse your lung there by injecting air between it and the pleura. In this deal, after the operation, they'll inject air between the pleura and the ribs."

"Why no pneumo for you?"

"Adhesions." Fawkes paused. "Yes, it's too bad, all right. But, we've got to hurry. My left lung is developing cavitation."

"Is your father coming?"

"No. It's not that important."

Eric nodded. He understood. This man, who had never irritated him, who had been a perfect roommate, who had been tolerant of every tantrum and idea of his, was a wonderful man to say that. And even now, dying perhaps, he had bothered to soothe a child. Eric remembered too that Fawkes had been willing to risk his precious lungs when Huck died. Eric thinned his lips to keep from blurting something sentimental. "What about a rib-sectioning for you?"

Fawkes gestured. "Too late for that. Bad heart. Just like father."

Tears circled Eric's eyes and gradually filmed them. He felt ashamed. Here he was floundering and roaring and crying around in this ward, thinking he was getting a pretty bad lashing from the Whipper, when all the while he had a roommate who, deathly ill, was not raising a hundredth as much fuss as he was. The Whipper was evoking from Fawkes no more than gentle comments. Eric looked down at his feet. "Tell me, how does this operation go?"

"Oh, it's really quite simple. Butcher Boy Stein'll cut off pieces of two ribs to make a hole just big enough for him to get his paw into my chest. Then he'll pull the pleura away from the ribs just like you would pull out a rubber inner tube that's stuck to the insides of an old tire casing. Then he'll fill the sack he's made with air and sew it up. When the wound's healed, you got a little pocket of air there, pushing the lung down."

"Say. I wonder. Why didn't Doc try that on me?"

"It's the last acey-deucey the doctor plays."

"Oh." He took a deep breath. "By God, Fawkes, I wish you a lot of luck."

"Luck won't do it. I've either got enough energy, or . . . I haven't."

"Man, you . . . " Eric turned to hide his face. He looked into the dark corner where Huck had died.

"Well, Eric, it's all right. I learned long ago to expect changes." He sighed. "And some of them are good. Like getting new roommates."

266

Eric caught at a word. "Say, that's right. We'll soon be having a new roommate, won't we?"

"You will, you mean. And two of 'em. I'm going up on Critical tomorrow. For two months."

"But Moses, man, I'd like to keep you."

Fawkes did not reply.

Eric stood up and went to his stand and poured out a glass of water from his water-bottle and drank a little. After the country water on Mary's farm, the chemically treated fluid was bitter.

He got back into bed and settled into his pillow, thinking. He worked at cleaning his wick. Presently his flame steadied and lifted, and his vision opened. What if Fawkes should die? Should never come down from Critical again? He wished he were a surgeon, skilled. He looked out of the window. Long ago September sundown had flown. Purples at the western horizon had deepened to black. Just above the rim of earth the planet of love burned whitely.

He nodded to himself. This flame of Fawkes should be saved and burned in an American Athens. Fawkes should have offspring. Children. Two boys. A girl. Cups to catch his fuels.

Yet a child could never be Fawkes. The moment Fawkes died he would be gone. Just as one could not move a piece of flame from one place to another without moving the wood that burned, or the oil, or whatever the fuel might be, so no one could move a piece of a man's spirit without moving too, a piece of his flesh.

Besides, it would be terrible punishment for the child. One soul is burden enough for any temple, crumbling or gleaming in the sun. Two souls in one body would double the tears. The child would become twice as desperate to avoid a death. He would be twice as anxious to foist his spirits upon his children.

No, when a temple fell, the spirit in it should vanish too. It was best that a man returned to the universe the dust he had borrowed to live in and the ideas he had learned to live by.

267

Eternity. Eternity. Who knew the word? The idea? For each man, forever lasts from the moment he is born until the moment he dies.

He moved his head to look at Fawkes. Why, the man had returned to his reading. That Fawkes. Imperturbable orb of fire. And the book? Doughty's *Travels In Arabia Deserta*. That scripture cut from basalt by the fragile fingers of a poet equipped with the brain of a Zeus.

Eric stirred and sat up. He made up his mind that the flame of Fawkes should not vanish. His knowledges, his gifts, his spirit, had to be saved. They had to be captured into imperishable cantos. If Fawkes were but a man who had merely discovered a specific cure for tuberculosis, mankind could let him die with only a few tears trembled. But Fawkes was more. He was the hardy flame up front taking the first leap into the darkness ahead. It was he who really met the Whipper face to face.

Eric sat stilled for a moment.

Then an anguished flame leaped to the roof of his skull. It could not be. It could not. If Fawkes should die on the table tomorrow, he would live on. He had to.

Eric swore an oath to himself. He swore that he would get Fawkes down on paper and pass on to others the prevailing attitude of this man's noble wonder at life, his gently critical spirit, his unprejudiced curiosity, his roving mind quietly asearch for pure truth, little caring what the Whipper might say or do. Fawkes was the silver-brained Poet that had been wrestling for expression in the fleshes of mankind. Fawkes was the evidence that Chaos, the Whipper, could be encroached upon.

"Fawkes, man, can I see your operation tomorrow?"

"Why, I dunno. It's against the rules, I think."

"But, I . . . Look. If you request it, I can see it. You know that. You're a doctor too. And I want to see it."

There was a long silence.

Then Fawkes moved in his bed and put aside the book that he had been waiting to read and turned off his bedlight and said, "I understand. Of course you can."

# M XXXII—THE WHIPPER STRIKES AGAIN

**M**AN IS A sealed lamp.

At birth an infant is given a certain measure of oil, a certain length of wick, and a spark. The oil is energy, the wick hunger, and the spark enjoyment.

The father and mother and the uncles and aunts of the little infant fan the spark into the flame of manhood.

The flame burns, varyingly, for a lifetime.

When the oil has burned, or the wick shortened, the old flame fluts. It dwindles to the infant's spark again. Presently it dies.

Sometimes, when the flame is fading, a lamp-trimmer with a cunning hand will come. He will remove a little of the carbon. He will jostle the last few drops of oil against the wick. He will stretch the wick. And the flame will live a moment.

But after the extra drops have burned, the flame will die.

In each man there is only a certain measure to burn.

The walls and the floor of the operating room were of green tile. Indirect lighting came from the north window. Except for the sliding doors that opened upon an observers' gallery, it was the same room where Eric had been given his pneumothorax, and where the negro in his wrath had flicked a razor at Dr. Abraham.

When Eric slipped into the gallery above the table, he found two young University internes, cynical Dr. Sauer and hearty Dr. Hansen, watching the operation, which had already begun. Eric sat down quietly. He straightened the long white smock that a nurse had given him to wear. He adjusted the germ-collector mask.

Stiffened by a local anesthesia, Fawkes lay nervelessly on a table. It was tipped so that the left side of his chest lay four inches higher than his right. He lay with his head toward Eric. Eric could barely catch the vivid dart and flash of his eyes past the prominent brow.

269

To Fawkes' left stood the butcher-big Dr. Stein; to his right, gentle narrow-lipped Dr. Price. Both were clothed in white from their eyes to their elbows and ankles. Both wore opera-long rubber gloves. Nearby hovered Dr. Abraham, his face wrinkled, his brow bubbled with sweat. There were three nurses.

Dr. Stein wielded the the scalpel, and talked. "Ted, you got the skin of a toad. Gray, and rotted t'hell."

Fawkes grinned a little.

Dr. Stein swore on. He cursed his luck. He wondered, aloud, when he would once again have the pleasure of cutting up the gentle flesh of a woman or of a sixteen-year-old lad. He cursed. He swore he was tired of cutting into the gray, dead, tubercular flesh of Phoenix patients. Christalmightygodtohellanyway.

For a little while, Eric inwardly condemned the braying, ass-eared Dr. Stein. But presently, as the operation progressed, and after he had studied Dr. Stein's orange pumpkin face, he began to understand that behind those craggy molds of flesh lived a kindly man who was continually being shocked by new hurts.

Peach-faced Dr. Price, in the meanwhile, stood by, blandly smiling.

Dr. Abraham leaned near, alert, silent.

No one else moved or spoke.

Eric watched so intently that his fisted hands soon pained him and he exercised them to ease the strain.

As Dr. Stein plowed on, he did not wait to hand the attending nurse his fouled instruments. Finished with a knife, he tossed it over his shoulder as if it were a corn ear and he an old-time cornshocker, and snatched at a fresh gleaming one.

Soon Dr. Stein picked up an instrument resembling a pair of wire nippers. He gritted his teeth into a ferocious square as he tried to snap off the first rib. He growled, "Fawkes, your ribs are as tough as oak roots."

Fawkes barely flinched. His brown eyes were alight with interest.

*Aawwwrrrk.*

"There. What a tough son of a bitch you are, Fawkes. Well, let's try the other end of it." He set the pincers and gripped.

*Aawwwrrrk.*

The bloody rib snapped over Dr. Stein's shoulder. It clattered to the floor, where a darting nurse jumped on it with a white napkin and covered it and covertly dropped it into a waste can.

*Aawwwrrrk.*

"Damn good thing we're not cannibals. How we'd cuss you if we were. Imagine having these god-damned ribs for supper."

Dr. Price laughed for the first time. "You know, the patients kid about that. When they're served spare-ribs, they always say, 'Yep, somebody's had a rib-clippin' today.' "

Dr. Abraham grinned momentarily.

Fawkes made a move as if he were about to say something.

Dr. Stein lifted his bloody nipper menacingly, and roared, "Acccl Shut up, damn you. Save your breath."

After a silence, Dr. Price chuckled, and mused, "You know, Stein, it's a good thing you're not in private practice, cussing the way you do. After a month of it, you probably wouldn't have a patient left."

"Oh yeh? I suppose you want me to operate like that suck-hole Dr. Sittaroni? What a racket he's got."

"Well, at least he makes a good living."

"Yeh. And how."

"Takes care of a lot of people. Averages a dozen an hour."

"Huh. And how. Look. Let's suppose you're a patient. All right. You come in. Okay. Sittaroni throws you up on a table. He rams a rubber glove up your sport, twirls it around a couple of times, says, 'Ten bucks. Come back Thursday. Next?' "

Everybody laughed.

**271**

"Sure he does!"

*Aawwwrrrk.*

"There. There's the son of a bitch." Dr. Stein heaved the second rib to one side. Like a foetal rabbit, it hopped around on the floor until a quick nurse caught it.

Fawkes moved a little.

"What's up?" Dr. Stein leaned over him.

"Right lung. Short there."

All three doctors moved forward. The nurses moved nearer. Silent.

"Better?"

"No. It's a . . . spontaneous." Fawkes gasped. "It's tight!" He sucked wildly for breath. He wrestled like an infant being choked in its blankets.

"Catheter," snapped Dr. Stein.

Quickly Dr. Abraham pulled up a stand to the operating table near Fawkes' head. He plunged a catheter through the ribs and the pleura of the right chest. He pressed down firmly, drew air as rapidly as he dared.

The surgeons waited. Dr. Stein's brow wrinkled. Dr. Price remained bland.

"Better?"

"Much."

"All right. Now," said Dr. Stein, moving in again. "Now." He cut through the opening he had made in the chest barrel; then started his hand up underneath the uncut ribs.

Fawkes moved.

They stopped again.

"Hurry," whispered Fawkes.

"Adrenalin," ordered Dr. Stein.

This time Dr. Price moved in.

After a long moment, Fawkes whispered, "That's better." Shifting his body a little, he whispered, "God. Now I know how a patient feels. Now I know. I can use that."

Eric became conscious of a movement somewhere above Fawkes. He looked up. He was startled to see a reflection of Fawkes in a mirror above the table. Fawkes was looking into it, and at him, smiling.

Eric sat, stilled.

The men were silent. They hurried. There was a tense-
ness in the room, a tautness.

Again Fawkes gasped, "Spontaneous."

Dr. Abraham leaped forward to the right chest.

"Acccc . . . no.The other . . ."

Dr. Stein jerked away. "No!"

Eric stared. He had an impulse to jump up and tear
the doctors away from Fawkes. He knew now why doctors
were loath to let husbands see their wives in the act of
giving birth to bloody babies.

Fawkes lay motionless.

In a calm voice Dr. Stein called out directions to the
doctors as one calamity after another hit Fawkes. The doctors were servants to a king.

"Adrenalin."

Yes. Yes.

"Left lung now."

Yes.

"Vomiting."

Yes.

"Adrenalin."

Yes.

How cool they all were. How calm Fawkes was. Eric almost gurgled with talk, with irrepressible excitement.

There was a sound of a door gently opening, of someone silently entering, of a faintly chuckling whisper.

Eric looked up at the mirror. Slowly Fawkes' bright,
brown eyes became smoky, as if he had a thought and were
searching for words to explain it. Then the smoke vanished
and the eyes were blank.

Dr. Stein turned away. Slowly, almost casually, he drew
the rubber gloves off his arms and hands and fingers, and
took off the germ-collector mask, and walked heavily out
of the room. A moment, and Dr. Price followed, mincing
out on stiff thin legs.

Dr. Abraham glanced up, wild-eyed.

Eric closed his eyes and saw, a little to the right, and in a front row seat, the Whipper.

The Great Cat of the universe, stupid in its blinking and timeless repose, had opened its Pa-cold eyes, thrown out a paw, and slapped to death a tiny inquisitive ant.

# A
## XXXIII—LAMENT

FTERWARDS, alone in his room, 176, Eric lay in the dark black night.

He felt he should write a poem of Fawkes, of Ted, of Theodore.

And long after the ill in the wards along the corridor had barked and coughed themselves to tired sleep, long after the womb-dark night had enfolded the stabbed with his wounds, at a time when words and verse well readily upward into the red consciousness of the sleepless seeker like slow blood rising on mashed capillaries, Eric thought, how utterly curious that the words so bright and literate in my mind have so little resemblance to the pain and love I feel.

My friend has gone.

Today I watched the burning sumac run enraged over the fall hills. I saw the leaves tremble red-gold beneath the trees. I discovered the lemoned poplars lonely in their tapered dignity. I rubbed my eyes to see the red-oaks blowing rusty purples. I filled my fever-swollen lungs with autumn's rain-washed air. All these were mine and yet . . . my Theodore is dead.

He is gone. Weep, weep, eyes. Eyes fixed unseeingly on his stone, weep. For you, Mary, and Pa, and I, all of us, have lost a mind that was nearest the clear, clear answer to this burning here; who rejoiced to see the Poet singing amidst the howling hungers of nature. All this he had . . . and yet, your Theodore is dead.

Because the feet of a million ants scratching on a single

stone cut a deeper language than all the talk of all the men since talk began, he was often silent. But when he did talk, his low words leaped. His story of the day when the sun first splashed the earth with energy and first stirred its atoms into a turbulence from which were born the fish and birds, and mankind with its First Words, was so real that I was able to live a billion years in a day. A billion years. And now, my Theodore is dead.

He knew, and was himself, the child wonder of the ancient Greeks, of Newton, of Darwin, of Eir tein. Like them he sat, a smiling friendly god on a parapet of history, contemplating the lanterns of mankind moving about in the dusky plains below while the stars circled in the great skies above. Like them he smiled and, neither condemning nor praising, offered comment.

Theodore, I shall never forget, how, when the Great Whipper swiped you bluntly across your chin, you still were smiling. And wondering.

O Theodore, I loved you because you had for the ghostly person of truth a greater friendship than you had for the fleshly person of man. And thereby loved man more. I loved you because you taught me that the Whipper does not exist except in ourselves, and that we find order or chaos just as we choose. I loved you because you opened a door for me, because you taught me to use myself as a pivot from which to strike for life.

Theodore, I swear it: someday I'll know the answer to this riddle of living. I swear it.

Yes, Theodore was dead. Gone.


# XXXIV—LONELINESS

LIKE AN enormous cauldron of metal, molten and smoldering, he swelled with a tumescing ache and wildness.

It was in the middle of rest hour, after a whole day of

snapping at nurses, of grabbing at things to do, of here and there a-flying and retreating, that he suddenly could stand it no longer. He leaped up and drew on his blue bathrobe and strode out of his room with its two empty beds. He went up tall and determined upon Miss Berg, the rest-hour nurse for the day. He ignored her fluttering questions and hands, her desperate telephoning of the head nurse, Miss Globe. He did not care that he was breaking the most hallowed law of the Phoenix, the absolute dictum that life in it must settle down to quiet near-death, to life fifteen-breaths-a-minute, during rest hour. What was a mere sour chokecherry added to the mouthful of alum that was his existence?

He took the stair-turn down and strode toward Dr. Abraham's door in the Main lobby. Out of breath, and swollen with unexploded emotion, he pounded on the door. There had been voices inside, but upon his sudden tempest of thunder strokes, they were silent. He burst in. Both Dr. Abraham and Dr. Stein looked up from smoking cigars.

A glance, and Dr. Stein stood up and left. Eric hardly noticed his going.

Dr. Abraham rose too, his eyes widening behind his blinking glasses. "What's wrong, my boy?"

"Doc, I came here to tell you I'm going. Going. You understand? Going!"

"Good."

"I mean right now. Not tomorrow, nor the next day. Right now. Going, I tell you. That room of mine, it's where things are always being dreamed of, but never done. I got to get out of it. I'll go nuts if I don't. You understand?"

"Sure."

"So, I'm going."

"Good. But is my office the exit?"

"No. I came here because I owe you at least a handshake and a thank-you. You've played it square with me, so I had to play it square with you."

"Thanks."

"But just the same, I'm going."

"All right, Eric. All right. Maybe it's a good thing." Dr. Abraham drew deeply on his cigar. "Won't you sit down a minute?"

"Now, Doc, don't get it in your head you can talk me out of it. Just as I said, I came down here because I thought I owed you an appearance, owed you a thank-you."

Dr. Abraham shot, "Couldn't you have sent me your thank-you by mail?"

"And felt a coward ever after? No, I came to tell you personally. With my own tongue."

Dr. Abraham nodded. By now his eyes had lost their startled, wide-eyed expression.

"So, I'm going. Well . . . "Eric paused. He was about to thrust out his big hand when he saw tears in Dr. Abraham's eyes. He started. Was the doctor the heart-friend he had been looking for? He let his hand fall. "Aw, Doc, I . . . I guess I've just been a lot of trouble to you. Not worth your time."

Dr. Abraham rolled his cigar between his fingers. He fumbled with the paper band. "My boy, has it ever occurred to you that trouble is my work?"

"Yes, but . . . just the same, I'm no good."

Dr. Abraham narrowed his eyes. "Well, I tell you, I tell you . . . I've been reading this record here." He drew out a black book from among the pigeonholes on his desk and opened it. "Look, read."

Curious, but ready for a trick, Eric read a few pages. Then, a new anger rising in him, he blurted, "Why, these are reports from Miss Mitchell on First East."

"Precisely."

"And . . . why, Holy Moses. She even put down when I went to the can."

"Sure." Dr. Abraham's face beamed like a cat's.

Eric leaned forward. "No wonder you docs know so much about us poor dogs. No wonder." He thinned his lips. "That's what I mean about this place. They pry into you so here. It's like living in a dictatorship, with spies running in and out of your ears like flies."

Dr. Abraham laughed. "Go ahead. Read a few more reports."

"More?"

"Sure. Page back a little. There, for instance."

Eric read. The passage described his skipping out with Mary on movie nights. "Why, those shaggy tattletales." He drew in a breath. "Those goddamned shaggy tattletales. Why, then you knew?"

"Sure I knew."

"Those damned tattletales."

"Hah. Yes. By the way, how's Mary?"

"Good. She's gone right now. For three weeks."

"Oh?"

Eric paused. Was the other wondering if this was another transient love affair? "Yes, she left for the North Shore of Lake Superior. With some girl friends of hers. I hated to see her go, was even envious of her being up in that cool, blue-smoky pine country. But, after this jail here, she had it coming. Lord, how she had her heart set on it. Lord."

"I can just imagine. She's all right?"

"Sure. Sure. What you getting at?"

"Nothing. Nothing." Dr. Abraham drew in a breath. His dark eyes narrowed behind the spectacles. "Eric, I think you are a coward."

Eric jumped back on the track. "Doc, don't try tricks."

Dr. Abraham puffed on his cigar, swelled up as if the breath he was taking in would lift him out of his chair; then slowly subsided, letting it escape in little shudders. "Okay, go then."

"I am. Don't rush me."

"Too bad. Too bad. Up to now you've been a good patient too."

"Huh. That's just talk, Doc. Talk. You know it."

"No, it's not talk."

"Aw, hell, look at the rules I've broken."

"But they were the right rules to break . . . for you. That's the thing about it. If you hadn't broken 'em, I would have worried."

Eric hesitated. He wondered. "Worried?"

"Sure."

"Oh."

"Look, before you go, how about taking another X-ray?"

"Well . . . "

"In the meantime, I'll try to get you into another room."

Eric pondered. He could see again, vividly, Fawkes' black mustache darkening against his paling skin. He shuddered.

He felt caught. No matter which way he ran now, this keen-eyed doctor would catch a glimpse of his awkward, heavy-footed stride.

Eric hesitated. Then, before surrendering, drew up his chest. "Well . . . if you do get me another room, make it a single."

Dr. Abraham jumped up, exasperated. He waved an arm. "Look. Do you want the nurses to take over my practice too?"

"How do you mean?"

"Look. To save ourselves time, we docs let the nurses house the patients. We just take care of their bodies. And brains, if they have any."

"But if you wanted to, you could get me a single room in a cottage, couldn't you?"

"You're not worth it, Frey."

"Well, hell, if that's the way you feel about it. I'll go see Miss Globe myself."

Dr. Abraham quieted. "Wait. Don't. That'll ruin everything."

A fagot of rebellion still glowed in Eric. "Doc, when can I start writing?"

Dr. Abraham sat down in his chair. His eyes became as wise as a cat's. "Are you ready for it?"

"Oh, then I can?"

"Well, when do you want to start?"

"Tomorrow? Or as soon as I've moved . . . or . . . next week . . . " Eric looked down at his pantofles. He scuffed them a little.

Dr. Abraham said abruptly. "Well, sir, I absolutely forbid you to write. Understand? First: it's too upsetting. Second: it's too much of a strain. Remember, you have a long way to go yet. Those TB equilibriums can still be tipped." He gestured as if he were weighing him and TB in a balance.

Eric peered at the other. The doctor was plying his trade again. Tricks. "But, anyway, if I get a good X-ray, I can move to a single room?"

"Yes. And start the next bank of privileges."

Eric jumped up. "You mean, meals? I can start meals in the main dining-hall?"

Dr. Abraham nodded. A covert smile wrinkled his face. "In two weeks, yes."


# H

### XXXV—REBUFF

IS X-RAY showed no change. He could move. He could go up to meals.

On the way to the Emporium to celebrate with a bottle of pop, he saw Miss Mitchell sitting at her desk, writing in a black book. He saw her shove it under a newspaper.

Anger erupted in him. "Well, Miss Mitchell, I see you're still working on my case history."

She stiffened.

"Yes, and I do mean trips to the bathroom," he added.

She turned. Her face flamed, became as red as her hair. "Mr. Frey, I'll thank you to mind your own affairs."

"Okay. But one thing I'd like to ask you. Did you ever read the Bill of Rights?"

She drew in her breath, stood up. "Did you ever reread that *Pauper's Oath* you signed when you came in?"

He straightened. A sulphuric lava of hatred for all white-gowned creatures rose in him. As he stood glaring at Miss Mitchell, he decided to see Miss Globe despite Dr. Abraham's warning. He made up his mind to humble these imperious, ubiquitous amazons, by striking at their head. "Miss Mitchell, I was on may way to the store, but, instead, I think I'm going to call on Miss Globe. Mind?"

Abruptly her manner changed. She hesitated, asked, "Is it anything I can do for you?"

He gloated. "No. This is a private affair."

She clicked her teeth, narrowed her lips. "All right. Be sure to sign out when you leave the floor."

"I'm not signing out. I'm telling you."

"Sign out. On that sign-out sheet right there."

"Oh, all right."

As he stepped into Miss Globe's office, the tall, black-eyed woman was listening to the telephone. "Yes?" she asked, looking up at him. Then she frowned. "Just a minute. Could you wait out in the hallway a moment?" She put down the receiver and stood up and closed the door behind him.

When she asked him in again, he pointed to the telephone and said, "I hope Miss Mitchell tattled the truth."

Her eyes gleamed blackly at him and he knew he had hit. "What do you want?" she asked, standing as tall as she could.

He shifted on his feet. His arches were still weak. He wished he could sit down but felt he could not give Miss Globe the advantage of looming over him. "Well, has Dr. Abraham told you I'm to move?"

"Yes, he has." She glanced up and down his long frame, and backed away a step.

He smiled. "Well, I'd like to get a single room in the cottage. I want to study. Write. And I need privacy for that."

"Huh. What makes you think your problem warrants a single room?"

"I'm a writer."

"Does that make you any different from any other patient?"

"Well, I've seen some things and I want to put them down."

"Huh. That doesn't mean much to me. We've had all kinds of hoboes here who thought they could write." She pointed to a chair.

He shook his head. "But I can write."

"They all think that." Again she pointed.

Again he refused.

Then she sat down.

He followed and folded his long bathrobe neatly over his knees. He fumbled with the silver tassels at the end of the belt.

She went on, tartly, "Mr. Frey, you know we can't go out of our way and play favorites with every fool who thinks he can write. We've had all kinds of them here and none of 'em ever wrote anything. Now, if you were a genius, somebody well-known . . . why . . . "

Abruptly he felt sad, defeated. He looked down at the floor. Yes, really, just what had he written so far? Nothing but a manuscript that had been rejected.


# XXXVI—RE-ENTER SATAN

THE ROOM Miss Globe assigned him was a six-bed ward in the East Cottage.

For a time the excitement of moving opened his lips with smiles. The wide sun burned golden upon the land, on the grass still green, on the leaves of molten red-brown and purple and dull gray-yellow.

But when night came, he was lost. The six-bed ward, he discovered, was full of chronics, men doomed like Deeble to stay out the rest of their lives in the care of the county because they turned up a positive sputum occasionally. That first night in the cottage his compassion for the humble people almost vanished. After 9 p.m., when the lights went out, the man next to him began to snore like the bass in an old accordion. Five minutes later, the old papa in the next bed started up his distinctive tremulo, his blursting, mouth-cleaning snorts. "Snortcchh . . . hacctthh. Snortch . . . hacctthh." Then the third papa started off. The fourth. The fifth. The whole ward rocked and tumbled and boiled. He did not sleep that night.

The next morning, feeling very white, he met Satan Deeble in the hallway. He tried to smile. He was glad to see someone he knew.

Satan's brown eyes glinted in his blue-milky face. "You here too?"

"Yeh. And how."

"What's up?"

"I'm in with those prehistoric chronics there," he said sourily, pointing. "It's like living in the Black Hole of Calcutta."

Satan laughed and slapped his back. "I can just imagine."

Eric went on, observing, "If the good angel Gabriel had called last night, I wouldn't have heard his trumpet."

Satan guffawed.

Though Eric was exhausted and drawn from lack of sleep, he grimly refused to complain to Miss Hatchett, his new charge nurse. He would give those power-mad females no satisfaction.

A week later, a patient escaped through a bathroom window. Eric was assigned to the man's single room. It was on the second floor, directly above Satan's, and overlooked the porch from which Satan sometimes peered through his cheap telescope at the strewn worlds mounted in the sky.

It was Satan who told him one night that Old Fawkes had died of heart failure just three days before Young Fawkes had gone. Eric paled. While he had been gorging himself with the blood-red life on Mary's farm, the tottering white-haired giant had fallen. Two flames of genius, gone. And never a word from Young Fawkes.

Eric looked up and around, half-expecting to see the Whipper hovering near. Then, remembering that Fawkes would have shrugged at such fiction, he tried to laugh at himself.


# I

## XXXVII—SATAN TEMPTS ERIC

T WAS EARLY evening. The sun was setting. Clad in his long blue robe with its silver-tasseled belt, Eric paced his single room. Occasionally he glanced out of the window to study the downward falling hill to the south, and the swamp and lake below. Early October sunlight was falling obliquely across the dull-green lawn and building white fires in a row of birches along the east road. The purples in the burr oaks were fading to dull brown and the once-scarlet sumac bushes to orange. Mournfully, lonesomely, he realized that winter was near.

There was a knock on the door. It creaked and opened. Eric turned. "Oh . . . it's you."

"Yes, me. Satan," smirked blue-skinned Deeble, standing in the doorway. He was wearing hard-red pajamas.

Eric glanced at him and shivered. Five stages of rib-cutting had certainly caved in his left chest and back. "What's up?"

"Why, I thought maybe you'd like to hear a little Wagner, or some Franck or so. And have a cracker and sardine with me. I got a little bottle of urinated nearbeer too. How about it?"

Music. Food. Talk. "Why, Deeb, I'd be tickled t'death to come."

As they tramped down the old wooden stairs together, it occurred to Eric that Deeble might be up to something. He remembered that Deeble had walked with Mary. He became alert.

Entering the room, exactly like Eric's above, Deeble

snapped on the overhead light. He set out the sardines, crackers, and beer, and put a record on the electric phonograph. It was Ravel's *Bolero*. "Well, make yourself t'home," Deeble said, waving his thin arm, and settling himself on the bed.

Eric sat down on the bed too, slowly eating and sipping, and listening to the rising strains of music.

But Ravel irritated him tonight. He did not care to be reminded of the aching days when he was first getting up and slowly climbing the long tedious stair of the body-rebuilding program. He twitched on the bed.

Satan tried to entice him into an argument about Dr. Stekel, Jeans' concept of the universe, astronomy, sex, and women. But Eric felt no impulse to argue.

A wise look narrowed Satan's eyes. He quieted and shut down the phonograph.

The crackers were noisy. A sardine slipped from Eric's fingers. He cursed.

Deeble's dark, subtle eyes flicked at him. "Got something on your mind?"

"No. Nothing."

Satan drew a wafer from the box and carefully loaded a slippery sardine on it. "Look, I've been here long enough to know a guy shouldn't force his friendships. But, just the same, I'd like to give you a piece of advice."

"Oh?"

"Yeh. Why don't you get drunk?"

"Drunk? What good'll that do?"

"Relax you."

"And the cure-taking?"

"Balls, who cares about cure-taking. Hell, you'll probably hemorrhage within the hour anyway."

"What're you trying to do, Deeb, break down my health again?"

"No. I begrudge no man his health."

"Look, Deeb. I don't want you to think I'm a prude. I like liquor, I like cigarettes, I like women. I like them as much as you do, perhaps. But it also happens I like some-

285

thing else better. I like to suck on a certain big red bone, suck on it for its yellowest most delicious marrow. And the only place I can get that certain bone is on the outside. So, dammit, I want to get out of here and have it."

"Are you sure you'll find that red bone outside?"

"Yes."

"Huh. I got a feeling that with a little coaching" . . . Satan drew a fifth of whiskey from his stand . . . "I'm sure I can make a first class IWW out of you. Because I know you really hate society. Don't you?"

"No."

"The hell you don't. Here, take a slug."

"No."

"No? Well, then I will." He guggled at the bottle a few moments; smacked his lips. "Sure you don't want a slug?"

"No."

"You're missing something. Really." He swigged again. "Balls of fire, what a first class IWW you'd make. It wouldn't take you long to grab The Brain by the beard and revolutionize the world."

"I don't get you."

"Look. You're one of these birds that could out-talk Apostle Paul himself, once you got the faith."

"Well, who doesn't live by some kind of faith?"

"Me."

"Huh."

"You see, I'm a philosopher. I don't need faith." Satan drank again. "C'mon, get drunk with me. We'll quote each other Shelley and have a helluva time. C'mon."

"No."

Satan grinned. He offered Eric a cigarette and, the offer refused, took one himself and lighted it and blew out an enormous cloud of smoke. He leaned back across the bed and said, smirking, "You sure think you're pretty good, don't you?"

Eric stood up. "I think I'll go to bed."

"What's the hurry?"

"Oh . . . it's time for cure-takers to sleep."

Satan sneered. "Teacher's pet."

"Harsh teachers, these damn bugs."

"Bugs, bugs, bugs! Who the hell gives a damn about bugs, anyway. It's only a fiction of the mind. Sit down. Here. Take a drink. Be a man. T'hell with TB. Let's have some fun."

"No . . . thanks." Eric rubbed his nose. "I'm sorry."

"What are you anyway, man or mouse?" Satan demanded angrily.

"I dunno, Deeb." He was sorry he had stirred the hardstone on the other's heart. "Good-night, Deeb." He left.


# E

## XXXVIII—THE WAY WIDENS

RIC longed for Mary's return from the North Shore. He wrote her letters.

I've tried to read a book, Thoreau, Cristo; I've tried to imagine you coming suddenly, miraculously, into my door . . . but the door does not open to my desperate willing. I've tried to play games, checkers, chess . . . but each checker becomes you smiling there and each queen so real I lose her.

He wrote a poem—

> *I've read, I've mused, I've read.*
> *I've learned of sex and bread.*
> *I've even reaped a crop,*
> *And learned to taste each drop,*
> *Each grape, each plum, each man*
> *As near the pit as can.*
>
> *Yet, I can sing no song*
> *To tell you what is wrong.*
> *I've but a taste or two*
> *To smile about with you.*
> *Go you to crows and Shaws*
> *To get you croaks and saws.*

> *. . . And anyway, our flock*
> *Wili take to flight, I think.*

And everywhere he looked, he saw momentary images of Fawkes: a gesture, a smile, a brushy pair of brows, a dark square moustache, a thought.

He griped about in his room. Now that he was an ambulant, he had to make his bed and clean his room. He performed these chores so half-heartedly that Hatchett, the squash-shaped East Cottage nurse, wrote furious stories about him in her black book.

It was dinner time and he was going up for his first meal. For the first time too, he was dressing in civilian clothes: underwear, blue trousers, shirt and tie, sweater, socks, and shoes.

Coming down the stairway he met blue-skinned Satan Deeble.

Satan croaked, "Huh. Dressed up, you look human."

Eric growled.

"It's going to be fun to see you when the dining-room anvil-chorus starts giving you the raspberry."

"They won't bother me none."

"Mister, not even Socrates could keep a straight face when they begin to whistle and hoot and holler and scream, and pound the plates with their forks."

"Sounds like a nut-house."

"What else is the San?"

"What a helluva custom."

"My boy, it's as hallowed as Christmas."

"Aw, hell, they probably won't notice me anyway."

"My boy, there's always somebody there who'll notice the newcomer. For instance, there's me."

Eric shrugged and went over to a small white table near Hatchett's desk. He picked up a pencil to sign out.

"Hey, what you doing that for? Nobody signs out around here," Deeble said. "You sure are a hound for rules, aren't you?"

Eric hesitated; then dropped the pencil. If he had to break a rule, this might be a good one to try it on.

They walked to the end of the hallway. Before them were two doors. Satan asked, "Which way, by land or tunnel?"

"Huh?"

"Oh, you don't know that yet? Well, we can go by tunnel, or we can go over the top and walk on the grass outside."

"Give me the grass. I want no tunnels today."

"Lots a fun, them tunnels. Full of little nooks and crannies, and ninnies getting their nookies."

"Huh."

"No?"

"No."

The sea-green grass soothed him. He looked up at the sun sitting athwart the vast sky. The hill behind the cottage with its purpled white-oaks was a giant cluster of tokay grapes.

The burr-oak leaves, though brown, were crisp. Familiar was their rustling over his shoes. The birches were white. A few northern pines stood up on orange legs and held out needled wings to the sun. Down along the rim of the east road, standing apart, young maples burned like matches just put to flame and thrust, end down, into the earth. And near the main buildings, some of the sumac leaves, stubborn, hung stiffly burnt, so purple they were almost black.

Beneath his black-dark mood he felt his body singing, exulting, his animal nature bounding. He had a sudden hunger for pancakes fried over red oak leaves. He could smell the smoke of an imaginary fire.

He entered the building with Satan, went up to the third floor on the elevator, and passed through a wide door opening into an enormous dining hall.

Two long, winding lines of hungry patients, one on either side of the hall, had already formed. Food was being served cafeteria-style over a long counter on the east side.

He and Satan joined the nearest line-up.

He glanced about the hall. There were exactly fifty tables. Each one could seat six people. Some of the patients, already served, were walking out among the tables and looking for their places. He remembered, just now, that yesterday Satan had invited him to sit with him and two others, Dr. Sauer and Dr. Hansen, the same young medics who had seen Fawkes die.

A half dozen floor-to-ceiling windows opened up the west wall to the countryside. He could see rolling hills and occasional farms. He saw again the barn where the lad, after he had chased the cows inside, had mused long and long over the lower door. Where had that flame flown by now?

Eric turned to study the waiting people. At the head of the lineup were the chronics. They had come down twenty minutes early to be the first at the food. He saw twos and threes of comely women laughing and giggling at gibes thrown them by speculative-eyed men. Many of the women wore bright colors. The line shuffled forward, an enormous coiling caterpillar.

No matter how he tried to ignore the stares of the patients, he felt self-conscious. He had the feeling that a game warden had just dropped him into a pen of dart-eyed minks. He turned, to catch Satan staring and smiling at him too. "What the hell's so funny, mister?"

"Nothing. Nothing. Except that you're just about the tallest pair of stilts in human form that I've ever seen. And, I think the women agree with me."

"Satan, I think maybe you're a bit off the beam."

"Maybe so." Satan's grinning eyes surveyed the hall. "Look, take a look over there," he whispered. "See that pair of gals? Well, that quarter-blood there is slung in oil."

"You mean that cripple?"

"She may be crippled, but boy!"

Eric saw a short, bright-eyed maiden of sixteen with dark straight hair drawn over her forehead like a hood.

She had very wide hips. She tittered constantly, and carried on a half-dozen flirtations at once.

"What's her name?" Eric asked.

"Fork-in-the-Willow."

"Oh, go on."

"No. Really. She was raised by an Indian tribe up north until somebody found out she was feeble-minded. She was sent down to an institution for a while, got TB, came up here." He grinned. "Say, by the way, she's safe. She's been spayed."

"You mean . . . ?"

"Sure. She's the one I was thinking about when I mentioned that the tunnel was full of ninnies. Almost any evening of the week you can find her in that short tunnel leading off into the repair shop there."

Eric grunted. "Huh. And who's her steadiest customer?"

"Laric the Chronic."

"Not you?"

"Well . . ." Satan licked his lips. "I've split black oak, but it wasn't as good as that piece of red willow."

They moved along, shambling slowly.

A thin pole of a woman over six feet tall joined the line.

"Look," whispered Satan. "See her? How do you like her?"

"Huh."

"Well, you know what they say: an old maid's kiss is best because she thinks every one may be the last one and wants to make it the best she's ever had."

"Oh shut up, Deeb."

Satan pulled at his arm again. "Just as I thought," he muttered. "There comes Old Silas. There. At the end of the other line. See how he stands there? Everybody hates the old mole."

Eric looked over; and instantly felt pity for the bowed, aged creature. An incredible hump-back thrust Silas' head forward like a gobbler's. Suspicious, jerky eyes moved behind shy eyelids. Swaying, trembling, he stood nearly ten feet behind the last patient in the line.

"See that black coat he wears? Those fat bulging pockets?"

"Yes."

"He's got them filled with bread crusts and scraps of meat, the old miser. Those pockets sometimes stink so bad with maggots, Old Hatchett has to tear the clothes off him."

Eric, though cumbered by a tray and a set of eating utensils, turned away. "Oh, come now, Deeble."

Satan went on as if he hadn't noticed. "There's an interesting story about that bird. When his father died, his mother grew him up too close to her button and made an incestor out of him. And an imbecile. When she died, they found him buried in crumbs and Russian novels. Funny guy. As twisted as an Arabian figtree."

"The Russians, huh? He's got some intelligence then."

"Sure."

Eric filled his tray with steaming food, followed Satan to a table in the southwest corner of the hall. Dr. Sauer and Dr. Hansen were already there, eating. Recognizing him, they nodded. Eric sat down, arranged his plates, and began to eat. The constant thunder of noise rolling about them—shifting chairs, clanking ware, laughter, loud talk; and the savor of warm food, baked potatoes, pigs-in-blankets, red beets, orange carrots, milk, a dish of fresh pineapple—banished all thoughts of the old hump-back from his mind.

Presently, hunger quieted, he began to study his table-mates. Dr. Hansen was the most easily read. From his hearty face and dark hair and easy manners, Eric could see that he had never known a sick or hungry day. Eric decided he liked the man. He soothed his ego. Hansen was the kind that always had a gentle word for everyone. It was his task in life.

But Dr. Sauer was more of a mystery. Sauer, he had heard, was part-Jew. And an orphan. He had never found within the rigid walls of Judaism, nor among the gentiles outside, a kind word spoken directly, or an opened heart,

292

or an unprejudiced mind. All through his young life he had hungered for love, and for a chance to love someone. Yet, when he reached out a hand, he found men laughing at him and women eyeing him with apprehension. By the time he had grown up, he was bitter. He began to seek revenge. Men he tricked; women he debauched. He was a huge muscular bull; and once in his presence, every good heifer and every good cow thrilled and shivered and succumbed. He gamed to see how many he could violate before he died. He did not fasten himself to any one more than twice.

There was a scream in the dining-hall. Silas, who had gone to his solitary table with his usual six slices of toast, two cups of coffee, and egg, had just discovered that his toast was cold. Like a child, he boiled up into quick uncontrollable anger, and ran shuffling and squirreling across the hall to the counter, scolding shrilly, demanding fresh toast.

The male cook laughed.

Again Silas screamed. He stamped.

The diners, seeing how things were going, began to stir, then to cheer. In a moment the whole room was a-thunder with claps and hisses and roars, and forks clanking on china.

Silas turned. With venomous eyes he studied his tormentors. Reluctantly he backed away and started for his table again.

Fork-in-the-Willow, seeing how the tide had run, darted her red tongue at him as he went by her table. Instantly Silas leaped forward. He shook his wriggling withered fingers in her face.

Everyone in the hall quieted; some sucked a quick breath.

Silas approached her. His claws worked slowly, closing in on her neck, his eyes wide and rolling like yellow-rimmed black susans. Fork-in-the-Willow's eyes swirled, animal-wise. She leaped at him. Nimbly Silas jerked back and escaped her slashing fingernails. She ran hobbling after him a few steps and, suddenly laughing, returned to her table.

For a few moments no one at Eric's table offered a word.

Then Sauer said, "Well, Hansen, taking up an old bone of ours, I guess that just about proves my argument. When you're down, you can't expect mercy from your fellow animals, human or otherwise." His dark restless eyes flickered. "Poor bastard. He hasn't got the chance of a thin snowball in hell. No one'll ever love him, or give him a chance. No one. And, he'll be lonesome until he dies." He added bitterly, "It would be a kindness to kill him."

Hansen reddened, said nothing.

Sauer burned on, sulphurously, looking at Satan Deeble. "Just wait until Satan gets his hands on Silas' lungs down in the Morgue. Won't he chuckle that another poor bastard has gone to hell without a stroke of joy."

Eric looked up startled, worried that there might be a fight at his table. But Satan, like a pleased ghoul, only grinned.

Eric finished eating, and remembered that he was due for an initiation. His tablemates, he saw, were already eyeing him with glimmering mirth.

Satan said, "Aw, c'mon Eric, get up and take your medicine."

Knowing he could not escape, he swallowed, stood up, and was immediately overwhelmed by a tumult of clanking and whistling and braying asses. He flushed. He grinned. He looked down at his feet as he hurried for the tray-racks. He shelved his dishes and turned for the door. He stroked his dull-straw hair and nervously hooked his finger over his nose. He grinned like a yokel caught in a watermelon patch.

# T

HE NEW FACES stirred him. And just as once
before, when he joined the bathroom forum, he began to
hunt for the bright, clear, high-flaming wick.

Evenings he searched the cottage. Out in the lounging
room, Laric the cornstalk-thin Chronic and his four cronies
played at an endless game of rummy. Each night one of the
men took a turn at kibitzing. Of the four, Bloomquist was
the oldest. Seventy, in his nods, and wrinkled, he played
a cunning game and sat until bedtime as silent as an animal. He had been a farmer once, and the callouses on the
palms of his hands were as thick as the pads on a turtle's
foot. He had never been hurt, nor hungry, nor idle. He had
gotten from life what he wanted of it. And more: ten
years ago he broke down with slow tuberculosis and so had
become eligible to live off the county.

Another was Popeye the Sailor, an incredibly cadaver-
ous fellow, who bragged good-naturedly about the cards he
had held the night before. He was so blue with disease that
his face was purple, his eyebrows faintly mauve.

And there was Andy Dirkens, shell-shocked in World
War I, who liberally spilled dung stories which nobody
smiled or laughed about. He slapped his cards down on the
table as if his life depended on them.

Pat was stone deaf, and was jammed with strange lore.
He was an "aginer." He was an authority on the white
man's maltreatment of the Indians. He gave little presents
to Fork-in-the-Willow and tried to get her to accept him as
a foster-father. Sometimes, to gain attention, he got drunk
and roared with sodden repetition the ribald ditty—

> *Frankie and Johnnie were lovers.*
> *O lordy how they could love.*
> *They swore to be true to each other,*
> *As true as the stars above.*
> *But he was a man,*
> *And he done her wrong.*

One night Eric caught him fumbling, ineffectively, with Fork-in-the-Willow. Laric the Chronic was coaching him. A passing impulse had stirred the stilled knob his stone-head.

Then there was the hearty visitor, Hoyt Murphy, ex-patient, who came into the lounge casting wary glances over his shoulders as if he too had a personal Whipper. He wanted to know where all his pals had gone. He had been to Californier, he had, and by jinks, he had to know what had happened to Pete Katrush.

"Oh," said Laric the Chronic, glancing up from a hand of rummy, "oh, he diedt last year."

"No. Dead, huh?" Hoyt staggered a little. Then, haul-ing up a grin, and looking about for Deputy Brannon, he drew forth a hipflask of whiskey, swigged it, and snorted to clear his head. "And Hank Matly? Geez, there was a helluva nice feller. Could lie like a whore, he could. What happened to him?"

"Oh, he diedt too. Two, three year ago. Hemritch."

"Hemorrhage, huh?" Hoyt staggered again; and braced himself with a snort. "And that, that . . . aw, you know who I mean. He had a white beard. We called him Gram-paw. A helluva nice feller too. You know, Old Jiggs?"

"He diedt this spring."

"Ssst, he too, huh? Jissus." He nipped again. "And old Judge Cripps, the guy with the meanest tongue in town?"

"Well, I dunno. I guess maybe Satan's got him down in the Morgue there. Ya, he is pickledted too."

"Ssst."

Hoyt stood for a moment, sniffing; and, looking around, muttered, "That smell. No matter how much I drink be-fore I get here, I always smell that smell. I sure feel low when I smell it." And turning, he hurried away.

Laric the Chronic went on with the game of rummy. Not once during the colloquy had any of the others looked up.

Sometimes to pass the time away, when he tired of reading, Eric sought out Satan and two others, Guster the Boaster and quiet Andy Rykov, to play a few hands of whist.

The first time Eric saw Andy, he liked him. An epileptic, and a tubercular, he also had arterio-sclerosis; and to the question, "How're you today, Andy?" he would always reply, mournfully, shaking his round Slavic head, "Well, I made it up to that last hypo, but I don't know . . . maybe I won't make the next one." His life was a thin cord. Every two hours, when Hatchett gave him a hypodermic, another short string was knotted to it. Eric peered at him. Through the gray lustreless eyes and falling lard-colored hair, the man's continual smile was the breaking of light through fog.

Guster the Boaster, however, irritated Eric. He teemed with schemes to cheat his fellowman. He spent so much time devising schemes that with his ordinary brain he was more than a match for the genius who gives only passing attention to such knavery. When he stood talking, he rolled about on short legs, swaggering and stomping and swearing, and busily annoucing some fresh enterprise that would bring him "plenty of big potatoes, by God. You bet." Probing Guster the Boaster's past, Eric found that he had been an orphan in a religious institution. Once, as a lad, he had kicked a nun in the shins. She had scolded him for stealing. For many days thereafter he had spent sleepless nights, sure that he was doomed to go to hell because he had kicked a bride of Christ.

Once, returning from a dinner, he discovered a lovely woman. She was a Phoenix doctor, convalescing from a broken leg. She had been in bed a couple of months and now sat weakly in a wheelchair in the auditorium, listening to an organ rendition of Handel's *Largo* on the phonograph. Earlier, he had heard that she was so shy that she never looked a patient in the eye. Looking at her now, Eric could imagine her whispering away on her rounds, as quiet as a sigh in a cathedral. Yet, there were evidences of a fine flame in her. Within the walls of her person he could see a tall flower burning. He stood beside her, talking, warmly smiling, and looking off to one side so he would not embarrass her.

Suddenly she asked, "You write, don't you?"

"A little. It's nothing, though. Nothing." He was surprised at his own words. Her shyness had been catching.

"What about?"

"People hoping."

"My father wrote about that too," she said.

He watched a flower opening in her eyes. He wondered what childhood fancy, or memory, was stirring her. But he could not catch the falling petal.

One noon a young woman named Clara took his arm in the dim tunnel on the way back to the cottages. The tunnel from the dining hall led directly north, and then, half-way, branched to the right and left; the left leading to the women's cottage, the right to the men's. She walked tipping along on high heels, gushing of "literacha" and using the word "satisfaxtion" in every other sentence.

"Did you ever read the *Forsythe Saga?*" she asked.

"Yes. I . . ."

"Oh, I got considerable satisfaxtion out of that."

He noticed the straining eyes, felt the clutching fingers on his arm.

"And Tolstoi? Oh, I got considerable satisfaxtion out of him too."

An anger rose in him. She sucked her bone too loudly. He turned away. He hurried through the dimly lighted tunnel toward the men's cottage.

Down on the lower floor of the San where the auditorium opened into a foyer he had often seen a fearfully crippled woman, Minnie. Though only thirty, her hair was so grayed it was as white as skimmed milk. For eyes she had holes through which one could see flames leaping from the furnace inside her skull. Some great paw had swiped her head deep back into the barrel of her chest, had crumpled her backbone into three vicious curves, and bulged her bowels and stomach outward. Inside her crutches her legs were thin dangles. Her toes and arches were so folded that she wore baby shoes.

Every time Eric saw Minnie he smiled at her, warmly, as though she were a good acquaintance of his. Because Minnie had been robbed of so much, he felt she had a friendly nod coming. But she only scowled at him. He thought his efforts wasted until he was startled to notice one noon that she seemed to make a point of being near the auditorium every time he came along to go to dinner. Puzzled, he decided to test her. He entered the rear of the auditorium and stood behind a pillar. He observed her for a while. She stood near the door, hobbling around, obviously watching for someone to come. Sure that she was waiting for him, he strolled into view. Instantly her face broke into a full scowl and she began to wriggle excitely on her crutches. He waved to her and entered the elevator. As he entered the dining room, still wondering why she should always scowl at him, he suddenly straightened. Why, why, Minnie couldn't smile! Her face was too contorted. That fearsome scowl was a smile. Quickly he turned and ran downstairs. But when he reached the first floor, she was gone.

Oddly enough, a day later Satan came into Eric's room, laughing and waving a sixteen-page letter. "Eric, read this. Minnie brought it to my *Drums* office this morning. You know I help edit the paper, don't you? Well, are my efforts appreciated. And how. She came on her crutches and started to tear down the joint. Man, she actually whacked me over the head." He whistled and with his finger outlined a bump above his ear.

Eric sat up. "What'd you do to her?"

Satan drew back. "Nothing. Nothing. We got a correspondent on every floor, you know. Also from the mental case floor where she's located. And some biddy up there

299

wrote some stuff about her, I guess." He narrowed his eyes. "Balls of fire, man, you don't think that I would stoop to malign that poor creature, do you?"

"What're you laughing about then?"

"Why . . . this letter."

"Let's see it."

He read:

To the Drums Editor: You & your
(bunch) of white—washed hypocrites, I'm
sick & tired of your rotten cracks etc.
...in your old Drums, lay off me will
you ! ? or else...as for meeting Dale
Carnegie thank you, I've already made
his acquaintance & of all his works
before you were dry behind the ears,
that's forsure! It might do you some
good to meet him your selves, and be—
cause I don't believe in being a two-
face hypocrite & have courage & nerve
to come out in the open with frank,
honest truths & facts in plain bold
english, with my opinions & experiences
& to tell certain people what I think
of them is o. k. & I mean just what I
said, that's forsure! I can get along
with any body till they start annoying me
with a lot of mental & physical abuse &
anguish, & petty sarcasm here, & being
around this "hashhouse" of "Doom" has
cured me of a lot of people & things.
I'm not scared of nobody & that goes
for all the crepe hanging "stuffed—shirt"
imperialists & their Hitlerized methods
around here, & all over the states.
They hate Hitler around here & around

the states, but I notice they are doing
all they can to employ Hitler's Methods
around here & all over the U. S. A.
All the blankety blank imperial—minded,
power & money gluttons ought to be
pulverized, pickled in brimestone &
boiled in oil & kicked slick & clean off
the face of the earth, since they are
worse than a pain in the Neck.

Eric flipped over a few pages—

then when somebody who has crust enough
to fight for their rights in self—
defence & defending somebody else's
cause & purposes, then they are called
an "emotional tirade," phooey, bah!
I'm an American, and that's forsure,
& nothing else, etc....If some of
these conceited head—nurses, superin-
tendents, directors, & supervisors paid
more attention to donating better care,
service & treatments of the poor,
needy, & sick patients & less to their
d—a—r—n infernal overdone dogmatic
rules & "Correction Measures" & exper—
iments there would be far less deaths,
etc. they run this place like a "House
of correction" for outlaws & desper-
adoes, instead of a hospital for care &
treatment of the sick & tuberculous
patients & show favoritisms to their
pet snobs & high brows who haven't even
got horse—sense let alone a heart, that's
forsure.  I have too many out side
bigger & better influential friends
else where, that these (false prophets)

301

around <u>here</u> don't know about & never
will, because I won't ever give them
any satisfaction <u>who</u> & <u>where</u> they are,
but my friends all agreed with my
editorial I wrote in the <u>Mpls Star</u>
<u>Journal</u> not long ago, & and if they don't
<u>look</u> out around <u>here</u> & treat <u>me</u> <u>better</u>
than they have in the <u>past</u> & <u>mind</u> their
own <u>d----n</u> business, they're going to
get <u>more</u> & <u>double</u> lambasting, & get
their ears <u>pinned</u> back besides, <u>s000...!</u>
Again Eric turned over a couple of pages—

....those <u>dirty</u> <u>rats</u> like Dr. Dallesandro, Miss <u>Valery</u>, Miss Globe, & sev-
eral others will get put in the hoosegow
where they belong & HOW &  that's
forsure. <u>This is it.</u> A den of <u>snakes.</u>
This hole <u>tkes</u> the <u>prize</u> for dis-
tributing all the mental & physical
cruelities & punishments they can
muster & think of.  I know what I am
talking <u>about.</u>  I'm not <u>crazy,</u> nor one
single <u>bit</u> feeble-minded either, that's
forsure.  I had a fine Christian mother
and she raised me <u>right.</u>  These dirty-
low-life, dogmatic domineering, (imperialists) do everything under the sun to
humiliate & disgrace me before the Public
& all Society by their false brandings,
<u>lies</u> in their yearly campaigns & lec-
tures & conventions, while organized
labor, shorter hours & sanitary conditions have done more to eradicate
T. B. & diseases than all the "Phoenixes"
have ever or ever will.  They've <u>killed</u>

302

        more people around here than they have
        cured, they've been dying around this
        place like flies....

Eric shivered. The whirling vortex made his mind reel.
He felt himself slipping off a precipice. He collected himself. He felt embarrassed to have looked so long at the open
sore of so pitiable a creature. He turned severely on Satan.
"I hope you're not passing this around?"

"Balls of fire, no. What do you think I am?"

"I don't know. You let me read it."

"Well, you're intelligent, aren't you?"

Eric turned away. Take away a little education, he
thought to himself, the more obvious parts of it and he
could have written the letter himself a year ago. He recalled his tirade the night hard-nosed Miss Haxxo burst into
his room. Yes, Minnie, the Whipper is fierce, no man can
face Him alone.

Oh, where was there a fellow lamp?


The more he heard and saw of Satan Wybren Deeble,
the more he became interested in him. Eric put together
the parts of the puzzle of his life. As a lad, Satan had loved
his mother because, despite her fragile health, she had pro-
tected him from his father, a Jehovah-hard domeny, and
because he admired her for spending most of her spare
time helping the unfortunate in St. Paul. She asked him to
go to a theological seminary. He acquiesced. She wanted to
show her husband that a servant of God could be tender
and loving. But Satan, his heart given to stars and poesy,
flunked exegetics in his second year. Again, to please her,
he tried another seminary. Again he flunked. Not daring
to face her, he went on the bum. Five years later he popped
up in Minneapolis one day as a butcher. For three years
he was known as an honest, jolly meat-man. Then a
close friend, an artist, died of tuberculosis. Affected griev-
ously, Satan became interested in doing something for the
suffering patients in the Phoenix. He decided to work

there. He took a course at the University of Minnesota in laboratory technique, managed to memorize the habits, routines, formulas necessary to become a good technician, and was appointed to the staff of the laboratory.

He was a model technician for a year. He was considered a simple, kindly fellow. He was assigned the job of slicing excisions from the lungs of just-dead patients for microscopic examination.

He broke down with tuberculosis; and it took him four years to get back on his feet. To keep himself amused, he began to play cruel practical jokes on new patients. He was nicknamed Satan. When he was well enough to work as a patient-employee, though not well enough to leave, he was reassigned to his lab work. His co-workers soon noticed that when the lungs of certain patients came down to the lab, he manifested too lively, too mocking an interest in them. It was to this that Dr. Sauer had referred.

Curious to know what the Morgue was, and the lab, and how Satan worked in both, Eric made up his mind one forenoon to visit him. On legs that were still weak, he followed the long tunnel under the main building until he reached a point where, like a small intestine entering a colon, the tube sloped into a wide passageway. He stopped to rest. He looked around. Already the white-washed asbestos-covered steampipes, which had been threaded through the tunnels to heat the buildings from a central heating-plant, were sizzling against the fall chill.

Rested, he passed many strange dark doors. Wondering what was hidden behind them, and trying them, he found them all locked.

He came to a door that smelled strongly of formaldehyde. He tried it, found it locked too. He was about to turn away when, abruptly behind, a voice sounded. "You looking for somebody?"

Eric leaped, and stuttered, "Yes, I . . . " Then his eyes tightened. "Why, Satan! Moses, man, you almost scared the stuffings out of me." He looked around, uneasy. "By God, Satan, this is a spooky hole."

304

"It should be, considering what's down here."

"So this is the Morgue, huh."

Satan nodded. "Want to see it?"

"Yeh. I'm curious to see what it looks like."

"Well, you asked for it. Come." Going to the door, Satan entered a key into the lock and opened it. He snapped on the light. He motioned for Eric to enter first.

The Morgue was nearly forty feet long, twenty feet wide. Its walls were lined with shelves. Large glass jars filled with formaldehyde and floating slabs of human flesh were stacked in orderly rows.

"You see," said Satan, his eyes boring into him, "this place should be spooky. A lot of our friends are pickled in those jars. It always reminds me of the story of Ali Baba and the Forty Thieves."

Eric stared at the floating slabs of flesh. Some were purple, some had aged to a deep frayed gray. "Holy Moses, Satan, do all TB lungs wind up here?"

"If the docs can get permission from the relatives, sure."

"Lord." Something clicked in Eric's mind. Satan's eyes were like Pa's at the height of rage: deadly cold.

Eric glanced around in the room. He pointed to a slab of gray marble supported by heavy cast-iron uprights. "What's that?"

"The post mortem table."

Eric winced. He could visualize the white-gowned, white-masked doctors working over a dead man, the nickel in their spectacles and instruments glittering steel-like in the blue light. Eric remembered something. "Say, come to think of it, I don't ever recall having seen a hearse."

Satan grinned. "No, I guess not. They come at night, out of deference to people's feelings."

Again Eric winced.

"Well, let me show you my library. As you'll notice, some jars have other parts of the human anatomy in them besides the lungs. This, for instance, is the Tongue Row."

Eric stiffened.

"Sure. You wouldn't know it, but a lot of your bud-

305

dies've got tongue and throat TB." Satan grinned. "As a matter of fact, I got a little myself." He opened his mouth wide. At the end of his tongue was a small red hole as if an acid had eaten into it. His throat was inflamed too.

Eric glanced nervously to one side.

"And this is Kidney Row."

Eric started to edge toward the door.

"What's the matter?"

"Oh . . . nothing. By the way, this isn't where you work regularly, is it?"

"Scared?"

"Hell no." Eric took a firm grip on himself. "Except that I think I am going to vomit."

"Well. Let's get out in the hall, my friend. I wouldn't want you to mess up this Hall of Fame." Satan glanced at him enigmatically. "Does the smell get you?"

Eric said, "Well, it isn't exactly roses." He stepped out quickly as Satan locked the door behind him.

"Want to see the lab too?"

"Well . . . "

"Sure. Now that you're down here, you might as well."

Satan led the way, his lab coat flapping around his thin, striding legs.

They fronted a short rise of steps in the dark tunnel, went up. They passed through a short right-angling hall, and went up a few more steps, turned through a large door, and entered a wide well-lighted laboratory. Eric sighed with relief. Compared to the tomb below, this was a friendly farm kitchen. Six technicians, three cold women and three mosquito-quiet men, were busy at work, some bent over microscopes, some mixing colored fluids.

Eric followed Satan to a bench. On it lay a fresh pair of cheesy lungs, sliced open. Eric drew back. "TB?"

"Yes. A far advanced case."

Eric blinked.

"Look at this pair," said Satan, lifting a napkin off a tray. The lung tissues were BB-ed with little white stones of calcium.

"Yes."

"And look. Here's a pair you should recognize. Not? They're Huck Olson's. A no-good bum, just like me. A failure."

Nausea rose in Eric. He remembered.

And that odd smell! Through his mind there flashed the memory of Ma Memme's death. The mortician, busy preparing her body, hadn't known who Eric was, and had asked him to help embalm her. The same smell was in this laboratory.

"Look at these. Odd fellow."

Again Eric held his stomach against a vomit.

"Look. Here is an interesting pair of lungs." Satan lifted a glass jar from a shelf on the wall. His eyes were as enigmatic as the Whipper's. "Very interesting. These lungs belonged to a brilliant man. A scientist. You'd never know it to look at them though, would you?"

"Not Fawkes'?"

"Yes. Our very good friend, Dr. Theodore Fawkes."

"Oh my God God God . . . " Turning and rushing past the six technicians, who looked up startled as he went by, Eric burst through the door at the end of the laboratory into the open air. Bent over he stumbled vomiting through the white birches. He ran down the hill. His breath came in blursts. He crossed the road and tramped into the long gray weeds near the edge of the swamp. He felt the swamp sucking at his shoes and veered to the left, stumbling his way out of the black muck onto sturdier ground. He stopped beneath a huge scarlet-oak and fell on the grass, gasping. He crouched on his knees, puffing, and fighting occasional vomiting spasms. An October wind rattled dried old leaves in the branches above.

He clutched at the grass, ripped up a handful of the fall-toughened blades. He smelled them.

A long time later, the twelve o'clock whistle swelled from a gurgle to a high shrill scream. A slim plume of smoke lifted above the towering smokestack behind the Phoenix.

# H

E LAY FLAT on his back in the dark room. Staring through the posts of his bed and through the window, he watched the sharp stars thicken in the night sky.

He could hear the boys on his floor stirring around. He moved a trifle in his bed. Lifting a sleep-prickling arm, he looked at the radiant dial of his wrist-watch. It was five minutes to seven. The evening rest hour had almost ended. In a few minutes Satan and Guster the Boaster would be in to see him.

He stirred again and rubbed his brow. The boys had invited him to go prowling with them out at the Rambling 'Reck, a nightclub located just two miles from the San. Guster the Boaster, like a physician with pat pills, had suggested that he go "case the joint with me. C'mon, you need a good snortin' drunk, man. Do you good, yessir." Satan had put it another way. "Balls of fire man, why don't you come with me and see how the world really lives? The reason you got so goddamned upset down in the Morgue there was that you don't know what life's all about. You got to be able to laugh at it. C'mon, I'll show you. Take a beer or two with me, and then stand back. Watch the other bastards make asses out of themselves. It's great sport." Tempted, Eric had said he would think it over.

He heard music buzzing faintly in the earphones hanging on the wall. It sounded like a crowd singing a hymn; and, curious, he fitted the phones over his ears. He nodded. It was the weekly devotional services sent over the San radio system by a small broadcasting set in the auditorium.

In a moment, Reverend Herder interrupted the singing to bring his message. "Dear frens. Tonight we come to bring you light from heaven . . . " A picture of the minister giving a talk to the movie crowd one night arose in Eric's mind. Herder had delivered his message with the trembling precision of a screwjack. His eyes had resembled a pair of deviled eggs, large orange blobs surrounded by whites. "Dear frens. Tonight we come to bring you light from heaven." Light indeed. Eric flicked off the switch and hung up the phones on the wall.

Again he heard the boys down the corridor. It was then, in a flash, that he realized he had neither smoked nor drank hard liquor for almost two years. He opened his eyes, astounded. Why, other years, on hot summer days, he had always liked a glass of strong beer; and on cold winter evenings, a glass of wine to warm the bones within his lean fleshes. He was an odd one, he was. Why, all the while that he had believed he was on the verge of becoming a no-good, he had really never been inclined to break the cure-taking. The thought was comforting: he had come to see that, while the Phoenix speeded up the unraveling or the knitting of a man, more people broke in it than healed.

He turned in his bed and abruptly got up, snapped on the overhead light, and put on his blue robe. He looked in the mirror to comb down the rooster tail on the back of his head. He shook his head at the image of himself in the mirror. "No, Deeb, not tonight. Or any night. No, sorry. I want to get out of here."

The visiting hour whistle blew up. And the door opened.

"Eric. Eric!"

For a long second he wasn't sure of his identity. She couldn't be real. How could Martha Lonn, ice-blue-eyed Martha, be standing there in the doorway? Dressed in blue? With the Pa-cold eyes? How could it be she when it was Mary he had desperately willed should come? A gale coiled around his flame, and bent it back, and almost tore it from the wick. The Whipper had come to play again.

But his flame held. He narrowed his eyes defensively. Inside, he trimmed his wick. He cautioned himself about how he should talk and act before her.

"Aren't you going to invite me in?" Her eyes were glowing.

"Come in." He stepped aside. "You'll have to pardon me. I'm not dressed. Just this bathrobe."

"Oh, that's all right. I only want to see you. See you.

309

Oh, Eric, you don't know, you'll never know how much I've missed you." She stood looking at him, her eyes running over him like excited flies. "You look so well. So healthy." She tried to push her ample bosom against him.

He stepped back. "Huh. What'd you expect, a cadaver?" He toyed with the silver tassels of his belt.

"Why, and you're a fatty."

"Aw, hell, I . . . "

She pinched his arm and, alert for his reaction, touched his cheeks. "Why, you're a regular chub."

He brushed her off and growled. He looked directly into her pale eyes.

"My, my. You're still in that ugly mood."

He shrugged. He pushed a white chair toward her. "Sit down."

She took the chair. She sat on its edge. She opened her coat. He recognized the tight blue skirt, the light blue blouse.

He felt tempted to smirk at her uneasy gestures.

Just then a chatter of feet came up to the door. There was a knock. Satan came in with a flourish. "Well, Jesus, get your duds on, and I will take you up to the exceeding high mountain, and shew thee all the kingdoms of the world, and the glory of . . . oh, I see. I guess you won't be going then?"

Eric waved at his company. "What do you think?"

Satan lifted his brows. His lips twitched in an amused smile. "Well, my Nazarene, that will be an even better remedy. Who am I to cast the first stone?"

Martha stood up. "Am I upsetting any plans?"

"Oh no." Satan laughed. "It won't be any plans you'll upset."

Eric glared at Satan.

Smirking, Satan took the hint, nodded, and left.

Martha sat down again. She appeared to be offended that he had not presented Deeble to her.

"Well, tell me, what's on your mind now?" Eric asked, leaning back across the bed, and flipping the tassels over his leg. He felt an impulse to make her crawl. "What's your trouble now?"

"My God," she said, her eyes blazing, "you're still too damned blunt."

He chuckled. It occurred to him that his not loving her was revenge enough.

"Couldn't you let me build this thing up?"

"I don't like your build-ups." He narrowed his eyes. "Say, just what the hell're you doing here, anyway? Your husband know about this?"

She whitened a little. "Yes. I told him. I made it a point to tell him. But you don't know. You'll never know."

"Really."

"Oh, Eric, let's . . . let's go for a walk somewhere." She jumped up and rubbed her hands nervously.

He studied her rubbing hands. He was quite pleased that this time, tonight, he saw no blinding aura circling her head. He was probably seeing her at last exactly as his friends had always seen her. He curbed an impulse to murmur Macbeth's "Out, damned spot; out, I say!" It would be cheap. And, he felt sorry for her. She had probably gone through a nervous period of daring, hesitating, daring, before she had finally come out to see him. "Sit down, Martha," he said kindly, "I can't go walking. Not yet."

She turned quickly. His kindly tone evoked tears. She sat down, and said, "Really, Eric, really. I did tell Russell I was coming."

"But why?" The moment he shot the question at her, he was sorry. He had given her a chance to rake over the dead ashes.

"Because . . . oh, Eric, it didn't dawn on me right away, but about a year ago I began to realize you were right when you said, 'Some day, some day, girlie, you're going to realize how much you missed not keeping me. I know how men are. And I know your mind. In time you'll hunger for men like me.' Oh, Eric, you were so right. I did miss you. So much. So very much." Her eyes fired with harsh desire.

He recalled that Adele had said she was a mother.

He wondered if she were a good parent. He looked at her and snorted, "Aw, hell, woman, you're just tired of Russell. You're just looking around for a change."

She jumped up. "I didn't come here to be insulted."

"Of course not. You came here expecting me to swoon in your arms. You're pretty clever, you are. You knew I'd be ripe for seduction about this time, after all these months in the monastery. Well, if you're so damned interested in me, why the hell didn't you come when I needed you most, those first months I spent in here? Then I was really the lad who needed a woman's arms. But now? Hell, now I'm okay again."

"But I've just told you. Told you."

"Look, girlie, let me tell you something. There's somebody else now."

She stared at him.

"And now you'd better go. I don't want her to be hurt. Go. Maybe it's too late already. The rumors're probably flying now."

She drew up tight. She asked, "What's she like?"

"Oh no you don't, lady. I'm not talking about her."

She glanced about, saw Mary's photograph on his bedstand, leaned forward in her tight blue skirt, peering greedily. "That her?"

Reluctantly he nodded.

"She's cute."

"Huh."

Martha sat back slowly, almost sullenly.

He composed himself and studied her. He began to understand why his friends had not liked her. She was a shade too strident in the way she sat, moved, waved her hand, talked. He watched her. It occurred to him that she must have come out of guilt, not out of love. Or to make sure she had not made a mistake in marrying Russell.

Under his hard eyes she suddenly hid her face. She began to cry.

Coolly he examined the texture of her sobs. Yes, his rolling waters had stilled.

After a few minutes she looked up from her tears and moaned, "Oh, if only my mother had left us alone. Maybe we'd have made it out." She wept. "But she kept encouraging me to cheat on you."

"Huh."

"Oh, if only she'd left us alone. We could have made it out. But, I was weak. I was too much a child to be loving then. Too young." She began to dry her eyes with a monogrammed handkerchief. He recognized her husband's initials, R. B.

"Maybe." He switched his leg with the silver tassels.

She blew her nose. "The difference between doing and not doing hangs on so slim a thread. So slim."

"Yes."

"And then, oh, if you hadn't've been so tall. Maybe that might have helped."

He sat up. "Tall?"

"Yes. Oh, you don't know. You were so tall. I didn't know how to take it. I was always worrying that people would think you a freak."

His eyes narrowed. What were Mary's inward, secret thoughts about his stilt-long body?

"And then you were so strong. So strong. Oh, I don't mean your muscles. I liked them. They were wonderful. But it was your morals. Why, you were so honest I was afraid of you."

He laughed. "Me strong? Oh my God."

"So strong you terrorized me."

He wondered.

"You seemed so sure of where you were going. Why, you were a fanatic in demanding that the common man should be given a chance at ideas, at the music and the dreams you had found and loved."

He was dumfounded. Couldn't people see that he had a flucting light on his candle? Weren't his vacillations apparent to others? "Holy Moses, woman, this is getting embarrassing." He cleared his throat. "Tell me, did you have a good trip down?"

She laughed. "You're still the blunt little boy, aren't you? There never was any deftness about you."

He growled to himself.

"You cute kid." She laughed. "Well, I really didn't have such a very good trip down. It's wartime and the only train I could get was a local."

He nodded. Those locals had a way of stopping at the least sign of a station, like a dog stopping at every tree. He stood up and said, "Look, Martha, you'd better go. Please."

She bowed her head.

"Please, Martha."

She jumped up and stood up to him. She lifted her chin and made a lovely oval of her mouth. Again she tried to push her apple-large breasts against his arm.

He felt embarrassed for her. He looked off to one side.

"Tell me . . . have I grown since you last saw me?"

"Well . . . yes." To himself he thought: "Martha, there's one kind of fire you'll never know about. It's a fire that, once fastened upon your wick, burns forever; once aflame upon you, makes you a world's wanderer. It is something that impels you to divine, to create, to record."

For a second a moving smile made her face very beautiful. She said, "Well, I see you don't at that."

Suspicious, he asked, "Don't what?"

"Love me. Or you would have told me what you were really thinking just now."

"Look, girlie, look. I feel . . . I feel very humble about your coming here."

"Did you ever find that dollar bill I tucked in your coat pocket? That day I went to *Of Human Bondage* with you?"

He looked at her coldly.

"Sure. I dropped one in your pocket then."

"What for?"

"Somehow to tell you something. You see, you never knew. That is, really knew what I thought."

"Come," he said after a moment, "come. I'll take you

down to the door." Saying good-bye to her was saying good-bye to Pa's cold eyes. And to the bosom of Ma Memme.

# M

## XLI—SPARKS

OMENTARILY he was tempted to hide Martha's visit from Mary. He did not want to hurt her. He did not want to unsettle her faith in him. He knew too well how easily a blind lover could become a bitter one. Yet he knew, too, that he would never be able to live with himself if he were to hide it from her.

He wrote her:

> You must come home. I've many, many things to tell you. First, starting tomorrow, I'll be eating all three of my meals in the dining-hall. That'll give me greater freedom to see you when you come to visit me. Second—and don't scare now—Martha was here. Yes. I sent her away. I've always hoped she would never come. But now that she's actually come, I'm glad. Now I know something for sure. While she was here in this room, and you a hundred miles away, you were nearest me, you were the one who possessed me. Mary, come. Hurry!

Her letter came by return airmail. Nervous, he drew up his chair to the window to read:

> I suppose there's no need to hide from you that her coming disturbed me greatly. You see, I shall never be able to forget those teal-blue eyes of yours, sometimes so slumbrous with little boy dreams, sometimes so afire and piercing with the wisdom of an old Indian. Those eyes of yours will haunt me forever. So I've been terribly upset since I got your letter. Sometimes I wonder if I should trust anyone any more. You write you sent her away. I hope that's the truth. It must be the truth! But other thoughts come to my mind. Are you sure you did not choose to send her away because you thought that going back to her would be too messy? Too late? I want to know that. I must know

that! I want some truth now. I'm tired of indecision. I must know. You've mentioned that sometimes my eyes look sad. Can't you guess why? I used to believe that when people talked, they meant exactly what they said. But to my growing rue, I learn they often don't.

Her passionate plea to know the truth made him feel uneasy. He nodded to himself. She must have had some sorry experience with another male. He twisted in his chair and looked out over the wide lawn darkly green in the twilight. He sighed. Martha had cursed him forever with a little distrust.

He sighed again, involuntarily.

He read on; and was surprised to see, at the end of the letter, a suppressed thought which had leaped from her subconscious mind to the page:

I suppose you enjoyed yourself with her. Men usually never let such opportunities slip. We poor women are always getting cheated. We don't dare to operate like men. Well, don't expect me to be anxious to fly into arms warmed by another.

He chuckled, read on:

I just wonder sometimes if you really want me. Really.

He chuckled.

Maybe I'm not good enough for you. Maybe you're too good for me.

He frowned. He recognized it. Would she be the kind that would sulk until he reassured her that he had always, always, been completely hers and that she had been blindly mistaken? He narrowed his eyes as he thought about it. Well, he would admit something like that but once; that road could not be traveled too often.

He sent her a reassuring telegram.

SATURDAY. A sleepless rest hour, a little coughing and an anxious look for the speck in the sputum, a long rising whistle, a leaping and a hobbling about to get into the long blue trousers and the red slip-over sweater, a hurried combing of the hair, a little touch of face lotion, and he was ready for Mary.

He waited. The room was brilliant with long, striking afternoon sunlight.

She came. When she entered, he was not ready for her glories. He was stunned that she should actually have come, that her grave blue-grape eyes were alight and upon him. She came toward him, shyly as of old. A running of quick feet, a gesture of the lonesome child, and her body was fierce against him.

But the moment she touched him he found himself tightening. He felt his mind drawing back, found it looking her over cagily. This time he had to make sure. Quite deliberately he fought back tears at the sight of her, repressed an impulse to laugh, to sob, kept himself from searching through her shoulder-length hair for her throat.

"Well," he growled, "well."

She said into his shoulder. "That telegram. I got a wonderful telegram."

"Oh. Yeh. Well, sometimes people get excited."

He felt her laughing against his arm. "Oh, you wouldn't relax and admit and be sentimental, would you? Oh no. You hard-heart."

"Well," he mumbled.

"Such a man. Mister Hard-Heart." She stood back a step. "And you've really got three meals now?"

"Lady, you're way behind. I've got a half-hour walk already. Doc says I'm as healthy as a horse again."

She stood back farther to admire him.

He forced himself to study her oval face, her skin, her nose, her spread and lifted forehead, her emphatic silhouette, her dark brown hair with its vanishing and reappearing bronze shades, her child-soft hands.

She came close and reached up and pulled at his hair. Some of it hung in his eyes. She laughed, and said, "You've got a thatch there, a straw thatch." She tugged at his hair again and drew him close and kissed him and looked into his eyes and jerked at his hair. "You know," she said. "I really believe your hair is changing color."

"Aw . . . "

"Why yes," she said. "When I first knew you it was faded, it had lost its sparkle. But now its sort of . . . well, strawy, with a faint red in it." She smiled. "A little boy with a straw-thatched roof."

He looked down. He was bewildered by the sudden warmth of her this day. It was her good day. She was inordinately close-pressing. Her eyes dared him to touch her. Her grave ways had vanished entirely.

He said suddenly, drawing her beside him on the bed. "Mary, look. I'll soon be leaving this dump. And you know, we'll have to start thinking about how we'll live. Marry, I mean." He paused, his brow troubled. "Dear, I want to marry you."

"Why . . . of course. Yes!" she ejaculated. She twined herself about his arm, and looked at his lips and his eyes and his forehead.

The little girl gestures touched him. He trembled. "Marrying will be a double responsibility because we'll be doubling up our weaknesses."

"And our strengths," she added quickly.

"Well, yes. Anyway, we'll each have to find part-time work." He narrowed his lips. "Just so I can find some kind of work that I'll like." He brooded. He felt her observant eyes upon his. "But I don't suppose I'll get much chance to choose." He thought a moment. "Those cold-hearted captains of industry should have a little mercy, shouldn't they, now that I've served some time in here?"

"I should think so. Now that we've declared war on Germany and Japan, 4F's will be needed to keep up the home front. Sure."

318

"Still, I dunno. I'm doubly blacklisted. You see, as I told Fawkes once, I'm both a liberal and a lunger now."

Her eyes sobered.

"Maybe I should give up writing."

"Never!" she exclaimed.

"Maybe I should get a full-time job and let you take it easy at home."

"No, no. I'm going to work too. Just like you said. I hate being a cook, an' such."

He studied her. "I'm glad you said that. I'm as willing as the next man to earn a livelihood for the family. But if my wife has brains, I want her to use them."

"Most men don't want their wives to feel their equal," she said, smiling a little at his theories.

"Most men are savages. Barbarians. Bulls. Mere impregnators."

She twinkled. "And who'll do the dishes? And wash the diapers an' such?"

"Both of us. We'll share the work. Besides, there are laundries."

She patted his arm. "Such a serious boy. So serious. Dishes an' such." She pulled at his hair. "I'll bet a month after we're married, my darling barbarian will stomp off after dinner and let me wash the dishes all by myself."

He growled, "Don't you hate those jobs?"

"Sure. Sure. I'm not saying anything."

"Well?"

She drew close to him. "You're sure you want me? And not Martha?"

Solemnly he looked into her eyes. "Lady, if you were a man, I'd knock you down for asking that."

"You're sure you're not lonesome? This Phoenix distorts people's judgments, you know."

"What're you trying to say?"

"Nothing."

"After your vacation and being outside and all, did yours seem distorted?"

"No."

"Are you sure?"

"Of course. But are you sure?"

"Holy Moses, yes."

She drew his head toward her.

He lay in her arms, thinking about his stay in the Phoenix, trying to estimate its impact on his personality. "You know," he said aloud, "I just wonder if we won't be much more greedy, more grabby, more self-centered than we ever were. We've been so used to taking things for granted, to having things thrown at us without our even asking for them, that we'll probably demand the same kind of treatment for the rest of our lives. Two years of it can really drill it in."

"Maybe."

"I'm sure of it. And starting today, I'm going to begin thinking about other people. Do something for them."

"Like what?"

"Oh, like . . ." He cleared his throat. "Well, what I really mean is, I've been worrying too much about justice for myself and not enough about justice for others. People like Minnie, Calisto, Deeble, Silas, and others. They should get a break, too."

"But suppose they don't want your help?"

"Well . . . even if they don't, I still ought to get out of the habit of being so selfish. For two years now I've done nothing but contemplate my navel." He rubbed his nose self-consciously. "It's time I grow up out of the Oh-God-the-pain! age."

She laughed. "Ah! now you're beginning to tick. Really tick."

He mused on. "There's one thing I am going to miss."

"Yes?"

"Crumbs. Those lousy crumbs you always found in bed after eating. Remember how they always felt like rocks? When you were about ready to go to sleep?"

She laughed at him.

He asked, "Mary, what if the docs say we can't have children?"

"I don't know."

He glanced down at his knees. "It would be nice to have a couple of little jiggers running around."

They were silent.

He stirred. "Mary, did you ever stop to figure I'm too goddamned big for you?"

She drew back. "You . . . I don't understand. You mean, how tall you are?"

"Yes."

"I think it's wonderful."

"Huh."

She pressed against him now, lifting his chin. "You self-conscious about your long legs?"

"Well, I don't exactly feel like a kangaroo with 'em, but . . ."

She laughed. "I can see you. I can just see you. I'll bet you were shy in college. You hardly dared to breathe. You thought everybody there a fancy stepper and you a clod-hopper from the country, didn't you?"

"Well," he growled uneasily, "it was something like that."

She studied him. She became serious. The smile vanished from her lips. "Look, Eric. Haven't you known you were a Saul among men? A tower? Eric, didn't you know that the higher the eyes the wider the vision?"

"Hooey!"

"Eric, be proud of your power. Your size. Why, you're so mighty, you practically function out loud."


# T
## XLIII—LABOR PAINS

HE NEXT DAY, Sunday, they went for a step-by-slow-step, half-hour walk. The road led to the east, toward Little Switzerland, a township filled with high hills.

The sky was overcast with a vast tarpaulin of gray. A slow wind breathed in their faces. Faintly the sugar maples whistled. The clinging red oak leaves rustled. A row of murmuring pines settled back to await winter's christening. Mourning, the black-banded white birches gently threshed their silver whips about.

They walked slowly. Eric sensed a different mood in Mary today. She was snapping her red nails. Scuffing at the weeds along the edge of the macadamized road, he looked up to ask, "Well, what's wrong now?"

"Nothing."

"Then take those nails out of my eyes."

She humphed.

"Are you always like this on Sunday?"

"Oh, don't be silly."

He tossed his shoulders. Damn her caprices. "Aw, nuts."

She said nothing. There was a small hole in her sock and every time her foot lifted it looked impishly at him over the edge of her shoe.

"Or did you get out of bed on the wrong side?"

"Oh, leave me alone."

"All right, all right." Who was she to have the right to flick her whip of words on his opened palm?

Ten minutes later they came to a country crossroad. The road going west fell away to a small 8-shaped lake, the one going east lifted slowly into a cluster of hills. Ahead rose the first steep bluff of Little Switzerland, an enormous rupture out of the earth. Trees were skewered into its steep chest.

He glanced briefly at her walking by his side; then leaned forward to start the climb. He nodded to himself. He would rush the hill until she cried uncle. He would make her talk.

But the climb stiffened and his breath came fast. The hill rose under his feet, swelled like bread dough. The top, which a moment before seemed but a few steps up, was now a mile away. He slowed his pace. To ease his weight ahead, he bent farther into the hill. He sweated. His leg muscles began to tremble. His knees sagged.

He glanced at Mary. She still walked along stoutly. He

bit his teeth. He rushed on. In a moment he was breathing hoarsely through his open mouth. Air rasped his throat.

He pushed on until his right leg buckled. He stumbled.

"Eric, you fool you, stop."

He took a few more steps and then, turning, puffing, looked down at her from a height. "Give up? Say uncle?"

"Oh you fool."

"Uncle?"

"Oh you . . . "

He coughed. Then she did. They looked at each other. He laughed. Then she did.

He took her hand and drew her to one side and sat down with her on the shoulder of the road. They sat wordlessly until they had calmed and caught their breaths.

"Well," he said after a while, "I guess we better go back, huh?"

"Wait," she whispered, "can you wait a moment? I . . . "she blushed and then, very much the girl whose mind is a web of vagary and impulse, rustled down into the head-high weeds in the ditch and disappeared.

In a few moments she was back. She smiled at him. They had a secret now.

They stepped along briskly. She took his arm. She looked up gaily. "You know, Eric, I always have fun when I'm with you."

He smiled and said nothing.

"You're the first man I've met who let's me feel free. With you I can do anything I want to."

He swallowed and cleared his throat.

"No, really. Probably it's because you're like me. I mean, you were born on the farm and so was I. And you like to dream. Or something. I don't know what it is. But I feel free around you."

"Well, if that's true, that's wonderful," he said quietly.

"It is true."

They stepped along, hand in hand.

"Funny thing is, I almost missed you," she said, laughing disarmingly at him.

"Oh?"

"Yes. You see, I had already given up trying to find somebody like myself. I mean, somebody who liked to dream. Who would understand me. I was about to take the first decent man that came along. Had my eye set on one already. Then, you came. Well, at first I wasn't sure of what I was seeing. I wasn't sure I wanted you."

"Why not?"

"Because you were too much like a boy who needed a sister, or a mother. But not a wife." She paused, wrinkling her brow, thinking. "But then, after a while, when I saw what was behind that hair hanging in your eyes, I saw it."

"Saw what?"

"The power of long dreams."

Eric didn't know whether to leap or run.

She went on, still probing. "Yes, that's it. You see, the only man I really ever knew was my cousin Ray. And for a long time I thought I wanted him or somebody like him."

"Oh?"

She grinned at him. "You're not jealous?"

"Well . . . "

"Really?" She seemed pleased.

"Well . . . it's nice to know other men want you, but . . . that's far enough."

She pinched his arm and laughed gaily.

He said, collecting himself, "You know the old saw—

> *In part she is to blame*
> *For having been thus tried.*
> *He comes too goddamn close*
> *Who has to be denied,*

don't you?"

"Of course. But you needn't worry about him. Oh sure, he is very dear and restrained and knowing and tender. But, deep inside, he makes the mistake of laughing at me. He doesn't like my dreams, doesn't respect my coming forth out of humility."

He nodded, holding himself against an impulse to say something sentimental.

"No, Eric, believe me, he means nothing to me now. You've meant far more to me than he ever did."

Eric said nothing.

She said, her voice rising, the fire in her eyes lifting, "Eric, let me tell you. My life has been one of terror, really. This Phoenix here, standing on these hills like a monument to the dying, it's been the only home I've ever had. It's been a family to me. Before that . . . when I was a little girl . . . my wonderful father and . . . you see, he killed my mother. He went crazy. Mad. He was a dreamer who never found his dream. He brewed about it. And slowly he went mad. And then one day, he shot Momma. And then himself. I saw him. He was going to kill me too, but he couldn't. I saw his eyes. I was only a little girl then, but I saw his eyes."

He turned and took her in his arms.

# XLIV—CAST FROM THE MATRIX AGAIN

H E STILL felt restless.

And when Dr. Abraham sent for him, he got ready at once, dressing in his red sweater and blue trousers.

He went down through the long tunnel that coiled within the hill like a slow intestine, down past the auditorium, past the X-ray room, until, turning, he entered the hallway where the doctors' offices were located.

Before Dr. Abraham's door he found three people waiting on folding chairs, strangers he had never seen before. They were thin, and their manners despondent. He decided they too were awaiting Dr. Abraham's advice and he sat down beside them with a kindly smile by way of greeting.

And they, warmed and stirred by his smile, grinned, and shifted in their seats, the two women folding their dresses modestly over their knees and the man recrossing his legs and combing his hair with his fingers. Eric was pleased with the response. He reflected on the good spirits of the common people. Their lights might be tiny embers, but the breath of a genuine smile could momently kindle them.

He wondered if they were really awaiting Dr. Abraham, for one of the women, gossiping, mentioned Dr. Stein. Eric asked, lifting his brows, "You waiting for Dr. Stein?"

"Yes," she said, and the man nodded with her, "yes, we're waitin' for Stein."

"For the Butcher Boy," the man added, "and a good doctor."

Ignoring the gentle challenge to brag about his physican, Eric stood up and knocked upon Dr. Abraham's door. Hearing a muffled response, "Come in," he opened and entered.

"Hah. There you are. I've been waiting for you."

Eric settled on the offered chair. "Well, those people in the hall, I thought they were waiting to see you. That's why I'm late."

"Oh, that's all right. Well, how do you feel?"

"Feel? Why, I feel fine, I guess."

Dr. Abraham studied him from beneath drawn brows, his eyes steady behind the blinking lenses of his spectacles. "You know, Eric, your ears are positively pink. That's a good sign. Good."

Eric stirred and his big hands wrestled with each other.

"Well . . . " and Dr. Abraham slowly turned in his squeaking armchair, "well, I guess it's time to give you another half-hour exercise. Only this time you're going to get work, not walk, exercise."

Eric still fumbled his hands.

"Well?"

"Well, what?"

"Well . . . " Dr. Abraham scratched his bald head. "You know the exercise schedule here. One hour walk, three hours work. We usually start off a patient with a half-hour walk and then work him up the next three hours in the work he's going to do after he leaves here. He doesn't get his second half-hour of walk until the end."

326

Eric nodded. "Well, if it's all the same with you, I'd like to take that second walk now."

"Hah, I thought so." Dr. Abraham shook his head. "Eric, what's wrong?"

"Nothing," He sighed. "Doc, look. I know you're wondering when I'll get busy and write again. Well, tricks won't get me started. I . . . I appreciate the psychology of saying 'no' just at the right time. But . . . tricks won't do it. Nor candy. No, there's a deeper problem."

"What, for instance?"

"I . . . anyway, just give me that second walk. I do my best thinking walking, and I need to do some of that."

"My boy, really, what's wrong?"

"Nothing. It's only . . . you see, I'm like a dog. When I've been hurt, I like to get off by myself until I'm completely healed."

"Well . . . " Dr. Abraham turned his chair. He reached forward and drew out a file. He glanced at a few pages. He laid the file on his desk and said, "All right, take it. I guess you can stand it. Go ahead."

Eric, still fumbling his fingers through each other, suddenly asked, "Say, Doc, tell me, what do you live for?"

Dr. Abraham drew back. "I . . . I don't know. I never thought to think about it."

"Really. Tell me. I'd like to know."

Dr. Abraham closed his eyes and rubbed his forehead. "Well, first point: because I enjoy the fighting. Second: because I like to help people."

Eric nodded. "You like people?"

"Yes. Don't you?"

"I . . . guess so. Except that they never behave the way I want 'em to. I can't make up my mind if we're human beings unlucky enough at times to act like crocodiles or crocodiles lucky enough to act like human beings. Why, take myself. I get the damnedest, meanest thoughts in my head. Really."

"You? Oh, no. Not you."

"Yes, me. Oh sure, overall. I'm not so bad. But, what

gets me is that no matter how much I train myself, with morals, and truths, and rules, there's a power in me that just grins at my good intentions. It's . . . it's just like a dog that's . . . that's been trained to stay away from the cat's milk, and yet slinks in and goes and gets it anyway."

Dr. Abraham's chair squeaked. He looked out of the window. A few flakes of snow touched deftly on the pane outside and fell on the ledge. "I know just how you feel, Eric. Sometimes I get a terrible impulse to tell all of you patients to go straight to hell. You seem so goddamn childish to me. And I get so goddamn mad at you." He paused.

"Doc, you sound like Pa."

"Hah. Well, I get mad for other reasons, too. At myself, I mean."

"Oh?"

"Sometimes, sometimes, I think I make a mistake to get so tied up with your lives. It almost kills me to see you die, and it almost kills me to see you live." Dr. Abraham sat tensely. "Sometimes . . . sometimes I think I should hate you patients, and develop a cold cynical attitude to destroy any false optimism I might have about your chances to lick this bitchy TB. As it is, I'm too willing to believe you're all going to make good, with the result that I pronounce you cured too soon and discharge you. And then you come back and you have to battle it all over again. And dammit, I don't ever want any of you to have to fight this TB twice. Yes, I should hate you. Hate you."

Eric's hand stilled.

"But, I can't learn to hate."

Eric nodded.

There was a short silence.

"Doc, tell me. Am I in pretty good shape?"

"What way? Physically? Sure. Very good. Good."

"But . . . the other?"

Dr. Abraham leaned forward. "Eric you're as blind as a bat. Haven't you learned anything? Look. First: remember when you came in, when I told you that you were right in the middle of the toughest battle you'd ever gotten into?"

Eric nodded, wonderingly. The flame on his wick lifted a little.

"Second: remember when I said that if you could lick this TB you'd win the greatest battle any man could win? Because there were forces in you that could easily destroy you?"

"Yes, I remember. Sure. The Whipper."

"Well . . . you dumb fool you, you've gone and done it. Done it! Don't you understand? You've made a conquering. Look, from now on, you can do anything. Oh yes, you can't run or jump, or take two seven-mile walks a night. But that's a small loss compared to what you can do. Any man that can control as boyish and as impetuous a nature as yours, that can train it to take each day as it comes, and who can, though the mists of his feelings and egotism, keep his eyes glued onto the next objective, such a man can conquer the world. My boy, a man may have the passion of a stallion, but until he's learned to discipline it, he can never hope to become a lover, an artist."

Eric clenched a fist. He felt like the bumbling private in a vast army who has been suddenly chosen by a shrewd major to captain a sortie into an alien land. He had trouble believing he had the bigness to do it.

"And you've done it. My boy, when you came in, I worried more about you than I do about most patients. Oh, I didn't worry too much about your unraveling body. But I did worry about you. For you hadn't learned to do first things first. But now, well . . . off hand, I can't think of a thing you can't do or get . . . if you use your head." Dr. Abraham added, after a pause, "You see, you've taken the cure long enough now to have started a new momentum in your life. And, if you keep it up another two or three years, you'll never have to worry about a collapse, mentally or physically."

"Oh."

"Boy, I envy you. I wish I were as strong as the man you are today."

"Why, Doc, I used to envy Fawkes for the same thing."

Dr. Abraham stared at him with narrowing eyes. He took off his spectacles. He rubbed his brow. Greatly agitated, he stood up. "Go," he said, quickly turning, looking out of the window. "Go. Get the hell out of here before I change my mind."

Eric stood up. He walked through the door. He was being born again. The placenta that had been mothering him within the Ma Memme San was breaking up at last.


# XLV—BRIEF VICTORY

HE RETURNED to his room. He drew up a chair to the window and sat down. He held his head in his hands. He found his thoughts diffused. He could not form them into an orderly procession. He threshed about in his mind. Dr. Abraham's words rose and droned and re-echoed through his skull like the chords of a symphony beating on the high-thrown walls of a temple. "Off hand, I can't think of a thing you can't do or get. Do or get." He was too stunned to grasp the hosts of meanings leaping from the doctor's benediction.

He looked up, and drank from the thermos bottle on his stand. Still his head rang. He went to the bathroom and washed his face in running cold water. He combed his hair. He shaved. He blew his nose again and again, trying to rid himself of the ringing in his ears.

He went back to his room and lay down. Gradually his beating heart quieted. His scattered attention drew together. Slowly the ringing faded.

He heard a train whistling in the Little Switzerland hills to the north. Listening, he recalled the many times, in his white bed, half-waking, half-dead, he had heard the engines go thundering over the frozen ground, had heard the sounds go rumbling down into the bowels of the earth. Often, in his mind's eye, he had glimpsed the fleeting train, spinning down the two long glistening spider threads into the distance. What had been the destinies of the passengers? Why had they come and gone? What mysterious cities and strange coasts had the peering faces at the coach windows seen?

He glanced at his watch. It was an hour before supper. There was still time to take his first full hour's walk and see the train. He looked through the window at the weather outdoors. It looked like snow. Rubbing his nose, he remembered the hill that he and Mary had failed to climb a few days ago. Beyond it rolled the train.

On a sudden impulse he decided to test himself. If he could pace himself he might be able to conquer that hill. The other day he had tried to rush it, and failed. Quickly he drew on the old felt hat and long gray topcoat that he had not worn for two years and went downstairs and outdoors.

As he strode along the east road past the thin maples, past the big elbowed oaks and the green-black needled pines, a testy north wind began to drive little flusters of November snow across his path. The snowflakes disappeared at the touch of warm air close to the ground.

Again the train whistled; this time faintly. He listened a moment and knew that he had missed it. He looked at his watch. Another train, also south-bound, was due in a half-hour.

He turned up the highway that he and Mary had walked wordlessly along. He strode on, steadying the light of his lamp, leveling the fluttering, sputtering fire on the wick.

He beat along with powerful steps. He drew in marvelous drafts of fresh, crisp November air. His cheeks glowed with new life. His eyes watered against the brisk wind.

The snow began to fall heavier now, in flakes as large as ruffled goosetail feathers. They swished against his face. They caught in the tufts of his camel's-hair coat like playing children caught in weeds. The flakes did not reach the earth. They came near to it and then curved away, borne upward on little breaths emanating from the warm earth. The land did not whiten.

He pushed along. There were strands of buff amongst the once-green grass; and there, where the shoulder of the road turned sharply down, the faded grass and the weeds were brown. And gray were the fenceposts and rusted the barbed wire strung between.

He pressed sideways against the rising north wind, through the whirling, shirring snow.

When he reached the crossroad, he paused to listen. The first train was whistling far to the south. Snowflakes clicked faintly against his ear. He went on, approached the hill.

He faced the hill and stopped to study it. Even for normal lungs, the lofty bluff was a struggle. And now, with the lungs he had . . . yes, he would have to play a cautious game, or the Whipper would have him cornered again. He nodded to himself. This time he would fix various points on the hill and at each of them stop to take a breath. And he would gain each point without troubling himself about the others. He studied the hillside and selected a boulder for the first goal.

He climbed. He controlled an impulse to charge. He crept up, slowly, a half-step at a time, slowly. He bent over to watch his feet. They rose and fell in lazy hammer strokes. He listened to his breathing. Like a child learning to walk, he picked out each coming step.

He examined himself. He wasn't breathless. His legs felt clean. He nodded. He was taking the first lift of the hill in stride.

He drew in huge breaths of November air. His cheeks tingled, swelling warmly against the cold. Blood rushed through his fingers.

He looked up, peering through the turning snow. There, to the left where the road cut into the hill a little, a clump of scrub oak fluttered stiff old leaves. The wind seared his eyes. He bowed his head and forged sideways into the wind.

332

The wind came up stronger. Snowflakes began to fall heavy enough to cover the ground; though the flakes were so cottony light that, when his foot started down to earth, the downward-rushing wind beneath his leather sole breathed the flakes away in every direction and cleared the earth of them.

He drew his coat about him. He enjoyed the tussling against the north wind's strength. He remembered the day, a year ago now, when he had hungered for a chance to battle the snow and the wind of winter, remembered that Fawkes and Huck had laughed at him. Well, he was in it now and it was good. He stepped faster. He strode along powerfully, exulting in this new power, smiling and grinning to himself. He enjoyed the feel of his cheek against the back of his wrist. With a snort he blew his nose into the wind and walked on, his eyelids narrowing and forming little defenses against the cold. Behind these defenses he sat warm by the fire that was alight in the room of his skull. He rejoiced that he had a place to live this cold-weather day.

He looked up. There was the boulder. He was a third of the way up the hill. He stopped, and found, to his dismay, that he had suddenly begun to puff. Mouth open, his breaths cutting harshly into his lungs, he sagged forward on tired legs. His flame subsided. He waited, hoping to overcome the breathlessness.

But he was still puffing a few minutes later. Strange, he thought. In the old days he could catch his breath in a couple of seconds no matter how long or how wildly he had run down a basketball court.

He stood breathing heavily. He bent toward the hill's incline. He turned his back to the wind. He pulled up his coat collar around his ears and face to warm the gnawing air before it entered his tender lungs.

It began to darken. It was near five. In a little while the sun, hidden now behind the white-gray mop-rag clouds, would set.

Then, and he could scarcely believe his senses, his heavy

breathing slowly quieted, his lungs began to feel warm, his throat soothed. Once more he could draw a good breath through his nostrils. He closed his mouth. He waited until he was calm again. He stood bowed. He waited until his flame spurted beneath his bent and cup-curved fingers. It rose. He spent another moment nursing the fire and warming himself beside it, and then looked up and picked a crooked fencepost for his second goal. He stepped on.

This time he watched his movements. He was an engineer nursing along an over-worked boiler. He checked the pressure of his heart, observed the volume of the white puffing breaths, gauged the pouring out of his power. He studied his impulses. He played with the throttle. He poked the coals. He threw the best fuel in the center of the firepot. The smell of the working engine, its roll and toss of belly, its noisy puffing, were marvels to him, the engineer.

Yet, soon he was out of breath again, and he stopped. Wondering how far he had come along, he flicked up his eyelids and looked out into the world of falling snow. He glanced along the line of fenceposts ahead, and then back.

He straightened, surprised. There it was, the crooked fencepost. He had passed it. While he had been fussing with his cranky machine, he had overshot his second goal by a long way, a good twenty steps. He turned and looked toward the crest of the hill. Well, the way was not far now. Just a little trotting out of half-steps and he would have whipped the Whipper. Just a few more big little-steps, the kind nature used to build civilizations out of ignorance, and he would have gained the knowledge of a new land.

He breathed easily for a few moments and then, dipping his hat into the wind, trudged on, slowly, slowly.

With the door closed, the flame rose again and he warmed himself.

The fire in his skull was burning merrily, and, as he strode along, he was not surprised to discern three figures sitting around the fire, nodding, warming themselves.

There was pale-faced, blue-eyed Huck, the dead one,

334

the one he could have been had his body failed him or had he failed to lock himself into a discipline.

There, to Huck's left, was the Woman, in whose face he found combined the features of Ma Memme, Martha, Miss Berg, and Mary: Ma Memme, who had given him creamy memme to drink and who had emboldened him with soothing hands; Martha, the warm-blooded heifer, who had attracted him with her Ma Memme bosom and sickened him with her Pa-cold eyes; Miss Berg, who had helped him bridge the long way from Martha to Mary; and Mary, the understanding one, who had opened her child hands, her Ma Memme hands, and taken him for what he was, a man, yet a little boy, a child crying in the wilderness, a prairie senna trembling at every contact with life.

And there, to one side, was Fawkes. From him he had learned to see the Whipper as He was, an impersonal chaos; from him had learned to accept the grim fact of it with serenity.

Eric strode along. And nodded his head. Fawkes had also agreed with a dim intuition of his that there was a nervous impulse in man seeking expression, that there was a potential light. The wicks were there, and the bowls were filled with fuel.

Light was the beauty in the beast. How could people be envious of each other's brains, as they often were? A man might reasonably hate another man for loving his woman, because every bull wants to make sure that his seed shall impregnate the heifer. But envy of another's light? No. The more it was shared the nearer the approach to the Answer.

Eric nodded. Having talked with Fawkes, he was sure that he would find, in the depths of the human body, a lamp that could be kindled there. He was sure that he would find, threshing blindly about in the soil of mankind's fleshes, a hope, a life, a dream. Give the Calistos, the Deebles, the Minnies, a society in which they could develop naturally, give them a little prodding, a wick-trimming, and their fuels would flame up clearly. He might have to wrestle the truth of it out of himself to prove it, but it would be there. For a little while there could be a little holding of the flame in the circumambient dark.

And yet, and Eric narrowed his eyes upon the leaping thought, and yet, it was the eternal tragedy of man, that though light emerged from the very act of his struggling flesh, light was alien to it. For a few moments, while the flame crept along the edge of his wick, man could have joy. With rapture his eyes might behold the light. But later, after a look around, the bitterness came. In the end, after either he or the world had been blown up in fire and smoke and thunder, it would be as if it had never been.

Eric swore to himself that, to make up for the loss of life at death, he would fill all the moments before it with all the exultation he could muster. He would see, leap, sing.

When he looked up, he had reached the top.

It was wonderful. He had won.

He paused, and, filling his lungs, trudged forward. Ahead was a short flat plateau that had been cut out of the top of the hill by highway engineers. Peering down the left side of the hill, and observing to the right the sweep of the major portion of it, he saw that he had been crawling up one end of a loaf-shaped hill.

He strode along. In the thickly falling snow, he could not find the outlines of the Little Switzerland across the gorge ahead.

A few steps more, and he saw a bridge. He narrowed his eyes. It was an overpass spanning the gorge. The railroad tracks ran below.

And now the snow began to fall very heavily. It squinched beneath his soles and spilled into his trouser cuffs. In the falling snow the world outside his skull had shrunk to a circle of a hundred yards. He looked up to see the leaf-sized flakes twirling toward him. First, as they appeared from nowhere in the sky, they were gray; and then, gradually, they lightened to blue-white; and then, white, they fell silently upon his face. They tumbled along his clothes and settled at his feet.

He bore on and walked onto the bridge. He went to the north railing and brushed off the snow. Hurling his legs over, he sat in the cleaned spot. He drew in a deep breath and shrugged his shoulders and pulled his hat low over his eyes and down in back to keep the snow out of his neck.

He peered into the gorge below. He could just see the tracks.

He heard the second train whistling to the north. A moment later the first train whistled far to the south, very faintly. The whistling reminded him of his father's farm where the sheik of the roosters lifted his wings in the morning and let fly a challenge to the world. And a moment later, across the road and down the valley, the neighbor's rooster rose to the tips of his orange toes too, and lifted his wings and hurled the challenge back up the valley.

Again the whistle sounded ahead. Again a whistling came from the south. Men were playing.

The north whistling drew near. He could hear the rush of the train. The tracks below began to quiver. He brushed the snow off his knees and shook his shoulders and head. He was excited. It was like seeing his first train.

And there it came, spewing black smoke against the white varying veils of snow, rushing and ramming its hot fires forward into the wind.

The train came so fast he could not adapt himself to it, could not study it in detail. Fleetingly he noticed an arm protruding from the window of the engine cab. And then the hot, smoke-erupting engine was gone, and after it followed a few coaches, rattling along like children led, never fearing where the power ahead might go.

For a little moment there had been a thundering, a great noise, a great fire, a great smoke. And then a silence; as if the train had never been.

"Strange," he muttered, "strange." He shook his head. "And yet it is the truth."

He kicked his foot out over the abyss.

He felt rested, and swung his feet up and over the railing and down onto the wooden floor of the bridge. He stood up. He brushed the snow from his coat. He took off his hat, shook it briskly, shook his hair, and replaced his hat. He turned and started back. A few large flakes had fallen on his thatch of straw hair and melted against his scalp.

Lightning Source UK Ltd.
Milton Keynes UK
UKHW010411260821
389497UK00001B/45